PENGUIN BOOKS

TANTRAS

THE AVATAR TRILOGY: BOOK TWO

The Avatar project, which consists of both game and
book releases, is the combined effort of a number of TSR
staff members and talented freelance authors. Richard
Awlinson is TSR's pseudonym for *Tantras*'s author, Scott
Ciencin, and editor, Jim Lowder.

The Avatar Trilogy

BOOK ONE: SHADOWDALE
BOOK TWO: TANTRAS
BOOK THREE: WATERDEEP

TANTRAS

by Richard Awlinson

**Cover Art by
CLYDE CALDWELL**

PENGUIN BOOKS
in association with TSR, Inc.

PENGUIN BOOKS

Published by the Penguin Group
27 Wrights Lane, London W8 5TZ, England
Viking Penguin Inc., 40 West 23rd Street, New York, New York 10010, USA
Penguin Books Australia Ltd, Ringwood, Victoria, Australia
Penguin Books Canada Ltd, 2801 John Street, Markham, Ontario, Canada L3R 1B4
Penguin Books (NZ) Ltd, 182–190 Wairau Road, Auckland 10, New Zealand

Penguin Books Ltd, Registered Offices: Harmondsworth, Middlesex, England

First published in the USA by TSR, Inc. 1989
Distributed to the book trade in the USA by Random House, Inc.,
and in Canada by Random House of Canada Ltd
Distributed in the UK by TSR Ltd
Distributed to the toy and hobby trade by regional distributors
Published in Penguin Books 1989
1 3 5 7 9 10 8 6 4 2

TSR, Inc.
PRODUCTS OF YOUR IMAGINATION™

Printed and bound in Great Britain by
Cox & Wyman Ltd, Reading

To family and friends who make a difference.

Special thanks to:

Anna, Frank, Bill, Martin, Michele, Patricia, Greg, Marie, Millie, Christine, Joe, Mary, and Jim.

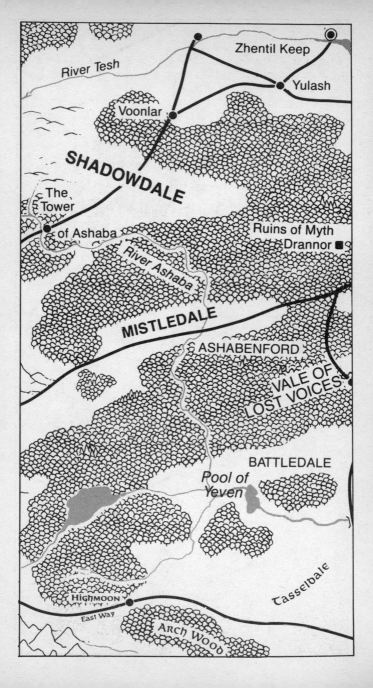

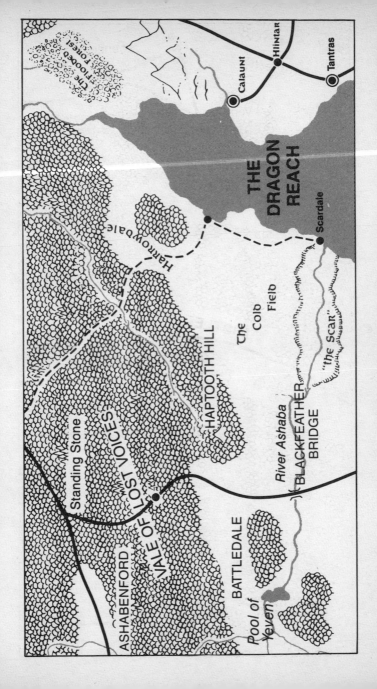

Prologue

Forester had lived in Shadowdale all of his life, and in the recent battle against the forces of Zhentil Keep, he had fought bravely to defend the bridge over the Ashaba River on the western edge of the dale. Now he toiled alongside his friends and neighbors, hefting bodies onto carts, trying to identify dead dalesmen. A cleric of Lathander who could write almost as well as Lhaeo, the scribe of the late Elminster, took down the names of the dead as the burly fighter called them out.

"Here's Meltan Elventree, Neldock's son," Forester said flatly as he grabbed the dead boy by the arms. The fighter had ceased to feel miserable after he'd moved his dozenth corpse. Now, after having hefted over fifty dead bodies, including close friends and even relatives, Forester really only took particular notice when someone was noticeably heavy or light.

"Poor lad," the cleric sighed. He moved his face close to the wax tablet he held and inscribed the name of the farmer's son. "Neldock will be heartbroken."

"He has another son," Forester said coldly as he lifted the body into the rough wooden wagon that stood next to him. "You know, Rhaymon, I thought you'd handle this much better. Lathander is the God of Renewal, right? You should be happy all these men are getting a fresh start."

Rhaymon ignored Forester's sarcasm and read over the list on his tablet. "So many young lads," he said softly. "So much wasted potential."

After placing Meltan Elventree in the wagon, the giant-sized fighter stopped for a moment and wiped his long, stringy black hair out of his eyes. Like everyone else on the corpse detail, Forester was covered with sweat and blood and smelled of smoke and death. He brushed his calloused hands over his dull brown tunic and looked out over the scorched area around him.

A blue-gray haze hung over the forest outside the small town of Shadowdale. The fires that Lord Bane's troops had started with their flaming arrows and foolish magic had been doused by a miraculous rainfall, but smoke still hung in the air. Forester didn't even wonder about the huge eye that had suddenly appeared over the dale and shed a tear that saved the town and the forest from fiery destruction. After all, the gods now walked the Realms, and such wonders were almost commonplace. The tear from the heavens was no more or less awe-inspiring to the dalesman than the attack on the town had been, even though the God of Strife himself had led the enemy army to their doorsteps.

In fact, the residents of Shadowdale, like most of the men and women who lived on the continent of Faerun, felt numb, almost oblivious to the chaos that had surrounded them since the time of Arrival. On that day, all of the gods were cast out of the Planes and took over human hosts, or avatars, in various places throughout the Realms. Since then, everything that people had always regarded as constant had proved to be unstable.

The sun was erratic in its course. On some days, it didn't rise above the horizon, while on others four suns would appear and rise into the air like fireworks. One moment snow fell from the sky, and the next it was literally raining cats and dogs. Plants, animals, and even people were totally unpredictable—sometimes mutating into beautiful, magical things, sometimes changing into terrifying abominations.

Worst of all, the ancient art of magic had become completely unreliable, even dangerous to those who tried to use it. The mages, who should have been the ones to rectify the mysterious chaos in the Realms, instead became feared harbingers of it. Most magic-users simply hid away to meditate about the problem, but those who were reckless enough to try to cast a spell—any spell—found that their art was more unpredictable than the sun. There were even rumors that Mystra, the Goddess of Magic, was dead and that the art would never again be stable throughout the land of Faerun.

Even the great Elminster, the most powerful mage in the entire Realms, had fallen victim to the chaos. He was dead, supposedly killed by two strangers to the dale who had been sent with him to defend the Temple of Lathander. People all around the small town were demanding that the strangers be punished for the murder, that Elminster be avenged. Unlike the chaos rampant in the world around them, this crime was something the people of Shadowdale felt they could do something about.

For most people now accepted the chaos as a part of their lives. It only took a few scant days after the fall of the gods for the men and women of Faerun to realize that they had little control over their world, so they had best get on with their lives. Farmers once again tried to grow their crops, and craftsmen returned to their trades—even though their plants now talked to them occasionally, or their tools suddenly turned to glass and shattered to pieces.

In Shadowdale, the dalesmen had learned of the impending attack from Zhentil Keep, their ancient enemies from the North, and fought the battle with the evil armies as they did any other. Many brave men had died, and had it not been for the Knights of Myth Drannor and the Riders of Mistledale, Shadowdale itself might have been overrun. But the dalesmen had somehow managed to drive the invaders off. Now, as with any battle, the survivors were left to bury the dead and repair the damages.

The trade road leading northeast from Shadowdale, little more than a well-used dirt path, was filled with townsfolk and soldiers as they solemnly moved into the forest to stack corpses and dismantle the traps they had set for the Zhentish. The road crawled through the worst of the scorched forest and, since it was the site of much of the daylong battle between the dalesmen and the army from Zhentil Keep, most of the destruction wrought by the combatants was centered upon it.

As some of the men from the dale used teams of draft horses to topple barricades, others, like Forester, handled the unlucky task of gathering the bodies of their comrades and loading them onto the wagons. Most of the wounded dalesmen had already been moved from the battlefield to a makeshift hospital in the center of town, but occasionally someone would start to clear a stack of bodies only to find someone alive underneath the pile.

Forester realized he was staring at a pile of bodies and shook his head, as if to dislodge any unwanted thoughts from his mind. The fighter rubbed his dirty, sweaty neck and turned to the next corpse.

"Hey, Rhaymon! I need your help to move this one," the fighter called to the cleric. "He's too heavy for me to lift."

"Who is it?" the cleric of Lathander asked softly. Ash and sweat covered his square jaw and wavy blond hair.

"I think it's Ulman Ulphor. No, wait . . . it's Bertil, not Ulman," the fighter grunted as he took the sword out of the corpse's hand and took a firm grip on the body. "I thought he wasn't trusted with weapons."

"He wasn't," the cleric sighed. "But everyone who didn't leave town before the battle was armed."

Rhaymon carefully placed the flat scrap of wood that held his wax tablet on the wagon, along with his stylus. The tablet held a list of the dead who had been identified, which Rhaymon composed in rough shorthand. Later he would transfer the list to parchment. That would normally be done in his room at the Temple of Lathander, but the temple had been destroyed in the battle. The cleric frowned as he thought of the ruined temple.

"Let's get at it," Forester snapped. "I don't want to be out here when darkness comes."

Rhaymon grabbed the rotund corpse by the feet and helped the fighter toss it onto the wagon. As the cleric picked up his tablet and stylus again, a howl echoed through the woods. Rhaymon looked around nervously, but Forester chuckled softly and wiped his hands on his tunic.

"It's only a scavenger . . . some big cat or a wolf drawn by the smell of blood." Forester shook his head and turned to the next body. When he saw that it was a young Zhentish soldier dressed in the black armor of the Zhentilar, elite army of Zhentil Keep, the fighter cursed. He dragged the body to the side of the road, where it would remain until the men collecting the corpses of the Zhentish picked it up. But as Forester turned back toward the cleric, the Zhentilar moaned softly.

"Damn!" Forester hissed. "He's still alive." He moved to the unconscious Zhentish soldier, took out his dagger, and slit the young man's throat. "There's another who won't get away."

Rhaymon nodded in agreement and motioned for another dalesman to come and move the wagon a little farther up the road. Forester sat on the back of the wagon as it lurched into motion, and the cleric walked wearily behind, checking and rechecking his list. Before they had gone more than a few yards, though, they heard a shriek from the area they had just cleared. Rhaymon turned in time to see a ghostly image of the Zhentish soldier Forester had just killed rise above its corpse.

"You'll pay for what you've done!" the ghost cried, staring grimly at the man who had murdered him. "All the Dales will pay!"

Forester lost his balance on the wagon and tumbled into the road. Rhaymon tried to help the fighter to his feet, but before either of the dalesmen could flee, the ghost floated to their side. Forester looked up into the pale, angry eyes of the dead soldier and uttered a silent prayer.

Rhaymon, however, was not so quiet about it. "Begone!" the cleric shouted, holding his holy symbol—a rosy pink wooden disk—out toward the undead creature. "Lord Lathander, Morninglord, God of Spring and Renewal, help me to banish this undead creature to the Realm of the Dead!"

The ghost merely laughed, and Forester felt dizzy when he realized that he could see through the undead soldier to the charred ground and burned trees at the side of the road. He considered reaching for his dagger, but he knew that it would be of little use against a spirit.

The ghost smiled broadly. "Come, come, Lathanderite. The gods are here in Faerun, not in the Planes. Lord Myrkul doesn't inhabit the Realm of the Dead now, so you shouldn't expect me to run off to an empty hell. Besides, since I don't see your god nearby, why do you expect your prayer to be answered?"

A small crowd of dalesmen had gathered around Forester, Rhaymon, and the ghost. Some had their weapons drawn, but most simply stood, watching the spectacle as they would a play at a fair. One man, a lean, hawk-nosed thief in a dark cloak, moved through the crowd to stand at Forester's side.

"So what are you going to do to us?" Cyric asked the ghost, spreading his arms wide. "No one fears a live Zhentish soldier here. A dead one is even less of a threat."

Forester looked up at Cyric. The dark-haired thief had been the fighter's commander during the Battle of Shadowdale. Cyric was a brilliant leader and had rallied the dalesmen against a huge force of Zhentish cavalry—a force led by the powerful Zhentish wizard, Fzoul Chembryl. Though Forester considered Cyric a great man and a champion of the dale, there were many who thought him suspect because of his friendship with the cleric and magic-user accused of Elminster's murder.

Rhaymon, who still held his holy symbol in front of him, and Forester, who still sat unceremoniously upon the ground, his hand near his dagger, felt a burst of cold air rush from the ghost as it moved toward Cyric. The crow's-feet around the thief's eyes deepened and multiplied as his eyes narrowed to slits. The ghost spread its arms wide to embrace Cyric as it moved toward him.

Cyric laughed as the ghost passed right through him.

"You're not a real undead creature," Cyric said through an evil grin. "You're just another product of the chaos in the Realms." The thief turned and started to stroll away.

The Zhentish soldier screamed once more, longer and louder than he had when he first emerged from his corpse, but no one paid any attention. Most of the dalesmen returned to their duties. A few headed back toward town. Rhaymon helped Forester up, and as soon as he was on his feet, the fighter ran down the road after Cyric. The apparition of the Zhentilar simply faded from view, whimpering and moaning as it disappeared.

"How . . . how did you know?" Forester gasped between panted breaths.

Cyric stopped for a moment and turned back to face the fighter. "Did you see anyone running away? Do you feel any older?"

A look of complete confusion crossed Forester's face. "Older? Of course not. Do I look older?"

"No. That's how I knew it wasn't an actual ghost. A real ghost, created when a truly evil man dies, is so frightening that those who look upon it age ten years in an instant. Ghosts radiate fear, too." Cyric shook his head when he saw that the fighter still didn't understand.

"Since you didn't look any older than you did when we were defending the bridge, and since none of the other dalesmen were running away, I figured it couldn't be real."

Forester still looked confused, but he nodded his head as if he understood completely. Cyric scowled. These dalesmen are idiots, he thought. "Look," the thief said at last, "I don't have time to give you a treatise about the undead. I need to find Kelemvor. I was told he came this way about two hours ago."

"He was here," Forester said, "but he disappeared into the woods some time back. I haven't seen him since."

Cyric cursed softly and headed for the trees.

"Be careful!" Forester called as Cyric walked toward the smoky forest. "We heard some kind of wild animal in there a little while ago."

Most likely a panther, Cyric thought. At least that means Kelemvor's not far away. The thief drew his sword and cautiously moved into the forest.

Smoke hung in the air deep into the woods, so that Cyric found it difficult to breathe at times. His brown eyes reddened as stinging tears ran down his lean face and streaked the grime still caked there from the battle. The thief squinted and continued to press on through the groves of oak and tangles of vines that filled the forest around him.

After moving east for about an hour, Cyric noticed that the air was clearing and he could breathe more easily. He discovered a tuft of black fur on a large thorny bush, but as the thief was examining the fur, he heard a branch snap loudly to the south, then another. Quickly he ducked behind a tree and gripped his sword more firmly.

Within two minutes, a blood-spattered Zhentish archer rushed past Cyric's hiding place. The archer was breathing hard, his arms and legs pumping frantically. After every two or three steps, he threw a worried glance back over his shoulder. Birds of various shapes and colors erupted from the bushes and shot noisily into the sky as the soldier passed.

Cyric started to scramble up the tree, hoping to avoid whatever was chasing the young archer. Halfway up, thoughts of the Spiderhaunt Woods, where Cyric had tried to escape from some giant spiders by climbing into the treetops, rushed into his head. Perhaps this is a mistake, he thought.

Before Cyric could leap to the ground, a large black panther burst from the trees and headed north after the Zhentish archer. The creature's beautiful green eyes were sparkling with malevolent glee as it raced through the forest and out of Cyric's sight.

"Kel," Cyric muttered softly and started to climb down from the tree. He heard a short, high-pitched screech to the north, followed quickly by the roar of the panther as it savaged its victim.

Cyric's eyes glazed momentarily as pity welled inside him for Kelemvor Lyonsbane, the powerful, highly skilled fighter who had been his companion for nearly a year. Kelemvor had traveled alongside him, along with Adon, a cleric of Sune, and Midnight, a spirited, raven-haired magic-user, on a quest to rescue the Goddess of Magic. Now Adon and Midnight were imprisoned in the dungeon of the Twisted Tower, awaiting trial for the murder of Elminster, while Kelemvor roamed the woods in the form of a panther. But the fighter had no control over his transformation into a beast.

The Lyonsbane family was cursed.

Long ago, one of Kelemvor's ancestors had abandoned a powerful mage during a battle, choosing instead to strike out after a treasure. The mage's dying curse made it impossible for the Lyonsbanes to do anything for less than altruistic reasons. However, over time, the curse reversed itself. Now a Lyonsbane could not do anything *except* what was in his own best interest. To aid another, he must receive a reward. Kelemvor had no choice but to become a hardened mercenary—or turn into a monster until he killed someone!

I wonder what activated the curse this time? Cyric thought as he crept through the underbrush.

The panther was lying down, licking the blood from its claws, when Cyric entered the small clearing. The torn body of the Zhentish archer was stretched out in front of the animal. As soon as the panther saw Cyric, it tensed, started to rise, and bared its perfect, white teeth in a savage snarl. Cyric leveled his sword defensively and backed up a cautious step.

"It's Cyric, Kel! Stay back! Don't make me hurt you."

The panther growled deep in its throat and crouched, as if it were about to pounce. Cyric continued to back up slowly until he felt a large oak behind him. Grimly he prepared to run the panther through if it leaped at him. The panther appeared ready to pounce at any instant, but instead it suddenly became very still, then threw back its head and gave a high, piercing yowl.

As Cyric watched, the panther's fur rippled spasmodically. The beast spread its jaws wide, wider than should have been possible. Two hands, covered with gore, reached out from inside the creature, grabbed its jaws, and forced them even wider. There was a sickening tearing sound, and suddenly the panther's body, starting at the mouth, split in half. The animal half dropped to the ground and instantly started to disintegrate.

A shivering, naked, manlike creature collapsed on the ground beside the pile of disintegrating animal flesh, where the panther had crouched only seconds before. Cyric stood frozen in awe. Though he had witnessed Kelemvor's transformation from panther to man once before, in Tilverton, the thief was both fascinated and revulsed by the spectacle. He found it impossible to turn away. Soon the shape on the ground became thoroughly human.

"Who—who did I kill this time?" Kelemvor asked softly. He tried to lift himself off the ground, but he was too weak.

"A Zhentish soldier. The dalesmen will thank you for it later." Cyric removed his cloak and wrapped it around Kelemvor's shoulders. "What caused you to change, Kel?"

"Elminster," Kelemvor said, shaking his head weakly. "He promised to remove the curse if I fought for Shadowdale in the battle. But if Elminster's dead, I can't receive my payment." The fighter glanced at the body of the Zhentish archer and shuddered. "I'm just glad it wasn't one of the dalesmen."

"Why? The dalesmen are no different from the Zhentish." Cyric scowled at the fighter. "Do you know what I just saw? I saw Forester, that big oaf who fought with me at the bridge, slit the throat of a helpless, wounded Zhentilar rather than take him prisoner."

"Remember, this is war, Cyric." The fighter flexed his arms. Finding his strength returned, Kelemvor pushed himself up from the ground. "You can't expect the dalesmen to tie up troops caring for the wounded of their enemies. Besides, the Zhentish started this. It serves them right."

"And does it serve Midnight and Adon right to be locked up in the Twisted Tower, waiting for the dalesmen to find them guilty of Elminster's murder?" Cyric snapped. "You and I know that they didn't kill that old man. It was probably Bane's avatar or a misfired spell. But the villagers need someone to blame, so they'll undoubtedly find our friends guilty."

"That's not true! Lord Mourngrym will give them a fair trial. Justice will be served."

Cyric stood in shocked silence for a moment. When he finally spoke, his voice was low, almost a growl. "Mourngrym will give the dalesmen exactly what they want. The justice served here will be the same as that given at the executions in Bane's temple in Zhentil Keep."

Kelemvor turned away from the thief and started toward the bushes. "I need to find my clothes and my armor. Are you coming?"

As the fighter disappeared into the underbrush, Cyric swore softly. Clearly Kelemvor had been fooled by the facade of law and truth the dalesmen had erected for themselves. "I'll just have to deal with this alone," the thief vowed to himself as he marched off after the fighter.

❧ 1 ❧

The Trial

There were depths to the darkness surrounding Midnight that she feared to explore. The room was perfectly black. It might have been a storage area at one time, or perhaps a large closet. The momentary glimpse that the magic-user had been given of the tiny cell when she and Adon were first locked away had revealed very little. The light from the torch their jailer held hadn't seemed to illuminate the room, and Midnight now wondered if the ceiling, walls, and floor of the cell had been painted black to keep her disoriented.

She'd been bound and gagged to prevent her from casting any spells, but the dalesmen had neglected to blindfold her. She had a horrible feeling of total isolation in the pitch-dark room. Only the sound of Adon's breathing reminded Midnight that she was not alone in the cell.

The network of ropes around the magic-user held her arms behind her back and bound her legs together tightly. Her wrists and ankles had been tied, too, and her fingers awkwardly touched the heels of her feet. Lying with her face pressed half against the floor was the only position that was remotely comfortable. At least it allowed her an occasional hour or so of sleep. Even then, though, pain constantly shot through her body.

After the first few hours in the black room, the magic-user's initial panic began to subside, only to be replaced by a numbing fear. Was it possible that she had been forgotten and left there to die? Again and again, she attempted to scream, but her muffled cries yielded no response. Occasionally she heard Adon shift in the darkness. Midnight wondered if the cleric was awake. He had said nothing since they were taken prisoner at the ruined Temple of Lathander. The mage knew the cleric hadn't been gagged. If he didn't speak, it was probably because he was unconscious or in shock.

As Midnight thought of all that had happened to her and her friends since they had left Arabel less than a month ago, she wondered why she hadn't gone into shock, too. First Mystra, the Goddess of Magic, had entrusted her with a shard of power in the form of a pendant. Then the gods had been thrown out of the Planes because of the theft of the two Tablets of Fate—ancient artifacts that listed the names of all the gods and their spheres of influence. Next Midnight had gone with Kelemvor, Cyric, Adon, and the goddess's intended avatar to save Mystra from Lord Bane, the God of Strife.

When they rescued Mystra, the goddess took back the power she had given to Midnight and tried to enter the Planes using a Celestial Stairway. The stairway, like many others throughout the Realms, was actually a path to the Planes, a direct link from the world to the homes of the gods. But before Mystra could climb the stairway and reach her home in Nirvana, Lord Helm, the God of Guardians, had stopped her.

Though Mystra tried to defeat Helm, the god would not allow her to pass into the Planes without the Tablets of Fate. And because Helm still had much of his godly power, he was able to stop the fallen goddess easily. In the end, Mystra had been killed, but not before she returned the pendant to Midnight, along with instructions to seek out Elminster in Shadowdale and find the lost Tablets of Fate before the Realms suffered even more damage.

While traveling through the chaos-ridden lands of Faerun, Midnight and her companions had been brought together as friends. The magic-user had gained Kelemvor as a lover, and Cyric and Adon as close allies. She had been lucky until now, although she felt she was a mere pawn in the conflicts of the gods, she had lost nothing. Not like Adon.

For clerics, the crisis in Faerun after the night of Arrival had been especially trying. Priests found that they could cast spells only if they were within a mile of their deity.

Worse still, they saw their deities take on flesh and blood to survive. Now the gods had all the limitations of a mortal frame. But Adon seemed to accept all this as the will of the gods.

Until the day the heroes left Tilverton.

On that day, a worshiper of Gond had attacked Adon with a knife and slashed him savagely across the face. Because Midnight and her allies needed to escape into the desolate area around the Shadow Gap in order to lose the mob that followed them out of Tilverton, they could not take the unconscious cleric to a healer. An ugly scar formed on Adon's face. Some might have considered this a mark of glory. Adon, however, was a worshiper of Lady Sune, the Goddess of Beauty.

Suddenly Adon felt as if he had been abandoned by Sune, as if he had done something terribly wrong and deserved to be punished. The once-joyful young cleric grew morose and sullen. Midnight had hoped that helping to save the Dales from the armies of Zhentil Keep would help Adon recover his spirit, but the incidents at the Temple of Lathander, when Elminster and Midnight battled Lord Bane, only deepened the cleric's depression.

And unless I can find a way to prove that it was Bane—not Adon and I—who killed Elminster, Midnight thought, things could get a lot worse for both of us.

Midnight reviewed the battle at the temple over and over again in her mind, examining each minute detail. She knew there had to be some way to prove that she and Adon had not killed the great sage, but she simply couldn't discover it.

She heard a noise at the door: the sound of keys rattling on a chain. The heavy door swung open, and Midnight was forced to squeeze her eyes shut as the bright flame from a torch nearly blinded her.

"Get them out." The voice was deep and resonant, but tinged with pain. "And be careful."

Midnight felt strong hands upon her, and she forced her eyes open. Guardsmen had grabbed her from either side. A powerful figure stood in the doorway, a torch held in one hand, a walking stick crowned with a small silver dragon's skull in the other.

"She's shaking," one of the guards said as they lifted Midnight from the floor. A muffled cry of agony rang out from the magic-user, and the guards hesitated.

"What do you expect?" the man in the doorway snapped. "You've trussed her up like an animal. Her limbs are sore."

As they dragged Midnight forward, her legs scraping along the floor, the bruised and scarred face of the aging warrior came fully into view. She did not recognize the older man, though she was immediately struck by his sharp blue eyes. He frowned slightly as Midnight was dragged past him.

The mage saw four other guardsmen in the hallway. Two of them entered the black room and retrieved Adon. Then the prisoners were taken past a row of barred cells, through a narrow hallway, and into the cavernous expanse of an outer chamber, where a table and three chairs had been set up.

"Remove the gag," the older man said as he helped the guards to position Midnight in a large wooden chair.

"But she's a powerful magic-user! Remember, she killed Elminster with her powers," a short, blond guard snapped as he backed away from Midnight. The other guards reached for their weapons. Adon simply stood where the guards had left him, a blank look on his face.

The older man grimaced. His blue eyes sparked with anger. "Has she been fed or given water?"

"No," the blond guard mumbled. "The risks—"

"The risks will be mine," the older man growled. He walked out from behind the chair and looked into the dark-haired woman's eyes. "She knows that I'm here to help her."

Suspicious glances passed between the guards.

"Do it now!" the older man bellowed. He clutched at the back of the chair as the strain of raising his voice took its toll, and he started to cough uncontrollably. Despite his impressive stature, the man was obviously recovering from a traumatic illness.

The guards removed Midnight's gag, and she opened her mouth wide, gulping in mouthfuls of air. "Water . . . water, please," Midnight croaked, her throat completely raw. The older man nodded, and a guard brought her a ladle full of cool water.

"Cut the bonds on her legs," the blue-eyed man ordered. "She can't cast spells with her feet. Besides, I want her to walk to the trial." The order was obeyed without hesitation, and Midnight relaxed noticeably as circulation began to return to her legs and feet.

"I am Thurbal," the older man said as Adon was seated next to Midnight. "I'm captain of the guard. It is important that you pay attention to my every word. In less than an hour, these men will lead you through the Twisted Tower to the audience chambers of Lord Mourngrym, our liege. There you will be tried for the murder of Elminster the sage.

"You must tell me all you can about the events leading up to the death of the mage. I need to know everything if I am to give you a proper defense." Thurbal gripped the dragon skull of his walking stick as if he were fighting off a wave of pain.

"Why are you helping us?" Midnight asked, curious.

"I was wounded on a mission to Zhentil Keep and lay deep in a healing sleep for most of the time you've been in the dale. Because of this, Mourngrym is convinced that I will be fair and impartial in this matter."

"But Elminster was your friend," Midnight said. Her gaze drifted to Adon, who sat staring at the wall behind Thurbal, his eyes glazed, his skin pale and taut.

"Elminster was more than just my friend," Thurbal replied. "He was a friend to all the Dales and everyone who loves freedom and knowledge in Faerun. Anyone who knew him would testify to that. That could prove to be unfortunate for you. Time is short. You must tell me your side of the story."

For the next hour, Midnight recounted the details of her involvement with the elderly sage. She focused on the events that led up to Elminster's death in the Temple of Lathander, of course, but the true story of her involvement with the mage had begun when Mystra gave her the shard of power to safeguard.

Midnight closed her eyes as she recalled Bane's attack on the Temple of Lathander. "Elminster tried to summon a powerful force from another plane to deal with Bane," she began. "But the spell went awry. The rift he opened allowed Mystra—or more precisely, a fragment of Mystra's essence—to escape from the magical weave around Faerun."

"But I thought you said Mystra died back at Castle Kilgrave in Cormyr?" Thurbal asked.

"Yes, that's right. But when Helm destroyed her avatar, her energy must have been absorbed by the weave. She was more like a magic elemental when she appeared . . . a force rather than a person." Midnight let her head loll back to relieve the tension from her neck before continuing.

"But even Mystra couldn't save Elminster from Bane. The Black Lord forced Elminster into the rift before he was destroyed. Adon and I tried to save him, but we couldn't." Midnight opened her eyes once more and found Thurbal staring at the cleric.

"Well, Adon," the older man said, "what have you to say? Did you try to save Elminster?"

Adon had remained completely still as Midnight related the story of Bane's attack on the temple. The cleric sat with his hands bound tightly together, resting on his lap. Occasionally Adon would reach up to cover the scar on his face, but a guard would quickly push his hands back down. When Thurbal addressed Adon, the cleric slowly turned to look at the captain and simply stared at him, glassy-eyed and silent.

Thurbal shook his head and ran his hands through his thinning brown hair. "His silence certainly won't help us during the trial," he said. "Can't you get him to talk?"

Midnight looked at the young cleric. The man she saw before her was hardly the cleric she had met in Arabel. Adon's face was pale, and his light brown hair was a mess, something he never would have tolerated before he was wounded. The most disturbing thing to Midnight, however, was the lifelessness in his once-shining green eyes. "No," she sighed softly. "It's probably best if I do all the talking."

"Very well," Thurbal said. He rose from the table and nodded to a guardsman who had moved behind the magic-user. The guard replaced the gag just as Midnight attempted a cry of protest. "I'm sorry," Thurbal said, "but I have my orders.

The town fears your powers, and Lord Mourngrym refuses to allow the possibility that you will create havoc at the trial with your spells."

The prisoners were taken up the stairway of the Twisted Tower. They passed through a stone arch and stood on aching legs in the central corridor of the tower as Thurbal conferred with one of his guards. The corridor led from the main entrance and traversed two thirds of the tower's length; its width was so great that five people could have walked side by side without difficulty.

Just then the door to Mourngrym's audience chamber burst open, and a chorus of outraged protests erupted from within. The prisoners were taken through the audience chamber with a show of force that brought cheers from the massive crowd gathered in the makeshift courtroom. Despite the thick stone walls of the fortress, the sounds of the outraged villagers outside added to the pandemonium. Chaos threatened to overtake the proceedings.

A dais lay at the head of the room, and Lord Mourngrym stood at the center of the platform, a small lectern before him. Dalesmen of noble blood were seated behind him. The ruler of the dales clutched the edges of the lectern until his knuckles grew white as the prisoners were prodded up the narrow stairs and deposited before him. Thurbal followed the prisoners and took his place at Mourngrym's left.

Storm Silverhand, the famous female bard and adventurer, stepped forward from the crowd and moved to Mourngrym's right. Light from the open shutters and the few torches scattered around the room reflected in her silver-hued hair, and hatred flashed in her blue-gray eyes. Storm and Sharantyr, a ranger with the Knights of Myth Drannor, had discovered Midnight and Adon lying unhurt outside the shattered Temple of Lathander. They also had discovered the fragments of a body that must have been Elminster's, along with cloth from his robe and pages from one of the sage's spellbooks.

As the prisoners knelt before Mourngrym, the noise from the crowd in the audience chamber began to swell. Much of the surviving populace of Shadowdale had turned out for the trial, and both the courtroom and the area outside the tower were crowded with angry men and women who shouted curses at Midnight and Adon. The soldiers of Mourngrym's guard found it difficult to contain the crowd.

Standing among the group of spectators at the front of the chamber, Kelemvor stared at the vulnerable form of his former lover as she was forced to kneel before Mourngrym. The fighter studied the cold, inaccessible expression of the dalelord and understood why his petition for a private audience with him the previous evening had been denied. Mourngrym's fury over the loss of his friend was obvious, though he was attempting to put aside his personal feelings and act with impartiality.

Mourngrym raised his hand, and silence fell upon the court instantly. "We have gathered here to perform a solemn duty, not to howl like hungry dogs in the night. Let us act like civilized men. Elminster would expect us to do nothing less."

A murmur rose from the spectators, but as the noise died down, the low, growling laughter of one man continued. Kelemvor turned to his left and jabbed his elbow sharply into Cyric's side. "Shut up, you fool!" the fighter whispered.

Cyric sneered at Kelemvor and shook his head. "Wait until the trial is over, Kel. Then we'll see what you think of the dalesmen's grand claims of justice."

When Cyric turned back to the dais, Mourngrym had his gaze locked on the thief. Raising one hand in mock apology, Cyric bowed slightly. A rumble of angry whispers was rising from the crowd again, but Mourngrym raised both hands to still the sound and cleared his throat noisily.

"Midnight of Deepingdale and Adon of Sune, you stand accused of the murder of the sage, Elminster," Mourngrym began.

The silence of the crowd was shattered like a fragile crystal by Mourngrym's words. Shouting for quiet, the dalelord unsheathed his sword and held it high in the air. Torchlight played off the blade and seemed to transform it into a mystic weapon, brilliant, hard, and unyielding. The guards all drew their swords and held them up in like fashion. The angry murmuring was silenced.

"Justice will be served," Mourngrym said. "I swear it!" There were cheers, and Mourngrym allowed the crowd to settle once more before he continued. "This is a military trial," he pronounced. "As such, there will be no jury. As lord of the dale, the responsibility of judgment is mine.

"Since magic is unstable, we dare not attempt to look into the minds of the accused. Facts alone will shape my verdict." Mourngrym gestured to the silver-haired woman beside him. "Let the prosecution introduce its case."

Storm Silverhand stepped forward. "There are two inescapable facts. First, a body was discovered in the Temple of Lathander. True, it was battered and torn beyond recognition, but the body was found near scraps of Elminster's robe and fragments from a number of his ancient spellbooks." The bard turned to the crowd. "Our sage and protector was missing, obviously murdered."

Storm Silverhand turned to the prisoners and gestured toward them. "Second, these two were seen running from the temple only seconds before it was leveled by magical forces. Yet they survived unscathed." The crowd's screams and threats echoed in the room.

Unlike Mourngrym, Storm didn't wait for the crowd to quiet down. "It is obvious that these two murdered our good friend," she cried over the noise of the spectators. Midnight tried to protest from under her gag, but it was no use.

"Hold!" Thurbal cried, waving his cane in the air. The captain of the guard turned to face Mourngrym. "We must not assume the guilt of these people. We are here to determine what happened, not to lynch these two!"

A storm of boos and hisses erupted from the spectators. Cyric glanced at Kelemvor, but the fighter was staring straight ahead. Thurbal shook his head and sat down, and Mourngrym rapped the lectern with the pommel of his sword.

"One more outburst like this and we will hold these hearings in seclusion!" the dalelord warned in a loud voice. The crowd quieted down while the guards removed a few spectators who refused to stop shouting.

"The prosecution calls Rhaymon of Lathander," Storm pronounced, and a blond man dressed in bright red robes with thick bands of gold trim was led forward by a guardsman.

"Tell us about the last time you saw Elminster alive," Storm said.

The priest frowned thoughtfully, then began to speak. "My final duty on the day of the Battle of Shadowdale was to stand guard at the Temple of Lathander until Elminster arrived."

"Stand guard? Against what?" Storm asked. "What were your fellow priests worried about?"

Rhaymon frowned, as if he had been asked a foolish question. "Earlier that day, the Temple of Tymora had been attacked. We were all badly shaken. The priests of Tymora were slaughtered, the temple desecrated, and the symbol of Bane painted in blood on its walls. Also the healing potions stored in Tymora's temple were stolen."

"So you feared, naturally enough, that the same thing could happen at your temple?"

"Yes, that's correct," Rhaymon said. "Elminster said he had something important to do at the temple. He said he would guard it for us."

"Even with his very life?" Storm leaned close to the cleric.

Thurbal stepped forward, gesturing with his cane in protest. "She's putting words in his mouth. Let the man speak for himself!"

Mourngrym's eyes smoldered. "Get on with it, Storm."

The silver-haired adventurer frowned and backed away from Rhaymon. "Was Elminster alone when he arrived at the temple?" the bard asked after a moment.

Shaking his head, the priest gestured toward the prisoners. "No. They were with him."

"Can you describe Elminster's mood at the time?"

Rhaymon seemed put off by the question. "Are you serious?" he mumbled quietly.

"I assure you, no one could be more serious," Storm said grimly.

The priest swallowed. "He was a bit cranky, but he *was* Elminster, after all."

There was some laughter from the crowd, but no hint of a smile crossed Storm's features. "Would it be fair to say Elminster seemed agitated? Did the presence of the prisoners upset him?"

Rhaymon looked serious. "I couldn't say what the cause of his uneasiness was. I do know this," the priest said quickly as he pointed toward Adon. "The one with the scar stopped me as I was leaving and told me to make Bane's soldiers pay for what happened to the worshipers of Tymora."

Stormed nodded. "I have one final question. Do you think the prisoners killed Elminster?"

Thurbal rushed to stand before Mourngrym. "Milord, this goes too far!"

The expression of the dalelord grew dark. "I will decide how far this goes." Mourngrym turned to the priest. "Answer the question."

The priest tensed as he looked down at the prisoners. "If I could run them through, here and now, I would gladly do so. Many men, some hardly more than boys, died to save this town. While those heroes were giving their lives, these two were making a mockery of their sacrifice!"

"That is all," Storm said, and she took her place beside Mourngrym.

Thurbal eyed the priest carefully before he spoke. "Did you see either the scarred cleric or the woman harm Elminster in any way?"

"Our way of life has been destroyed! We will have to rebuild the temple—"

"Answer the question," Thurbal said calmly.

Rhaymon shook with anger. "I saw nothing."

"Thank you," Thurbal said. "You may go."

A guardsman took Rhaymon's arm and led him away. The priest looked over his shoulder and wrenched free of the guard. "I did not see the sun rise this morning! Does that mean this trial should be cloaked in darkness because it did not rise?"

"Enough!" Mourngrym declared firmly, and two guards gripped Rhaymon's arms.

"They are guilty and deserve no less than death!" Rhaymon shouted. Instantly the crowd was stirred into a frenzy. As the robed man was dragged away, the guards grabbed several others from the crowd and forced them out of the audience chamber. The noise from outside the tower was growing steadily louder.

Cyric sat down on the bench and ran his hand through his brown hair. For this we risked our lives, the thief thought. We saved these cattle so they could put us on trial.

Then Cyric's attentions turned to Adon. The cleric was slack-jawed and seemed unaware of the gravity of the proceedings around him. There was no gag to prevent the cleric from declaring his innocence, but instead Adon chose to remain silent. Say something, you worthless slug! Cyric thought. If not for your sake, then do it for Midnight!

But Adon did not speak, even as Lhaeo was called to testify. The young man who stood before the court had brown hair and gentle green eyes. His back held straight, his concentration directed fully toward Storm Silverhand, Lhaeo stood with an air of royalty, a far cry from the simpering fop most denizens of the dale were familiar with. "I am Elminster's scribe," Lhaeo said. His voice was firm.

"When Midnight and Adon first arrived at Elminster's tower, they were in the company of Hawksguard, the acting captain of the guard." Lhaeo looked out into the audience. "The fighters, Kelemvor and Cyric, were also with them."

"Can you describe anything unusual in the exchange between Elminster and the magic-user, Midnight?" Storm asked.

Lhaeo swallowed. "Elminster indicated that this was not his first encounter with Midnight. He said something about the Stonelands."

"Where a strange disturbance was seen in the skies just days before the strangers arrived in Shadowdale," Storm pointed out. "Do you know anything about that?"

Lhaeo looked down into Midnight's eyes and saw the quiet desperation of the magic-user. Memories of Elminster teleporting from his tower in haste, then returning after nightfall, muttering something about Geryon's Death Spell, ran through the scribe's mind.

"Not that I recall," Lhaeo said, and Midnight's eyes closed slowly in thanks. "I wish to go on record that I do not believe Elminster is dead."

There were startled cries of outrage from the onlookers.

"We all know how close you were to the sage, Lhaeo," Storm said sympathetically. "I would not think it an exaggeration to say that he was like a father to you." Storm watched as Lhaeo stiffened. "But don't let that overwhelm your reason."

Storm bent over and picked up the tattered fragments of Elminster's robe and the pages from the ancient spellbooks. "These are Elminster's, are they not?" Lhaeo nodded slowly. "It is rather unlikely that your master would let artifacts such as these books be destroyed. And it is, in fact, impossible that he would allow the Temple of Lathander to be destroyed. If he were alive, surely he would have kept his promise to the clerics."

The bard paused for a moment before she spoke again. "What business did Midnight have with Elminster?"

"She claimed that she carried the final words of the goddess Mystra, as well as a symbol of the goddess's trust."

"Then she is a heretic as well as a killer!" Storm cried, and the crowd exploded.

"Enough!" Mourngrym shouted, and the spectators slowly grew quiet once more. "Control yourself, Storm, or I will be forced to find a replacement for you in these proceedings!"

There was silence from the crowd.

"You were not present at the Temple of Lathander?" Storm asked when she turned back to the scribe.

"No," Lhaeo said softly. "Elminster had sent me to contact the Knights of Myth Drannor. Magical communication with the East had been blocked. I was armed with Elminster's wards and traveled at night."

"You left the same day the strangers arrived," Storm stated sharply.

"That is true." Lhaeo said.

"Was it possible that Elminster did not trust the strangers and was attempting to protect you from them?" Storm asked.

Lhaeo hesitated for a moment, Storm's words striking him like a blow. "I don't think so," the scribe said slowly. "No, that would not have been like him."

"Yet you rarely accompanied him on his many ventures throughout the Realms. Why was that?"

Drawing a sharp breath, the scribe looked away from the bard. "I don't know," he said softly.

"I have nothing further to ask." Storm turned away from the glaring green eyes of the scribe. Thurbal gripped the handle of his walking stick, his fingers caressing the dragon skull of the handle. Perspiration trickled down his face as he spoke.

"Why did Elminster allow Midnight and Adon to stay at his tower?" Thurbal said.

"Elminster trusted them and felt they would be of valuable assistance in the Battle of Shadowdale," Lhaeo said.

"Elminster told you this?" Thurbal asked.

"Aye, and he allowed Midnight to assist him in the casting of many spells as the cleric researched mystical tomes."

"Did he seem frightened or suspicious of Midnight and Adon in any way?" Thurbal inquired.

"No," Lhaeo said. "Not at all. Quite the opposite."

Biting his lip, Thurbal asked his next question. "Is the goddess Mystra dead?"

Storm rose up to shout in protest, but Mourngrym silenced her and ordered the scribe to answer the question.

"According to Elminster, a horrible fate befell the goddess. Whether or not she is dead, I cannot say." Lhaeo sighed and hung his head.

"When Midnight arrived with her claims of a message from the goddess, Elminster did not laugh or send her away," Thurbal stated flatly. "He was convinced of her integrity and dedication to the Realms." Both Thurbal and the scribe remained silent for a moment.

"If you have nothing else to ask, Thurbal, I think we've heard enough from this witness," Mourngrym said.

Lhaeo quietly left the stand and returned to his seat. Storm moved forward and called a burly guardsman with hazel eyes named Irak Dontaele.

"Your patrol was on duty the night of the attack against the Temple of Tymora. You were the first to enter the temple and discover the bodies of the worshipers and the desecration of the temple itself," Storm said.

"No," Irak growled. "Not true." Quickly he rushed past the other guards, grabbed Adon by his robes, and lifted the cleric up off his knees. "This one was there before any of us!"

"Put him down!" Mourngrym said, and the crossbows of the guards who stood behind the prisoners were suddenly leveled at the witness. Adon's dull eyes swam in their sockets as he was lowered reluctantly to the ground. "What is the meaning of this, Storm? Are you trying to show some connection between the attacks on the two temples?"

"There's the connection!" Storm cried, pointing at Adon. "This man was present both times. They say he is a cleric of Sune, the Goddess of Beauty, yet look at his face. Even without the ugliness of his scar, he is hardly what one would expect. I submit that Adon of Sune and Midnight of Deepingdale are allies of the Black Lord, and their true allegiance is to that evil god and the city of Zhentil Keep. That is why they murdered Elminster!"

A roar erupted from the crowd. "Kill them!" someone cried.

"Yes!" screamed a woman. "Death to the servants of Lord Bane!"

Mourngrym struggled to maintain his composure. "Enough!" he ordered.

"No!" Storm cried, turning to face Lord Mourngrym. "What names did the adventurers give to the guards when they first arrived in the dale?"

Kelemvor winced. When they had arrived in Shadowdale, they had used a false charter to gain admission to the town. The fighter had been certain that the matter would be forgotten in the chaos caused by Bane's attack.

"They used false names . . . a stolen charter. If my words are untrue," Storm shouted, "why hasn't the cleric said anything in his own defense?" Storm now stood directly over Adon. "Speak, murderer! Tell us what you've done!"

Adon didn't look up to meet the bard's fiery gaze. He simply looked straight ahead and whimpered. "Sune," he said simply, and then he was silent once more.

"Thurbal, have you any witnesses to call?" Mourngrym inquired.

"I call Kelemvor Lyonsbane," Thurbal said, and the fighter was escorted forward from the crowd. "You led the eastern defenses near Krag Pool, where Bane's army suffered the greatest number of casualties and the decisive victory against our enemies was won. Yet you entered Shadowdale at the same time as the prisoners, and in their company. Tell us briefly how you know the accused."

"Midnight and Adon are of stout heart, and their loyalty to the Dales and to the Realms should not be questioned," Kelemvor said confidently.

"Tell him to answer the question," Storm snapped, turning to Mourngrym.

Kelemvor examined the striking, silver-haired woman. His gaze locked on her blue-gray eyes as he told the tale of his first meeting with Midnight in Arabel and the quest that eventually led them to the Dales.

"So this was a business arrangement," Thurbal stated. "You didn't know her before you met in Arabel."

"No, I didn't," Kelemvor said. "But I've come to know her very well since then."

"He's a consummate mercenary," Storm said. "He does nothing without some form of reward."

Passing his fingers over his mouth, Mourngrym spoke. "If you had not been called, Kelemvor Lyonsbane, if you had been forced to volunteer to testify on Midnight's behalf, would you have spoken for her?"

The fighter shook, his face growing dark. To lie in Midnight's favor would be an unselfish act he had not been paid for. And that would trigger the curse.

"Answer the question," Mourngrym said.

Kelemvor glanced at Midnight, and her eyes were wide with fear. With a heavy heart, Kelemvor turned back to Mourngrym. "I could not," he said.

"No further questions," Thurbal snapped, turning away from the fighter in disgust. Storm simply smiled and dismissed Kelemvor.

The fighter said nothing as he was led back to the crowd. Cyric stared at Kelemvor as he walked past. The thief saw the look of defeat in his friend's eyes. For some reason, it made Cyric feel a little better to know that Kelemvor now realized he was right about the dalesmen.

"This day grows long, Thurbal." Mourngrym folded his hands upon the lectern. "Have you any other witnesses?"

"Only you, milord," Thurbal said softly.

Mourngrym stared at the older man. "Are you well? Have you taken leave—"

"I call Mourngrym Amcathra," Thurbal pronounced distinctly. "By the laws of the Dales, you cannot refuse to testify unless you wish to declare this trial at an end and release the prisoners."

The eyes of the dalelord turned wild with anger, but Mourngrym nodded and said in an even voice, "Very well. Ask me what you will."

"Where was Lord Bane throughout the battle for Shadowdale?" Thurbal asked.

Mourngrym cocked his head slightly. "I don't understand."

"Bane led the attack through the forest from Voonlar. Our scouts can verify this. I will summon them if you wish." Thurbal leaned against the lectern as a coughing fit overcame him.

"That won't be necessary," Mourngrym said. "Bane led the attack."

"At Krag Pool, before the defenders of the dale toppled the trees upon Bane's army, the Black Lord vanished," Thurbal stated calmly. "There are dozens of witnesses I can present to verify this as well."

"Go on," Mourngrym said impatiently.

"The next time Bane was sighted, it was at the crossroads, near the farm of Jhaele Silvermane. The Black Lord appeared before you, Mourngrym Amcathra, and attempted to slay you. Mayheir Hawksguard pushed you aside and was fatally wounded in your stead. Is that correct?"

"Aye," Mourngrym replied. "Hawksguard died nobly in the defense of the Dales."

"Where did Lord Bane go after that?" Thurbal asked. "Weren't you quite vulnerable? Could he have not slain you then and there, despite Hawksguard's sacrifice?"

"I don't know," Mourngrym mumbled uncomfortably. "Perhaps."

"But he didn't. He vanished again," Thurbal said. "Bane's attentions must have been drawn elsewhere." The captain was seized by another coughing fit. Mourngrym drummed his fingers nervously on the lectern.

"I'm all right," Thurbal said, and he drew a breath before

continuing. "Now, where was Elminster throughout the battle for Shadowdale?"

"At the Temple of Lathander," Mourngrym replied.

"Why?" Thurbal asked. "Why was he not at the front lines using his magic to help repel Bane?"

Mourngrym shook his head. He had no answer.

"Didn't Elminster tell you repeatedly that the true battle would take place in the Temple of Lathander?" Thurbal asked.

"Aye, but he never explained what he meant by that statement," Mourngrym said. "Perhaps he had foreseen the danger to the prisoners and wished to draw them away from the true battle—"

Thurbal held up his hand. "I suggest that the true battle was at the temple, that Bane went there, and it was he who murdered Elminster the sage."

Storm stood up and threw her arms over her head. "All this is complete speculation. There isn't a bit of evidence to suggest Bane was at the Temple of Lathander."

Thurbal grimaced and turned to Mourngrym. "Before you can convict the prisoners, you must show a motive for their actions. Storm Silverhand claims they were agents of Bane. Yet there is no proof to support such allegations. I spoke to the prisoner, Midnight, before the trial, and she claims—"

Mourngrym raised his fist. "I don't care what she claims!" he snapped. "She is a powerful mage, powerful enough to slay Elminster. My orders were explicit: She was not to be allowed to speak to anyone!"

"Then how is she to defend herself?" Thurbal yelled.

"How do any of us know that she did not ensorcel you when you spoke, bending your will to hers?" Storm asked. "You are hopelessly trusting, my friend, and for your own sake, you should be removed as counsel."

"You cannot!" Thurbal yelped and moved to Mourngrym's side.

"You're wrong. I cannot let you be injured again by Bane's servants." Mourngrym gestured to a pair of guards. "See that Thurbal is well provided for. He is obviously fighting off the effects of powerful magic. Whatever guards were present when Midnight spoke should be relieved of duty, pending my later judgment. Take him away."

Thurbal cried out in protest, but he was too weak to stave off the guards that dragged him away.

Addressing the court, Mourngrym stepped out from behind the lectern. "I have seen all that I need to," Mourngrym said. "Elminster the sage was our friend and our loyal defender to the death. It was his blind trust in others that led to his demise. Yet we of this court are not blind. Our eyes are open wide, and we can see the truth.

"Lord Bane was a coward. He ran from the battle in fear when our forces overwhelmed his army. That is why we cannot account for his whereabouts. If Elminster were alive, he would appear before us now. But that cannot happen. There is nothing we can do to bring Elminster back, but we can put his tortured soul to rest by punishing his murderers."

The audience chamber had grown completely silent again. Mourngrym paused a moment and looked back at the noblemen seated behind the dais. Like the rest of the room, the nobles were staring at the dalelord, waiting for his verdict.

"I decree that at dawn tomorrow, in the courtyard of the Twisted Tower, Midnight of Deepingdale and Adon of Sune will be put to death for the murder of Elminster the sage. Guards, remove the prisoners." Mourngrym stood back, and guards grabbed Midnight and Adon and pulled them to their feet. The crowd erupted in a roar of cheering.

At first Cyric was swallowed up by the crowd, but the thief fought his way through the blood-crazed villagers in time to see Midnight and Adon exit the courtroom under heavy guard.

Justice will be served, Mourngrym had said. The words of Shadowdale's ruler echoed in Cyric's thoughts as he maneuvered past the remaining guards standing in Mourngrym's vicinity. As he drew closer to the dalelord, Cyric thought about exactly how quickly he could draw his dagger and slit Mourngrym's throat.

Mourngrym Amcathra felt a slight rush of air at his back, but when he turned to see what had caused the breeze, he saw only the back of a lean, dark-haired man vanishing into the crowd.

Once again lost in the throng of excited townspeople, Cyric contemplated why he had changed his mind at the last instant and spared the life of the man who had condemned Midnight to death. There were better ways to honor his debt to Midnight and make these contemptuous imbeciles pay, Cyric thought. Besides, the crowd would have torn me to pieces. And I'm not ready to die quite yet.

Quite the opposite, the thief thought. Quite the opposite.

* * * * *

The God of the Dead reached for the shard of red energy with his bony right hand. The fallen god chuckled softly as he held the fragment next to the foot-tall obsidian statue of a man he clutched in his left hand. There was a flash of brilliant white light as the statue absorbed the energy, and Lord Myrkul looked at the faceless figurine. A red mist swirled inside it violently.

"Yes, Lord Bane," the God of the Dead rasped through cracked, black lips. "We will have you whole again soon enough." Myrkul chuckled once more and stroked the smooth head of the statue as if it were a small child. The mist pulsed with an angry red light.

Myrkul looked around and sighed. Faint images of the real world hung in the air around him. The farmer's home in which he stood was dark, dirty, and bleak. The low-beamed ceiling was black from the greasy smoke of the peasants' cooking fires. Rats occasionally scurried across the floor, racing between the legs of the warped wooden tables and splintering benches. Two people lay asleep under stained furs.

Lord Myrkul, the God of Decay as well as the God of the Dead, rather liked this place. It was like a tiny, unintentional shrine to him. In fact, it upset Myrkul that he couldn't experience it fully. For Myrkul was in the Border Ethereal Plane, an area parallel to the plane where the Realms and its people existed. From the Border Ethereal, the things Myrkul saw around him—the furniture; the vermin; the grimy, sleeping peasants—appeared only as phantasms. And if the snoring farmer and his wife had been awake, they wouldn't have been able to see or hear Myrkul.

"If only they *could* see me," the skeletal man complained to the black statue. "I could frighten them to death. How pleasant that would be." Myrkul paused for a moment to consider the effects his avatar's visage, complete with rotting, jaundiced skin and burning, empty eye sockets, would have on the humans. "Their corpses would make this hovel complete."

Energy crackled and arced from the figurine.

"Yes, Lord Bane. The last shard of your being isn't far from here," the God of the Dead hissed. Myrkul cast one glance back at the hovel as he walked through the insubstantial walls. When he got outside into the ghostly moonlight that shone down upon the countryside south of Hillsfar, the God of the Dead shuddered. The filthy hut was much more to his liking.

Pulling the hood of his thick black robe over his head, Lord Myrkul stepped into the air as if he were climbing an invisible staircase. Gravity had no effect on him in the Border Ethereal, and it was easier to see his prize if he looked for it from a vantage point high above the ghostly hills and houses. After he had climbed a hundred yards or so straight up, Myrkul could see the final fragment of Lord Bane glowing in the distance.

"There lies the rest of the God of Strife." Myrkul held the statue up and faced it toward the pulsing shard that rested over a mile away. Tiny bolts of red and black lightning shot from the figurine and bit into the God of the Dead's hands. Slivers of pain raced up the avatar's arm, and Myrkul could smell burning flesh.

"If I drop you, Lord Bane, you will plummet back into the Prime Material Plane, back into the Realms." The tiny arcs of lightning grew smaller. "And I will not help you to recover the last piece of your essence. You will be unwhole— trapped inside this statue."

Myrkul smiled a rictus grin as the lightning ceased and the statue became black once more. "I am pleased to serve you, Lord Bane, but I will not be goaded into action." When the figurine remained dark, the God of the Dead started walking toward the shard of Bane's essence. After an hour, the fallen deities reached their destination.

This fragment of the God of Strife resembled a huge, bloody snowflake, almost three feet wide. It was larger and far more complex than any of the other pieces Myrkul had recovered. *How odd,* the skeletal figure thought. *Each shard is different. This one is the most intricate yet. I wonder if it could be his soul. . . .*

The God of the Dead shrugged and held the statue next to the snowflake. As before, there was a brilliant flash of light as the shard disappeared into the figurine. This time, however, the statue continued to glow brightly, pulsing red and black in a quickening pattern. Myrkul narrowed his eyes in pain as a loud, high-pitched shriek tore through his brain.

I am alive! the God of Strife screamed in Myrkul's mind. *I am whole again!* A pair of burning eyes and a leering, fanged mouth suddenly appeared on the smooth face of the statue.

"Please, Lord Bane, not so loud. You are giving me a splitting headache," the God of the Dead rasped. "I am pleased my plan succeeded."

How did you find me? How did you know I wasn't destroyed?

"I was monitoring the battle in Shadowdale as best I could. When that debased form of Lady Mystra appeared in the temple, it became clear to me that we gods cannot be destroyed, but merely dispersed." Lord Myrkul smiled. "And so, when your avatar was destroyed, I tracked one of the shards of your being into the Border Ethereal and started searching for the others there as well." The God of the Dead tilted his head slightly and tried to look into the obsidian statue. "Are you quite whole now?"

Yes, Myrkul, I'm fine. Do you understand what you've done? The voice inside Myrkul's head was growing loud again, and the God of the Dead winced at the noise. *You've crossed into the Planes! You've beaten Lord Ao! We have escaped from the Realms, and now we can go home and claim our true power!* The eyes on the statue were wide with excitement.

"No, Lord Bane, I'm afraid we cannot. I was ready to give

up when I discovered that you had been blown into the ether. I thought that Lord Ao had blocked all the existing planes from us." Myrkul rubbed his rotting chin with a bony hand. "I was wrong."

Wrong?

"Yes," Myrkul sighed. "As my high priest pointed out, none of the gods live in the Border Ethereal, so Ao had no reason to stop us from entering it. Of course, with magic being so unstable, three of my wizards died trying to locate all the fragments of your being and send me here to recover them." The God of the Dead bowed slightly, and all the vertebrae in his back cracked. "But I could not let you suffer here."

Please, Myrkul, spare me your flattery. After all, you need me to force my way into the heavens so you can follow.

Myrkul scowled. For a moment, he considered journeying farther into the Border Ethereal and dropping the statue into the Deep Ethereal, a place of swirling colors and mighty vortices. Bane would never make it back to the Realms—or his home—from there. But the thought lasted only a second.

Bane was right. Myrkul did need him. But not because the God of the Dead lacked courage or initiative. Myrkul wanted the God of Strife to lead the assault on the heavens because it was very dangerous, and it wouldn't do at all for the God of the Dead to be destroyed.

So Myrkul grinned obsequiously and again gave a slight bow to the obsidian statue. "Of course you are correct, Lord Bane. Let us exit this place so that we may find you a new avatar and proceed with your plans."

How will we return to the Realms?

"It seems that magic is more stable outside the Prime Material Plane. I should be able to cast a spell to send us home without error." The God of the Dead held the statue close to his face and smiled once more, so wide this time that the decaying skin at the sides of his mouth tore slightly. "I only await your command."

❧ 2 ❧

The Twisted Tower

The mystical wards that Elminster had placed throughout the Twisted Tower had begun to fail the night the Temple of Lathander was destroyed. The passageways within the tower that were cloaked to appear as part of the walls sometimes revealed themselves as open doorways, and during the first day after the Battle of Shadowdale, people passed through them without incident. By that night, however, an unwitting guardsman walked into one of the openings and was killed as the break in the wall sealed up by itself, trapping him within.

Outside the tower, the torches lit by blue-white eldritch fires either smoldered dimly or blazed with a light that blinded any who dared to look directly at them. Any attempts to remove the torches met with failure, since mortal hands merely passed through the torches as if they weren't there.

The mists that engulfed the upper levels of the tower were meant to stop any prying mystical eyes, but their nature had changed, too. Now the mists swirling around the tower caused a continuous, ear-piercing shriek. The shutters in the upper levels had been closed and heavily boarded over in an attempt to block out the noise.

Dressed completely in black, Cyric ignored the shriek as he stood in the trees at the far end of the tower's stables. Though it was night, the thief could see the guard who stood before the northeast entrance to the tower, near the kitchen. During his last night in Mourngrym's home, on the day Midnight and Adon had been arrested, Cyric had made a detailed study of the tower's defenses. Plying a disgruntled guardsman with gold and liquor, the thief had learned all he needed about the tower's secrets to formulate his plan.

A half dozen guards were always posted at the main entrance, while other soldiers patrolled the tower's perimeter. Security at the Ashaba bridge stations had been relaxed, since most of the bridge's length lay in ruins at the bottom of the river. The guard Cyric had bribed stood alone on the west bank of the river, but when the time came, he would be at the northernmost end of the bridge, investigating a "minor disturbance" that Cyric left to the guard's imagination.

The only other guards who had been posted near the boathouse were inside the tower, looking out from time to time through spy holes to verify that the quiet of the night held no hidden dangers. The workmen who sometimes prowled the boatyard long into the night had been ordered home to their families, so that they might be properly rested when they attended the execution of Elminster's murderers in the morning.

Inside the tower, a large number of Mourngrym's men had been assigned that night to the upper levels, to guard their liege. The magical wards that normally protected the dalelord were unstable. Worse still, the trial had raised concern about the whereabouts of Lord Bane, and Mourngrym was troubled over the welfare of his wife and child should the Black Lord seek revenge against him.

Cyric was certain that the lower levels of the tower, where Midnight and Adon were being held until their execution the next morning, would be occupied by quite a few guards, too. But Cyric was prepared to assault the Twisted Tower. He was armed with a pair of daggers, a hand axe, several lengths of blackened rope, a small black cylinder, and the skills that only training by the Thieves' Guild in Zhentil Keep could foster.

The light from the torches lining the tower wall suddenly flared intensely, and a series of brilliant flashes lit the streets. A string of curses erupted from a guardsman. His back pressed against the trunk of nearby tree, Cyric forced his breath slowly from his lungs as he waited for the lights to flicker and fail. He had been in full view of the rear guard when the torches flared.

The guard, a young blond man who reminded Cyric of Adon, rubbed his eyes. Silently hurrying for the cover of the stables, Cyric glimpsed a pair of eyes in the stable and tensed, but he did not break his stride. He sighed with relief when the huge whites of the eyes merely revealed a pony that had wandered to the doorway.

"Here, now!" a deep, age-withered voice called. "You come back here!"

The pony pranced closer to the stable door, and the footsteps of the stablemaster sounded inside the building. Cyric unsheathed one of his daggers, angled to his left, and doubled up into a crouch, ready to spring at the man and silence him before he could raise an alarm. Another voice cried out abruptly as the guard from the rear entrance turned the corner.

"Manxtrum! You've got a runaway, it seems," the guard shouted. "Better get a tighter rein on your charges!"

The man from the stables walked past the pony and stood at the doorway, oblivious to the dark figure who crouched in the shadows a few yards to his right. Cyric was not facing the guard, and the thief couldn't tell if he'd been spotted. He didn't dare to turn around, but since no one had cried out yet, he assumed neither the guard nor the stablemaster had seen him.

"Ah, this little beauty is the one Mourngrym promised to your daughter last week," Manxtrum said. "Care to come over and take a look?" Cyric gripped his dagger more tightly.

"Can't now," the guard said. "Perhaps after my shift."

"Decent folk will be asleep!" Manxtrum said, waving his finger at the guard like an angry parent.

"Then you should be wide awake," the guard called, laughing at his own joke, then suddenly bursting into a coughing fit.

Manxtrum shook his head and led the pony back into the stable. Counting to twenty, Cyric slowly looked over his shoulder and saw the guard cough again. The man's back was to him. Cyric shifted position slightly and, with a deft flick of the wrist, hurled his dagger.

The blond guard's arms jerked backward as the blade pierced his neck. He went down, falling backward with a gurgling, strangled cry that was cut short when he landed.

Cyric waited for any sign that the guard's cry had been heard. After a moment, the thief scrambled to the servants' entrance to the tower, near where the dead man lay.

Took care of that nasty cough, now, didn't we? Cyric thought grimly as he turned the corpse over to pull his blade from its throat. The thief grabbed a plank left over from some work on the shutters and placed it next to the guard. Uncoiling three lengths of rope from his waist, Cyric laid them out horizontally, then placed the wood plank over the center of the ropes. The thief rolled the corpse onto the plank, tying the ropes around his thighs, waist, and chest, then propped the dead man up in his usual station, visible from within the shadowy confines of the tower as well as the stables. His head hung limply upon the man's chest, concealing the bloodied throat.

Cyric entered the alcove that housed the servants' door. When he looked back toward the stables, the thief saw that the light from within the building revealed no sign that his actions had been detected. He then looked up to check where he had removed the large stone block in the alcove's ceiling several hours earlier. It had not been sealed up. Cyric silently climbed up the wall into the indentation, took a breath, then, reaching down with one leg, gave the wooden door a kick.

Moments later, he heard a muffled voice call from the other side of the door. "Segert?"

Cyric frowned, lowered his leg once more, and kicked the door once again, this time adding an exaggerated cough. Drawing back up into the indentation in the ceiling, Cyric watched as the door opened and a short man with a gray mustache stepped out into the alcove.

"Segert?" the guard asked as he moved toward the still figure that leaned against the wall just outside the alcove. Muscles straining, Cyric prepared to drop on the guard, but froze when he heard a second guard approach from inside the tower.

"Trouble, Marcreg?" the second guard asked, his voice

high and trembling. Cyric could barely see the younger guard's face in the doorway.

"Guess not," the guard with the gray mustache snapped impatiently. "Better get back to your post. We'll continue your training later."

"Aye, sir," the other guard said and hurried away.

Marcreg shook his head and stepped forward. "Now, what's your problem, Segert? There'll be no sick leave until after the prisoners are executed. I told you that—"

Cyric relaxed the pressure on his braced legs and allowed his body to fall. The thief landed with his legs around the neck of the gray-mustached guard and twisted hard until he heard the sound of cracking bones. Marcreg fell into the door, nearly slamming it closed. In a moment of blind panic, Cyric let go of the guard and jammed his foot in the upper corner of the door. Suppressing a cry of pain as the heavy door pressed against his foot, Cyric wriggled out of his boot and landed beside the corpse.

Cyric dragged Marcreg's body away from the door, then slid his boot to the bottom of the doorjamb. The thief unraveled his last section of rope, set it aside, and arranged Marcreg's body like that of the other guard. After propping up the corpse outside the door, Cyric entered the tower.

The service hallway stretched in both directions, following the curvature of the tower. Cyric knew that he would have to search out the guard who had spoken to Marcreg. The younger man wouldn't wait for his tutor forever. When the older man didn't return, he would certainly raise the alarm.

There was a clanging of metal bowls and a whispered curse from off to Cyric's right. The thief followed the noise to the delivery entrance to the kitchen. A sign had been tacked up above the open doorway, marking it as a portal safe from magical chaos. Cautiously he peered around the corner. Inside the kitchen, the young guard stood in semi-darkness. The dull orange glow of a lantern revealed the furtive motions of the guardsman as he gorged himself on a rare delicacy, a chilled bowl of chocolate covered with cherries and cream. He had his back to the door.

Drawing a dagger, Cyric advanced on the guard. This is too easy, the thief thought. He noticed, a moment too late, that the young man was gazing at the flickering shadows on the shiny metal surface of the bowl.

The cold metal bowl flashed in the dim light as the guard whirled and hurled it. It struck Cyric full in the face, but the thief managed to catch the bowl before it could clatter to the floor. Cyric's blade flew by his head as the young guard turned to run. The dagger missed completely, thudding dully into the wall beyond.

Drawing his hand axe, Cyric leaped upon the guard, slashing with the axe and driving his knee hard into the man's back. Cyric grinned as he heard the crack of breaking bone. The guard's legs twitched for a few seconds, then were still.

Rising from the dead man, Cyric glanced around for any signs that a disturbance had taken place. After straightening a few stools and clearing away the spilled chocolate, Cyric dragged the guard's body down a flight of stairs to the food storage cellar. Then the thief took the lantern and went back up into the hallway.

Following the layout of the tower from memory, Cyric skirted the north wall, passed through a series of interlocking chambers, and emerged near the southwest hallway, leading to the boathouse. The information Cyric had been provided was accurate so far. Only one guard was stationed at the far end of the hallway. However, Cyric was trapped in a single moment of indecision as he stared at the nearly seven-foot-tall guard. It was Forester, a man who had served under him at the Ashaba bridge.

Forester turned sharply, then relaxed as he saw Cyric emerge from the shadows.

"I've been sent to relieve you," Cyric said, smiling. "You're needed on the upper floors."

"But I just got here," Forester said as he approached Cyric. "Where have you been all day? I sent word for you to meet me at the Old Skull—"

Forester didn't even scream when Cyric's dagger pierced his heart.

Just according to plan, Cyric thought as he dragged the body through the hallway. The thief had to remind himself that the battle was only two days ago. It might as well have occurred in another lifetime.

Once Forester's body was safely hidden away, Cyric returned and began to search for the secret entrance to the dungeon level. Following the explicit instructions of his contact, Cyric pressed the uppermost edge of the twenty-eighth wooden panel from the west door. Nothing happened.

Cyric frowned, then counted off a half dozen paces, crouched down, and located a small opening in the wall, just above the floorboards. Easing his dagger into the crevice, the thief heard the telltale clicks of some kind of mechanism working back and forth as he gently moved the hilt of the dagger. The door still didn't open.

A heavy weight seemed to fall on Cyric's shoulders, and he wondered if the guardsman who had given him the information had neglected to mention that both means of entry had to be performed simultaneously. Cyric drew another dagger, counted off the floor panels once again, then threw the blade at the upper edge of the wood panel as he yanked the floor release back.

The hilt of the dagger struck the panel. There was a slight hiss as the door opened and cold air escaped into the hallway. Cyric retrieved his second dagger and moved toward the darkened passageway, holding the blade out before him.

According to Cyric's informant, the long, winding stairway led to the rear of the dungeon, where the holding cells were located. The hidden stairway had been installed as a fail-safe, in case the main entrance to the dungeon was ever blocked or overrun. A single guardsman, if he was unable to reach the alarm gongs, could quickly reach the ground level by the stairs to get help.

Cyric descended the stairway until he came to the landing and a second door. The thief knew he would be spotted the moment he opened the door and stepped off the landing, but he was not concerned about the lone guard stationed below an alarm gong at the far end of the cells. However, the hallway took an abrupt right after that guard station and opened into a large hall, where six more men apparently were gambling. They were swearing so loudly that Cyric could already hear their voices.

Cyric withdrew a small black cylinder from the sash at his waist, then used his remaining dagger to ease the metal cap from its end. He wrapped his fingers in the sash and felt for the sharp point of the Gaeus Thorn.

Cyric's knowledgeable informant had made a pastime out of exploring the ruined hut of an alchemist and selling his finds on the black market. The Gaeus Thorn was very rare, possibly one of a kind, and Cyric smiled at the irony that Mourngrym's gold had paid for the item.

A moment passed as Cyric allowed all emotion to drain from him. He drew a deep breath, put the cylinder to his lips, and threw open the door. The guard was staring in Cyric's direction and immediately stood up to raise a cry of alarm. The thief blew hard into the barrel of his weapon and watched as a tiny dart pierced the guard's throat.

The wounded guard fell instantly into a stupor and sank down onto a stool, his head lolling back and forth. Cyric waited until the guard looked at him again, then gestured for the man to leave his post and come closer. Lifting himself from the stool with a flourish, the guard complied.

"Listen very carefully," Cyric whispered as he placed his hand on the guard's shoulder. "Lord Mourngrym has sent me to get one of the prisoners slated for execution in the morning, the dark-haired mage. He wishes to question the woman. Take me to her."

"I should inform my captain—"

"There's no time," Cyric said quickly. "Keep your voice low. You don't want to wake your other charges."

Many of the cells had been filled with mercenaries who had been hired to fill out Bane's forces in the Battle of Shadowdale, then surrendered themselves to the dalesmen when the battle was lost. Cyric heard the sound of a boot scuff the floor, and he tensed.

A pair of dirty hands protruded from the iron bars of a nearby cell, and a dark, sweaty face peered out. The prisoner laughed once, then nodded to Cyric and gestured for the thief to proceed.

"Let's go," Cyric said. The guard led him past the twenty cells that lined the corridor's north bank. An ugly stone wall on the southern side of the hallway was the only view afforded the prisoners. Finally the guard stopped before a storage room adjacent to the final cell and unlocked the door.

"Wait," Cyric said as the guard's hand reached for the heavy wooden door. "If anyone should ask, I am over six feet tall, with fiery red hair, the build of a wrestler, and a strange foreign accent."

"Of course you are," the guard murmured flatly. There wasn't a trace of emotion in his voice.

"Describe me," Cyric whispered as he gazed into the guard's face. The dalesman described the thief exactly as the hawk-nosed man had instructed. Satisfied that the effects of the dart were all that his informant had promised, Cyric gave the guard a few final commands and watched as he returned to his station.

The thief opened the door with care, fearful that the sound might alert the other guards. Cyric gazed into the confines of the black room and saw the object of his search lying on her side in the corner.

"Midnight," Cyric whispered as he entered the cell and went to work on the bonds of the dark-haired magic-user. He left the gag for last. "Keep it to a whisper," he cautioned.

As soon as the gag was removed, Midnight drew a deep breath, then looked at her fellow prisoner. The cleric sat with his knees drawn up before him, his forehead pressed against his knees to hide his face.

"Adon!" Midnight whispered. The mage rubbed her arms and legs, trying to massage some feeling back into them.

"Can you stand?" Cyric whispered as he got up and moved to the door. "We must leave quickly."

"We've got to take Adon," Midnight hissed urgently. She crawled toward the cleric.

"Your ordeal has left you confused," Cyric said. "Leave him."

Placing her hands on the cleric's shoulders, Midnight shook Adon, attempting to wake him. Shadowy, bloodshot eyes rose as Adon looked up, but the young cleric didn't seem to see his friends. He simply stared at the wall behind Midnight.

"He's useless!" Cyric hissed. "Besides, he betrayed you with his silence at the trial." The thief glanced nervously into the hallway, but no guards had noticed the open door yet.

"No!" Midnight declared, her voice cracking with pain and fear.

"Every moment we delay here increases our risk," Cyric snapped. He turned from the door, grabbed Midnight's arm, and tried to drag the magic-user to her feet.

"Get away from me," Midnight whimpered, but she was too weak to resist Cyric's less–than–gentle urgings.

"I came back for *you!*" Cyric hissed.

"You'll take us both, or I'll start screaming until even the gods know you're here!" Midnight warned. "He's sick. Can't you see that?" The mage ran her hand through Adon's tangled hair.

"I see only his cowardice," Cyric growled. "That and nothing more. But if his life truly matters to you, even after what he's done, I suppose I have no choice."

Midnight stumbled back as Cyric tore into Adon's bonds with an alarming fury. The tip of the thief's dagger drew a few drops of blood from Adon's wrists as Cyric hurriedly cut the last bit of rope and reached down to pull the cleric up by his filthy robes.

At the end of the corridor, the drugged guard waved stupidly as Cyric dragged Adon from the black room. Midnight stumbled along behind the thief.

Every step was a struggle for Midnight, and it became worse when they reached the darkened stairway. Cyric contemplated dropping Adon down the stairs, hoping that the cleric would break his neck in the fall. But Midnight walked close behind him, as if sensing the thief's intentions.

"Where's Kel?" Midnight gasped through sharp breaths as they struggled up the stairs.

Cyric hesitated as he decided which lie would serve his needs best. "He refused to join me. He said he 'couldn't interfere with justice.'"

"Justice!" Midnight spat out in amazement.

"I told him he was a blind fool," Cyric said, shrugging. The thief waited for a response from Midnight. When none came, he assumed the lie was enough to satisfy the mage—for now, at least.

At the top of the steps, Cyric saw the soft orange glow of torchlight from the hallway and wondered if he should warn Midnight about the dangers of the randomly solidifying doors. He decided against it and secretly hoped that the wall would reappear just as he pushed Adon through.

Shoving the cleric through the portal first, Cyric quickly hurried through the narrow passage. "Make haste," he hissed into the darkness. Midnight dragged herself through the doorway and stumbled along behind the thief.

At the end of the corridor, Cyric looked out through a series of spy holes to verify that the boatyard was still deserted. Midnight helped to support Adon as Cyric unlocked the door with the key he had taken from Forester's body.

The boatyard was quiet. Only the sounds of the gently lapping waves from the Ashaba and the conspiratorial creak of wooden boats rubbing against the dock helped to cover the plodding footsteps of the escapees as they followed Cyric. A host of blue-white torches illuminated the arched wooden ceilings of the boathouse and the vast array of craft docked nearby.

Making his way toward a twenty-foot skiff at the south end of the yard, Cyric imagined the boathouse in flames. The chaos such an event would create was exactly the distraction they needed to ensure their safe escape. With the destruction of Mourngrym's small fleet, the repairs to the Ashaba bridge would be stalled and any pursuit of the escapees would be severely restricted.

Much to Cyric's regret, however, they didn't have time for such an elaborate operation.

Cyric stood before the boat and looked around quickly. "Can you spellcast, Midnight? We might need a diversion."

Midnight shook her head from side to side. "I would need to study first, and my spellbook was left in Elminster's Tower."

Cyric was about to speak when he heard the soft padding of footsteps. Someone was leaping from boat to boat, carefully avoiding the dock where his footfalls would give him away. "What do you think of this boat?" Cyric said as he made an exaggerated motion with his right hand, hoping to draw attention away from the quicksilver motion of his left hand as he drew out one of his daggers. Suddenly the thief whirled on the intruder.

Midnight grabbed Cyric's hand before the dagger could fly. One of the torches on the tower flared, and the heroes found themselves gazing into the searing green eyes of Elminster's scribe, Lhaeo. Midnight softly breathed his name, and the brown-haired young man gracefully leaped from the bow of a nearby boat to the dock. A huge sack was slung over the scribe's shoulder, but he carried it without effort. An elegant black cloak hung rather loosely around his shoulders.

"What do you want here?" Cyric hissed, suspicion burning in his eyes. The thief held his dagger pointed toward Elminster's servant.

"I'm not about to give you away, if that's what you mean," Lhaeo whispered, then carefully set his canvas bag down on the dock. "Do you have any idea how annoyed Elminster will be if the first thing he learns upon returning home is that you've been executed for his murder?"

"But we saw Elminster die, Lhaeo," Midnight said, hanging her head. "He was drawn into that horrible rift." Adon winced slightly, but the cleric didn't speak. He just stared at the boat, slowly bobbing in the water.

Lhaeo rubbed his chin. "I don't believe it," the scribe said as he opened his sack. "Elminster's disappeared before— many times, in fact. I would know . . . somehow . . . if he were truly gone."

"If you're not going to stop us, then what do you want?" Cyric growled quietly. He continued to point his knife toward the scribe. "If you haven't noticed, we're in a bit of a hurry."

Lhaeo frowned and pushed Cyric's dagger aside as he approached Midnight. "I'm here to help you. It's the least I can do after the trial."

The scribe gestured for Midnight to look into the sack. "Your spellbook is here, along with some provisions for your journey." Lhaeo reached into the bag and withdrew a beautiful orb that glowed with an amber light. Strange runes had been wrought in the surface of the glass, and a golden base, marked with intricate designs that were covered with fine, sparkling diamond dust, had been added since the last time Midnight had seen the orb in Elminster's study.

"Do you remember this?" Lhaeo said as he held the sphere toward Midnight. A slight smile played across the scribe's face.

"Aye," Midnight said as she reached out to stroke the glowing sphere. "The globe was made to shatter if any powerful magical object comes within its range."

"This should help you find the Tablets of Fate," Lhaeo said quietly and put the globe back into the bag.

Midnight and Cyric looked shocked, but Lhaeo continued to smile. "There is little Elminster keeps hidden from me. He even told me that the first tablet is in Tantras."

"We have to go," Cyric hissed to Midnight. "You can go through your bag of gifts later." The thief grabbed Adon and moved toward the boat.

"One last thing," the scribe whispered as he removed another, smaller bag from his shoulder and handed it to the magic-user. She opened it and saw a metal vial.

"The mists of rapture," Lhaeo said. "Perfect for disabling a large group of guardsmen without causing lasting harm." Cyric pushed Adon into the boat and started to untie the skiff's moorings.

"You were going to try to rescue us yourself!" Midnight gasped. Adon looked up from the boat, and for an instant, his gaze seemed to focus on the scribe.

"Oh, perish the thought!" Lhaeo whispered and turned away with mock indignation.

Midnight grabbed Lhaeo by the shoulder and spun him around. The scribe's expression was serious, almost hard, as he gazed into the mage's eyes. "Why?" she said. "The townspeople would kill you if they found out."

Lhaeo stood up straight, and his voice deepened slightly. "I could not allow you to be injured. I could not condone such a travesty of justice, milady." The scribe took Midnight's hand and kissed it. "Elminster trusted you to help him at the temple. You must be worthy of that trust."

Cyric looked up sharply. "Midnight, I might just leave you here with him to face Mourngrym if you don't hurry!"

"He's right," Lhaeo said softly. "You must go."

Midnight climbed into the boat. Lhaeo helped Cyric release the boat from its remaining moorings, and the scribe pushed the craft away from the dock. Then Lhaeo stood on the pier and waved once before disappearing into the darkness.

Cyric manned the oars at the center of the boat, his back turned to Midnight. As he rowed, the thief was forced to stare into the vacant eyes of the scarred cleric, who always seemed to avoid Cyric's angry stares. Utilizing the hand-over-hand method of rowing he had been taught during his years of traveling, Cyric started the boat moving, but, much to his surprise, not very quickly.

"What's going on here?" the thief cursed as he looked into the water. "Are we caught on something?" As he dropped his hand into the cold water of the Ashaba, Cyric realized what was wrong. The current was traveling in the wrong direction, forcing him to paddle against the flow of the river, even though they were moving downstream, away from Shadowdale.

Cyric cursed and slapped an oar against the water. A small wave sloshed into the boat, soaking Adon and Midnight. The mage cried out in surprise, but the cleric just sat there, letting his wet tunic hang on his slouched shoulders.

Cyric looked at Adon and cursed again. "This lump is only so much ballast," he sneered and flicked water into Adon's eyes. "All he'll be good for on this trip is making the rowing harder."

The hawk-nosed thief started to row again, and Midnight used a cloak to dab some of the water from Adon's face. "I know you can hear me, Adon," the mage whispered. "I still care. I won't let you get hurt."

When Adon failed to respond, Midnight frowned and wiped more water away from the cleric's face. She didn't notice the salty tears mixed with the cold drops from the Ashaba.

*   *   *   *   *

Kelemvor had stood in the windy courtyard much of the night. Sleep had been out of the question. Besides, the fighter had not been alone. Guards had been stationed to watch over the courtyard of Midnight and Adon's executions, and a small crowd of rowdy gawkers had decided to keep an all-night vigil. Watching the dalesmen laugh and make disgusting jokes about the event scheduled to occur at first light made Kelemvor sick at heart. The festive atmosphere that pervaded the killing grounds was horribly out of place.

The fires of Kelemvor's anger were fanned into a blaze of rage as workmen arrived at the courtyard and began to assemble a complex stage for the executions. The spectators had evidently been taken into prime consideration in the design of the stage. It was composed of two circular platforms that moved like opposing gears, constructed to display the victims for all who cared to see them. Columns jutted from the center of the platforms, with crude, metal hooks where wrists and ankles would be bound. There was a circular opening, not unlike the knot of a tree, midway down each column. Kelemvor realized with a shiver that the executioner's spikes would be driven through the holes, and into the bodies of the condemned—his former allies. It would be a slow, horrible death.

Kelemvor wasn't sure what he planned to do when the time for the execution actually arrived. He felt that he had to atone somehow for his failure to help Midnight at the trial. Still, the evidence given against Midnight and Adon at the trial had been so conclusive that the fighter was not even convinced that his friends were really innocent. It certainly was possible that Midnight had lost control of the powerful magic she wielded and accidentally caused Elminster's death. Kelemvor simply couldn't decide.

The first hint of dawn played across the horizon as a band of reddish gray light appeared in the distance. Kelemvor found himself standing beside a pair of guardsmen who struggled to hold back their yawns.

Suddenly a series of alarm gongs sounded from the Twisted Tower, and the guards shook themselves to battle readiness in a matter of seconds.

"The prisoners!" someone shouted from the tower. "They've escaped!"

"Kelemvor, come on!" one of the guards, an obese young man, shouted as he headed for the Twisted Tower. "We need every man we can get!"

The dalesmen still think of me as one of them, Kelemvor realized as he followed the guards to the main entrance of the tower and was admitted without a second glance, even though the irate villagers were held back. The door leading to the dungeon stood open, and Kelemvor and the overweight guard raced to the landing. From there, they saw a congregation of dalesmen in the cavernous chamber. Forcing his way through the crowd, Kelemvor stopped abruptly as he saw the solemn faces of Lord Mourngrym and Thurbal.

The reason for their distress sat propped upon a small stool at the head of the corridor leading to the holding cells. Kelemvor studied the wide-eyed expression of total bliss that graced the dead man's features, then looked down to see the hilt of the man's short sword protruding from his neck. The blade had been driven through the man with such force that the tip had pierced the mortar of the wall behind him, pinning the dead guard in place.

"Who killed him?" Kelemvor growled. His words broke the silence on the landing, and everyone turned to him.

"He killed himself," a red-haired guard said as he nervously rocked back and forth on the balls of his feet. "When I came to relieve him, there was this mark on his neck. I asked him what had happened to him, and he rattled off some story about a man that was big, about Forester's size, with red hair like mine, and an odd accent."

The guard stopped rocking for a moment and turned to Mourngrym. The dalelord nodded, and the guard continued his story. "He said this man came down the back stairway and took the prisoners to see Lord Mourngrym." The redheaded guard paused for a second, then started rocking again. "When he finished telling me that, he took out his sword, smiled, and rammed it through his own throat, right where the mark was! That's just how it happened. I swear!"

The dalesmen remained silent but became aware that the prisoners were shouting from their cells. One voice was louder than the rest.

"I saw it!" a filthy, dark-haired mercenary shouted. "I saw it all!"

Mourngrym turned away from the dead man and walked to the cell of the prisoner.

"Cover him," Thurbal said, gesturing with his dragon's-head walking stick, and followed his liege to the cell. Kelemvor was close behind.

"What did you see?" Mourngrym said.

"Not so fast!" the prisoner snapped, his hands dangling from the bars. "What's in it for me?"

Mourngrym grabbed the prisoner's hand and yanked it sharply. The prisoner cried out as his face slammed against the rusted iron bars. Mourngrym's sword left its sheath with a blinding motion and stopped, poised just over the man's wrist.

"You get to keep your hand," Mourngrym snarled as another guard grabbed the prisoner's other hand before he could gouge Mourngrym's face. "Speak quickly, or I'll take you apart, starting with this hand!"

The prisoner stared into the blood-red face of the ruler of Shadowdale and quickly told all that he had witnessed the previous night.

"Cyric," Kelemvor said, hanging his head. "It must have been Cyric!"

There was a hoarse shout from the top of the stairs. "More bodies up here! Forester is dead!"

"Come with me," Mourngrym said to Kelemvor, and they hurried up the narrow stairway, crossed the hallway, and entered the audience chamber, where the trial had been held. A short, bald guardsman stood in the middle of the room, his sword drawn as if he expected trouble at any second. The guard's pudgy hands trembled as he led the dalelord and the fighter up a few narrow stairs to the rear of the small stage. Curtains bearing Mourngrym's coat of arms hung against the back wall. There was a small stain at the bottom of the red curtain. Forester's body had been left in the space directly behind Mourngrym's throne.

"Calliope, the maid, noticed the stain," the bald guard mumbled softly.

The dalelord shook with anger. "Search the tower!" Mourngrym said, wringing his hands. "I want to know who else is . . . missing."

Within the hour, Cyric's movements had been mapped out, and the missing boat was discovered. Mourngrym was suspicious of the guardsman at the bridge. The bodies of Segert and Marcreg had been discovered near his post. The guard was led away to the dungeon for interrogation.

"Does this look like the work of your friend?" Mourngrym said as he crouched over Segert's body. He exposed the wound on the corpse's neck for emphasis.

"He was not a friend," Kelemvor said as he surveyed the corpse's wounds. "And, yes, it looks like Cyric's work."

There were shouts from the kitchen, and Kelemvor accompanied the dalelord back into the tower, to the kitchen. They found the cook pointing at the stairs that led to the storage room. The body of the young guard-in-training had been placed on a hook and dangled beside a number of butchered slabs of meat. Smears of chocolate and cherry still covered the lad's ashen face.

"Come with me," Mourngrym said, but Kelemvor remained standing at the door, staring at the young man's corpse. The dalelord gently put his hand on the fighter's shoulder and turned him away from the body. "We need to talk," Mourngrym said softly as he led Kelemvor to his private audience chamber.

The two men climbed a set of stairs. At the first landing, the dalelord unlocked a large oaken door and ushered Kelemvor into the room. Mourngrym's audience chamber was small but comfortable, with a few pieces of dark wooden furniture scattered about the room and brightly colored tapestries on the walls. A single, small opening admitted the weak morning sunlight from outside the tower.

The dalelord collapsed into a chair and started to wring his hands. "I need someone to find them, Kelemvor. Someone who is loyal to the causes of the Dales—freedom, justice, honor—and someone who knows how to find the butchers who did this to my men." Mourngrym stopped speaking, but he continued to wring his hands.

Kelemvor was too distraught to answer. Midnight, Cyric, and Adon had played him for a fool all along. That was the only thing that could explain their leaving the dale without him. Perhaps they were murderers after all.

"Your service in the cause of the Dales was exemplary," Mourngrym said after a moment. "You are a good man, Kel. I believe you have been deceived." The dalelord stopped wringing his hands and stood up.

"Aye," Kelemvor said as he ran his hands through his hair. The fighter sat down in a large, high-backed chair across from the dalelord. "That may be so."

"You spent time with them," Mourngrym said as he moved to the fighter's side. "You know how they think. You may have some idea where they've gone."

"I may," Kelemvor mumbled.

Mourngrym paused for a moment, then put his hand on Kelemvor's shoulder. "I want you to track down the criminals and return them to Shadowdale. I will give you a dozen men, including a guide who knows the forest."

"The forest? But they left by boat," Kelemvor said, confusion showing on his face.

"They have a considerable head start. The only way to overcome their lead is by land," Mourngrym said with a sigh. "Will you do it?"

Kelemvor roughly brushed the dalelord's hand from his shoulder and stood up. But before the fighter could speak, the door to the chamber suddenly burst open and Lhaeo stumbled into the room. "Lord Mourngrym, your forgiveness!" the scribe said and fell to his knees before the ruler of the dale. "I did not know! I believed in their innocence! But they have spilled innocent blood and soaked my hands in it!"

"Slow down," Mourngrym said as he reached down and grabbed Lhaeo's shoulders. "Tell us everything."

Elminster's faithful scribe sighed and looked up into Mourngrym's eyes. "As I said at the trial, I thought Elminster was alive. I—I went to the tower, thinking to help the magic-user and the cleric escape before they were executed. . . . But Cyric had already done that." Lhaeo bowed his head again and covered his face with his hands. "I let them get away—No. I *helped* them get away. I gave Midnight her spellbook . . . and some other things."

Mourngrym frowned and turned to Kelemvor. The fighter stood silently over the scribe, his face devoid of all emotion.

"I should have realized that the guard inside the tower was dead," Lhaeo snapped, suddenly angry. "Someone should have seen us and sounded the alarm. I never thought that they . . ." The scribe shuddered and looked up at Kelemvor. "I can never forgive myself for what has occurred!"

Mourngrym tried to remain calm, but anger marched across his features like a rampaging army. "The killings occurred before you arrived, Lhaeo. You must not blame yourself."

Lhaeo swallowed and bowed his head again. "You must place me under arrest."

Mourngrym stepped back from the scribe. "Consider yourself under house arrest," Mourngrym said flatly. "Do not leave Elminster's Tower unless it is to procure food and drink for yourself. That is my final word."

The scribe lifted himself from the floor, bowed before his liege, and turned to leave. "One other thing," Mourngrym snapped before Lhaeo could leave. "Do you know where the criminals were headed when they left?"

The scribe turned. Kelemvor could see that his face was white, and anger clouded his eyes. "Yes," Lhaeo said through partially clenched teeth. "They are going to Tantras."

Mourngrym nodded, but Kelemvor held up his hand. "Wait, Lhaeo. You just said that you *thought* Elminster was alive. Don't you believe that anymore? Do you think that Midnight and Adon . . . murdered him?"

Shoulders drawn tight, the scribe stood up straight. His voice was barely louder than a whisper as he spoke. "After what they did in the tower, I believe they are cold-blooded killers. Worse still, they have fooled good men—like Elminster. Like you, Kelemvor. They must be brought to justice!"

❧ 3 ❧

The Nereid

In the privacy of his own thoughts, Cyric had murdered Adon well over a hundred times. During the trip down the Ashaba, the thief often imagined himself bashing the cleric with an oar and watching as the pathetic, weak-willed man allowed the river's current to swallow him up without a fight. But the sudden, unwelcome intrusion of reality would always shatter Cyric's daydreams. Adon would begin to weep, and Midnight would try to comfort him by stroking his hair and whispering into his ear. At those times, Cyric quivered with anger and thought of even bloodier ways to dispose of Adon.

Still, travel down the river was generally quiet and un-eventful. Since they rarely spoke, these lulls gave the heroes far too much time to think. At the moment, highsun was approaching and Cyric's stomach growled as he contemplated a fine banquet. The food they had taken from Shadowdale was filling but far from appetizing, and so the thief didn't relish the thought of eating, even though he was hungry.

Midnight shared Cyric's feelings. As she sat in the bow, trying to study her spellbook, swatting away annoying, bloated mosquitoes, thoughts of fine meals drifted through her head, too.

"A few more hours of this and I'm going to become deliri-ous," Midnight said at last, slamming her spellbook shut. "We need to eat something."

"No one's stopping you," Cyric croaked, his throat dry from the intense heat of the midday sun.

Midnight frowned. She was hungry, but she wanted Cyric to rest for a while and eat, too. The thief hadn't allowed her to take a turn at the oars since they left Shadowdale, and he just snorted and shook his head when Midnight had suggested Adon try to row. "You need to rest, Cyric. Why don't we pull in to shore and all eat something?"

"Because the dalesmen might catch up to us, and I, for one, don't want that to happen," Cyric said. Midnight crossed her arms and leaned back into the bow. The thief scowled and turned away from the raven-haired mage. When he looked over his shoulder, though, Cyric was startled to see Adon holding out a large chunk of bread to him. A warm, foolish smile, like that of a simpleton, flickered across the cleric's face.

"Get away from me!" Cyric growled and slapped the cleric across the face with the back of his hand. Adon fell backward in a heap, and the bread flew from his hand. The boat rocked from side to side as Cyric made a grab for the oar he had released and Adon crawled as far away from the thief as he could manage inside the skiff.

"Damn you!" Midnight cursed. She climbed over Cyric and moved to Adon's side. The cleric was quivering, his knees drawn up to his chest. A strange mixture of fear and anger lingered in his eyes.

"Why did you do that?" Midnight snapped to Cyric as she caressed the cleric's shoulders.

Cyric thought of making a nasty retort, but instead he only narrowed his eyes and remained silent as he watched Midnight brush the hair from the younger man's face. Adon had pulled himself up into a ball, his hands covering his face as he rocked back and forth, humming an unfamiliar song.

"Answer me!" Midnight hissed. She leaned closer and glared at Cyric.

The thief was silent. There was no answer he could give that Midnight would be able to accept. Ever since Arabel, where their journey began, Cyric had viewed Adon as a liability. Very little had happened to change his opinion. The cleric could not call on his deity for spells, so he was useless as a healer. Adon's fighting skills, when they had been employed, were adequate but not exceptional. We can get along perfectly well without him, Cyric thought. That's why I hate him. I just don't need him.

"Tell me about Tantras again," Cyric sighed, anxious to change the subject.

Adon stopped rocking and looked up at Midnight. Any anger in his face had disappeared, and now only fear showed in the cleric's features. Don't tell him, Adon whispered in his mind. He doesn't need to know.

However, Midnight didn't see Adon's expression. The mage stopped caressing the cleric's back and looked down at the bottom of the boat. "One of the Tablets of Fate is hidden there. At least, that's what Elminster told us at the Temple of Lathander before the battle with Bane."

All emotion drained from Cyric's face. "Where is it hidden in Tantras?"

"Elminster didn't know." The mage sighed and looked up at the hawk-nosed thief. "All the sage could tell us . . . before he died . . . was that one of the tablets was hidden there."

At mention of Elminster's death, Adon started to rock again and began to whistle a mindless tune. Cyric scowled at the cleric. He probably would have slapped Adon again if Midnight weren't sitting in his way. "So how are we supposed to find it? I'm not even sure I know what the tablets look like."

Midnight shivered. When Mystra, the Goddess of Magic, had been destroyed in her attempt to enter the Planes without the Tablets of Fate, she had granted Midnight a vision of the artifacts. Now the tablets and the death of her god were irrevocably linked in the magic-user's mind. "They look like simple clay tablets," Midnight said with a sigh. She closed her eyes, and an image of the Tablets of Fate formed in her mind. "They're a little less than two feet high. Runes naming all of the gods and their duties are etched upon the stones. The runes are magical. They glow with a blue-white light."

Cyric tried to picture the tablets. However, each time he tried to form an image of them in his mind, thoughts of what he could do with the Tablets of Fate, or, more precisely, the power they could give him, charged into his consciousness. The thief saw himself as a powerful ruler, with armies strong enough to trample the mighty forces of King Azoun of Cormyr into the dirt. The tablets will give me the power to do what I want, the thief thought. At last I will be free to run my own life!

"Cyric?" Midnight said and leaned over to tap the thief on the shoulder. "I said, let's forget about the tablets for now. All right?"

Cyric frowned. "Yes, yes. Whatever you say." The thief paused for a moment, then attempted to smile warmly. "We should eat something. We need to keep our strength up if we're ever going to reach Tantras." Adon whimpered softly.

Midnight relaxed a bit and nodded. "I'm glad you agree. We need to start acting like friends again."

Cyric guided the skiff toward the shore. Thick forest flanked the river, and when they got close to the bank, Cyric leaped into the shallow water. The thief guided the craft close to the shade of a large, gnarled tree. Securing the boat to the base of the tree, Cyric reached out to help Midnight climb to shore.

When she got a firm footing on the boggy shore, Midnight turned back to the skiff and held out her hand. "Come on, Adon."

The cleric did not move.

"Adon, get out of there and join us!" Midnight snapped and put her hands on her hips. The cleric trembled, then rose to his feet.

"And bring us some food while you're at it!" Cyric yelled as he searched the shore for a likely campsite.

Adon reached down and picked up the smaller of the canvas bags that lay near his feet. He handed the sack to Midnight, then grabbed the mage's other hand and climbed from the boat.

"We're a good little dog, aren't we?" Cyric said in a high-pitched, taunting tone. The cleric's shoulders sagged.

"That's enough!" Midnight snapped. "Why do you keep badgering him?"

The thief shrugged. "When he acts like a man, I'll treat him like one. Not before." Cyric dusted off a small rock and sat down.

"There's no need to be so cruel," Midnight said. "When you were wounded in the Stonelands, Adon stayed with you. He did all he could to help you. The least you could do is return the favor." The mage threw the bag of food to the ground.

Instead of responding, Cyric leaned forward, grabbed the sack, and started to rummage through it. In the rough canvas bag, the thief found carefully wrapped preserved meats and flasks filled with mead. "At least you could see my wounds, when we were ambushed in the Stonelands. Adon's are merely in his head."

"That doesn't make them any less real," Midnight said coldly. "You could at least make an effort to be pleasant . . . if our friendship means anything to you. A little compassion won't kill you."

Cyric looked up and saw Adon leaning against the tree their boat was secured to, one arm around the warped and knotted trunk. The cleric's eyes were filled with apprehension, and he was standing on his toes as if he were prepared to jump out of the way instantly if anything threatened him.

Digging into the canvas sack, Cyric found a chunk of bread and brought it to the cleric. Adon wiped his hands on his tunic. His entire body quaked as he cautiously reached out and took the bread from the thief. Staring at the offering in amazement, the cleric looked as if he were going to burst into tears. "Thank you," Adon said in a small, broken voice. "You are kind."

"Aye," Cyric mumbled as he exchanged glances with Midnight. "I am far *too* kind."

They ate quickly and in silence. When they were done, Cyric went to the boat and withdrew the oars. He found a tree stump and set the oars down, then searched until he found a fallen branch the width of his thigh and chopped the log into two even pieces. These he sunk into the earth on either side of the stump. The thief sat down and positioned the oars, using the stumps as the oarlocks in their boat.

"You've trained with a staff," Cyric said as he led Midnight to the stump, "so the basic movements of rowing should be easy for you to master."

"Just a minute, Cyric," Midnight snapped as she brushed his hand away from her arm. "I've rowed a boat before. You don't need to teach me."

"But do you know the best way to row, the most efficient technique?" When Midnight didn't respond, Cyric grabbed her arm again and almost pushed her down onto the stump. "If you row the wrong way, you'll only tire yourself out, and you won't be of much use to anyone then. Sit down and pick up the oars."

For the next fifteen minutes, Cyric taught Midnight the proper rowing technique for their skiff. The mage learned quickly, and soon Cyric leaned back and let her practice on her own.

As he lounged against a rock, twirling his dagger, Cyric noticed Adon staring at the oars. "You'll learn next, cleric. I want the boat in motion as much as possible."

Adon nodded slowly and a half-smile crept across his face. Cyric continued to look at the cleric for several seconds, but the thief turned away quickly when he realized that he had balled his hands into fists. "Midnight can teach you later, when we stop for eveningfeast."

The heroes packed up quickly after that, and Cyric was careful to hide any evidence of their presence on the shore. Midnight took a turn at the oars for several hours that afternoon, and the thief seemed to relax a bit when he saw that Midnight had learned to row properly. In fact, Adon and Midnight were more comfortable, too. The cleric even laughed once when Cyric stretched after a long yawn and nearly fell out of the skiff.

While Midnight was rowing, the boat passed into a section of the river where there seemed to be no current at all. That made rowing quite a bit easier for a while, but the current picked up again suddenly—still in the wrong direction, of course. Though this was disheartening for the heroes, they tried to be cheerful. That was difficult, though, and tempers were flaring again by the time Cyric headed toward shore for eveningfeast.

When they docked, Midnight let Cyric start a small fire while she waded into the river to cool off after a long afternoon of rowing. Adon sat on the mossy bank, dangling a long stick in the water as he daydreamed. But as the mage stood in the chilly water of the Ashaba, a sharp pain bore into her leg. She let out a sharp cry and nearly fell over.

Cyric rushed into the waist-deep water and steadied Midnight as she tried to regain her footing. "What's wrong?" the thief asked as he helped the raven-haired mage toward shore.

"I don't know," she gasped through clenched teeth. "I think something bit me." Midnight felt another spike of pain shoot through her leg. When she looked down, the mage could see a pair of shimmering, crimson lights darting back and forth beneath the surface of the water. Cyric cried out then, too, and a third blood-red glow blinked to life in the Ashaba.

On shore, Adon paced back and forth, holding out his hands. "Get out," he said softly, over and over again.

The water churned as Cyric and Midnight rushed to shore. The tiny, lancing pains came more frequently, and more than a dozen of the strange blood–red lights were visible in the river now. The number had doubled before the heroes reached the bank and Adon helped them to shore.

The cleric stood by, smiling contentedly as Midnight swabbed a myriad of tiny cuts on her legs. Cyric crouched over the edge of the water, his right hand poised to snatch something from the river. The thief plunged his hand into the water once, then stepped back from the bank. When he opened his hand, a small, wriggling fish dropped to the ground. The glowing creature's razor-sharp teeth accounted for half the length of its body, and its tiny body seemed to have been set afire with the blood it had stolen.

"The river!" Midnight gasped as she pointed to the Ashaba. There was a large concentration of the glowing parasites, and the water roiled where the creatures attacked one another. More than a hundred had entered the bloody frenzy. Even as the heroes watched, the patch of red luminescence from their gorged bodies continued to spread.

"There must be thousands of them," Cyric said as he moved back to the bank. "I can see them swarming." The thief paused for a second, then turned back to Midnight, a sardonic grin on his face. "Rather reminds me of the dalesmen after your trial in Shadowdale."

"I can't see a thing other than the glow," Midnight replied, turning away from the thief.

"I have very good vision, even at night," Cyric said as he stared at the fish tearing each other apart.

Midnight didn't look at the thief. "Just like Kelemvor," she said absently as she started to break up the camp.

"You're still thinking about him?" Cyric's voice was suddenly as cold as the river's icy water. "What's wrong with you?"

"Cyric, I'm grateful for all that you've done for me, and even for Adon," Midnight sighed. "I'd be dead right now if it weren't for you. I know that. But I felt something for Kelemvor that I can't even explain." The mage shook her head and carefully placed her spellbook into a pack.

Cyric was very quiet. His attention seemed to be riveted on the glowing parasites. The blood pool was widening steadily.

"Even in Shadowdale, before the battle, Kel refused to stand with me," Midnight said flatly. "Then at the trial, I was certain I was going to die, and—"

"Say, Adon, why don't you take a dip!" Cyric yelled, gesturing for the cleric to come closer.

"Don't start in again, Cyric," Midnight snapped wearily as she tied the drawstring on the pack she was filling. "Why do you even talk to me at all if you don't care to hear what I have to say?"

"You know what I care about?" Cyric growled as he crouched beside the river, the blood-red glow from the fish reflecting in his eyes. "Getting to Tantras alive. Those tablets are important, and together we can find them." He turned to look at Midnight, but the red glow seemed to linger in his eyes even after he'd turned away from the river.

Adon had wandered over to Midnight and now sat huddled at her feet. The cleric was staring at Cyric as if the thief were some horrible creature that had crawled from the forest. Midnight stopped fidgeting with the pack and stood shaking her head. "Even with Elminster's help, we barely managed to defeat Bane. The three of us are going to be hard-pressed to succeed on this quest."

Cyric smiled. "On the journey to Shadowdale, you performed some pretty impressive acts of magic. Spells you had never studied were suddenly at your fingertips. Incantations far beyond your training seemed to trip off your tongue with ease." The thief stood up and spread his arms. "You have all the power we need—if we stay away from the gods. Even then . . ."

"The power was in Mystra's pendant," Midnight mumbled. "And the pendant was destroyed in the Temple of Lathander. The power you speak of is gone."

"Have you attempted any spells since then?" Cyric asked as he walked toward the mage. "Who can tell what powers that trinket may have left you?"

"I have no desire to court disaster," the raven-haired mage snapped. "Magic is still unstable. I don't care to attempt a spell unless I need to."

"Is that your only reason for holding back?" Cyric asked. "Or is it that you're just afraid?"

"I'm not on trial anymore." Midnight hefted the pack and tossed it into the boat, but before she could walk back to Adon's side, Cyric grabbed her by the arm.

"Just answer one question," Cyric began slowly. "How did you survive the destruction of the temple? I stood in the ruins and examined the very spot where you and Adon were found. There was wreckage all around, yet you escaped without a scratch."

"Tymora's luck," Midnight mumbled as she pulled away from the thief's grasp.

Suddenly Adon stood up and walked to Cyric's side. "Tymora is dead," he whispered. "All the gods are dead." Both Midnight and Cyric stared at the cleric as he walked to the boat and climbed in.

"Only magic can account for what happened at the temple, Midnight," Cyric said at last. "*Your* magic. I don't know how, but you gained some kind of power from that pendant. And we need that power to recover the Tablets of Fate."

"Why are you so anxious to find the tablets?" Midnight asked as she picked up a sack of food and tossed it to Adon in the boat.

"Because others will want them. Many others. That makes them valuable." Cyric looked back toward the river.

The blood-red pool had dissipated. "Perhaps even price-less."

"What about Mystra's warning?" the mage asked. "She said the tablets must be returned to the Planes, to Lord Ao, before the gods can go back to their homes and the Realms can return to normal."

"If Lord Ao has the price I seek, then I will gladly deliver them to him. But until then, there is the simple matter of survival." Cyric put out the small fire, and the camp was thrown into darkness.

"That's madness!" Midnight hissed.

Cyric stood close to Midnight. "No . . . not even close. We've battled the gods, Midnight. We've seen them die. They don't frighten me any longer." Cyric paused for a moment, then smiled and whispered, "The gods really are no different from you . . . or me." Even in the darkness, Midnight could see the sparkle in the thief's eyes as he spoke.

Less than a quarter of an hour passed before the heroes were on the river once more, the bright moon lighting their way. Midnight spent most of the night sitting in the bow or taking an occasional turn at the oars, all the while pondering what Cyric had said about the gods and about her powers.

Midnight slept little that night. However, the next two days passed quietly, so the mage had a number of chances to doze. Adon gradually became more responsive. When it came time for Midnight's next turn to row, the cleric held her spellbook open so that she could study, turning pages and searching out specific references at the mage's request.

Cyric grew tired of the preserved meats and cheeses they had brought along for rations, so he decided to fish from the bow of the skiff. Although he didn't have a bow and arrow, the thief tied their mooring line to the hilt of his dagger and successfully speared three large flounders on his first three attempts. Rather than enjoying the spoils of his skill, Cyric seemed disappointed, as if there were no true challenge in the sport.

With the exception of another skiff traveling upriver an hour after Cyric, Midnight, and Adon had passed out of Mistledale, they saw no other craft during those two days. As evening approached and the sky turned to a rich amber, Adon noticed a patch of golden angel seaweed trailing alongside their skiff, as if it had been caught on the underside of the craft.

The cleric's hand was steady as he reached over the side and dipped his fingers beneath the surface of the water to the seaweed. Its texture was like that of delicate human hair, affected by the strong current, but not snarled or matted. Memories of the sweet kisses and caresses he had been awarded by a host of beautiful women in his short time in the Realms engulfed the cleric, and a warm, knowing smile stretched across his face.

"What is he doing?" Cyric called from the bow.

Midnight looked up from her rowing. "He's not harming anyone," the mage said softly. When she noticed that Adon was smiling, she smiled, too. "It's nice to see him happy."

An almost imperceptible nod came from the cleric as he stared at the surface of the water, his hands tracing delicate forms upon the angel hair. But Adon tensed as he suddenly felt something solid beneath his hand. The cleric squinted into the golden, sparkling water and saw a lovely young woman floating underwater alongside the boat, her body translucent. The golden angel seaweed was in actuality her hair. As Adon watched, a pair of bright yellow eyes opened beneath the surface of the water, and the woman, as beautiful as any goddess, smiled up at the cleric and covered his hand with hers.

When the woman suddenly stood up, Adon gasped and Midnight nearly lost the oars. Cyric drew his dagger and crouched in a defensive stance, but the thief felt the fear and anger drain from his body as he gazed at the golden-haired woman. The dagger slipped from Cyric's grasp and dropped with a clatter to the bottom of the boat.

The woman, who seemed to stand waist-deep in the water, kept pace with the boat as it floated along on the river. She was clothed in a sheer gold and white gown that clung to her perfectly formed, statuesque figure. Her skin was pale, and she appeared vaguely wraithlike. A hint of the shoreline was visible through her stunning form. A white shawl was slung across her shoulders.

"Who are you?" she said in a remarkably resonant voice. Her words seemed to echo from the surface of the river and fill the cradle of water that was held between the opposing shores of deep green trees.

Midnight stopped flailing with the oars and spoke clearly. "I am Midnight of Deepingdale," she said. "My companions are Cyric, behind me, and Adon, beside you."

The woman smiled. "Would you . . . like to play?"

The surface of the river seemed to bubble as the golden-haired woman spoke. The skiff rocked back and forth unsteadily. "We don't have time for games," Midnight declared as she pulled the oars into the boat. "We are on important business."

The golden-eyed woman laughed, her hand rising to her face, the tips of her fingers brushing her lips. "Oh, that sounds exciting," she murmured. "But really, I think you should stay with me."

The air surrounding the boat shimmered with tiny, amber sparks. Adon and Cyric were suddenly transfixed by the pale-skinned woman. Both men stood, blank-faced and staring, as the boat rocked and bobbed.

Midnight glanced at her enraptured companions, then realized what it was she faced: a nereid, a strange creature from the Elemental Plane of Water. And it seemed that the legends the magic-user had heard about the capricious water sprites were also true. All men who gazed upon a nereid were mesmerized on sight.

Before the mage could break the nereid's spell, she heard a sudden roar behind her, and turned to see a huge tunnel form in the water directly in front of the boat. Fearing that the boat would be dragged to the bottom of the river by the tunnel, Midnight quickly turned back to the golden-haired creature. "If you kill us, we won't be able to play your games," Midnight shouted, her mind racing.

"I can play with you alive or dead," the nereid said, then stroked Adon's face and giggled. "It makes no difference."

In desperation, Midnight picked up one of the canvas storage sacks. "We can give you something of great magic. But only we know how to use it."

Suddenly the tunnel collapsed, just as the skiff was about

to enter it. The boat rocked violently, and a fine mist washed over the heroes. Neither Adon nor Cyric moved, nor did either stop staring at the woman.

"Show me," the nereid murmured. It rose to the top of the water and walked easily on its surface around the outside of the boat, oblivious to the craft's motion. The creature seemed to glide over the waves, so that its feet never left the Ashaba.

Midnight contemplated the amount of time she would need to cast a single spell, but she decided against it. If only there were something in the bag I could use against this creature! Midnight thought desperately. Or better yet, something I could use to grab that shawl! If the legends were correct, then the nereid's soul was encased in that piece of cloth. If Midnight could grab it, then she could command it to leave them alone.

"Show me!" the golden-haired creature cried, and the river came to life. Suddenly the water congealed into a dozen sparkling mirror images of the nereid. The water sprite's doubles rose on either side of the small craft and grabbed the sides of the skiff, halting its motion completely.

As the golden-eyed sprite drew closer, Midnight noticed that it was not made of flesh and blood. Swirling, sparkling water, alive with streaks of lightning that darted back and forth, lay behind the sprite's delicate features. The bright glow of the sky was trapped within the nereid's body and shifted lazily as the creature moved. The sight reminded the mage of light passing through a large block of ice.

Midnight raised her hands to cast a spell.

"Wait!" a voice cried weakly, and Midnight turned in surprise to see Adon reach out toward the nereid. The golden-eyed creature seemed intrigued and held its ground. "You are so beautiful," Adon murmured softly. Thoughts of Sune Firehair, the Goddess of Beauty, the goddess he once served, floated through the scarred cleric's mind.

The nereid smiled and reached back, running its hands through its hair. "I am indeed beautiful," the creature said. Suddenly its features began to run like wax beneath a flame. The youth and vitality drained away from its form, leaving the image of a withered hag in its place. "And now?" the nereid asked.

Adon seemed to straighten, and the amber sunlight fell upon his features, filling in the depression of the scar that lined his face. "There's no difference," he said. "None whatsoever."

Again the nereid's form turned waxen until it returned to the shape of a beautiful young woman. "You're in love with me," it stated matter-of-factly. "You would do anything I say."

Once, when Adon, Midnight, Kelemvor, and Cyric had entered the ruins of Castle Kilgrave on a mission to rescue the Goddess of Magic, the God of Strife had assaulted the heroes with visions of their fondest desires. Adon had seen Sune Firehair—and he had nearly succumbed to the illusion. Only the intervention of his friends had saved him.

Now, as Adon stared at the nereid's beautiful, mesmerizing eyes, something deep inside his mind recalled the memory of that illusion back to him. The cleric felt his lower lip tremble. "No . . . ," he growled. "No, I don't think I would." Adon sprang into lightning motion and quickly tore the shawl from the nereid's shoulders.

"No!" the creature screamed as it tried to snatch the shawl back. As it did, the watery doubles of the nereid lifted the boat from the surface of the river.

Adon tumbled into Midnight, and they both fell to the bottom of the skiff in a tangle of arms and legs. Cyric, on the other hand, still stood in the stern. He, too, was reaching for the nereid's shawl. Seeing the thief's dagger within reach, Midnight grabbed the weapon, then snatched the shawl from Adon.

"Put us down!" Midnight cried as she folded the shawl over the sharp blade.

All at once, the water creatures dropped the boat to the river. Cyric fell backward, bumped his head, and stopped moving. The nereid cried out in pain. "Please!" the sprite screeched piteously. "Leave my shawl alone!"

"I thought you wanted to play," Midnight said, her voice low and cold.

For a moment, the only sound Adon and Midnight could hear was the steady gurgling of the river. Then suddenly a fine mist struck the back of their necks. The cleric turned to see the nearest of the nereid's doubles contort its face into a terrible visage and hiss threateningly.

"Dispel your servants!" Midnight demanded, pressing the dagger against the shawl. "Let us go in peace!"

A series of strangled gasps escaped from the watery constructs as they dispersed with a muffled splash. The golden eyes of the nereid narrowed, and suddenly the skiff was in motion once again. The creatures flanking the boat had returned to their original watery state.

"Adon, take the oars!" Midnight shouted as the flow of the river spun the boat around and dragged it upstream. The cleric grabbed the oars and tried to control the craft.

Cyric groaned and sat up in the stern of the skiff. Suddenly the nereid was beside the thief, clutching at his arms, trying to pull him out of the boat. Before the creature could claim its hostage, however, Adon locked both his hands tightly around Cyric's right ankle.

At that moment, Midnight drove the dagger through the shawl.

The nereid froze in place momentarily, holding on to the groggy thief's arms. Then violent, painful shudders wracked the creature's body. Finally the sprite let out a high-pitched, whining sigh and collapsed into the water.

Adon dragged Cyric back into the skiff. The thief was badly shaken. The cleric stood over him, smiling, as Cyric rubbed his bruised head and looked around, trying to remember what had happened to him after the nereid had appeared.

The beautiful white shawl in Midnight's hands gradually grew black, then started to crumble. The mage looked into the water, but the nereid was gone, returned to the Elemental Plane of Water. Shaking her head, Midnight dropped the decaying shawl into the Ashaba and watched it float away upstream.

* * * * *

Fzoul Chembryl lay, close to death, upon a rough straw mattress, staring up at the fading amber light of the afternoon sky through the shattered ceiling of a deserted farmhouse in Zhentilar-occupied Daggerdale. Despite the casualties to Bane's armies in the Battle of Shadowdale, the dalesmen had not tried to drive the Zhentilar from their neighboring settlement to the west. For the moment, Fzoul felt safe.

What an ignoble place to call my tomb, the wounded man thought. I, a powerful priest of the God of Strife, leader of the Zhentarim, second only to Manshoon, am to die in a stinking, burned-out hovel in a captured territory. For a moment, Fzoul wondered if the Zhentarim, a massive, largely secret organization loyal to the God of Strife, would send someone to search for him. The priest smiled grimly and dismissed the idea, certain that most of the Zhentarim would be happy to see him dead.

"Our overconfidence cost us everything!" the red-haired priest muttered aloud, although he was alone. "And your greed, Bane. Your madness and your greed. . . ."

Fzoul attempted to move, but he could not. The pain in his chest was not unlike a huge, vicious watchdog that pounced on him whenever he was foolish enough to forget the wound he had suffered in the attack on Shadowdale.

The high priest of Bane slipped into delirium, as he had done frequently in the last few days, and events of the recent past played through his mind. Fzoul suddenly remembered discovering that Tempus Blackthorne, Bane's chosen assistant and emissary, had died, a victim of the omnipresent instability in magic. Bane then had chosen to split Blackthorne's duties between Fzoul and his sometime rival, Sememmon of Darkhold.

Filled with plans of how he could exploit his new position and solidify his own power base, Fzoul had accepted the post with an enthusiasm he had not felt in years. But that enthusiasm faded quickly as he learned the secrets of the god-made-flesh. The Black Lord was forced to eat, drink, and sleep, like any other man. Wound the god, and he would bleed like any other man. Fzoul, much to his disgust, was forced to tend to his master's human needs and protect the Black Lord's secrets at all costs.

Fzoul's mind raced ahead. Suddenly the preparations for the Battle of Shadowdale were underway, and Sememmon was chosen to ride with Lord Bane through Voonlar. Fzoul was assigned the task of leading a five-hundred-man contingent across the Ashaba bridge to take the town from behind and capture the Twisted Tower.

The defenders of Shadowdale had destroyed the bridge rather than allow Fzoul's forces the easy victory that had been expected. Worse still, the priest had been trapped on the west side of the bridge when it fell, away from most of his troops. Then the lean, hawk-nosed, dark-haired leader of the dalesmen at the bridge fired an arrow into Fzoul's chest. The high priest fell from the bridge to the roiling water below, where the unnatural tide swept him upstream, along with a handful of other survivors. The small band of soldiers struggled together to stay alive until they got to shore and found a squad of Zhentilar that had been posted to watch the supply route.

The wounds of the red-haired high priest had made travel back to Zhentil Keep impossible; Fzoul knew that he'd never survive the journey. The farmhouse was the closest shelter the Zhentish soldiers could find.

"I have spilled my own blood in your name, and you desert me!" Fzoul railed. "Damn you, Bane!"

Now, forced to place his life in the hands of his subordinates, Fzoul lay upon the dirty heap of straw and tried to force his thoughts away from the near certainty of his approaching demise. As he stared at the amber sky through the ruined ceiling, the high priest realized that the light was growing brighter and more intense. Finally the color of the sky deepened to blood red, and streaks of light pierced the darkness of the farmhouse as if the boarded-up windows had been torn open.

"Attend me!" Fzoul shouted as he tried to rise, despite the pain in his chest. A skeletal hand fell upon Fzoul's chest, gently forcing him back down. The high priest found himself staring into a face that belonged more to a corpse left on a field of battle than to a living creature.

"Zhentilar! To my side!" Fzoul yelled as he tried to back away from the horrible, rotting thing that stood before him, its hand on his chest. The priest's chest convulsed in pain after the effort of shouting.

The skeletal figure smiled a rictus grin. "Alas, Fzoul Chembryl, High Priest of Bane, the Zhentilar who were camped outside this hut are . . . gone." He removed his hand from the priest's chest. "I trust you know who I am?"

"You've come for me at last, then," Fzoul whispered and closed his eyes.

"No need to be so melodramatic," Myrkul said. "All men know my touch sooner or later. But this need not be your time to enter my kingdom."

Fzoul tried to hide his fear. "What do you propose?"

The God of the Dead raised his bony hand and drummed the tips of his fingers against his bleached white chin. The sound was high-pitched and sharp. "It is not *my* proposition you must entertain," Myrkul sighed. "I'm here as, let us say, an agent of your lord and god, the immortal God of Strife."

A short laugh escaped from the high priest. "Look at me," Fzoul said. "What could Lord Bane want with me? I can hardly breathe anymore."

"Lord Bane's avatar was destroyed in the Battle of Shadowdale, in the Temple of Lathander," Myrkul stated flatly. "You have been chosen for the high honor of being host for Lord Bane's essence." The God of the Dead looked around the ruined hut and grinned again.

"But my wounds—," Fzoul began.

"Are as nothing to a god. You can be healed, and you can live out the glory you dreamed about all your life," Myrkul sighed as he turned to look at the high priest.

Concern flashed across the features of the priest.

Myrkul shook his head, and a stray, fleshy strip flapped against his cheekbone. "Spare me your denials. Your self-serving machinations are well known."

"Why doesn't Bane just take me?" Fzoul said. The high priest tried to sit up again, but he couldn't. "Obviously I could do nothing to stop him."

"If *Lord* Bane simply possessed you, your identity and memories would be compromised. The Black Lord wishes to assimilate your being into his, but he cannot do so without your cooperation," Myrkul said, yawning.

The pain in Fzoul's chest was terrible now, and the priest

was panting hard. "Why—why didn't he come himself?" he gasped between breaths.

"He did," Myrkul said softly, chuckling. "Look around you."

The blood-red haze that Fzoul had taken for the sky now flowed into the hut through the opening in the ceiling and slowly drifted toward the high priest.

"Death or life?" the skeletal man asked. "The choice is yours."

Fzoul watched as the red mass grew brighter, then started to pulse in time to the rhythm of his own heart. A black flame emerged from the center of the red cloud.

"I want to live!" Fzoul screamed as the flame shot through the air. The black energy entered his body through the wound in his chest.

"Alas, I knew you would," the God of the Dead sighed as he stepped back and watched Fzoul's body writhe. Streamers of black and red light burst from the high priest's eyes, nose, and mouth.

The high priest felt his flesh become numb as Bane's dark essence coursed through his body. The flow of Fzoul's blood slowed, then stopped for a moment as it was overwhelmed by the presence of the evil god. Then the priest's internal organs were violated as the spark of godhood merged with humanity. Fzoul felt the tide of Bane's evil rise within him, and he welcomed the sensation.

The pleasant feeling was short-lived, however. A sudden agony pierced Fzoul's consciousness as his memories and desires were laid bare to the Black Lord. Then the pain subsided, and Bane's voice eased into the high priest's mind.

Have no doubts concerning who is in control, the God of Strife growled. The god's mind stretched and shifted as it tried to grow accustomed to its new home. *Your tasks will be simple. Fail me, or act in rebellion even once, and I will destroy you.*

Muffled sensation returned, and Fzoul vaguely felt the chill of the night air as it drifted in from above. How long has this taken? he wondered, and he attempted to put voice to his query. Fzoul was only mildly surprised when the words did not come.

The high priest watched from somewhere deep inside his

own mind as his hand rose up before his eyes. The hand clenched and became a fist, then opened and passed over the priest's bloody, wounded chest. Instantly the wound was gone, and Fzoul realized that he was sitting up.

"Myrkul," the Black Lord said with the voice of the high priest. He sat upon the rough straw mattress and stretched. "Attend me."

"There is no longer a need, Lord Bane," Myrkul said calmly as he bowed. "Once I have delivered you to Zhentil Keep, you will need to attend to your own needs. It is best you start now."

The Black Lord snarled. "You go too far, Myrkul! I will not stand for this insubordination!" As the God of the Dead bowed once more and spread his arms wide, Lord Bane considered striking the skeletal god. Or perhaps, he thought, I should cast a spell. Nothing too powerful, of course, but something strong enough to show Myrkul who is in command.

Looking out through eyes that were no longer his to control, Fzoul tried to scream. Bane would destroy them both if he attempted a spell and it backfired!

"Remember your place," Bane snapped. Myrkul nodded, and Fzoul found himself tumbling back into the recesses of his own mind.

"My apologies, Lord Bane," the God of the Dead murmured. "This has been a very difficult and tiring time for me. Are you ready to return to the Dark Temple in Zhentil Keep?"

Bane ran his hands over the body of his avatar. He had altered his previous incarnation into something more than a man, a horrible creature with sharp talons and hard, charred skin that only the sharpest of instruments could penetrate. The pale, vulnerable flesh of the high priest made the Dark God uneasy. Myrkul had argued in favor of Bane's new appearance, reasoning that humans would trust the god more readily if he appeared to be one of them. Bane had reluctantly agreed. After all, his previous tactics—trying to frighten his forces into submission—had been a rather decided failure. After the defeat at Shadowdale, he would need to regain the confidence of his followers.

The God of Strife shivered as he realized that his power in the Realms was nothing more than the sum of all his worshipers. The thought was revolting. "Yes," the Black Lord sighed after a moment. "Take me to my temple in Zhentil Keep."

Creating a mystical gate, Myrkul stood aside and beckoned to Bane to come forward. Through the opening, the Black Lord saw the seemingly deserted streets of Zhentil Keep. Bane stepped through the opening. In a moment, the Black Lord was standing in a dark, rat-infested alley. A cutpurse let out a yell as Bane's avatar suddenly appeared nearby. The grimy thief scurried out of the alley and ran down the street in panic.

"So it begins anew, Myrkul," Bane said as he gazed at the partially constructed spires of his temple in the distance. When he received no response, the Black Lord turned to find that the gate had vanished and the God of the Dead was nowhere to be seen.

It hardly matters, Bane thought as he left the alley. Myrkul has served his function for now.

Bane traveled through the city, shunning the poor and homeless people he passed. Sounds that might have come from thieves or slavers falling upon new victims drifted from nearly every shadow and caused Bane to quicken his step, until finally he was running through the streets, the spires of his temple fixed in his eyes. As he turned one last corner and approached the temple, Bane spotted the figures of several temple guards ahead.

"Guards!" the Black Lord shouted with Fzoul's voice, then stood motionless as one of the watchmen stepped forward, his weapon drawn.

"You'll get no free meals here!" the guard growled, looking out at the tattered clothes of the avatar from under a black hand on a red field—Bane's own symbol. "Off with you now!"

"Don't you recognize me, Dier Ashlin?" Bane asked, running his hand through the tangle of red hair on his head.

The guard squinted as he examined the tired, grimy man who stood before him, wearing the tattered remains of an officer's uniform. Blood spattered the redheaded man's shirt, and his face was covered with sweat and dirt. But even the grime and blood could not hide Fzoul Chembryl from the guard for long. "L—Lord Fzoul!" Ashlin shouted and lowered his sword.

"Indeed," the God of Strife grumbled. "Get me inside. I have traveled all the way from the Dales since the battle."

"The slaughter, you mean," Ashlin mumbled as he turned and headed for the front of the temple.

The Black Lord longed to kill the guard without another word, but something inside him—Fzoul, perhaps—told him that now was not the time for bloodshed. Now was the time for the God of Strife to rebuild his kingdom.

As they entered the partially finished Dark Temple, Lord Bane was impressed with the amount of work that had been accomplished since he had last been there. Unfortunately, the Battle of Shadowdale had diverted many of his men from the task of rebuilding his temple. In fact, now, with the exception of the guards, the wounded who had survived the journey from Shadowdale, and a handful of devout worshipers, the temple was deserted.

"Who is in charge, now that Bane has disappeared? I assumed Sememmon had taken the reigns of leadership," Bane said as he stopped and looked out a window.

Ashlin shrugged. "Sememmon was wounded on the field of battle in the Dales. Some of our men said they saw him dragged off, and that was the last anyone saw of him."

A chill ran up the avatar's spine. "Then the city is once again in the hands of incompetents!" the God of Strife growled. Balling his hands into fists, Bane turned to the guard. "Lord Chess?"

"Aye," Ashlin muttered. "With Bane gone, you and Sememmon missing, and Manshoon off in hiding somewhere, Lord Chess could see little reason to continue work on the temple, and so it sits. Rumor has it that Chess, the filthy orc, wants to turn it into a brothel!"

The shoulders of the avatar tightened. "I would like to see Lord Chess," snapped the Black Lord. "Tonight." The God of Strife turned back to the window and looked out on the dirty, rubble-strewn streets around the Dark Temple.

"Yes, Lord Chembryl," Ashlin said, and he turned to leave.

"Wait! I haven't dismissed you yet!" the Black Lord shouted without turning from the window. The guard froze in his tracks. "There are others who I wish you to summon. . . ."

* * * * *

For the next several hours, Bane retired to his private chambers, hidden behind the throne room, and prepared himself for the meeting he had called. The ceremonial robes Fzoul had left in his quarters before the battle were brought to the Black Lord. He bathed, then dressed as his guests began to arrive.

When the noise from the outer chamber became a roar, Bane opened a small secret panel to the room and listened to the crowd. The members of the Zhentarim—Bane's Black Network, some called them—were silent. Lord Chess's men, the high-ranking city officials and the heads of the militia, were not.

"Lord Bane has forsaken us!" they cried. "Lord Chess should rule the city now!"

"Bane betrayed us!" another voice shouted. "Our forces were led into a deathtrap in Shadowdale! Then he abandoned us to be tortured by the dalesmen!"

A roar of approval went up from a group of militia standing close to Bane's listening post. It's time I made my entrance, the God of Strife thought. Now that they've worn themselves down, it shouldn't be too hard to manipulate them.

As Bane's avatar emerged from behind the large black throne that dominated the room, some of the cries were silenced. Still, a loud hum of conversation hung over the room, punctuated occasionally by a curse or threat. The Black Lord raised Fzoul's hands, and the hum died away, too. "I am here to unify Zhentil Keep once again!" the avatar cried.

Slowly Bane walked to the black throne. He turned to the crowd, which was now almost completely silent, and flashed a wide, malicious grin. Then he sat down upon the throne.

The room erupted in a wave of gasps and cries of outrage. "This is an insult!" a dark-haired priest called out. "Have we been summoned from our homes in the dead of night to witness sacrilege? How do you explain this, Fzoul?"

"With blood," the red-haired priest said as he raised his hands again. "I answer your call with blood. For I am not Fzoul Chembryl, although his flesh hosts my essence. I am your lord and master, and you will bow before me!"

The dark-haired priest screamed, clutched at his eyes, then fell to the ground. Visions of a world controlled by the God of Strife filled the priest's mind. The rivers of Faerun ran with blood, and the land itself shook under the tread of Bane's mighty armies. And there, in the middle of the carnage and ruin, the priest saw himself, covered with the blood and jewels of the defeated.

Rising to his knees, the priest removed his hands and revealed glowing, blood-red eyes. "Bane has returned!" the priest screamed. "Our god has returned to deliver us!"

"All my children will know my glory," Bane said, and in moments the entire chamber was filled with the screams of his followers as they reveled in Bane's vision of conquest and power. Looking out through a blood-red haze as a reminder of their true allegiance, Bane's faithful stood before their lord, awaiting his orders.

"We must first discover the strength of our enemies. Recall our spies from Shadowdale," Bane cried, pointing to a greasy-haired city official who cowered near the throne. "I wish to learn the fate of those who stood against me in the Temple of Lathander. If Elminster or that raven-haired lackey of Mystra still live, I want them brought before me!"

The minister of defense bowed before the Black Lord, then hastened from the throne room. "Of course, Lord Bane," the minister whispered over and over as he fled from the chamber.

"And now we must address the state of Zhentil Keep," the God of Strife growled and turned to once again face the crowded throne room. "The discontent, fear, and confusion of our people must be put to rest before we may achieve the greatness that is our preordained future.

"We will proceed through the streets of the city this very night, spreading the news of my return. The flames of hope that light your eyes will be fanned into an inferno. Together we shall sweep away the people's doubts and begin a new age!" The audience chamber was filled with cries of thanks and shouts of support for the Black Lord. Bane allowed a slight smile to work its way across his face. Once again, he held his followers in an iron grip.

When the frenzy reached a peak, the God of Strife held his fist aloft and spoke again. "Together we shall triumph where gods alone would fail!"

Bane's worshipers parted as their god rose from his throne and walked to the center of the room. The God of Strife stood among his screaming followers for a moment, then led the multitude out of the temple and into the night.

❦ 4 ❦

Pursuit

The edge of the forest was over an hour away, and Kelemvor and his men could hardly wait to leave the slow travel and the many obstacles of the woods behind them. The sun had risen, and the last of the magical crystals Lhaeo had supplied the riders with had failed. The light from the crystals had pierced the veil of night and allowed Kelemvor and his charges to keep moving along the river almost constantly. In the days since they had left Shadowdale, the riders had stopped only twice to rest, for a few hours each time.

Kelemvor reached for the small purse tied to his belt and jostled it slightly. The jingle of gold coins against one another rose above the sounds of the dalesmen as they made their way along the rough path. A few men glanced at the mercenary, then quickly looked away when Kelemvor scowled in their direction.

I wonder if Cyric and Midnight received this much money to work against the Dales? Kelemvor thought for the fourth time that day. *They probably got paid off when we were in Tilverton.*

Letting the purse drop to his side, Kelemvor glanced around at the men Mourngrym had sent on the hunt with him. They were, all in all, a less than remarkable lot. The fighter saw them as typical residents of a farming town: narrow-minded but sincere. The men had done little to impress or surprise the experienced adventurer during the long journey from Shadowdale, but that was fine with him.

The only thing about the party that *had* surprised Kelemvor was Mourngrym's insistence that Yarbro, the young guardsman who had taken an instant dislike to Kelemvor and his companions when they had first arrived in Shadow-dale, join them. But there had been no time to argue about personnel if the hunters wanted to catch the escapees, so Kelemvor had reluctantly agreed.

"A cold heart is needed for this task," Mourngrym had said as Kelemvor prepared to ride after his one-time allies. "Your rage might blind you to justice. I want the criminals returned alive, unless there is absolutely no other choice." The dalelord paused for a moment, then handed the fighter the purse full of gold. "Yarbro will see that reason prevails."

Kelemvor snorted. Placing "Yarbro" and "reason" in the same sentence was almost a joke. It seems far more likely that Mourngrym wants someone to keep an eye on me, the fighter thought. He pulled up on his reins, and his horse jumped over a fallen branch. Kelemvor looked around again and sighed. At least the rest of the men seem relatively trustworthy.

The guide chosen by the dalelord to lead the hunters through the forest was Terrol Uthor, a veteran of several battles against the drow and a scholar steeped in the ancient lore of the elven clans that once claimed the forest around Shadowdale as their own. Uthor was a short, powerfully built, square-shouldered man in his late thirties with blue-gray eyes and thick, black hair that he wore slicked back.

A common bond of hatred for the escapees was the one thing that united the remaining members of Kelemvor's charges. Gurn Bestil, a woodsman in his fifties with a shock of white hair, had lost his twenty-year-old son in the Battle of Shadowdale. Kohren and Lanx were priests of Lathander. Kohren was tall, and all that remained of his dark hair was a widow's peak. Lanx was of moderate build, with thin, curly blond hair and dull brown eyes. Both priests wore the red crest of their order on their clothing.

Bursus, Cabal, and Jorah were soldiers who had watched comrades and friends die in the battle. Of the three, Cabal was the oldest, with a gray beard and thick white eyebrows. Tired, jet-black eyes and deeply tanned skin distinguished Bursus. Jorah was of slender build with wild, auburn hair. All three were archers as well as swordsmen, and they carried spare bows and arrows for the other huntsmen.

Mikkel and Carella owned the fishing skiff that had been stolen by the escapees. No one knew their last names, but in appearance, they could have been taken for brothers. Their faces were baked red by the sun, and their builds were rugged and well toned. Both their heads had been shaved. They even dressed alike. The only thing that really set them apart was the sparkling prism that dangled from Mikkel's right ear.

Since the trip through the thick woods along the Ashaba had been uneventful so far, Kelemvor had no idea how the men would react in a battle. Not that he was worried about their fighting ability. The battle against Bane's troops had given the adventurer enough proof of the dalesmen's general fighting prowess. Still, the fighter wondered how his pack of huntsmen would work as a team.

"Until we run into a stray band of Zhents or a wild creature that is addled enough to attack a party this size, or those butchers we're chasing, we won't know how the men will fight," Yarbro said snidely when Kelemvor had posed the problem to his second-in-command. "But I wouldn't worry," the soldier added. "We'll all pull together when we catch up to that witch and her friends."

Even now, as he rode through the forest with the troops, Kelemvor was not reassured by Yarbro's confidence. Or perhaps it was the knowledge that the soldier was right— that the dalesmen's hatred would pull them together when they finally caught Midnight, Cyric, and Adon—that troubled the fighter the most.

Kelemvor shook the thoughts from his head. I'm doing the right thing, he growled to himself. They betrayed me. They murdered innocent people. They killed Elminster.

The fighter spurred his horse and raced down the path. His men pushed their horses on as well, and soon the company was out of the forest and on the edge of the open fields of Mistledale. So far, they had seen no sign of the skiff or the escapees. Unless they got lucky or did something drastic soon, the huntsmen were in danger of losing their quarry.

"Halt!" Kelemvor called as he held up his hand to signal the troops. When all the men got close enough to hear, the fighter added, "We need to decide where to go from here."

"We follow the river," Yarbro snapped. "What else can we do? In fact, we're wasting time even talking about it. We should be charging across Mistledale as fast as we can. It's open land, and—"

"The road to the Standing Stone," Kelemvor interrupted flatly. The fighter dismounted and stretched. "We can ride even faster on the road than we can across open fields."

Gurn ran his hand through his white hair. "But the road angles to the north and east, away from the river."

Kelemvor fished a piece of dried meat from his saddlebag. "And then it turns to the south, all the way to Blackfeather Bridge. We know they're going to Scardale, following the river. They have to pass the bridge eventually."

Yarbro cursed. "How will we know they haven't already passed the bridge when we get there?" A few of the other men mumbled in agreement.

"We won't," the green-eyed fighter said as he stuffed the piece of meat into his mouth and mounted his horse again.

"Kel's right," Terrol Uthor said over the mumbled curses of the two fishermen. "We'll never catch up with them if we continue along the river. Once we've crossed the dale, the woods between here and Battledale are very thick. At times we wouldn't even be able to ride."

Kelemvor smiled and turned his horse to the east. "That's it, then. Our guide has spoken." The fighter kicked his horse into a gallop and headed east, toward the road. A few of the men looked at Yarbro, who cursed again, then spurred his horse and raced off after Kelemvor. The rest of the men followed.

It wasn't long before the huntsmen reached the wide, well-traveled road that led from Hillsfar in the north to Tilverton, Arabel, and eventually even the great city of Suzail in the south. To Kelemvor, the open road seemed to carry the sweet scent of freedom and release. Even the mood of Kelemvor's fellow hunters seemed to improve.

By midafternoon, however, the dry heat of the sun had managed to burn off whatever good cheer the dalesmen had felt. As was becoming common on the journey, the men vented their ill humor by suggesting new and inventive means of dealing with the escaped criminals once they were caught. Yarbro's fertile imagination accounted for fully half of these.

Kelemvor's anger grew as the day went on. *If Mourngrym thinks that these men will support his justice*, the fighter thought, *he's a fool! They're a bloodthirsty lynch mob, no more or less vicious than the wild-eyed fanatics in Tilverton who tried to kill Midnight, Cyric, Adon, and me because they thought the God of Blacksmiths wanted us dead.*

Kelemvor knew that he should remind the men of Mourngrym's orders that the prisoners were to be returned to Shadowdale alive, but he couldn't. Instead, he brooded silently, and his refusal to contradict the hunters' angry threats and boasts was taken as unspoken consent. The tales became wilder and more cruel as the day went on.

As the fighter looked around at the leering, cursing men he commanded, he remembered Cyric's tirade against the "justice" the dalesmen would provide to Midnight and Adon, and for the first time since Lhaeo had burst into Mourngrym's chamber, Kelemvor wondered if he was doing the right thing.

The fighter turned the idea over and over in his mind all day, until finally the sun became a low, blinding orb at the hunters' backs, and the road ahead was blanketed by the first hints of nightfall. The food reserves had not been replenished in the last few days, and Kelemvor gave silent thanks for a task that would take the dalesmen's minds off their murderous imaginings.

The fighter signaled the company to come to a halt. "We'll need to forage here," the fighter snapped as he dismounted. "Perhaps the earth has not yet turned sour from the chaos in this part of the Realms, and we will find healthy game."

Dividing the hunters into three groups, Kelemvor led Bursus, Jorah, and Terrol into the south woods while Mikkel, Carella, and Gurn went to the north. Yarbro, the priests of Lathander, and the remaining soldier, Cabal, stayed behind to guard the camp.

Half an hour later, as night was beginning to fall in earnest and a dark blue veil hung over the woods, Kelemvor and his group emerged from the forest. They were carrying the carcass of a deer that had been felled by one of Jorah's arrows.

A few minutes after that, Mikkel and his men exited from the thick, dark woods north of the road. The fisherman carried the still form of a jackrabbit in his hands. His look of triumph faded quickly as he saw the meal Kelemvor had secured. The hunters laughed at the sight of Mikkel, standing alone and dejected with his prize, then welcomed him and his party to join in the meal. The hunters feasted on the fresh deer meat, then lingered around the fire at the edge of the woods.

Well fed if not well rested, the hunters buried the deer's remains and took to the road once again. For a short time, Kelemvor sensed a camaraderie that he had never before associated with the grim, disparate band of hunters. Stories of past adventures, real or imagined, were traded as they traveled through the moonlit night on their way to the Standing Stone.

As always, however, the topic of Midnight and her accomplices soon became the central focus of conversation, and the veneer of civilized behavior disappeared, to be replaced by the bitterness and savagery of the hunters' threats and curses. Kelemvor realized that, no matter how much he might hope otherwise, it was the common hatred of the three criminals, whom most of the hunters had never even met, that truly bonded the men.

The moon was high when the hunters reached the Standing Stone, where the road split, one branch continuing northeast to Hillsfar, while the other ran south, past the town of Essembra, to Blackfeather Bridge. The stone itself was a huge, glossy gray square that rose twenty feet into the air. At its base, elvish runes were inscribed in a series of bands that wound around all four sides of the stone.

There was a clearing behind the stone, a perfect crescent of brownish black earth where nothing grew. The trees farther back behind the Standing Stone were unlike any others the hunters had seen this side of the Great Desert, which lay far to the west. The bases of the trees were wildly knotted, with their roots twisted forward and dug into the ground like an old miser's fingers in a pile of gold. The trees' branches grew away from the stone, curving strangely midway along their lengths so that they remained generally parallel to the earth instead of growing straight and proud. The trees were a dull orange, while their occasional leaves appeared yellow and sickly.

Some of the men were obviously nervous about being so close to the Standing Stone, which was known to hold extraordinary reserves of magic, especially now that the art was unstable. Others did not care to remain so close to the ruins of Myth Drannor, which lay to the north. Indeed, stories of the creatures that stalked the land around the ruined city made most of the men jumpy. Still, the hunters were exhausted, and when the issue was put to a vote, the dalesmen chose to make camp beside the stone, despite their fears.

Kelemvor and Yarbro took the first watch along with Bursus, one of the archers from the dale. Although Yarbro's open hostility toward Kelemvor had ceased, the fighter still didn't trust the young guard. Bursus sat beside the fighter, and they gazed at the mystical stone before them as it reflected the soft moonlight and the flickering flames of their fire.

"There's something I've never understood," Bursus sighed as he turned to face the fighter.

"What's that?" Kelemvor asked, absently tossing a stick into the fire and watching as a tiny explosion of sparks floated into the air.

"The murderers we're chasing were once your friends. You fought at their side." The archer paused for a moment. "Isn't this difficult for you?"

The fighter's eyes were fixed on the fire. "They betrayed me," Kelemvor growled. "They lied to me right from the beginning." He turned to look at Yarbro and found the guard staring at him.

"I shouldn't have doubted you," Bursus said, nodding. "You have as much cause for revenge as any of us. Perhaps more."

Revenge? Kelemvor thought. Is that all the motivation I have for this quest? Perhaps that's not reason enough. Midnight certainly wasn't given a proper chance to defend herself at the trial. Justice wasn't served . . . and these dalesmen certainly aren't going to see that Midnight, Cyric, and Adon are treated fairly.

Kelemvor cursed silently and shook his head. When he looked up again, the fighter saw that Yarbro was still watching him, except that now the guard had a curious, sly look on his face.

"Yes, Bursus," Yarbro murmured, never taking his eyes off Kelemvor. "He *should* have more incentive for hunting down that witch than the rest of us put together." A grin slowly worked its way across the guard's face.

Looking into Yarbro's eyes, Kelemvor decided that he would prevent the dalesmen from harming Midnight and her allies . . . if that proved possible. He couldn't hinder the hunters or help his former friends directly. That would activate the curse. But he could try to hold the dalesmen to Lord Mourngrym's instructions. After all, that's what he was being paid to do.

Suddenly there was a sharp snapping sound from the twisted trees behind the hunters. It didn't take Kelemvor's enhanced senses to detect the sound. Each of the sentries had heard the noise and was looking to Kelemvor for orders.

The fighter paused for a moment, then, from the woods at their backs, heard the sound of branches snapping and leaves rustling underfoot.

"Wake the others," Kelemvor whispered. "Let's hope it's nothing more than some harmless beast that got curious about the fire." The fighter stood up slowly and drew his sword.

Yarbro stood beside Kelemvor. "Put out the fire," the green-eyed fighter said calmly. The young guard complied without question, which surprised Kelemvor. More sounds came from the forest as Yarbro extinguished the flames. Standing out in the open, bathed by firelight, the hunters would have made easy targets. If the watchers in the woods had hostile intentions, they had just lost part of their advantage. Still, the cover of the woods would be in the hidden creatures' favor. Kelemvor urged the hunters to pack their belongings as quickly as possible.

"If we keep our wits about us, we may be able to get to the horses and outdistance whoever is out there," Kelemvor said, slinging his pack onto his horse with one hand and brandishing his sword with the other.

Suddenly there was a piggish grunt from the forest, and one of the horses whinnied in terror. The horse rose up on its hind legs and threw its rider, Jorah, to the ground. Then the frantic horse raced onto the Mistledale road and vanished into the night. There was a hiss, like the whisper of a sudden gust of wind, and Gurn, the white-haired woodsman, grunted and fell forward.

One of the fishermen, Carella, was near Gurn, close to the Mistledale side of the crescent-shaped clearing. He leaped from his mount and rushed to the woodsman's aid. Gurn lay on his chest, writhing in agony. A three-inch dart protruded from the back of his neck. The fisherman reached down, grabbed the woodsman's arms, and tried to drag the white-haired man to a horse.

"Kelemvor!" Carella shouted between puffs of breath. "They're using some kind of darts. They could be poisoned. They—"

The fisherman's words were cut short as a dart pierced the side of his face, passed through his cheek, and impaled itself into his tongue. Despite his absolute horror, Carella was quickly satisfied that the darts were not poisoned. He felt no sensation other than intense pain. The fisherman lost his grip on Gurn and fell to the ground, clutching at his face. As Carella quickly struggled to his feet, another dart pierced his throat, and the fisherman fell backward, his body quivering as death claimed him.

Rough, snorting laughter erupted from the forest. For the first time, Kelemvor saw something—a few faces—in amongst the trees. The creatures had large, watery eyes, set irregularly over a piggish snout. The fighter knew immediately what the hunters faced—orcs. Probably a dozen, at least.

"To the road!" Kelemvor shouted and wheeled his horse around. Several darts and two or three black-fletched arrows flashed from the trees. Cabal pulled Jorah onto the back of his horse, and the other two archers raced after Kelemvor.

Near the center of the clearing, Mikkel screamed as he saw Carella fall. They had been childhood friends and inseparable for most of their lives. Mikkel started to move quickly to help his friend, but Yarbro grabbed the red-skinned fisherman from behind and dragged him back toward the horses. Arrows flew all around them as they mounted and made for the south road.

No one was there to stop Terrol Uthor from rushing to Carella's side. However, as the guide crouched over the fallen fisherman, an arrow flew out of the darkness and pierced Terrol's chest. The guide gasped once, then fell onto his face in the dirt.

Five orcs, wearing dirty, rusted armor and carrying swords, burst into the clearing near the Standing Stone. Two immediately ran toward the bodies of the dalesmen, but the other three rushed toward Kohren and Lanx, the two clerics of Lathander, who were still fumbling with their saddlebags.

"Forget your books!" Bursus screamed as he spurred his horse down the south road. "Hurry! We—" A black arrow pierced the fighter's leg, pinning it to his horse. Bursus careened down the road after Kelemvor, gritting his teeth in pain. Five more orcs, most carrying bows, leaped from cover. A few stray arrows and a larger number of curses screamed in Orcish followed the dalesman down the road.

Kelemvor reined in his horse and stopped around a bend in the road. Cabal and Jorah, riding the same horse, quickly joined the green-eyed fighter, as did Yarbro and Mikkel. The hunters sat silently for a moment, listening to the orcs cursing in the distance. Only Kelemvor could understand what the orcs were saying, but all of the riders shivered. The meaning of the threats were clear enough, despite the difference in language.

In another second, Bursus's mount cantered into sight. The black-haired dalesman was lolling in the saddle from the pain of his wounded leg, but his horse had continued down the road. Jorah jumped down from Cabal's mount and stopped Bursus's horse from continuing past them.

"The Lathanderites . . . ," Bursus mumbled. "Save them!" The archer tried to raise his hand, probably to point back at the Standing Stone, but couldn't. Cabal dismounted and examined the arrow wound in Bursus's left leg.

Kelemvor turned his horse away from the Standing Stone. "Let's go," he muttered. "The clerics are lost. There's no way they can escape those orcs."

Yarbro drew his sword and looked at Kelemvor. "Sometimes orcs let their victims live . . . for a while." The young guard paused for a moment. Mikkel drew his sword and Cabal remounted. "We're going back for them."

Kelemvor closed his eyes. Even if he wanted to, there was no way he could go back for the clerics. It simply wasn't in his best interest to endanger his life for them. "Do what you want, Yarbro. I'm not going to help you." The fighter got off his horse and walked toward the trees. "I'll wait here until you get back."

"I'll look after Bursus," Jorah said flatly. "I'll try to get that arrow out and bind his leg." The slender, auburn-haired archer turned to Kelemvor and spat, then turned back to the others. "If that's what you want me to do, that is, Yarbro."

The young guard narrowed his eyes and stared at Kelemvor for a moment. "Yes . . . it is up to me now, isn't it?" Yarbro said slowly. "Fine, Jorah." The guard spurred his horse and headed back toward the Standing Stone. "But I'd keep Kelemvor in front of you at all times."

Yarbro, Cabal, and Mikkel raced back down the road, whooping and yelling. Kelemvor heard a few squeals and cries in Orcish as the fighters rounded the bend, then nothing but the sound of something running through the woods.

This is the end, Kelemvor thought as he sat under a tree and watched Jorah pull the arrow from Bursus's leg, then dress the wound and even tend to Bursus's wounded horse. There's no way I'll ever be able to stop these men from killing Midnight, Cyric, and Adon.

The fighter kicked a stone into a rut in the rough dirt road. It would all be so simple if it weren't for my damned curse! I could do what was right. I could give up this hunt.

But that wasn't possible, and Kelemvor knew it. The moment he sided with Midnight, Adon, and Cyric, he broke his pledge to Lord Mourngrym and would lose the reward the dalelord had promised him as incentive to finish the quest. He would have endangered his life on the hunt for no reward—an act that would surely cause the curse to go into effect. Then Kelemvor would transform into a panther until he killed someone.

Jorah turned to Kelemvor and scowled. Kelemvor saw the hatred in the archer's eyes. For a moment, he felt afraid. It's far more likely they'll kill me, too, Kelemvor suddenly realized. I'm no better or worse to these men than Midnight.

Before Kelemvor could think about that too long, he heard the rumble of hooves on the road. The fighter jumped to his feet and moved behind his horse. If the orcs had taken the dalesmen's mounts, they'd likely try to shoot a volley of arrows at him as they rode past.

But it wasn't the orcs coming down the road—it was Yarbro and the two other archers. They had one other riderless horse in tow. All three men were sweating profusely, and Cabal had a nasty slash across his upper arm, but they were alive. Jorah helped them to dismount, and Yarbro immediately went to check on Bursus.

As soon as Jorah and Cabal had placed Bursus onto a horse, Yarbro walked over to face Kelemvor, his sword drawn. "The orcs ran, you coward. Just like you did!" The young guard held his sword up to Kelemvor's face. "I ought to kill you right now, but we'll need you as a shield in case we're attacked again. You ride in front, alone, from now on."

Kelemvor pushed the guard's sword away. "And were you right about the clerics?" Yarbro snarled, and his sword flashed out toward Kelemvor's chest. The fighter slapped the sword aside with his own blade, however, and Yarbro was knocked backward a few feet by the blow. Jorah, Cabal, and Mikkel drew their swords.

"See?" Yarbro hissed as he sheathed his weapon and held up his hands. "You're alive only because I say so." The other dalesmen sheathed their swords as well. Kelemvor turned away and readied his horse for another long ride.

The ride to Blackfeather Bridge was long and silent for Kelemvor. The dalesmen stopped in Essembra only long enough for supplies and to have a local healer look at Bursus's leg. The wound was not too serious, and after a few poultices, Bursus was ready to ride on to the bridge with the other hunters. All along the road, Kelemvor rode far out in front of the others, hoping that something would attack them from behind.

The green-eyed fighter knew that if the dalesmen were ambushed, he wouldn't lift a sword to save them. There was nothing but Mourngrym's gold and his promise holding him to the quest now, and even that was proving to be little incentive.

Kelemvor had expected that the shock of losing their companions to such a horrible fate would cause the dalesmen to withdraw into themselves, to tone down their viciousness. At the very least, he thought they would stop dwelling on ways to torture Midnight, Adon, and Cyric. But Yarbro and the other hunters—even Bursus, when he was well again—spent much of their days plotting horrible fates for Kelemvor's friends.

Occasionally Yarbro would catch up to Kelemvor and tell him the latest cruel imaginings, just to taunt him. The fighter always remained silent, but it never stopped the young guard from telling him over and over again how the dalesmen were going to kill the magic-user and her allies.

Eventually the hunters arrived at Blackfeather Bridge, where they secured their mounts in the forest on the north bank of the Ashaba, then took up positions on the bridge.

As the dalesmen set up a rough camp, Kelemvor stood at the northern end of the bridge and cleared his throat loudly. "Yarbro is now your leader," the fighter began, "and rightly so. However, I have something to say to you all." A low rumble of mutters ran through the camp. Yarbro eyed Kelemvor suspiciously, then nodded to his men, letting them know that they had his permission to listen to the fighter.

When the dalesmen had all turned to glare at him, Kelemvor continued. "This is the last time I'm going to remind any of you of the explicit orders of Lord Mourngrym." Yarbro frowned deeply. "Our orders are to *capture* Midnight, Cyric, and Adon, and return them to Shadowdale, where they will pay for their crimes. They are to be taken alive unless there is no other option."

The cold stares of the hunters seemed to bore through the fighter. His words were stated calmly and without passion.

Kelemvor knew they would have no effect, but he could not stop trying. When he was done speaking, the fighter slowly walked back to his horse and unpacked his gear.

After almost an hour had passed and the dalesmen were beginning to get restless, Mikkel asked, "What if they've already passed this way?" The archer kicked a pebble off the bridge and watched it plummet into the Ashaba.

"Impossible," Yarbro snapped, trying more to convince himself than his men. It was entirely possible that the hunters had arrived late. Their quarry might be miles away by now, perhaps in Scardale already.

Sitting on the north end of the bridge, Kelemvor felt his heart jump at the archer's question. By all the gods, Kelemvor thought, let it be so! Let the decision be taken out of my hands!

*   *   *   *   *

The God of Strife summoned his sorceress, Tarana Lyr. Moments later, a beautiful young woman wearing the ebon robes of Bane's dark order entered the massive throne room of the god's temple in Zhentil Keep. Her long, blond hair was regally styled and held in place by a silver headpiece. A red sash pulled the robe tight about her slim waist, and a slit up the side of the robe allowed a glimpse of her long, shapely legs. Her eyes were a deep, unearthly blue.

"Milord," Tarana purred, her voice rich and melodic. "I am at your command."

"I have summoned you to open a scrying portal to Scardale," Bane said. "I wish to contact our garrison."

"Of course," Tarana murmured and immediately started the spell. The instability of magic did not trouble the sorceress. She relished the thrill of tampering with forces that might one day destroy her. Taking risks had been an integral part of her upbringing, and the magical chaos since the time of Arrival had allowed her many talents—and her madness—to be put to full use.

The Black Lord stepped back cautiously from the enchantress as she released her spell. A fiery frame was carved in midair, and through the portal, Bane saw three men in soldiers' garb seated around a wooden table. It was obvious from the dice and coins strewn over the table's surface that they had been gambling. At the moment, the men were arguing over a bet.

"Gentlemen!" Bane growled. His voice brought the soldiers to instant attention. News of Bane's acquisition of Fzoul's body as an avatar had spread to Scardale quickly, and these soldiers knew Fzoul's voice well from past dealings with the high priest.

"Lord Bane," a stocky, red-bearded soldier named Knopf said as he quickly shoved his chair back and rose from the table. The other soldiers, Cadeo and Frost, hurried to do likewise.

"I see that you have been 'busy,' " Bane snapped, gesturing toward the table.

As the Black Lord glared at the dice and money, the face of the red-bearded soldier paled. "The occupation of the dale has been very quiet of late," Knopf said, trying to placate his master.

Actually, the occupation of Scardale had been very quiet for several years. It hadn't been long ago that Lashan Aumersair, a young, aggressive lord of the dale, overran Harrowdale, Featherdale, and Battledale with his armies. But Lashan's empire hadn't lasted for long. The Dales, Cormyr, Sembia, Hillsfar, and even Zhentil Keep all banded together to halt Scardale's expansion. Now each of the kingdoms that had supplied troops to defeat the young lord had a garrison in the city. Like the other garrisons, Zhentil Keep's contingent of soldiers was limited to twelve men-at-arms. The balance of power among the garrisons in Scardale shifted from one day to the next, but little of consequence ever happened to change the status quo in the occupied city.

"In other words, there has been no progress!" Bane exploded. "I expect you to be doing more in Scardale than playing dice and keeping the peace!"

"Actually, we engaged the Cormyrian soldiers in a small skirmish only last week," Cadeo mumbled, trying to smile feebly.

"Any casualties?" Bane asked, encouraged.

"Cadeo broke one of their thumbs," Knopf muttered as he pointed to the young, flaxen-haired soldier. "I'm afraid there really hasn't been much excitement here recently, Lord Bane."

"I see," Bane said slowly. "That sounds like something we can remedy. Where is Jhembryn Durrock?"

"Lord Durrock?" Knopf asked. He shifted his feet nervously for a moment, then ran his hand through his beard.

"If that is the pompous title he has assumed, then, aye, 'Lord' Durrock," the God of Strife growled, his voice hardening. "Find him and bring him to this portal immediately! I will be waiting."

Bane folded the arms of his avatar as the three soldiers hurried from the small room. Looking away from the magical opening, he cocked his head slightly and glanced at his sorceress. "I suppose every moment this portal remains open increases the risk to you."

"It is not a problem," Tarana responded. Her eyes narrowed to mere slits, and a mad smile stretched across her face, marring the illusion of delicate beauty. "I enjoy the danger."

Moments later, a huge, dark-skinned man appeared before the scrying portal. His flesh had been seared almost black, and severe burns grossly disfigured most of his face. A thick beard and mustache succeeded in hiding only some of the damage. A black-visored helmet, which had been removed in respect for the Black Lord, acted as a mask to further conceal the worst of the assassin's deformities. In fact, the other garrisons had demanded that Durrock wear the helmet at all times inside the city, since the assassin's appearance had been known to give nightmares to Scardale's children.

"I live but to serve you, Lord Bane," Durrock said, his voice a hoarse whisper. The assassin bowed slightly, but he didn't allow his eyes to wander from the scrying portal.

"Yes, Durrock. I know that you do," Bane said in a low voice. "And that knowledge pleases me—especially in light of what I am about to tell you." The God of Strife smiled an evil grin.

"My spies have informed me that a mage, a raven-haired worshiper of Mystra who opposed me at the Battle of Shadowdale, is heading toward Scardale. She is traveling down the Ashaba." The God of Strife paused for a moment and let the smile melt from his features. "Capture her . . . alive. I am coming to Scardale to interrogate her personally."

A scowl crossed Durrock's ravaged face, and the assassin bowed again. "As you wish, Lord Bane," he said flatly. "How will I find her?"

"That is not my concern!" the God of Strife screamed, curling his right hand into a fist. "If you cannot accept this mission, 'Lord' Durrock, then tell me now so that I can find someone more suitable."

"That will not be necessary, Lord Bane," the assassin replied. "I will find her."

The Black Lord smiled again. "Good. You will find her on the Ashaba River itself. I understand that a contingent of dalesmen are heading toward Blackfeather Bridge to intercept her flight. You may wish to begin there." Bane turned to Tarana and waved his hand. "Oh, by the way," the God of Strife said as the scrying portal started to fade. "She has two others with her. Do with them as you please. . . ."

The portal vanished, and Durrock found himself staring at a circular, polished shield on the wall of the soldiers' quarters. He scowled again and headed for the door.

As he left the hastily constructed barracks, Durrock allowed the full effects of the sun to play on his ruined face for only a moment. Then he heard footsteps approaching and lowered the visor. Greeting a pale-skinned fighter from Hillsfar with a brief nod, the assassin passed him by silently. As he walked, Durrock surveyed the port town that stretched before him.

The Scar, the steep ravine for which the town was named, lay to the north. Port Ashaba, the town's busy harbor, was to the south, at the other end of town. In between the two landmarks, a host of buildings ran the gamut from functional houses where hardworking residents of Scardale raised their families, to abandoned shacks and workhouses that had fallen into various stages of disrepair since the war. There were also gigantic warehouses, where supplies for ships preparing to cross the Dragon Reach were plentiful. One such warehouse was Durrock's present destination.

The guards who stood watch before the warehouse

moved aside quickly when the assassin approached. "Lord Durrock," one said humbly, opening the large wooden door for the forbidding, black-robed figure.

"I ride in an hour with my lieutenants. Inform the necessary parties," Durrock snapped to the guards before he dismissed them and entered the warehouse alone.

The warehouse was almost empty. A rickety, rotted wooden staircase led to an open trap door at the top of the stairs. A single shaft of light shone through the opening, bathing three suits of armor that lay in the lower room's center in an intense, macabre brilliance that almost made them seem attractive. On closer examination, though, the armor's appearance proved more ghastly than attractive—night black, covered with rows of razor-sharp spikes. Durrock and two of his most trusted men would don that armor soon.

Next to the armor lay three fine leather saddles. They were magnificently crafted, but far too large for any normal steed. As Durrock waited for his fellow assassins, he busied himself with checking the armor and tack.

Within five minutes, two more assassins quietly entered the empty, cavernous warehouse. Durrock nodded a silent greeting to the two men and moved toward the armor. The other assassins followed. Soon all three were fully clad in the frightening, deadly mail.

"Summon your mounts," Durrock said flatly as he placed a thick metal chain around his neck. A glowing black pendant hung on the end of the chain, in the shape of a small horse with glowing red eyes.

In unison, all three assassins held up identical pendants and slowly repeated a series of powerful commands. Bolts of red and black lightning flashed across the room. A swirling blue cloud appeared in the center of the room, high in the air, accompanied by a wave of noxious-smelling mist.

Three sets of glowing red eyes appeared in a rift in the cloud, and the assassins could hear the sound of heavy, thunderous hoofbeats. Their mounts were approaching.

First one, then another, then a third gigantic black horse leaped through the swirling rift and landed heavily on the floor of the warehouse. Fire flashed from the horses' hooves, and the creatures' nostrils flared orange. The huge ebon steeds reared and bared a set of perfectly white fangs.

"You are ours to command!" Durrock cried, holding the pendant out toward one of the nightmares. "Lord Bane has given us the tools to call you from the Planes to do our bidding!" The nightmare mounts reared again, breathing clouds of smoke from their nostrils.

The nightmares whinnied nervously as the assassins moved toward them, but the horses could do nothing to prevent the humans from saddling them. The special magical pendants Bane had provided for Durrock and his men gave them complete control over the strange otherworldly beasts.

Durrock wheeled his nightmare around and spurred it toward the huge double doors at the front of the warehouse. The nightmare reared up and gave the doors a mighty kick with its flaming hooves. The doors burst open, and the three assassins raced out into the street. At the sight, the nearby villagers gasped and shrieked. Several fainted dead away.

Durrock laughed and pulled up on his nightmare's reigns, and the creature leaped into the air. Within a few minutes, the scarred assassin and his lieutenants were racing across the sky, the nightmares' hooves pounding flaring gouts of fire into the air as they flew toward Blackfeather Bridge.

* * * * *

Earlier in the day, Cyric had made the decision to portage the skiff around the dangerous rapids that lay ahead, where the horseshoe curve of the Ashaba led southwest and sprouted two tributaries before finishing its arc and traveling northeast. Midnight gazed at the violently churning water and felt relieved that they weren't going to attempt the passage. Fallen trees groped over the shoreline, their branches half buried in the water. The trees looked like gnarled gray hands with thousands of skeletal fingers. Large, craggy rocks rose up out of the water in the distance. Clouds of froth gathered before the rocks, calling attention to areas where the flow of the river was temporarily slowed by the stones.

Heavy woods stood sentinel on either side of the Ashaba, but there were occasional clearing on the shore, left, perhaps, by fishermen or other travelers. Cyric guided the skiff toward the eastern bank, where a small clearing was visible. As the heroes approached shore, the thief barked out orders for his companions to get out of the boat and guide it toward land.

Cyric jumped out of the boat, too, and together the three heroes dragged the skiff to shore. Beyond the small clearing lay a path that followed the bank of the river. Obviously they weren't the first to choose not to brave the rapids downstream.

"We'll have to carry the boat awhile," Cyric grumbled as he pulled his pack from the skiff. "That path should take us to the edge of the woods. We can follow the Ashaba for a little ways, then cut overland through Battledale and get the boat back into the water beyond the bend." The thief paused to wipe sweat from his eyes. "Is that simple enough for everyone to follow?"

Midnight flinched. "You don't have to treat us like children, Cyric. Your meaning is quite clear." The raven-haired mage grabbed the sack containing her spellbook and slung it over her shoulder.

"Is it?" Cyric said, then turned his back on the mage and shrugged. "Perhaps . . ."

Placing her hand on Cyric's upper arm, Midnight gave a gentle squeeze, then rested her forehead on his shoulder. "Cyric, I'm your friend. Whatever is troubling you, you can tell me about it if you need to talk."

The thief pulled away from Midnight's comforting touch with obvious repulsion, as if her fingers were the legs of a spider. He refused to look at her. "I don't need to talk to anyone," he snapped. "Besides, you wouldn't like what I had to say."

Behind Midnight and Cyric, Adon trembled and climbed into the boat. The cleric pulled his knees up to his face and closed his eyes. Midnight took a step back toward the skiff, then stopped as she saw the thief's back tense, as if he were preparing to attack Adon. Instinctively, the mage stepped in front of the thief, blocking the quivering cleric from view.

"Cyric, you can say anything you want to me," Midnight pleaded. "Don't you know that by now? When you were wounded, on the ride to Tilverton, you told me so much about yourself, so much about the pain and the heartache that's driven you. I know your secrets, and I—"

"Don't badger me!" Cyric hissed as he moved closer to Midnight in a rage. The hawk-nosed man pointed at Midnight with his right hand, his fingers thrust forward like daggers. The mage backed away slowly.

"I—I wasn't," Midnight whispered. She looked into Cyric's eyes and shuddered. There was something in the thief's eyes that frightened her, something she had never noticed before.

"I know your secrets, too," Cyric growled. He stood only a few inches from the mage. "Don't forget that, *Ariel!*"

The mage stood perfectly still. Cyric had learned her true name on the journey to Shadowdale. With that information, in league with a powerful mage, the thief could, if he chose, hold dominion over her soul. Midnight knew she should have been afraid, but she was simply angry.

"You know *nothing* about me!" Midnight cried and turned to the boat. Adon stood up and held his hand out toward the mage.

"I know you," the cleric said softly and moved to Midnight's side. He pointed to Cyric, who was still glaring at the dark-haired magic-user. "I know you, too, Cyric."

The thief narrowed his eyes, then looked away and walked to the clearing. "We have a long journey. We should go now if we're going at all." After a moment, the thief cleared his throat and spoke again. "Are we going, Midnight?" he asked.

The mage trembled. "We're going. Let's go, Adon."

Smiling at the mage, Adon gathered the remaining gear and got out of the skiff. Both he and Midnight turned to Cyric, who was still standing a few yards away. The thief muttered something, walked to the skiff, and grabbed the bow. Midnight and Adon took hold of the stern, and together the travelers flipped the surprisingly light craft upside down and held it over their heads. They followed the path through the woods, parallel to the river, for nearly an hour, speaking only when necessary.

As the thief had suggested, the heroes soon broke from the woods to take the more direct route past the rapids. Soon, they were in view of the low, rolling hills of Battledale. For hours they were surrounded by lush green rises as they carried the boat over the soft ground. The hills in the distance seemed to melt, losing form until they became a hazy, greenish white wall on the horizon. A soft wind whispered over the dale, and occasionally a sound from the river made it to their ears.

The heroes found a path that lay between a series of hills and followed it. On either side of the travelers, the rising earth was marked by ridges that angled up to the top of the hills, then blended into the soft, brownish green of the landscape. As they progressed through the dale, the hills that were closest came into sharp focus, while those in the far distance lost their form and melted into the sky. Slow-moving, puffy clouds drifted past.

The work was tiring, but it was a pleasant break from the steady toil of rowing the skiff down the Ashaba. The heroes set a strong pace, and soon after highsun, they were once again nearing the river.

"The Pool of Yeven should be very close," Cyric said flatly. "The river's usually calm here, but who knows what it'll be like now? Be ready for anything."

The heroes reached the shore, and Midnight and Adon lowered their end of the skiff as Cyric did the same. Midnight was exhausted, and her muscles ached. She sat on the ground beside the skiff, and Adon knelt beside her. The thief stood with his arms crossed, tapping his foot impatiently.

"What do you want from me?" Midnight cried. "Do you want me to cast a spell that will take us to Tantras? I only wish I could. At this moment, I'd rather be banished to Myrkul's realm than take on the Ashaba again." The mage put her hands over her face. "But I don't see that we have a choice."

Midnight stood and walked toward the thief. "We're just as worthy to make this trip as you. In fact, I don't know who put you in command of this little expedition in the first place." Cyric started to speak, but Midnight cut him off.

"The point is, Cyric, I'm not going to be treated as your baggage anymore. Neither is Adon. If you want to continue alone, then I won't stop you. I'm sorry that I couldn't be whatever it is you wanted me to be. I tried to be your friend, but that doesn't seem to be enough for you."

Cyric's arms had fallen limply to his sides. There was nothing he could say, nothing he wanted to say, to make up for the pain he had caused Midnight. That simply didn't matter. Cyric wanted the Tablets of Fate. The desire for the power and the glory they would bring burned inside him. All other considerations paled beside his need for control of his own fate, and ownership of the tablets would buy him that control.

Cyric had begun his life as a slave, and until he confronted and killed his former mentor from the Thieves' Guild, just before the Battle of Shadowdale, Cyric had never felt like a free man. Phantom chains of servitude had hung around his neck, wrists, and ankles all his life. Now, however, he had a purpose, a quest for his own gain. And if he succeeded, no one would ever control him again. The chains would be removed once and for all.

But Cyric also knew that, for now, he needed Midnight, and perhaps even Adon, to make it to Tantras, to recover the first of the missing Tablets of Fate. He simply couldn't allow the mage's petty anger to spoil everything.

"I'm . . . sorry," Cyric lied as he pushed the boat into the water. "You're right. I have treated you both badly. It's just that . . . I'm frightened, too." Midnight smiled and threw her arms around the thief.

"I knew you'd come around, Cyric!" she said happily. Smiling, Midnight removed her arms from around the thief's neck, helped Adon into the skiff, then threw her gear in the bottom of the boat. "We're all in this together."

Neither Midnight nor Adon could see the expression on Cyric's face as he turned his back to them and reached for his own pack. A peculiar smile crossed his face—a smile born not of happiness, but of victory. And contempt.

As the heroes rowed toward the Pool of Yeven, Adon sat near the bow of the skiff, his hand hanging over the edge. The cleric watched the rushing, quicksilver lines of current in the blue-green water, and a slight frown formed across his face. "The direction of the river is changing up ahead," Adon said softly. His words were smothered by the sounds of the river, and the cleric was forced to repeat himself.

Cyric looked back over his shoulder and gazed toward the vast lake downriver. Adon was correct; the current was changing. A wall of pure white froth arose at the barrier where the river met the lake, obscuring the swirling chaos beyond.

The Pool of Yeven had become a huge whirlpool!

The thief looked to either shore and realized that he could never guide their fragile craft to land before the pull of the current caught them and capsized the boat. The only chance the heroes had was to guide the boat to the outer channels of the violent water and attempt to ride it out.

The thief shouted hurried orders to Midnight and Adon, but his words were lost in the roar from the vortex. As they got closer to the whirlpool, Adon stared at the maelstrom as if it were somehow familiar. Midnight, on the other hand, seemed paralyzed with fear. With only Cyric's frantic efforts to slow them down, the heroes soon passed through the barrier of mist where the river entered the pool. Although they were all soaked to the skin, the skiff did not take on enough water to cause alarm.

Midnight was shocked from her paralysis by the splash of the ice-cold water. When she saw the gigantic, gaping maw of the whirlpool in the center of the once-placid Pool of Yeven, she couldn't hold back a scream.

Cyric couldn't hear her. There was a wall of sound rising up from the center of the vast maelstrom that grew louder as the skiff was pulled into the outer rings of the madly swirling water. The thief jammed a single oar over the right side of the boat to steady the craft, but the tiny skiff spun and bobbed as it was dragged toward the maelstrom.

In a matter of moments, the heroes were poised at the very top of the whirlpool, and they could see down into its lowest depths. A blinding blue-white luminescence was visible at the very bottom of the vortex. Using the oars as rudders, Cyric tried to keep the skiff steady, but the boat was lurching violently. A fine mist surrounded the heroes, and they occasionally caught glimpses of a landmark on the shoreline as they sped dizzily past it. The boat lurched, leaving the water for a brief moment, and Midnight had to force back a wave of nausea. Cyric fought with the oars, cursing loudly. Tears were streaming down Adon's face as he stared at the swirling vortex of water.

"Please, Sune!" the frightened cleric cried as he reached out and nearly fell from the boat. The skiff rocked, and Cyric shot a look over his shoulder.

"Can't you control him?" Cyric shouted, then turned back to the oars to compensate for the disturbance Adon had caused.

"What is it, Adon?" Midnight screamed. "What is it you see?"

Adon whimpered for a moment, then spoke softly, barely audible above the roar of the whirlpool. "Elminster's in the rift. I want to save him, but I can't reach him."

Images of their final moments in the temple returned to Midnight. Bane's avatar had been defeated, and Mystra's essence had vanished in the explosion that destroyed the Black Lord's avatar. During the battle, Elminster had been driven into a swirling vortex he himself had created. Neither Midnight nor Adon could save the old sage when the rift closed.

"I—I tried to save him!" Adon cried. "I tried to cast a spell. But Sune refused to hear my prayers. She deserted me and let Elminster die!"

"It wasn't your fault!" Midnight screamed. The frame of the skiff was beginning to shake violently under the assault of the surging water.

Adon turned to Midnight. Though his eyes were red from crying, Midnight saw clarity in them, a spark of understanding that had long been missing. "It *is* my fault," the cleric said calmly. "I was unworthy. I deserved to be forsaken by my goddess." Adon paused for a moment, closed his eyes, and pointed to the jagged scar that ran down his cheek. "I deserved this!"

The boat shook violently, pitching the cleric forward. Midnight grabbed Adon and pulled him back from the gunwale. Midnight looked up at Cyric and saw that he was still fighting with one oar, using it as a rudder. The boat was now more than halfway around the outside of the whirlpool, but it hadn't seemed to descend any deeper into the vortex.

Midnight grabbed the other oar. "What can I do?" the mage screamed. "How can I help?"

Cyric nodded toward the southern edge of the vortex. There the Pool of Yeven opened onto the Ashaba again. "We've got to break out of the curve!" Cyric yelled. "It's either that, or we die right here!"

The mage plunged the oar into the water. Adon grabbed the end of the shuddering oaken oar with Midnight, and together they held the second makeshift rudder in place. Together the three heroes forced the craft to break free from the ring of the whirlpool. In a moment, they had passed through another wall of froth and were moving downstream, away from the Pool of Yeven, toward Scardale.

The whirlpool had apparently somehow corrected the misdirected current, and now the river was running as it should, though it was still dangerously swift. As they moved farther away from the Pool of Yeven, Midnight gave a hearty yell, happy just to be alive. The others didn't seem to share her enthusiasm, however. Cyric simply scowled at Adon and turned away from the cleric, who sat quietly in the bow.

This partnership has to end soon, the thief thought. I was wrong to believe I needed these fools to make it to Tantras! Cyric glanced over his shoulder at Midnight. In fact, he growled to himself, they practically killed me in that whirlpool with their whining, while I risked my neck to save them!

The heroes continued down the Ashaba for several hours more, Midnight lounging happily in the stern, Adon silently staring at the water from the bow, and Cyric moodily handling the oars. Finally Cyric spotted a huge wooden bridge spanning the river in the distance. "Blackfeather Bridge!" Midnight called.

"Perhaps we can rest here," Adon said softly as he turned to gaze at the bridge.

As they approached the bridge, however, a flicker of movement alerted Midnight. She quickly called a fireball spell to mind, but when she saw that the figures were men and not some strange creature lurking on the bridge, she hesitated to cast it. The spell could fail and destroy the skiff. Or it could succeed, and Midnight might learn that she had harmed an innocent group of fishermen or travelers like themselves.

The hesitation proved costly.

Cyric, too, saw the movement on the bridge, but he had also glimpsed sunlight glinting from steel. The three men standing on the structure were joined by two more. All had weapons. The thief turned quickly and shouted for Midnight to cast her spell.

On the bridge, Kelemvor and the group of dalesmen stood waiting, arrows knocked, ready to fire at the skiff.

❦ 5 ❦

Blackfeather Bridge

The surviving members of the hunt were lined up in a row upon the bridge, their bows ready. Kelemvor stood next to Yarbro, and the two men looked out onto the Ashaba. A skiff rushed toward them, three people frantically scrambling about inside it.

"Look at them!" Yarbro snarled, the muscles in his lean arms tensing as he prepared to loose an arrow. "They're trying to turn around. They'll never be able to do it in this part of the river. The current's too fast." The young guard's flesh was pale, and his eyes were bloodshot. His lips pulled back in a grimace, the guard trembled with anticipation.

The killing time had come.

"I can see them," Kelemvor snapped. Below, on the river, Midnight, Cyric, and Adon struggled to turn their boat to shore. The fighter glanced across the bridge. The men were all like Yarbro, barely hiding their glee as they held their bows ready to fire. "No one shoots without my order!" Kelemvor shouted.

A few of the dalesmen laughed. Yarbro turned sharply to the fighter. "You don't command us any longer. The men follow my orders now!"

Sweat was streaming down Kelemvor's face. "Our orders are to capture the prisoners, not to kill them on sight."

"Unless there's no other choice," Yarbro growled bitterly as he turned back to face the river. "Unless you want me to have you shot full of arrows, I suggest you either grab a bow or get off the bridge!"

The small boat rocked violently in the fierce current as the escapees tried unsuccessfully to turn their shuddering craft. Kelemvor silently stared at Midnight and felt a strange pressure upon his chest.

I can't do this! the fighter cursed to himself. I simply can't let these lunatics hurt my friends . . . and my love.

A few feet away from Kelemvor, Jorah laughed. "Let them get to shore . . . if they can. I don't want the river to sweep them away after we shoot them. We can have them stuffed and hung like scarecrows on the road to Zhentil Keep." Bursus and Cabal chuckled and nodded.

"That'll let any Zhentish scum who might plan to attack the Dales again know exactly what we'll do to them," Bursus agreed. The wounded archer hobbled to Jorah's side and patted the younger, auburn-haired man on the shoulder.

"Let's just kill them now," Mikkel suggested. As he looked down at the fishing skiff, images of the countless days he had spent on that boat with his partner flooded into his mind.

The skiff was within range now. The hunters watched as Adon stood up and grabbed Cyric's arm. The thief lashed out at the cleric, and Adon fell. The young cleric hit the side of the skiff hard, and Midnight and Cyric were unable to maintain their balance as the boat careened wildly and capsized.

Midnight screamed as she struck the water and sank as if a heavy weight had been attached to her body. Adon also plummeted into the Ashaba and vanished beneath the surface of the river. Cyric fell in the opposite direction, and the current grabbed him and began to pull him downstream.

"Fire!" Yarbro shouted, and a rain of arrows struck the river around the capsized boat.

"No!" Kelemvor screamed, but it was too late. Midnight and Adon had disappeared from sight, and Cyric was bobbing up and down in the strong current. The thief tried to plunge under the surface of the water, but he was helpless in the tide. The skeletal branches of a large, dead tree that had fallen into the river reached out from the shoreline, and the thief managed to grab a limb as he rushed past. As the thief hung there, suspended in the rapid flow of the Ashaba for a moment, an arrow struck the water mere inches from his face. Cyric let go of the branch instinctively, then sunk beneath the surface of the water.

Beneath the river's surface, Midnight flailed her arms and legs in a frenzied panic. Suddenly a large shape approached her out of the darkness. The cleric held one of their canvas bags in his left hand as he swam toward the mage. His eyes were wide with fear.

We're going to drown unless I do something! Midnight realized. The mage reached out, trying to grab anything on the bottom that would stop her from tumbling down the river. She came up with a handful of reeds. Unconsciously a spell thrust itself into Midnight's mind.

Pushing back her fear, Midnight recited the brief incantation in her mind as she plucked a reed from the riverbed. Before she could turn and cast the water breathing spell on Adon, a huge sphere filled with air flashed into sight around her. The shell surrounded Adon as well, who now lay on his stomach, soaked and gasping.

"Thanks, Midnight," the cleric groaned and rolled over onto his back. "I owe you my life . . . again."

Midnight smiled weakly, then looked shocked and fell to her knees as the bubble lurched into motion and quickly rose to the surface of the river. "Mystra, help me!" the mage cried as she looked up and saw the bridge only about twenty yards away. Arrows rained down from the bridge again, and she heard the curses of the dalesmen as the arrows glanced harmlessly off the sphere.

On the bridge, Kelemvor stepped back from the other men. The fighter watched as Yarbro swore and stamped around on the bridge in frustration, screeching orders at the other dalesmen. The group had degenerated into a band of killers, differing little from the orcs they had encountered near the Standing Stone. The fighter relaxed slightly. Midnight had managed to save herself, and in doing so, she took the need to act away from him.

As the sphere passed beneath the bridge, close to the southern bank, one of the archers ran to the shore to get a large rock. When the sphere emerged on the other side of the bridge, he was waiting, the rock held high over his head. The other dalesmen stood stock still, bows at the ready.

Midnight looked up as she passed beneath the bridge. She saw Kelemvor leaning over the bridge's edge, and her heart skipped a beat. For only an instant, the mage's attention was completely focused on her former lover. So when the large stone came hurtling down at her, it took the mage completely by surprise. The rock bounced off the top of the sphere, but Midnight lost her concentration, and the sphere disappeared in a flash. The magic-user and the cleric plunged into the water, very close to shore but also very close to the bridge.

I've got to help her! Kelemvor thought desperately as the sphere disappeared. At that moment, the fighter let out a terrible, high-pitched scream. The dalesmen loosed a volley of arrows at Midnight and Adon, but the distraction caused by Kelemvor's horrifying scream disturbed their aim. Three of the dalesmen turned in time to see Kelemvor's breastplate clatter to the bridge. Mikkel and Yarbro were too intent on their prey to notice.

Jorah, Cabal, and Bursus stood staring at Kelemvor as he let out a deep, long growl and tore at his face with his fingers. Then they noticed that the fighter's flesh was rippling. It was as if there were something inside him, struggling for release from his human skin. Kelemvor fell to his knees, threw his head back, and screamed once more as his chest burst apart and the paws of a sleek, black beast emerged.

Kelemvor's head seemed to collapse, and then the loose flesh tore open. Glowing green eyes and a gaping maw, filled with razor-sharp teeth, appeared visible as the head of the panther shook itself free from the glove of human flesh. In moments, all that remained of Kelemvor were a few bits of bloody flesh that soon dissolved. The fighter had moved to help Midnight with no reward in sight, and the curse had asserted itself.

"Shut him up or kill him!" Yarbro shouted without turning around. The young guard had drawn a bead on Midnight's head as she started to clamber up the southern bank. Anticipation rushed through Yarbro, and he reveled for a second in the knowledge that the fate of the sorceress was in his hands, that he was her judge, jury, and executioner. And the sentence is death, Yarbro thought as he steadied his arm and prepared to loose the deadly shaft.

Suddenly an incredible, bestial roar sounded from behind him, and Yarbro started in surprise. Distracted, he released the arrow, and the shaft flew harmlessly over Midnight's head. The young guard turned and saw the panther, and for a moment he believed that he had slipped into some kind of waking nightmare, that his lack of sleep was playing tricks with his mind. Still, his fellow huntsmen stood beside him and stared at the snarling beast with expressions of disbelief rivaling his own.

Yarbro and Cabal were between the panther and the other dalesmen, who were now backing away nervously toward the north end of the bridge. Kelemvor was nowhere to be seen, the young guard realized, even though the fighter's shredded clothing and discarded armor, stained with gore, lay in a pile just beyond the panther.

Yarbro stared into the creature's flaring, deep green eyes. They were so much like Kelemvor's. At that moment, the young guard understood, impossible as it may have seemed, that Kelemvor and the panther were one and the same! Just as the creature sprang toward Cabal, the closest of the huntsmen, Yarbro leaped over the side of the bridge and plunged into the Ashaba to save himself.

As the panther tore the aging archer apart, the man's screams for mercy echoed around Blackfeather Bridge and over the Ashaba. The two remaining archers, Bursus and Jorah, raised their bows and moved forward. Mikkel, on the other hand, was frozen by fear and held his bow limply at his side. The panther looked up sharply from its bloody feast and bounded toward Bursus and Jorah, as if it sensed their deadly intent.

Hands shaking, Jorah aimed and loosed his shaft. It flew high and scraped along the floor of the bridge until it came to a stop a hundred feet away. The slender, auburn-haired archer grabbed another arrow, but he never had a chance to fire it.

Standing next to Jorah, Bursus steadied himself on his wounded leg and tried to remain calm as the sleek, powerful cat raced toward him. The black-eyed archer got the creature in his sights, aimed between its eyes, and released his shaft. The panther dodged to the right at the last possible instant, just before it sprang toward Jorah. The sleek beast bowled the archer over with its weight, then clamped its teeth upon Jorah's throat.

Bursus stared at the creature in horror as he backed away, reaching for another shaft. His hands shaking as if he had been struck by palsy, the black-eyed dalesman found an arrow just as the panther looked up from the dead man at its feet. The shaft rattled against its sight as Bursus stopped limping backward and readied himself to fire. Before Bursus could let fly another arrow, though, the panther roared again, and the dalesman saw blood and bits of flesh in its open maw. The sight paralyzed him with fear, and the moment of hesitation was all the beast needed as it sprang from Jorah's corpse. The black-eyed archer saw the creature's one huge claw raised above his eyes, and then his world went black.

Toward the northern end of the bridge, Mikkel stumbled a few steps backward, away from the carnage. He was moving steadily, if slowly, away from the panther, his bow at his side. Still, he had only managed to travel a half dozen feet toward the end of the bridge when the panther turned and looked in his direction.

The green-eyed monster shook with anticipation as it slowly padded toward the fisherman. Fear radiated from the dalesman, and the scent of his panic rankled the beast's senses, filling it with an even greater rage.

Mikkel dropped his bow and moved away from the weapon, toward the edge of the bridge. The panther's gaze followed the red-skinned, bald fisherman as the dalesman's sparkling prism earring caught the attention of the beast. The panther's rage slowly melted away as it moved toward the shining object, its limited intellect lost in the multicolored display of light.

Noting that the panther had slowed its movement toward him, Mikkel broke into a run and flung himself over the edge of the bridge. There was a last, sparkling burst of light from the prism earring, and then the man was gone. The panther raced to the edge of the bridge and put its front paws up on the railing to search for its prey, but the dalesman was gone, lost in the the raging flow of the river. The beast roared and settled back on all fours.

In the trees beyond the south end of the bridge, Midnight and Adon felt a chill as they listened to the panther howling only a few dozen yards away from them. They sat huddled beneath a tree, scanning the water for signs of Cyric. As they listened, the panther's cries turned from roars of anger to bellows of pain, and Midnight's concern for their own survival and growing sorrow over Cyric's apparent death were pushed into the background by her concern for Kelemvor. Waves of guilt rushed through her, filling her soul with a horrible sickness. The man who rescued me from the Twisted Tower is probably dead, and I'm more concerned about the lycanthropic mercenary who led the dalesmen's hunt for me! the mage cursed silently.

"Cyric," Midnight whispered softly as she covered her face with her hands. "I let him die!" she said. "I should have saved him! I should have—"

"Don't punish yourself for being human," Adon murmured quietly. "You did what you could." The cleric put one arm around Midnight's shoulder. On the bridge, the panther howled once more.

"Kelemvor!" Midnight gasped. She pushed Adon away and struggled to her feet.

The young cleric grabbed the mage's arm and pulled her back to the ground. "Don't go up there!" Adon wheezed. "We can't face him while he's in this state. There's nothing we can do now but wait."

And so Midnight and Adon waited in the forest, shivering in their damp clothes. Although Midnight was wracked with guilt over the loss of Cyric and ached to ease Kelemvor's pain, she knew that Adon was right. Sometimes events got out of control and there was nothing you could do, no way for you to help.

There was nothing to do but wait for things to right themselves.

If only I could make Adon appreciate the wisdom of his own words, Midnight thought as she turned toward the scarred cleric. Adon sat huddled against a rotting log, his eyes closed as if he were daydreaming. However, Midnight could guess from the pained expression on his face that, in his mind, he was watching Elminster's death in the temple again. She thought of a dozen ways to start up a conversation with him, but she rejected them all as contrived or melodramatic.

Finally she put her hand on the cleric's shoulder. When he looked up at her, the mage smiled warmly and said, "Adon, you've got to stop punishing yourself for what happened in the Temple of Lathander!"

Adon frowned and turned away. The cleric drew his knees up against his chest, then wrapped his arms around his legs. "You don't know anything about it," Adon mumbled as he rocked back and forth, his gaze fixed on the churning river.

Midnight sighed and slumped down next to Adon. "We don't know that the old sage died in that rift. Elminster might have saved himself," the mage said as she caressed the cleric's back. "Lhaeo seemed convinced that his master was safe. That fact alone should give us hope."

When Adon didn't react to Midnight's words, the raven-haired mage put her hand under the cleric's chin and forced him to look into her eyes. "Hope has to be enough for us, Adon—for both of us." The panther roared again, and a tear welled in the corner of Midnight's eye. "It's all any of us really has left, isn't it?"

Adon gazed into Midnight's eyes. "But Sune—"

"I know," Midnight said softly. "It's hard to let go. When Mystra died—"

Adon pushed Midnight away and leaped to his feet. "Sune isn't dead!" the cleric snapped as he backed away from the mage.

"I didn't mean to imply that she was," Midnight said with a sigh. The magic-user stood up and took Adon's right hand in her own.

"If anyone is dead, I am—in Sune's eyes, at least," Adon mumbled. He ran his hand over the scar that lined his face and winced. "I've become as accursed as Kelemvor. I have been forsaken for my deeds, and this horrible scar is my punishment."

"What deeds?" Midnight asked. "You're one of the most faithful clerics I've ever known. What did you do wrong to deserve your scar?"

Adon sighed and turned away from the mage. "I don't know . . . but it must have been terrible!" The cleric put his hand over the scar and bowed his head. "This punishment is the worst thing Sune could visit upon me. I was once attractive, a credit to Sune. Now people cringe at my approach or ridicule me behind my back."

"I have never turned away from you, Adon," Midnight said softly. "I have never mocked you. The scars on your flesh can be healed, and if Sune won't have you, then perhaps she isn't worth worshiping. Besides, it's the scars that run beneath the flesh that concern me."

Above, the panther roared once again.

Adon turned, anger flaring in his eyes. "We should be quiet," the cleric growled. "We can't afford to have Kelemvor hear us."

Midnight nodded. It was obvious that her comment about Sune had upset Adon, and she did not want to force the issue. Not yet, anyway. So they spent nearly an hour sitting in silence, listening to the sounds of the river and the panther on the bridge. Finally, when the yowls and roars had stopped and they were certain the creature had changed back into a man, Midnight and Adon broke from their cover and approached the bridge.

The heroes felt their hearts sink as the scene of bloody carnage on the bridge was revealed to them. Kelemvor was lying on his stomach at the center of the bridge. He was naked, and his matted hair covered his face. Four badly mangled bodies lay nearby. Blood and bits of bodies stained long stretches of the bridge, as if several of the dead men had been dragged or tossed about by the animal Kelemvor had become.

Images of the clerics whom Bane's spies had slaughtered in the Temple of Tymora just before the Battle of Shadowdale returned to Adon, and he felt himself grow faint. However, the cleric fought back the nausea rising in his stomach and steeled himself for what he knew had to be done. The cleric wiped a thin film of sweat from his brow and moved to the first corpse. He grabbed the dead dalesman's arm, dragged the body to the edge of the bridge, and let the corpse drop into the Ashaba.

"To the sea our shattered bodies go, that our souls may take flight," Adon whispered as Bursus's body disappeared down the river. "May you find the peace you were denied in this world."

As Adon continued his bloody detail, Midnight dragged Kelemvor's heavy armor close to the fighter's side, then crouched down beside him. After a moment, she ran to the dalesmen's camp and grabbed a blanket to throw over her former lover.

"Don't wake him," Adon said as he dragged the second dalesman to the brink of the bridge. The cleric stopped for a moment and looked around. "Not until I've finished. It'll be . . . better that way."

Midnight nodded, then pointed to the daggers that hung from the dalesman's boots. "Take his weapons before you drop him into the river."

Adon gasped, and a look of extreme shock gripped his features. "I will not steal from the dead," the cleric snapped.

Midnight stood up and moved away from Kelemvor. "Take their weapons, Adon. We will have a greater need for them than the creatures that reside at the bottom of the river."

The cleric did not move. He just stood over the dalesman's body, his mouth hanging slightly open. Midnight went to the remaining bodies and gathered their weapons herself. After the mage stripped each man of his weapons, Adon pronounced a final blessing on them and dropped the corpses into the Ashaba. Although he did not know if his words would hold any true value in the realm beyond the living, Adon knew that he would regret it if he didn't even attempt a blessing.

As the last of the dalesmen splashed into the river, Kelemvor began to stir.

"Midnight!" Adon called from the end of the bridge, pointing to the fighter. The beautiful, dark-haired magic-user returned to Kelemvor's side and placed her hand on his sweat-covered face. Instantly the fighter's eyes flew open and he grabbed Midnight's hand.

Pain shot up the mage's arm. "Kel!" Midnight cried and tried to wrench her arm from the fighter's iron grip.

Kelemvor looked shocked for a moment, then recognition slowly filtered into the fighter's flashing green eyes. He relaxed his grip slightly, although he did not release his hold on the mage.

"Midnight!" Kelemvor murmured, his lips trembling. "You're alive!" The fighter's grip loosened even more, and Midnight stopped struggling.

"Yes, Kel," Midnight said softly. The mage looked into the fighter's eyes and saw pain and confusion.

Kelemvor turned away from Midnight, squeezed his eyes shut, and brought her hand to his lips. "I made a terrible mistake. I almost hurt you."

Adon approached the fighter's side. Midnight smiled and looked up at the cleric but said nothing.

"Are they . . . dead?" Kelemvor asked, his face still turned away from Midnight, his eyes still closed. "Are they *all* dead?"

"There were four bodies," Adon said softly as he pulled the blanket over the fighter's shoulders. "We saw two more men jump into the river during the battle."

Kelemvor opened his eyes once more and gazed at the cleric. "Adon," the fighter said softly. "You survived, too. And Cyric?"

Midnight shook her head. "He was lost in the river when the skiff capsized."

Raising himself on one arm, Kelemvor ran his hand through Midnight's hair. "I'm . . . sorry," he said flatly. Midnight turned to look at the fighter, but he was already standing up, surveying the bridge. Kelemvor saw the splatters of blood, the weapons gathered in a pile, and his own armor. Nothing else.

"I'll wager Yarbro escaped," Kelemvor growled. "That one'll be the death of us yet."

"He was the first one off the bridge," Adon mumbled as he handed the fighter a shirt Midnight had taken from the dalesmen's camp. "I saw him leap off just as I got to shore."

Kelemvor swore loudly. "He'll either return to Essembra to gather reinforcements or ride on to Scardale to warn the town of our approach. Either way, it'll mean trouble for us. The dalesmen wanted you, Cyric, and Adon dead, though Mourngrym ordered them to bring you back to the dale to receive your 'just' punishment." Kelemvor paused and turned to Midnight. "Anyway, I'm sure that my name will now be added to the ranks of the guilty."

The fighter paused as he continued to dress himself. When he was done, he reached out and took Midnight's face in both of his hands. "Why did you leave me behind in Shadowdale?"

Midnight pulled away, anger suddenly overwhelming her. "Leave *you*! You turned Cyric down when he asked you to help rescue us!" The mage slapped the fighter's hand away as he reached for her, then she moved to Adon's side.

A bitter laugh escaped Kelemvor's lips. "Just what did Cyric tell you?"

Midnight hesitated for a moment. Brushing the hair out of her face, she relived the pain she felt when she first heard Kelemvor's words of betrayal. "That you 'couldn't interfere with *justice*.' "

Kelemvor nodded. "Cyric chose his words well, don't you think? He knew you," the fighter growled, turning away from his friends. "He knew just what to say to make you believe him."

"He was lying?" Midnight gasped. "You never said that?"

"I said it before the trial," the fighter mumbled and hung his head. "I thought you were going to be found innocent. If I'd have known, I would have found some way to help you escape."

Adon shook his head. "What do you mean? Didn't you know about Cyric's plan?"

Kelemvor whirled around, anger flashing in his eyes. "By all the souls in Myrkul's Realm, what do you think I'm saying?" The fighter took a deep breath. "Cyric never told me about the escape. I found out the next day . . . when the bodies started to appear."

Midnight and Adon looked at each other, shock in their eyes. "What bodies?" Midnight asked. A dark, creeping fear was moving across her soul. Even before Kelemvor told her about the murdered guardsmen, she knew that Cyric had not told her everything about his plan.

Kelemvor studied Midnight's face for a reaction as he told her about the bloody trail of corpses he and Mourngrym had traced through the Twisted Tower. The fighter hoped that the mage would not be able to hide her guilt if confronted directly with the murders. As he told her of the crimes, the mage blanched, and her eyes revealed surprise and horror.

"I—I didn't know," Midnight stammered and looked again to Adon. The cleric was frowning deeply, and his eyes reflected the fury he felt.

Kelemvor sighed. They really are innocent, he thought to himself, relieved that for the first time in what seemed like years he had done something right, something good. "I know you didn't, Midnight," Kelemvor said at last. "But didn't you even think it odd that you were able to escape so easily?"

"He told us he used the Gaeus Thorn," Adon snapped. When Kelemvor looked puzzled, the cleric continued. "That's a magical weapon of sorts. You strike someone with the thorn—a type of dart, really—and they do anything you tell them to do." Kelemvor thought of the young guard who had impaled himself and shuddered.

"We assumed he had subdued the guards using the thorn." Midnight folded her arms and hugged herself tightly. After a moment, she turned to the fighter. "Are you sure that it was Cyric? Could it have been someone else?"

Kelemvor shook his head. "We both know it was Cyric. Who else could it have been?"

"I . . . I don't know," Midnight sighed. "But it's possible there was someone else, isn't it? Another killer could have broken into the tower that night. He might have found the guards in a weakened state, or—"

The mage stopped speaking for a moment and took a deep breath. "Could one of the other guards have done it? Perhaps he wanted to cover up his own inattentiveness. Or maybe he wanted . . . I don't know what he might have wanted. . . ." Tears were welling in Midnight's eyes.

Kelemvor reached out to take Midnight by the arm. The fighter drew her into his embrace and held the mage as her tears came. Suddenly she pulled back. "No," Midnight said. "I won't believe it!"

Kelemvor put his hands on his hips. "Midnight, the facts are—"

"I don't know what the facts are, and neither do you!" the raven-haired magic-user cried. "I refuse to condemn our friend the way the dalesmen condemned Adon and me for Elminister's murder!"

Adon put his hand on the mage's shoulder. "Midnight, you know he did it. He would have killed me, too, if you hadn't stopped him." The cleric turned to the fighter. "A sickness had taken hold of Cyric, Kel. It was as if he went mad," Adon said flatly. He paused then and looked into the churning river. "Perhaps it's better that he's dead."

Midnight slowly walked to the edge of the bridge. "No, Adon. Cyric would have been fine once we got to Tantras, once we had a chance to rest. He really was a good person, you know. He just never had the chance to prove it."

Memories of all the evil he himself had done in the past, things the curse had forced him to do and things he had only blamed on the curse, flooded into Kelemvor's mind. The fighter went to Midnight's side and put his arms around her. "Perhaps he was afraid to do what's right," he said softly. "That same fear nearly prevented me from rescuing you."

Looking into Midnight's eyes, Kelemvor sighed and was forced to look away. "I was standing near the tower, waiting for daylight, waiting to see you again," the fighter told her. "I didn't know what I was going to do. But I suspected that once you were brought out, I wouldn't have been able to stop myself from trying to help you, even if it cost me my life. I stood there waiting for the moment when I would learn what I was going to do.

"Then the bodies were discovered, and I let Mourngrym convince me that you were guilty, that you and Adon had killed Elminster and then the guards." Adon whimpered softly at Kelemvor's comments, and the fighter paused for a moment. "It was easier to believe them than to do what I knew was right.

"After I saw what the dalesmen really were, when your boat approached, I knew that I had to make a choice." The fighter turned and looked at the bloodstains scattered about the bridge. "My reaction was as I thought it would be."

"Then you believe we're innocent?" Midnight asked softly.

"Aye," Kelemvor whispered as he kissed Midnight full on the mouth. When the kiss had ended, Kelemvor noticed Adon crouching over the pile of weapons that had been appropriated from the bodies of the dead hunters. He suddenly looked tired, even withered. "What's wrong with him?" Kelemvor asked.

Midnight told Kelemvor all that had transpired in the Temple of Lathander, but especially how Adon had tried to save Elminster from the rift. "With his scar and his failure at the temple, Adon's certain that Sune has abandoned him," the mage concluded. "It's as if his whole world has been shattered."

"He still should have said something at the trial to defend the two of you," the fighter grumbled. "His silence helped to sway Mourngrym's verdict."

"Don't hold it against him, Kel. I don't," Midnight said, smiling. "Besides, the trial is over now. And after you're with Adon for a while, you'll know that he's paying the price for his silence at the trial . . . and much more." The mage turned and walked toward Adon. As the fighter followed her, she added, "Cyric found it almost impossible to show him kindness or mercy. If I can forgive him, then you should be able to do the same."

Kelemvor considered the magic-user's words, then crouched at the other side of the pile of weapons, staring at the cleric. "Our survival depends on being able to count on one another, Adon. We will be wanted fugitives."

"I know that," Adon snapped. His gaze failed to meet Kelemvor's. Instead, the cleric toyed with one of the dead men's weapons.

"We're going on to Tantras, Adon, but the dalesmen might try to capture us. They also may try to kill us. Will you pledge your life to help us?" Kelemvor asked.

"My life . . . ," Adon growled, his voice cracking. "For what it's worth, yes, I'll pledge my life for the two of you. Perhaps I can make up for what I have done." The cleric reached down and picked up an axe. He gazed at the weapon for a moment, frowned, then tossed it aside. "I'll find a way."

"Thank you, Adon. We'll need your help," Midnight said and started to walk toward the dalesmen's camp. Kelemvor quickly followed her. They could hear the sound of metal hitting metal as Adon picked up one weapon after another and tossed it back into the pile.

"The dalesmen hid their horses in the woods next to the camp. We should pick out a few mounts, pack up our supplies, and head toward Tantras while we still have a chance," the fighter said.

Midnight stopped walking and turned to Kelemvor. "Aren't you forgetting something?" Kelemvor smiled and shook his head. "Your reward," Midnight said flatly.

The fighter stiffened.

Gesturing at the blood stains on the bridge, Kelemvor spoke. "I'm a wanted criminal for aiding you and for killing the dalesmen. The curse only demands payment if I am not acting in my own best interest. Getting you to Tantras, where we may be able to hide from the long arm of the dale—or even recover the Tablet of Fate and magically clear us of all charges—is most definitely in my own interest. I don't want a price on my head for the rest of my life, however long that may be. It's no way to live."

"I see," Midnight said quietly.

Kelemvor frowned and closed his eyes. "That doesn't change my feelings about you," he murmured. "I have to look at things in those terms. Besides, it just simplifies matters."

"Well," Midnight sighed. "I suppose we should keep things simple."

Kelemvor looked at her sharply, and for the first time he saw a trace of the wicked grin Midnight had so frequently displayed to him on their trip to Shadowdale. He laughed and placed his hand on her waist. "Come," the fighter said, and they walked to the end of the bridge.

"Adon!" Midnight shouted. "We're leaving."

Footsteps sounded behind the mage and the fighter. Then they heard the clang of steel falling against steel and turned to see Adon gathering up the pile of weapons he had dropped.

"Hold it!" Kelemvor snapped. "Let's just take what we need." The fighter already wore his two-handed sword, but he grabbed an axe, a spare bow, and a cache of arrows to add to his arsenal. Midnight found a pair of daggers that suited her. Adon stared down at the collection, trying to find some weapon that was suitable. He was well trained with a war hammer and a flail, but sharp-edged weapons were frowned upon by his order. All the weapons that remained were edged.

"Take something and carry it for us," Kelemvor said at last, his patience reaching its end. The heroes quickly left the end of the bridge and entered the forest. After a few minutes, Kelemvor had led his companions to the spot where the huntsmen had secured their mounts.

The horses were gone.

"Are you sure this is the right place?" Adon asked as he looked around.

"The evidence is all about you, cleric. Open your eyes!" Kelemvor snapped. Adon shrank away from the fighter, and Midnight frowned. Kelemvor cleared his throat. "What I mean to say is that you can see the tracks that the horses, and whoever took them, left behind—the broken branches and the footprints." The fighter pounded his fist against a tree and swore. "It was probably Yarbro. Now he's got the gold that Mourngrym paid me, and we'll have to walk to Scardale."

Adon was struggling with two heavy swords he had found as the heroes prepared to leave the forest. Concern crossed Midnight's features. "Adon, where did you leave my spellbook and the items Lhaeo gave us?"

The cleric dropped the swords and the shield and backed away in terror. "I . . . I left them on the bridge," he gasped. "Sorry . . ."

Kelemvor's shoulders drooped, and he opened his mouth to spew out a tirade of angry condemnations. When he saw the cleric's frightened, childlike expression, he fought back his anger. "Go get them," Kelemvor said softly, his deep voice trembling with barely controlled rage.

As Adon ran back toward the bridge, the fighter set his bow down beside the swords that Adon had dropped and walked back to the bridge with Midnight. "He is trying, you know," the mage purred as she put her arms around Kelemvor's waist.

"No doubt," Kelemvor grumbled and tried not to smile.

"And you're trying, too," Midnight said. "I appreciate that."

The fighter and the mage broke from the forest and saw Adon near the middle of the bridge, crouching over the canvas sack he had rescued from the river. He seemed to be rifling through the sack, checking its contents.

Standing near the north entrance to the bridge, the fighter called out to Adon. "Come on, cleric! We don't have all day!" Midnight started slightly at Kelemvor's sudden outburst.

On the bridge, Adon suddenly stood up, the bag firmly in his hand. The cleric stared at the eastern horizon, pointing toward the sky. The sun was behind the cleric, so he could clearly see the three figures floating in the eastern sky, becoming larger as they approached.

"Riders!" Adon exclaimed. "Riders to the east!"

At the northern end of the bridge, Kelemvor shook his head. "What is he—"

Then the fighter saw what had captured Adon's attention. Three darkly clad soldiers were flying toward the bridge. They were following the course of the river and riding huge ebon horses that struck a trail of fire as they galloped across the sky.

On the bridge, Adon stood rooted to the spot. As the riders drew close, he was able to see them even more clearly. The armor of the riders was completely black and lined with razor-sharp ridges. Spikes the size of daggers jutted out from various parts of the armor. The riders' faces were hidden by helmets. Far more frightening than the terrible armor the mysterious riders wore were the mounts they rode. The creatures that carried them across the sky were nightmares—powerful and deadly monster horses from another plane.

As they came even closer, the heroes could see the weapons each of the riders carried. One was armed with a huge scythe, which he tested in the air as he approached Blackfeather Bridge. Another favored bolos, with a cutting silver wire laced between the heavy spheres. But the man in the lead, an imposing specimen who seemed best-suited for his horrible mount, carried a heavy, two-handed broadsword that was stained black and charged with blood-red runes.

From the north entrance to the bridge, Midnight cried out. "Run, Adon! Get off the bridge!"

Kelemvor grabbed the mage and dragged her a few steps toward the woods. "We have to take to the forest," the fighter growled. "They might not have seen us yet."

The magic-user dug her heels into the dirt and pulled away from Kelemvor. "They've seen Adon!" Midnight snapped. "We can't leave him."

"It's stupid to sacrifice ourselves, too. Let Adon come to us, to safety, instead of our running into danger with him," Kelemvor snapped. The fighter knew that they faced a trio of deadly foes. His enhanced vision—one of the only positive effects of his curse—had already revealed the crimson stains of the symbol of Bane over the hearts of the riders.

"You haven't changed at all, have you?" Midnight screamed as she ran from Kelemvor and stepped onto the bridge. "All you care about is yourself!"

The riders were no more than fifty feet from Adon and closing fast. Midnight approached from the north end of the bridge, yelling for Adon to move. The scarred cleric stood motionless, the bag containing the amber sphere from Elminster's tower and Midnight's spellbook clutched in his hands. All expression had drained from his face, and Adon stood as if he were a statue in the center of the bridge.

Before Midnight could reach Adon's side, the riders swooped in. The rider in the lead, the swordsman, aimed his nightmare directly at the cleric and held his sword thrust out before him. Seconds before the sword would rip through Adon's body, the rider drew up suddenly, and his mount veered up and over Adon's head as the other two riders sailed around the cleric on either side. The wind buffeted Adon, but he stood his ground. As the rider flew past, though, the canvas bag fell from Adon's hands, and the young cleric grabbed one of the hind legs of the monstrous horse.

"Adon, no!" Midnight cried, but it was too late to stop him. The cleric's body was yanked into the air above the bridge, twisting as he flew off into the sky.

The nightmare that Adon had grabbed let out an ear-piercing shriek and tried to shake the cleric off its leg.

Flames from the creature's hooves danced around Adon's hands, singeing them, but still the cleric didn't let go.

At the north end of the bridge, Kelemvor stood alone, struck dumb by Adon's unexpected actions. The fighter watched as the cleric not only held on to the monstrous beast, but also began to climb upward, ignoring the horse's wildly flailing legs and flaming hooves.

The fetid smell of the nightmare's hide had almost caused Adon to release his hold on the mount when he first became airborne, but he had ignored the stench and settled his attention on more important matters, such as helping his friends—and perhaps redeeming himself in their eyes. He started to climb toward the rider, in the hope of deposing the assassin and taking control of the mount.

In the air, Varro, the assassin with the scythe, laughed at the spectacle. "Shake him loose, Durrock!" Varro cried. "His life is of no consequence as long as we capture the woman!"

The other assassin reigned his nightmare in and dashed past his scythe-wielding friend. "Leave him to his sport, Varro!" Sejanus said as he stopped swinging his bolos. "Besides, Durrock may want to keep the scarred one alive. They have something in common!"

Riding the mount that Adon was holding desperately to, Durrock ignored the comments of his fellow assassins. He had no need to gloat; his unexpected passenger was completely at his mercy. And if the reports that the Zhentarim spies had sent to him as he flew toward Blackfeather Bridge were correct, the cleric had already handed the assassins the day. Guiding his mount in an arc that would take him back to the bridge, Durrock marveled at the simplicity of the task ahead of him.

Finding the mage and her companions had been child's play. The path the travelers were taking was known. All the assassins had to do was follow the Ashaba until they spotted their prey. Better still, the heroes were not hiding along the river's edge, but standing on a bridge, in the open, when Durrock and his partners spotted them. It was as simple as shooting arrows at a prisoner in a pit.

On the ground, Kelemvor rushed to Midnight's side, but not for any altruistic reason. The assassins would never let him live if they captured or killed Midnight and Adon. The fighter was simply protecting his own life. As he considered his options, the fighter cursed. They might have stood a fighting chance against the assassins under cover of the woods, but Adon and Midnight had taken that option from him, and now Kelemvor was sure that they would all be as dead as the dalesmen very soon.

Next to Kelemvor, Midnight was lost in the spell that she was about to cast. As the riders drew near, Midnight knew that she could not risk harming Adon, so she took aim at the rider with the bolos, the one at the back of the charging formation, and released a fireball spell. A crackling, blue-white pattern of energy formed before the mage's trembling hands, then collapsed.

Nothing else seemed to happen.

In the air, sailing toward the bridge, Sejanus had felt a moment of panic when he saw the mage on the bridge and realized she was attempting to cast a spell in his direction. When she completed the complex gestures and the spell seemed to fail, the assassin laughed and raised his bolos above his head. He prepared to throw the weapon and bind the woman's arms before she could try such foolishness again.

On the bridge, Midnight stared in shock at the flaming scimitar that hung poised over the head of her intended victim. No one else sees it, she realized as she watched the magical sword—the result of a spell called Shaeroon's Scimitar, if she guessed correctly—follow Sejanus. Midnight's spell had gone awry and had brought this force into existence by mistake. But the mage knew that she could profit from the error, and her eyes narrowed as she spoke. "Take him!" she whispered, and the scimitar descended.

A hundred feet above the Ashaba, with only a dozen yards between himself and the mage, Sejanus felt a searing pain begin at the base of his skull and race downward, through his spine, like a fire out of control. The agony flowed out from his spine, piercing every nerve in his body. He began to convulse, and his mount, confused by his motions, veered off at a right angle and raced upward toward the clouds.

As Midnight's errant spell struck Sejanus, Kelemvor stepped aside from the raven-haired magic-user and readied himself to face Varro, the scythe-bearing assassin. With his sword drawn, the green-eyed fighter prepared himself for the fury of the nightmare rider's descent. As the night-black horse came within twenty feet of Kelemvor, it opened its fanged mouth and belched out a foul-smelling cloud.

Now only a dozen feet away from the fighter, Varro gripped his scythe and prepared to match its steel against that of his prey's sword. The assassin leaned over the left flank of his nightmare as the creature arced upward, toward the right. The fighter's sword gleamed as it reflected the harsh sunlight at the assassin's back. Only a few feet from slicing his prey neatly in half, Varro was shocked as the fighter leaped forward, brought his sword down in a crashing blow against the assassin's weapon, then rolled to the bridge and out of Varro's view. As his mount rose to the east, over the bridge, the assassin looked at his weapon in shock.

"You'll pay for this, dog!" Varro screamed in disbelief, dropping the shattered scythe into the river. The assassin reined in the nightmare and drew a sword. The monstrous horse beneath him turned as sharply as it could, but as he turned back to the west, into the sun, Varro was shocked to see Durrock hovering over the bridge, not attacking, just hanging in the air. The image was both beautiful and terrible, a majestic silhouette in black against the blazing orb of the sun. The body of the cleric dangled from Durrock's hand, and the assassin's sword was raised high over his head.

"This game is over!" Durrock cried. "Varro, stay where you are!"

Varro dug his heels into the sides of his mount, and the nightmare reared once but held its position. On the ground, Kelemvor stood, his heart racing, as Midnight moved toward the center of Blackfeather Bridge.

Durrock's nightmare exhaled a cloud of smoke and snorted. The assassin brandished his sword and yelled, "Surrender now or your friend dies! Decide!"

Kelemvor heard a scream behind him and turned. In the sky to the east, the third rider, Sejanus, was slowly making his way back to the bridge. "What do you want with us?" the green-eyed fighter yelled.

Durrock's nightmare reared, and Adon twisted precariously in the air. "I'm not here to answer your questions," the assassin cried. "Lord Bane, the God of Strife, has sent us to deliver a summons. We are here to escort you to an audience with the Black Lord in Scardale."

"Oh, is that all?" Kelemvor snapped. His grip on the sword tightened. "Thank you, but we'll pass. You'll have to carry my regrets to Bane."

Durrock loosened his grasp on Adon, and the cleric slipped slightly toward the ground. The assassin grabbed the scarred cleric again before he could fall. "Do not tempt fate, fools. You have no choice!"

"We'll come with you," Midnight cried. The mage held her hands, their fingers laced together, above her head so the assassins would know she was not casting a spell. "You've won."

Kelemvor stared at the mage, then looked away and slowly lowered his sword. "This is insane!" the fighter hissed. "They will simply kill us in Scardale, once Bane is done with us."

Midnight sighed and turned to the fighter. "Perhaps. But we can't let them kill Adon now," she said. "We may have a chance to escape later."

"Ah, of course!" Kelemvor snapped. "It will be better if we try to escape. Then they can have the pleasure of hunting us down again before they kill all three of us!" The fighter reached down and picked up the heavy canvas bag containing Midnight's spellbook.

Midnight didn't answer the fighter. Instead, she looked up at Durrock, still hanging against the sun, and nodded. "We're ready," the mage said. The riders began to descend.

❦ 6 ❦

Scorpions

Cyric crawled through a tangle of heavy branches on the north shore of the Ashaba. The underbrush served to camouflage his quaking, half-drowned body as the thief heard the sound of the nightmares racing across the sky above the bridge, then watched as Kelemvor, Midnight, and Adon were taken away by the assassins.

I'm lucky I'm not with them, the thief thought. In fact, I'm lucky to be alive at all!

After the dalesman's arrow had caused him to lose his grip on the tree in the river, Cyric had been dragged beneath the surface by a powerful undertow. Only by grabbing for handholds and footholds along the steep, slimy wall of the riverbank had the thief been able to save himself. When he finally broke the surface of the water, he was past the bridge.

Cyric had remained hidden beneath an overhang in the bank and watched the events on the bridge unfold. He saw Midnight's protective sphere burst and Kelemvor become a panther and savage the dalesmen. Two men had escaped the creature's fury—the young, blond guard they had met in Shadowdale, and a shirtless, red-skinned, bald man. Cyric was uncertain of either man's whereabouts.

The hawk-nosed thief had seen Midnight and Adon resurface, then drag themselves up the bank opposite him to the woods at the southern end of Blackfeather Bridge. There had been a brief moment of relief as Cyric watched Midnight move toward the shore, but that feeling faded as he realized that Adon had survived, too. The very thought of the weak-willed Sunite infuriated the thief. Worse, he simply couldn't understand why Midnight protected him.

It was that kind of foolish behavior from both Midnight and Adon that made me realize I'd be better off without them, the thief decided as he crawled up the bank. And from Kelemvor's lame performance in the non-battle with the assassins—He gave himself up! Cyric cursed silently— the thief had added the fighter to his list of people too sentimental to be trusted.

Still, Cyric did feel some remorse over the fact that he couldn't help Midnight escape from Bane's assassins. She would be disappointed in me, the thief suddenly realized, then grew angry at himself for being concerned about the mage's feelings at all. Anyway, he concluded, wherever she's been taken, she probably believes that I'm dead.

Perhaps it was best that way. There had been a strong bond of friendship between the thief and the mage—at least there was before the trip down the Ashaba—and Cyric knew that that type of bond could easily get in the way of his plans. Although he didn't care if Adon's blood might have to be spilled in his pursuit of the Tablets of Fate, Cyric did not relish the idea of harming Midnight. She knew things about him that no one else alive would ever know. Still, he realized that he could trust her, that she would not betray him. Were situations reversed, Cyric was sure that his friendship would not prove as unshakable as the mage's.

As the thief moved some branches out of his way, careful not to allow them to snap and reveal his position, he pulled himself up the embankment. The small expanse of woods Cyric faced had to be an unnatural growth, a product of the physical and mystical chaos that was infecting the Realms. That was the only explanation the thief could think of to reconcile the presence of a grove of trees in an area that had appeared barren on all his maps. Although there had been no sounds that would accompany unusual activity in the woods—or signal the presence of the two remaining dalesmen—he was quite nervous about being discovered while he was still unarmed.

Making his way to the top of the embankment, Cyric found himself staring into the eyes of the blond guardsman, Yarbro. The younger man's armor had been discarded, probably to help him avoid drowning. He still had his sword, though, and that sword was now raised against Cyric, its point grazing the thief's throat.

"It seems there is going to be some justice served here after all," Yarbro hissed as he grabbed the thief by the arm and tossed him to the ground.

Cyric was about to leap at Yarbro in a last-ditch effort to bring the guardsman down when he heard the sound of a branch snapping off to his left. Out of the corner of his eye, the hawk-nosed thief saw the deep, red skin of the bald man who had escaped from the bridge. Mikkel raised his bow and nocked an arrow.

"You're making a mistake!" Cyric gasped. The thief quickly ran through a long list of lies and half-truths that the dalesmen might just believe. "I'm as much a victim as you are," he said after a moment, his voice full of emotion.

Yarbro's sword wavered for an instant. The young guard paused, then pulled his lips back in a grimace. "Oh, really?" he growled. "And why is that?"

"Kill him!" Mikkel snapped. "Just kill him so we can get to Scardale and try to catch the other butchers!" The fisherman took a step toward the thief.

"I don't think so," Yarbro said. "Not yet. Not until I hear a few more of this killer's fantasies."

"What I've been through is no fantasy," Cyric groaned. "The sorceress cast a spell on me. She made me her pawn. My will has not been my own . . . not until this very moment." The thief rose to his knees and looked up at Yarbro. "Think for a moment. I helped to save Shadowdale from Bane's troops. It was under my command that more than two hundred of Bane's soldiers met their deaths. I personally put an arrow in Fzoul Chembryl, Bane's high priest and leader of his clergy. Why would I have attacked him if I were a spy for the Black Lord?"

"Perhaps you wanted Fzoul's job," Mikkel scoffed. "I understand that assassination is the preferred method of advancing one's career in Zhentil Keep."

Cyric shook with barely restrained anger. "The Twisted Tower would have fallen into the hands of Bane's forces were it not for me!"

"That's ancient history." Yarbro feigned a yawn as he allowed the tip of his sword to ease down and touch Cyric's throat again. "More recently, you killed a half dozen of our men when you helped the mage and the cleric escape from the Tower of Ashaba." The guard paused for a moment, waiting for Cyric to respond. "Do you deny it?"

"No," Cyric mumbled.

Mikkel nodded and raised his bow once more. "Then you must die!" Yarbro said. "In the name of Mourngrym, lord of Shadowdale, I pass judgment on you!"

Yarbro started to back away from Cyric. The thief looked at Mikkel, who stood ready to fire an arrow into his heart. Cyric knew that if he didn't say something right now, he was a dead man. "It was the witch!" the hawk-nosed man cried. "You saw what she did to Kelemvor! She turned him into a panther, a mindless beast!"

Yarbro held up his hand and Mikkel lowered the bow. "How do you know that?" the blond guard asked, moving back toward the thief. "You were in the water. You couldn't have seen anything that took place on the bridge."

"That's right," Cyric said flatly. "The raven-haired sorceress boasted of what she was about to do when the skiff got close to the bridge. I tried to stop her and the cleric from harming you. That's how the boat capsized." Cyric paused for a moment and drew a deep breath. "She cast her spell anyway, and as a result, your men died."

Mikkel moved close to Yarbro's side. "Is it possible he's telling the truth?"

A spark jumped to life in Cyric's heart, and the thief silently breathed a sigh of relief. The fools had taken the bait. They were his. "Yes! You have to stop her!" Cyric cried as he rose to one knee. "Midnight cast a spell on me before you captured her at the Temple of Lathander."

"But you didn't see her between the end of the battle and the beginning of the trial," Yarbro said. "How could she cast a spell on you?"

"I didn't have to see Midnight for her to cast a spell over me," Cyric whispered. The thief held his hand to his side, over the wound he had received in northern Cormyr. "I was injured before we reached Shadowdale, and the mage kept the weapon—smeared with my blood." Though he knew little about how magic really worked, the thief knew enough about human nature and popular beliefs to create a sufficiently ominous spell to frighten the dalesmen. "She tasted my blood from the weapon. That allowed her access to my soul later on, after the battle. She twisted me, forced me to do what I would never do on my own!"

Yarbro looked toward the bald fisherman, then back again to Cyric. The thief bowed his head.

"You must believe me—I want her blood as badly as you do," Cyric growled, without looking up. "She and the cleric exchanged laughs over the dying men's screams at the tower. They told stories of how they had lured Elminster away from the battle and murdered him in the Temple of Lathander."

Yarbro's face turned white with anger. Cyric looked up at the dalesmen. One more item on the scales, the thief decided. That should tip them in my favor.

"The cleric boasted of leading Bane's spies into the Temple of Tymora. It was he who soaked his hands in the blood of the murdered priests and painted Bane's symbol on the wall." Mikkel gasped, but Cyric went on. The thief stood up now and held his open hands out to the dalesmen. "They are the killers, and they are the ones we must find and put to death for their crimes!"

Cyric paused for only a moment, then lowered his voice and spoke softly to the dalesmen. "And if you must kill me after we have found them, I will make no move to stop you," the thief murmured. "All I desire is to hear the screams of those two monsters before I die!"

Yarbro and Mikkel backed away from the thief. The guard lowered his sword. The fisherman put away his bow. Cyric smiled and put a hand on each of the dalesmen's shoulders.

"Come with us, then," Yarbro said. "Together we shall find the mage. Then we'll make her pay!"

Cyric could not believe his good fortune. The idiots actually believed his wild story! "She's already on her way to Scardale," the thief volunteered helpfully. "Bane's servants must have had orders to rescue them. We should follow them to the city."

Cyric and the dalesmen walked into the woods for a hundred yards, following the course of the river. They found the fishing skiff impaled on a thick branch. Obviously it would never be seaworthy again. Mikkel gazed at the small boat, thinking of the splendid times he had shared with his partner, Carella. Kicking the boat loose from the snag, the fisherman watched as it sank into the Ashaba.

"We take the road, then," Yarbro said flatly as he turned from the river and headed back into the woods. Cyric quickly followed the guard, and Mikkel soon joined them.

After leaping from the bridge, as soon as they had struggled to shore, Yarbro and Mikkel had rushed to the camp the dalesmen had established in the woods at the north end of Blackfeather Bridge. There they took three horses—one for each of them to ride and the third as a pack animal. The other horses they sent down the road, away from the bridge. Now the two survivors of the hunt, along with Cyric, found the proud animals and loaded the mounts with the few supplies they had gathered.

But as they got ready to ride, Cyric realized that Yarbro and Mikkel were exhausted. The lack of sleep they had endured during the ride from the Standing Stone and their frightening experiences of the last few hours had drained the last sparks of energy from the men. Cyric was still alert, though, and he knew that the men needed rest more than anything. So the thief set about to ensure that they would never get any if he could help it.

"We must ride hard and try to catch them before they're in Scardale too long," Cyric said hurriedly as he leaped onto his horse. "If they get to the city before we do, they'll have a chance to disappear in the crowds, perhaps even catch a boat to Zhentil Keep. Then we'll never find them."

The hunters nodded. "For now, you ride in front," Yarbro sighed as he mounted his horse. "You don't get a weapon until we say so . . . and never forget that our cold steel is at your back."

Cyric kicked his horse into motion. "Of course. I would feel the same way if I were you. All I ask is that you allow me the opportunity for vengeance when the time comes."

"Aye," Mikkel said, stifling a yawn. "That we promise."

Cyric sensed that Yarbro hadn't believed his story as completely as he first thought. It hardly mattered. They had allowed the thief to live. Once the party stopped to rest for the night, the hunters would belong to Cyric. After he dispatched the weakened, exhausted men, he would take their supplies and set off for Scardale alone.

After an hour's ride, the forest gave out, and the barren expanses of Featherdale loomed before Cyric and the two dalesmen. Looking back, the thief half expected the mysterious forest to shimmer and vanish, or the trees to uproot and follow them. Yet nothing strange occurred.

The riders left the riverbank to avoid a curve of the Ashaba to the north in order to follow the most direct route to Scardale. After an hour's ride over the dull flatlands of Featherdale, Cyric spotted a handful of riders in the distance, riding toward them. "What do you want to do about those riders?" the thief asked as he turned slightly in his saddle.

"We have no quarrel with whoever it is," Yarbro snapped, a slight tinge of nervousness in his voice.

Cyric reined his horse to a stop. "We could try to avoid them, but they might think us cowards or criminals and set out after us if we do."

A frown creased the young guard's face. "Just a minute! I'm trying to think," Yarbro growled harshly.

"There isn't much time, of course," Cyric continued. "If we ride right now, we might stand a chance of escaping from them."

"A moment ago, you seemed to favor facing them," Mikkel said, confused. He stopped his horse next to Cyric's.

The hawk-nosed thief smiled. "Well, either way might be dangerous. There are many things to take into—"

Yarbro shook his head violently. "Be quiet! I can't hear myself think!" Mikkel frowned at the blond guard.

The thief smiled. Good, he thought. This kind of conflict will make it easier for me to stay alive a little longer in the company of these yokels. Cyric turned back to Yarbro. "Aye," he said condescendingly. "That's the problem with these situations. You need a clear head, plus a bit of hindsight, to judge them properly. If I may be so bold—"

"You already have been," Yarbro barked. "Now shut up! You're making my head swim!"

"Am I?" Cyric said softly, almost meekly. "It's not my intention, I assure you." The thief turned away and did as he was told.

After a moment, Yarbro drew his sword and laid it across his lap. "We do nothing," he said, sounding pleased with himself. "We'll simply stay here and wait to see what they do."

In a short time, the riders had approached to within about a hundred yards. Their dark clothing and coats of arms became clearly visible, and Cyric identified them at once. "Zhentilar," the thief said flatly. "Probably just a wandering band. I doubt that they're on any special mission. All that should concern them is staying alive."

The dalesmen were tense and nervous as the riders approached. If they handled themselves properly, the dalesmen could avoid a conflict with the larger band. However, their frightened expressions and slightly quavering voices would probably give the hunters away no matter what they told the Zhentish troops.

The band of Zhentilar stopped about fifty feet from Yarbro, Mikkel, and Cyric. The leader of the company, a burly, black-haired man, rode forward a few steps. "I am Tyzack, leader of the Company of the Scorpions. These are my men—Ren, Croxton, Eccles, Praxis, and Slater."

Each of the black-garbed travelers nodded as his name was called. They were all well tanned from days of riding, and their clothes were worn and dirty. After a quick scan of the company, Cyric could not help but notice that one of the "men" in the company, Slater, was actually a woman.

Tyzack crossed his arms, and there was an uneasy silence for a moment.

Cyric leaned toward Yarbro. "You're supposed to respond," the thief whispered. "And I shouldn't be the one out front. It makes it seem as if I am in charge."

Yarbro led his mount past Cyric. The thief eyed the hilt of the guard's sword as he passed. Of course, Cyric didn't dare make a move for the weapon with Mikkel still at his back.

The blond dalesman cleared his throat. "I am Yarbro . . . a hunter of the Dales. With me is Mikkel, and Cyric." The nervous pause was far too lengthy to be missed by the Zhentilar.

Tyzack looked around at the barren fields surrounding the two parties and laughed slightly. "You're a bit out of your element, huntsman. Are you lost? Unable to find your way back home?" A low rumble of laughter ran through the Zhentilar.

"They mock us," Mikkel hissed in a hoarse whisper.

"Better that than attack us," Cyric hissed to the fisherman.

The leader of the Zhentilar eyed the dalesmen for a few moments, then looked back to his company. Ren, a wiry, golden-haired young man, nodded, and Tyzack smiled. "Heading to Scardale, are you?"

"That's correct," Yarbro said. "And we are in a bit of a hurry, if you don't mind."

"Not so fast, dalesman," Ren called from behind Tyzack. "Tell me, what is it you hunt? You've come a long way to track your game."

Mikkel moved his horse past Cyric. "We only wish to be on our way," the fisherman snarled. "Will you let us move along?"

Tyzack spread his arms in a flourish. "Was there ever any question?" The Zhentilar signaled his company to move forward. "I didn't realize you required our permission."

Cyric cursed softly. It was clear that the Zhentilar had no intention whatsoever of letting them go. I'd better make the best of the confusion, the thief thought to himself.

Yarbro turned to Mikkel and Cyric. "Ride on," the guardsman said, the words catching in his throat. Yarbro and Mikkel flanked the thief as they rode toward the Zhentish soldiers.

As the companies came close to one another, Eccles, a wild-eyed Zhentilar with flaming red hair, spat on the ground in front of Mikkel's horse. "I'd spit on you, dalesman, but it would be a waste of water," the fighter barked as he got close to the red-skinned fisherman.

Mikkel stiffened in his saddle. "Zhentish dog!" he cursed bitterly.

"What was that?" Tyzack screamed, holding up his hand. The Company of the Scorpions halted.

"He called your man a 'Zhentish dog!' " Yarbro said flatly and reached for his sword. The Zhentilar quickly unsheathed their weapons as well.

Cyric considered his position. Yarbro and Mikkel still were on either side of him. The Zhentilar were formed in pairs, with Tyzack and Eccles in the lead, followed by Croxton and Praxis, then Ren and Slater at the rear. There's nowhere to run to, the hawk-nosed thief realized, and I have no weapons.

Eccles held a broadsword in his right hand and ran his left, with the reins wrapped around his wrist, through his red hair. The fighter trembled with rage. "Well, Tyzack?" the wild-eyed Zhentilar asked breathlessly.

The black-haired leader of the Company of the Scorpions casually looked over his shoulder at his band. "Kill them all," he said calmly.

Fingers digging into the mane of his horse, Cyric prepared himself.

"You're dead men!" Eccles screamed as he kicked his horse into motion. "Dead men!"

Cyric had leaped from his mount before the first blow was struck. He landed on the ground near Croxton, a red-bearded man with a flat jawline and thick, bushy eyebrows. The Zhentilar's lips curled back in a grimace as he saw Cyric fall, but he ignored the thief and rushed at Yarbro. As he raced past the guard, Croxton struck the young man in the face with the back of his mailed hand. Yarbro fell backward off his horse and landed beside Cyric. The thief saw seething hatred in Yarbro's bloodshot eyes.

Slater, the only woman in the ranks of the six-member band of Zhentilar, produced a crossbow and leveled it at Mikkel's face. She was no older than Midnight, Cyric realized as he watched her take aim at the fisherman, yet her features were as battle-worn as any man's he had ever seen. Her eyebrows had been completely shaved off, and her brown hair was cut short. Lips that might have been full and sensual were dry and cracked. She bit one side of her lips as she smiled and prepared to kill the fisherman.

Eccles rode past Mikkel and slashed him across the arm with his sword. Croxton and Praxis flanked Cyric and

Yarbro. It was clear that the battle was over.

"Wait!" Ren yelled. "Where's the fun if we merely slaughter them? Let's give them a fighting chance . . . and *then* we can slaughter them!" The golden-haired Zhentilar turned to the company's leader. "Well, Tyzack?"

"I have no objections," the black-haired soldier said, a wolfish grin crawling across his mouth. "What do you propose?"

Ren pointed to Mikkel with his sword. "Get off your mount, dalesman."

The fisherman did not move. Ren leaned forward on his horse and pointed to Slater, who still had her crossbow trained on the red-skinned dalesman. Ren smiled, revealing a mouthful of rotted teeth. "If I tell her to *wound* you, it might take days for you to die. I'm about to offer you a chance to live."

Yarbro wiped the blood from his mouth. "Get off the horse, Mikkel. Let's hear what they have to say."

All eyes turned to Mikkel as the fisherman slowly dismounted and sat on the ground.

Taking advantage of the distraction, Cyric slowly started to creep backward, away from the hunters. Then a high-pitched whistle caught his attention. The thief looked up and saw that Slater had aimed her crossbow at his heart. She nodded toward Yarbro, and Cyric moved back to the young guard's side.

"So, the coward would leave his friends behind," Ren growled as he turned to Cyric. "I imagine your own skin is the one you value the most."

"Of course," Cyric hissed softly.

"By Bane's black heart!" another of the Zhentilar exclaimed. "A dalesman who speaks the truth!" The speaker was Praxis, a sandy-haired man with steel-gray eyes who towered over Cyric and Yarbro on his horse. "Perhaps we can have some sport from this after all."

"This is no sport!" Eccles snarled, nervously running his hand through his hair. "Dealing with dalesmen is only sport when it takes place in the arena." The wild-eyed Zhentish soldier turned to Cyric. "Do you know what we do to 'honest' dalesmen like you in the arena?"

As he looked into Eccles's eyes, noting the tinge of madness that lay behind them, Cyric suddenly thought of a way out of this dilemma. "I know a good deal about Zhentil Keep," the thief said, narrowing his eyes. "I was born there."

Both the dalesmen and Tyzack screamed "What?" at the same time. Cyric smiled a half-grin and nodded slowly. "I am an agent of the Black Network. These dalesmen held me prisoner and would be most happy to see you kill me."

"Prove it!" Ren snapped. "Tell us something only a Zhentarim agent would know."

"What I can tell you depends on your level of clearance for covert matters of state," Cyric said softly. "Not the tone of your voice or the number of threats you hold over me."

Mikkel cursed softly and shook his head. Yarbro was not so calm about the "revelation." The blond dalesman rose to a crouch and screamed, "You filthy liar!" Before anyone could act, the young guard launched himself at Cyric. "You were a spy all along!"

Croxton grabbed Yarbro by the hair and lifted him off the ground when the dalesman tried to wrap his hands around Cyric's throat. "That's enough from you!" the red-bearded soldier shouted, then tossed Yarbro to the ground.

Cyric withheld a smile. He could have blocked Yarbro's attack in any of a number of ways, but he chose to wait, hoping the Zhentilar would come to his aid. Although he despised the idea of allying himself with scum from Zhentil Keep, Cyric knew that it was far less objectionable than lying in the middle of Featherdale with his throat slit.

Tyzack dismounted and strolled toward Yarbro. "He was your prisoner?" the black-haired Zhentilar asked, his voice low and threatening.

"Why else would I have been unarmed?" Cyric said from Tyzack's left. The thief rubbed his neck, trying to make the dalesman's attack look far more serious than it was.

"Shut up," Tyzack growled as he turned to Cyric. "No one's talking to you . . . not yet, anyway." He turned back to Yarbro. "So tell me, dalesman, is it true?"

Yarbro hung his head. "I should have killed him the moment I saw him!" the guard hissed.

The thief smiled. "Yes," Cyric said. "That's probably true."

Yarbro started toward Cyric again, but both Croxton and Praxis thrust their swords between the dalesman and the thief. "So why was he your prisoner?" Tyzack asked gruffly as he grabbed Yarbro by the back of the shirt and whirled him around.

Yarbro wrenched free of Tyzack's grasp and turned to glare at the thief, anger narrowing his eyes. "That scum murdered six royal guardsman in the Twisted Tower of Shadowdale," the young guard snarled. "Then he helped two convicted murderers, the mage and cleric who killed Elminster the Sage, to escape from their executions."

Cyric wanted to scream in exultation. The idiot guardsman was making him look better and better to the Zhentilar with each word he spoke!

A murmur ran through the Zhentilar. "So, you're from Shadowdale," Croxton hissed. "You should have told us that first. We would have killed you on the spot and not wasted any time on you."

Tyzack frowned and held up his hand to silence his company. "I'd heard that Elminster was dead. But . . . where are these other criminals?"

"Yes," Slater chimed in. "We'd like to congratulate them!"

The muscles in Yarbro's face twitched, and he glared at the woman with the crossbow. "They escaped," he mumbled after a moment. "Bane's assassins, riding nightmares, rescued them."

"Don't tell them anything more," Mikkel said, shaking his bald head. The fisherman's earring dangled against his cheek.

"So you're a spy for Lord Bane, is that it?" Tyzack asked as he turned back to Cyric.

"Aye," the hawk-nosed man said flatly. "I was a thief—"

"Once a thief, always a thief," Slater brayed, her voice thick and raspy. She chuckled at her own attempt at humor, although no one else seemed especially amused, least of all Cyric. He had run from his past for years on end and finally thought himself free of it. Now it seemed that the only way to save himself was to embrace what he had denied for so long.

Cyric frowned and continued. "I apprenticed to Marek, an

important member of Zhentil Keep's Thieves' Guild. He trained me as a spy." The thief looked around at the Zhentilar and saw that they were all listening to his words closely, waiting for him to slip up.

Tyzack raised a bushy black eyebrow. "Marek, eh? I've heard the name. An older man?"

"That's right," Cyric said.

"What information did he uncover, thief?" Eccles asked as he shifted nervously in his saddle. "What did he tell you?"

Cyric laughed. "It is hardly likely that I would ever reveal important information to someone like you."

The wild-eyed Zhentish soldier growled, and Tyzack moved close to Cyric. The thief silently calculated how quickly he could take Tyzack's weapon from him. As he stared at the black-haired Zhentilar's sword, a glint of sunlight reflected from Slater's crossbow. Not quick enough, Cyric realized, and he relaxed his stance slightly.

"Telling us now might be the prudent thing to do," Tyzack said softly. "Especially if you're concerned with your own survival."

"No," Cyric said coldly. He turned to the other Zhentish soldiers and said, "My words are for Lord Bane alone. It was the Black Lord himself who gave me my orders. I will reveal what I have found only to him."

The Zhentilar mumbled among themselves or silently fidgeted at the thief's proclamation. At least I raised the stakes at the right time, Cyric thought. Now they're afraid to kill me.

Tyzack sheathed his sword and walked to Cyric's side again. "Well," the black-haired man said, "the Black Lord awaits us in Scardale, in the body of Fzoul Chembryl." He paused and looked at the rest of the Company of the Scorpions. "You'll have your chance to see him there, Cyric."

The thief was both relieved and horrified at the same time. Not only was he being taken to the God of Strife, who would certainly kill him, but the god's avatar was a man Cyric had severely wounded in the Battle of Shadowdale. The hawk-nosed man's mouth went dry as he remembered firing an arrow into Fzoul's chest at the Ashaba Bridge.

Tyzack moved away from Cyric and the huntsmen. The

leader of the Zhentilar addressed his second-in-command. "Do you have a suggestion, Croxton? For our guests, I mean?"

"Let them fight one another to the death," the red-bearded fighter snapped. "Whoever lives, we let go. But he'll have to kill his friend first."

"Splendid!" Tyzack roared and returned to his mount. Reaching into a pouch in his saddle, Tyzack withdrew a fresh red apple. The Zhentilar bit into the apple, his teeth piercing it to the core. He swallowed the bite and said, "We'll include our new friend in the game, too. After all, a properly trained *Zhentilar* should have no problems dispatching these two sorry dogs from Shadowdale. What say you, Cyric?"

The thief looked at Yarbro and Mikkel, then nodded. If they have to die for me to go on living, even for a little while, that's fine by me. "Just give me a weapon, and we'll get this over with quickly," he hissed. "But remember, Lord Bane will hear about this."

"Hmmm," Tyzack said and rubbed his chin. "I wouldn't want you to get hurt, but . . ."

Eccles snarled and yelled, "If he dies, then he was lying in the first place! The Black Lord will protect him if he really is a loyal Zhentilar spy!"

The other Zhentilar nodded in agreement. "It's settled, then," Tyzack muttered. The black-haired man leaned close to Cyric and whispered, "It seems that this is the only game available to you, friend. I would urge you to play it out." He paused for a moment, then added, "I won't let you get hurt. Remember that in your report."

Cyric looked at the company's leader and nodded. "Clear these horses away and give us some room."

Tyzack looked to Croxton. "Disarm the dalesmen."

As the last of the horses was led away, the Company of the Scorpions formed a circle around the combatants. Mikkel began to back away from Yarbro and Cyric. "We can't do this!" the bald fisherman said, his voice quavering with fear. "Please, Yarbro! Even if we manage to kill the spy, they'll expect us to turn on each other. Then they'll kill the survivor. We've got to fight them, not each other!"

Slater, still holding her crossbow, began to laugh. "Yes, come and fight us."

Yarbro's face was set. "Though you'll likely kill me for it, I'll not raise a hand against my comrade," the guard said as he turned to Cyric. "But I'll gladly see this one die before I rush to Myrkul's realm."

Moving toward Cyric, Yarbro reached out and tried to grab the thief. The dark, lean shadow of a man darted out of the way and moved past the young guard with ease. Yarbro cursed and followed. He reached for Cyric again, but again the thief avoided him.

"Look at them dance!" Croxton cried. The red-bearded fighter reached down and picked up Mikkel's bow. He smiled a vicious grin, then tossed the bow into the center of the circle. "This should liven things up!"

Mikkel, who was closest to the weapon, quickly grabbed the bow. As Cyric dodged Yarbro yet again, the fisherman swung the bow at the thief's head. Cyric ducked the fisherman's attack, then lashed out at Mikkel with his empty, open hand.

There was a sharp crack as the bow snapped in half where Cyric had struck it. Mikkel looked at the weapon in confusion for a second, until the thief snatched the shattered bow from his hand and thrust the jagged wood into the underside of Mikkel's jaw. The fisherman's eyes flashed open wide and his knees began to buckle. Cyric reached down as Mikkel fell, grabbed the bow, rolled to his left, then sprang up into a crouch, facing Yarbro. The guard screamed something incoherent in his rage.

"Come on, dalesman!" Cyric urged, brandishing the bloody, broken bow. "I could shove this stake into your throat before you ever saw me move. Give up and I'll make it easy on you."

"You killed him!" Yarbro wailed.

"That's the point, isn't it?" Cyric said. "And I don't expect you'll put up any more of a fight."

Yarbro moved toward the thief again. "If you hold still and fight like a man, I'll show you a fight!"

Laughter erupted from the Zhentilar. "Aye, Cyric," Slater called. "Hold still so the dalesman can relieve you of your head!"

To Cyric's right, the leader of the Company of the Scorpions stood with his arms crossed. "Aye, thief, give us a taste of blood!" Tyzack yelled. "Wound him before you kill him."

The thief forced a smile. "That would be too easy!" Cyric growled, thinking that he'd best end this contest quickly, before the Zhentilar got bored and tossed Yarbro a sword or something.

Yarbro swung out a fist wildly at the thief, adrenaline pumping through his veins. "I'll kill you!" he screamed, sweat pouring down his face.

The thief easily ducked the clumsy swing and kicked Yarbro in the stomach. "This *is* getting boring, isn't it?" Cyric said, circling around the guardsman and slapping him with the bow in the back of the head. The thief smiled at Yarbro, who was buckled over in pain, and tossed the bow aside. "I'll give you a running start," Cyric growled. "You can have fifty yards before I come after you."

Yarbro looked up at the hawk-nosed man, disbelief in his eyes.

"Make it a hundred, Cyric!" Ren cried.

Cyric bowed quickly to the golden-haired soldier. "A hundred yards it is," the thief said with a flourish. "Go on, run back toward the river. Maybe I won't catch you before you get to the water. Then you can escape and warn all the Realms about me."

Sweat was pouring into Yarbro's eyes. A lump was forming where the thief had smacked him with the bow, and pain exploded behind his eyes with every movement. "Damn you!" Yarbro hissed. "I'd kill you and everyone else from Zhentil Keep if I could!"

A rumble ran through the Zhentilar, and Cyric gritted his teeth. Yarbro was wearing the company's patience, such as it was, very thin. If Cyric didn't prove to the soldiers he was one of them—a brutish, bloodthirsty Zhentish agent—they might not let him live until Scardale. That just wouldn't do.

"Two hundred yards," Cyric said flatly. "That's my final offer." When the guardsman still didn't move, the thief narrowed his eyes and snarled, "Run, damn you! This is your only chance. I won't take a step toward you for two hundred yards."

Yarbro's breath caught in his lungs. "But *they* will," the guard whispered, nodding toward the Zhentilar.

"Scorpions!" Cyric called. "Will you honor my pledge? Two hundred yards before I move after him on foot. And you stay where you are."

"Done!" Tyzack agreed. The rest of the company nodded or grunted their consent.

Cyric smiled a wicked grin. "Go. It's your only chance. Go now!"

A final grimace of pure hatred crossed the blond guard's features as he turned and began to run. The Zhentilar parted for the dalesman as Cyric strolled to the edge of the ring. Yarbro had run for less than twenty paces when the thief grabbed a dagger from Praxis's boot and hurled it. Blinding pain coursed through Yarbro as the blade entered his back at the base of his spine. Then the guardsman collapsed.

Cyric turned to the stunned Zhentilar. "Come on. He's not dead yet." As the thief approached the place where Yarbro lay, he knew that the next few moments were all-important. By turning his back on the Company of the Scorpions, he had allowed himself to become vulnerable to their attack. For every step he heard them take behind him, some walking, others riding, Cyric's confidence grew. Every moment that Slater's shaft did not strike his back was a victory.

The thief bent down over the twitching body of the hunter.

"You promised . . .," Yarbro gasped, his teeth gritted in pain. "You promised!"

A chill ran down Cyric's spine. "But I didn't come after you, Yarbro. I didn't take a step. It was my blade that did the job." The dalesman started to moan, and Cyric felt a swirling anger growing in his soul.

The Zhentilar gathered around the thief and his victim, and Cyric stood up and started to walk away. "Wait a minute!" Eccles snarled. "You haven't taken care of him yet."

Cyric stood motionless for a moment and closed his eyes. "It's over," he hissed. "Leave him here to die."

"He might get away," Croxton roared, balling his hands

into fists. "You're no Zhentish agent if you leave him like this! You're not—"

They're not going to make this easy, the thief cursed. But I'll do what I must. Cyric whirled around, his face emotionless. "Give me another dagger," he murmured flatly and started back toward Yarbro.

As the Zhentilar watched, Cyric walked slowly to the suffering dalesman and kneeled beside him. As the thief looked into Yarbro's fear-filled eyes, he felt something die inside of him, some tiny spark go out in his soul. "You'd do the same to me," Cyric hissed. He pushed Yarbro over onto his face and quickly slashed the tendons at the backs of his ankles.

As the dalesman wailed in pain, Cyric stood up, tossed the dagger onto the ground next to Yarbro, and walked away. "Now he won't go anywhere," the thief growled as he approached the now-silent Zhentilar.

As the Company of the Scorpions prepared to ride to Scardale, Slater went to the body of the dead fisherman and bent over it for a moment. She gave a throaty laugh and snatched the prism earring from the dead fisherman. Yarbro continued to scream as the woman robbed Mikkel's corpse and the rest of the company packed, but no one seemed to notice.

Cyric mounted one of the dalesman's horses and rode up to Tyzack. The thief's expression was unreadable. Finally the leader of the Zhentilar patrol allowed a grin to spread across his face. "I'm sure Lord Bane will be pleased to see you when we reach Scardale," the black-haired man said and held his hand out to Cyric. The thief paused for a moment, then grabbed Tyzack's hand.

"Welcome to the Company of the Scorpions," Eccles chuckled as he rode past Cyric and Tyzack. And as the Zhentilar started on the long, hard ride to Scardale, the wild-eyed man's laughter drowned out the screams of the dying dalesman.

❧ 7 ❧

Scardale

Midnight used the time it took the assassins to fly back to Scardale wisely. Although she pretended to be asleep much of the time, the mage took advantage of the rough ride on the nightmare to conceal the tiny motions she had been making with her wrists, ankles, and face for almost the entire journey. A small piece of metal on the saddle allowed Midnight to gently saw away at the bonds that held her in place. The journey was long and tedious, and the mage had made some progress on her bonds by the time they reached Scardale.

Just after sunrise, the nightmares were in the right configuration and close enough together that Midnight could catch Adon's attention. She tried to let the cleric know surreptitiously, through subtle hand signals and gestures, that she was trying to cut through her bonds. The mage knew that Adon saw her, but if he understood what she was trying to tell him, it didn't register on the cleric's face.

When the port town came into sight, it was clear to the heroes that this was a place they did not want to be. Columns of thick, black smoke rose from various sections of the city. In the harbor, the heroes could even see huge fires greedily consuming some of the larger ships. Worse still, a number of Zhentish slave galleys cruised offshore.

"The city is under siege!" Durrock cried. "Scardale is at war!" He raised his sword high over his head and signaled the other assassins to hurry. The assassins urged increased speed from their mounts, but it was still almost half an hour before they were over the city.

The assassins laughed and cried out in joy as the nightmares raced over the city. Buildings had been set aflame. Corpses lined the street, and in a few places, the fighting was still in full swing. The heroes noted, though, that Bane's symbol had been painted in red on a number of the larger, more important-looking houses and buildings they passed over. Armed troops, wearing the black armor of the Zhentilar, marched through the streets unopposed.

Varro flew close to Durrock. "We should secure the prisoners," the assassin called. "Then perhaps we can aid the Zhentilar in the destruction of the garrisons—if that has not already been accomplished."

Durrock nodded, and the nightmare riders guided their mounts away from the heart of the city and flew toward the garrison of the Zhentilar, at the outskirts of town. A half-dozen buildings enclosed by a hastily constructed wall comprised the unimpressive fort. The warehouse to which Durrock had summoned the nightmare mounts was located just outside the newly constructed walls of the garrison. The few Zhentilar posted outside the garrison walls cheered when they spotted the assassins.

Kelemvor was amazed as the nightmares descended into the street with a grace and a sureness he never would have associated with the massive beasts. Once the assassins were safely on the ground, Durrock quickly dismounted and opened the warehouse doors. The assassins rode into the old wooden building, then dragged their prisoners from their mounts. Varro quickly untied the ropes that secured Kelemvor to the nightmare, but he left those that held his arms and legs in place. As he did so, Varro talked to the horrid beast with a soft, comforting tone.

Midnight remained perfectly still as Durrock approached his nightmare to untie the ropes that held her to the beast. The mage kept her ankles pressed tightly together, and the assassin did not seem to notice that the bonds around her legs were frayed and nearly severed. Midnight glanced at Adon, and the cleric moved his hands apart a little ways to show the magic-user that his bonds were cut through, too. Midnight's spirits rose, and she couldn't suppress a smile.

I'd best make good my escape now, before anyone catches on, Midnight thought as Durrock moved toward the front of the huge, jet-black horse. Entwining her fingers as if she were saying a prayer, Midnight raised her hands in a tight ball and struck the nightmare as hard as she could. The creature snorted in surprise at the blow and reared up, its forelegs hammering into Durrock, knocking the assassin to the ground.

Midnight threw her arms apart, and the bonds at her wrists snapped. The mage fell back and away from the nightmare, landing on the floor at the creature's rear. The raven-haired magic-user quickly untied the ropes around her ankles and tore the gag from her mouth. She was free!

Only seconds after Midnight struck Durrock's mount, Adon tried the same thing on Sejanus's. The second assassin's nightmare reared up wildly, too, and Adon was also thrown free. But Sejanus proved faster than Durrock. The assassin deftly avoided the wrath of his mount by tumbling away from its flaming hooves. Still, the panicked steed stood between him and his captive, so Adon had time to snap the bonds at his wrists and free himself.

Kelemvor was not so lucky.

Just as Adon struck Sejanus's horse, Varro pulled Kelemvor from his mount and knocked the fighter to the floor. Kelemvor's bonds were still secure. Then the third assassin reached for the dagger at his side, but Midnight was already gesturing a spell. Out of instinct, Kelemvor rolled away from Varro's feet. He had no idea what spell Midnight would attempt or if it would succeed or fail.

As Midnight cast a sleep spell, a pattern of blue-white light formed around her hands, wavered for an instant, and disappeared. Seconds later, just as Varro drew his dagger and prepared to throw the weapon, a sound like thunder ripped through the confines of the darkened warehouse as an invisible force struck the assassin squarely in the chest and drove him backward fifty feet. Varro hit the back wall of the warehouse with such force that the spikes of his armor were driven into the wall, pinning the assassin in place.

Midnight and Adon moved toward Kelemvor, but Durrock and Sejanus were already on their feet, rushing to head off the heroes.

"Run!" Kelemvor called, gritting his teeth as he struggled

with his bonds. "I'll be all right!"

"I doubt that very much," Durrock hissed as he stood over the green-eyed fighter. The scarred assassin drew his sword.

Midnight hesitated for a moment, wondering if she should attempt another incantation. The spell she had cast against Varro had gone awry, but nevertheless it had worked in her favor. However, Midnight doubted she would be so fortunate if she were to cast a second spell against the remaining assassins.

"Forget the fighter, Durrock!" Sejanus shouted as he raised his bolos over his head. "He's not going anywhere. Get the witch! She's the one we were sent for!"

"Run, damn you!" Kelemvor screamed, glaring at his companions. Durrock kicked Kelemvor in the side of the head with his heavy boot. The fighter was struck speechless by the blow, and his head swam in a sea of pain.

Adon grabbed Midnight's hand and pulled her toward the open door at the front of the warehouse. "You can't help him now!" Adon explained quickly. "We'll have to come back for him!"

A look of desperation crossed Midnight's features, and she allowed Adon to pull her forward. The bright sunlight from the doorway, no more than six feet away now, was nearly blinding as the mage and the cleric turned and ran for it. Then Midnight and Adon heard the sharp hiss of Sejanus's bolos slicing through the air as the assassin prepared to hurl them.

"Down!" Midnight screamed as she shoved Adon to the floor. The bolos whistled through the air just above the heroes' heads and went spinning down the street outside the warehouse.

Grabbing Adon's hand, Midnight jumped to her feet and yanked the cleric from the floor. Quickly they crossed the half dozen feet to the doorway, but the heavy footsteps of Bane's assassins sounded close behind the heroes as they leaped from the warehouse out into the light.

The Zhentish garrison was to her left when Midnight burst from the warehouse, so she quickly ruled out running in that direction and headed to the right. The dry dirt street that the mage and the cleric found themselves on seemed to lead into the center of town. As they ran deeper into Scardale, they heard the sounds of fighting grow louder and louder, although the closest skirmish they could see was a number of blocks away, off to their right. Behind them, the heroes could hear the cries of the assassins and the Zhentilar from the garrison.

The heroes raced through the narrow, twisting streets, looking for someplace to hide from their pursuers. They ran until the road they were following met another street to form a **T**. Midnight and Adon could hear the voices of the Zhentilar behind them, so there was no doubling back. The street to her left was lined with bodies and rubble from burned-out buildings. To her right, a huge, overturned wagon blocked the street, and a raging fire consumed a short, squat building. Thick smoke covered the road, obscuring everything that lay beyond the wagon.

"The Zhentilar are following us!" Adon wheezed between breaths. "Where can we hide?"

"How close are they?" a voice hissed from Midnight's left. Midnight looked sharply and saw one of the corpses raise his head. The corpse frowned. "From your expressions, I would guess they're right on your heels."

The "dead man" rose to his feet and dusted himself off. His violet clothing was trimmed with gold mesh, and blood-stains that had turned a deep brown covered him from head to toe. His yellow boots were almost brown with dirt, and he wore a cape with a crimson lining. The man's fine, golden hair was matted and tangled, but Midnight could see that it was very long, curling about his shoulders. He was armed with a short sword and a dagger. On his forehead was a large, ugly purple welt.

"Come on, then," the man said cheerfully as he gestured for Midnight and Adon to follow him. "Don't just stand there. You've already called enough attention to me. We might as well make a run for it."

Midnight looked back and saw Sejanus, Durrock, and a few Zhentilar approaching. Although the assassins were trying to run, their armor did not allow them much more than a brisk walk. The Zhentilar, on the other hand, broke into a sprint when they saw the mage and the cleric. When Durrock saw the heroes break into a run after the golden-haired man, he stopped and headed back toward the garrison.

Midnight glanced over her shoulder as she ran and saw the scarred assassin quit the chase. "He's going to get his mount!" the mage gasped. She tightened her hold on Adon's hand as they ran through the street lined with corpses.

After several hundred yards, the man ducked around a corner and led the heroes into an alley between two large buildings. As the shadows of the alley engulfed them, Midnight and Adon realized that they faced a dead end. Midnight was about to speak when the man turned, smiled, and said, "If we're going to die together, I'd like to know who I'm dying with."

"I'm Midnight of Deepingdale. This is Adon, a cleric of—"

"Adon," the cleric hissed and ran his hand over his scar. "Just Adon."

"Fair enough," the man answered, running his hand through his long, golden hair. "My name is Varden." The man turned toward the end of the alley, but Adon grabbed his arm.

"Why are you helping us?" the young cleric asked.

Varden turned back to face the heroes, the slight smile gone from his face. "You're being hunted by the Zhents, right?"

Midnight and Adon nodded. A handful of Zhentilar ran past the alley. The three fugitives held their breath and pulled farther back into the shadows. Luckily none of the soldiers stopped to investigate the alley.

The man nodded toward the street where the soldiers had just passed. "That's reason enough," Varden growled. Adon took his hand from the man's arm. Varden turned back down the alley. "Now let's get rid of your slow-witted pursuers so we can talk in less . . . stressful circumstances."

Adon and Midnight followed Varden deeper into the shadows. Soon the golden-haired man uncovered a side door to a building flanking them on the right. He yanked at the door and found that it was locked.

Just then, Sejanus appeared at the entrance to the alley,

bolos in hand.

"I hate working under pressure," Varden hissed as he pulled a small set of tools from a band at his wrist.

"You're a *thief?*" Midnight gasped, her eyes growing wide with disbelief.

"I assure you, I am fully licensed and accredited by the Thieves' Guild," Varden said as he fitted a skeleton key into the lock. He did not take his attentions from his work. "I suppose that lummox is still coming."

Midnight looked back toward the head of the alley and saw Sejanus approaching, the bolos whirling over his head. The assassin was less than seventy-five feet away. "Come, little mage!" Sejanus rumbled. "I have no wish to bring damaged merchandise back to Lord Bane. Make this easy on me, and I promise to return the favor later on."

Shuddering, Midnight looked back to the thief. "Hurry!" she urged.

"There! That should do it!" Varden cried. A series of tumblers fell inside the lock, and the thief grabbed the door's handle. Varden pushed Midnight and Adon into the darkened hall, then slammed the door closed behind him. Sejanus screamed in frustration and threw his bolos. The weapon crashed into the door.

In the semidarkness of the cluttered festhall, Varden struggled to find the locking mechanism on the inside of the door. It took him a moment to find the proper levers and lock the heavy oaken door. "That should hold him for a moment or two," the thief chuckled as he turned to survey the musty, deserted hall. "What have we here?"

A dull yellow light shone in the main room of the festhall, its source a rather large hole in the ceiling that had been partially covered with rotting timber. The light revealed a long room with a decrepit wooden staircase and a crumbling balcony that ran around the edges of the entire building. The ground floor of the hall was dominated by a large oaken table. The table was warped and decaying in places, and it ran for almost the entire length of the building.

Though the edges of the room on the first floor were hidden in deep shadows, Varden could see that at least twenty suits of armor lined the walls. All were rusted, half were incomplete. Above each suit, a few weapons, many twisted or broken, hung on display. Midnight thought she heard the hushed whispers of a dozen or more voices, but she decided that it must be the wind through the hole in the roof.

"Seems like we've stumbled across some old meeting hall," Varden said as he walked toward a shield on the wall. Any coat of arms the shield had once held had been erased by time and rust. "From the armor and weapons, I'd guess it belonged to some order of knights—maybe even paladins," the thief added.

There was a loud crash at the door through which the heroes had entered, and Midnight heard Sejanus curse loudly. Midnight and Adon quickly scanned the room for another exit. When she saw none, the mage turned to the thief, panic in her eyes. "Where can we hide?"

Varden laughed. "We need to escape, not hide. Any minute now, the Zhents who ran past the alley will come running back, looking for their leader." The thief paused and looked around the room. "If we hide here, we're as good as dead."

Sejanus crashed against the door again. "You cannot escape me, mage!" the assassin bellowed.

"That's just what you'd expect him to say," Varden chuckled. "Those Zhents have absolutely no imagination!"

"That's a clever observation," Adon snapped. "So use your imagination to find the other exits."

Varden leaned against the wall and shrugged. "I haven't the slightest idea where they might be."

"What do you mean, you don't know!? Then why did you bring us here?" Midnight cried.

"So we wouldn't have to face your friend out there," Varden growled, pointing at the door. "Believe me, I'm as much in the dark about this place as you are. Start searching the edges of the room for another door."

The crash at the door came again. This time the wooden door splintered slightly and bent inward on its hinges. As Midnight approached the edge of the hall, near one of the suits of armor, she heard whispering again. It seemed to come from the rusted suit of plate mail. In other parts of the hall, Varden and Adon heard the voices, too.

"Conflict," a battered suit of armor whispered. "We lived and died for conflict."

To Adon's right, a set of antique plate mail with a large hole in its ornate breastplate turned to face the cleric. "For law and the cause of good, we gave our lives. Fought rust and wear to save our masters. In Anauroch, my lord was slain. They bore me back, a monument to his greatness."

Varden started and began to back away, but a rusted mail hauberk coiled its chain sleeve around his arm. "At the foot of the Glacier of the White Worm I fell, unable to prevent a giant's club from bashing in my lord's skull." The thief tried to pull away from the ghostly armor, but it held him tight. "We serve the force of good," a voice whispered from the hauberk. "Whom do you serve?"

All around the room, creaking suits of plate mail stepped off pedestals and grabbed rusting halberds and swords. Chain mail hauberks filled out, as if worn by invisible knights, and stepped to the center of the room. "Yes, whom do you serve?" a dozen phantom voices rasped.

"We—we work for the good of the Realms," Midnight cried. The suits of armor paused for a moment, and for that moment there was silence in the festhall. The hauberk released Varden, and the thief hurried to Midnight's side. Adon walked slowly across the room, shaking his head.

"The whole world has gone mad!" the young cleric sighed. Before anyone could respond, though, the door to the alley splintered into a dozen pieces, and Sejanus burst into the room.

"In the name of Bane, what's going on here?" The assassin gasped as he looked around the room at the ten full suits of armor holding weapons, standing as if poised for battle. In the shadows at the edges of the room, incomplete or badly damaged suits waved their battered, rusting arms and turned toward Sejanus.

"Your armor gives you away, servant of darkness!" the suit of plate with the gash in the breastplate rasped and raised its bent sword.

Sejanus began to laugh nervously. "Little mage, is this your doing?" Midnight didn't answer, but she and her companions moved behind the advancing armor.

"Born in fire!" a set of armor whispered as it grabbed a halberd and pointed the poleax at the assassin. Sejanus glanced to his left and saw a second suit of armor approaching him.

"This is madness!" Sejanus growled and tossed his bolos at the suit of plate wielding the halberd. The armor easily deflected the bolos with its halberd and continued to advance on the assassin. Sejanus drew his sword. "I grow tired of your display, mage. Stop this at once or you will pay for your impudence later!"

As they backed toward the far end of the hall, Varden leaned close to Midnight and whispered, "*Are* you responsible for this?"

Midnight frowned and shook her head vigorously. "No. This is just another of nature's tricks or some ancient magic that was set here long before we stumbled across it."

Adon grabbed Varden's sleeve and pointed into the darkness at the end of the room. A small wooden door lay in the shadows, but a series of boards were nailed across it, holding it tightly closed. "We can escape through here while the armor keeps the assassin occupied," Adon said and turned toward the door.

Suddenly there was an explosion of wood from above. Sunlight flooded the warehouse as huge chunks of rotting wood fell to the floor. The heroes dove under the long table. Sejanus and the animated suits of armor stopped moving. All eyes turned to the roof of the festhall.

There, hung in the air above the hole in the ceiling, was Durrock, riding his nightmare. The horrible creature was shattering the boards that covered the hole with its flaming hooves. Obviously Durrock desperately wanted to get inside the warehouse. He wanted Midnight.

"We're leaving now!" Varden yelled as he grabbed Midnight's hand. "Cover your head."

Taking advantage of the confusion caused by Durrock's appearance, Varden, Midnight, and Adon broke from the cover of the table and rushed between two living suits of armor toward the door that led out into the alley. Sejanus was howling with rage as the ring of animated suits of armor tightened around him.

"Durrock, the mage is getting away!" Sejanus screamed as he parried a sword thrust from one of the suits of rusted plate. Durrock and his nightmare vanished from the jagged hole in the roof just as the heroes emerged into the alley. The sounds of swords crashing against one another echoed from inside the warehouse, mixed with Sejanus's screams of anger.

As the heroes ran down the alley toward the street, the sound of the nightmare snorting and whinnying drifted down from above their heads. Midnight looked toward the sky and saw Durrock and his mount hovering over the rooftops. "The alley is too narrow for his mount, but on the street we'll be at his mercy," the mage cried. "We're right back where we started!"

"Well, we can't camp here all day," Varden exclaimed.

Midnight turned to the thief. "I'm the one the assassins are after," the raven-haired magic-user stated flatly. "Lead Adon to safety. As long as I'm trapped in this alley, Durrock won't follow you."

"Don't be absurd!" Varden snapped as he grabbed Midnight's arm and tried to drag her forward. "The next thing I know, you'll want to try using magic! There's nothing more infuriating—"

Midnight shifted her weight away from Varden, dug her left leg into the ground between his legs, and shoved the thief over her leg against the wall of the alley. The golden-haired man struck the wall with such impact that he was momentarily stunned.

"*Never* put your hands on me like that!" Midnight growled, then backed away from the thief. "I know what's best. Now, go!"

Adon walked to Midnight's side and put his hand on her shoulder. "No," the cleric said softly. "We've got to trust Varden." The scarred young man paused for a moment and looked up at the assassin, still hovering over the alley. "We've got to stay together."

Midnight had run out of arguments. She considered their circumstances for a moment, then followed Adon and Varden down the alley. At the edge of the street, the thief paused and turned to the mage.

"I know where to go from here," Varden whispered. "We need to get to the alley five stores to the east of here." The thief looked up and saw the nightmare descending into the street. "Run!" he cried and bolted into the street filled with corpses.

"We still have your lover, Midnight!" Durrock shouted as the nightmare landed and started to race down the street after the mage and her allies. "Surrender now or he will pay the price for your foolishness!"

Chancing a look back over her shoulder, Midnight saw that Durrock had picked up a new weapon when he had gone back for his mount. In the assassin's hands was a black net, large enough to contain a man, with heavy weights secured to its edges. The scarred assassin was no more than twenty feet from Midnight and her companions, holding the net open wide, when Varden suddenly turned into another alley.

In the cramped lane that ran between two dilapidated buildings, Varden charged up a rickety set of stairs and dove into an open window. Midnight and Adon turned down the alley just in time to see the thief disappear. At the same time, Durrock released the net. The metal mesh struck the corner of the building as the heroes raced into the alley and climbed through the window.

Inside the building, Midnight and Adon found themselves in a small room that was covered in paper. The room looked as if a whirlwind had passed through the interior of the building and scattered pieces of parchment everywhere. Varden was lying in the center of the mess, lifting himself up from the floor, when the heroes entered. In the corner of the room, sitting cross-legged, with a large pile of papers in his lap, was a man in his early sixties, with two patches of white hair at the sides of his head and a shining bald pate between them.

Varden saw the older man and let out a cry of greeting. "Gratus!" the thief exclaimed happily, a smile on his face. "Why, it's my good friend and associate, Gratus!"

The old man looked up. He was wearing clothing similar to Varden's—violet pants and shirt with yellow boots— except that Gratus was missing the cape. An expression of sorrow and pain flashed across the old man's face as he squinted in the direction of the thief. Then Gratus spread his hands wide, and papers flew in every direction.

"Varden, you're still alive!" Then the old man's expression changed rapidly to one of anger. "Go away! Every time I see you, it's nothing but trouble!" Gratus croaked. The old man saw that the papers had scattered from his lap and tried futilely to gather them up again.

Varden's smile widened. "I can't really deny that, considering our present circumstances," the thief said as he flashed a glance back at the open window. "But I would very much appreciate it if you would stop complaining and give us a hand!"

Standing near the window, Adon ducked his head outside to take a look. "I don't see any sign of Durrock," Adon noted.

"He's probably calling the other Zhents, trying to cover all the exits," Varden said flatly. "He has no way of knowing what direction we'll take when we leave."

"Excuse me," Gratus said. "But did you say 'Durrock,' as in Bane's unholy servant? Black, spiked armor? Rides a horrid, monstrous horse with flaming hooves?"

Midnight drew a deep breath. "Yes. That's who's following us." The mage moved to Adon's side and glanced nervously at the window.

"Come now," Varden said cheerily, turning to Midnight. "Don't look so glum. We've already defeated Durrock's friend back in the festhall."

Gratus held his wrinkled hand in front of his face. "Fine!" he snapped and held up a single finger. "You defeated one." The old man paused and held up another bony digit. "Durrock's undoubtedly circling somewhere overhead, so that makes two." Gratus held up a third finger slowly and said, "But where is the third assassin? Durrock is always in the company of two others."

Midnight turned away from the window and fixed the old man with a cold stare. "I cast a spell at him when we escaped. He's probably still pinned to the side of the warehouse near the Zhentish garrison."

"A mage!" the old man cried as he lifted himself from the ground. "So this is what you bring me, Varden. Another mage!"

"What does he mean, 'another mage'?" Adon asked.

Varden tried to dismiss the question with a smile. "It's nothing," the golden-haired thief said. "Gratus's mind wanders sometimes, that's all."

The old man stood up straight. "Go on, Varden! Tell them!" Gratus put his hands on his hips. "I'm not lifting a finger to help until you do."

Varden sighed and hung his head. "A . . . former acquaintance of mine was a magic-user." All traces of the thief's good humor disappeared as he spoke.

Gratus nodded emphatically. "Note the word 'was,' " the old man cackled, wagging his finger at the younger man.

The thief spun to face the older man. "It's not my fault that Dowie tried to light that torch using his magic! It was a very stupid thing to do."

Gratus chuckled. "Did either of you happen to notice a pillar of flame that rose to the heavens a week ago?" the old man asked.

"We're new in town," Adon said.

Gratus nodded and continued. "You should have seen the look on Dowie's face right before—"

"The two of you can trade stories all you want later," Midnight growled. The mage trembled with barely controlled anger. "Right now, we need help. Durrock will be back any second now with those Zhentilar that passed us a while back."

Varden held up his hand to calm Midnight down. "Gratus, I think we should go to the garrison." The thief turned to Midnight and Adon. "We're merchants here in Scardale, but it recent days, we have found it expedient to seek the protection of the Sembian garrison here," Varden explained. "the outfits are the garb of our illustrious employer."

The old man nodded. "That's fine with me." Gratus paused and idly kicked a pile of paper aside. "Unless the fair lady of magic wants to use her great power against the assassins and turn Scardale into a smoking pit in the process. I heard about a mage who reduced an area outside of Arabel to—"

"How do we get there? To the Sembian garrison?" Adon growled. "And please make it quick, before the Zhentish decide to storm the building."

Gratus looked at Varden. "Impatient, isn't he?" the old man sighed. "Do you expect us to simply dance out of here into the streets and stroll to the garrison? The Zhents would be on us in an instant."

Even Varden was growing impatient now. "So how *are* we going to get out of here?" he snapped.

Gratus smiled a crooked smile, exposing his yellowed, crooked teeth. "I've been holed up in this place, sifting through papers, because I'd heard rumors that the old government installed a number of secret tunnels beneath the city."

Midnight could not contain a sarcastic laugh. "And you expect the plans for them to be lying around here, waiting to be found by any old cutpurse who can find his way into the building?"

Gratus continued to smile. "Why *not* hide them in plain sight?" the old man said. "That's what I would do."

"And that's why you aren't ruling this city," Varden growled. "This is a terrible time to be relying on rumor, Gratus."

The old man ignored Varden and continued, the crooked smile still on his face. "I have made some rather interesting discoveries." Gratus withdrew a set of documents from his waistband and gestured with them. "Like these plans for a proposed sewage system that—"

Moving forward, Midnight reached for the stained, crumpled parchments. "Give them to me!" the mage growled. After studying the plans, Midnight shook her head, then returned Gratus's smile. "According to these, there should be an entrance to the sewer right beneath this building."

"That is correct," Gratus said smugly. "If the government installed the secret tunnels, then it would make sense that there are entrances to all public buildings. This building used to be a sort of hall of records."

"Your luck seems to be holding out, old man," Varden said, shaking his head in disbelief.

"Luck!" Gratus exclaimed, balling his hands into fists. "Suddenly I no longer feel guilty about leaving you for dead in the street after that band of Zhentilar attacked us."

"I wasn't going to mention that," the thief stated flatly. "Besides, you couldn't have known that I wasn't dead. After all, I was unconscious for a while." Here Varden rubbed the bruise on his forehead. "Anyway, I was perfectly safe as long as the Zhents thought I was dead."

Gratus stiffened at Varden's words, then turned to leave the room. "You didn't know?" the old man mumbled as he moved into the hallway. The sounds of Durrock barking orders to the Zhentilar drifted in through the open window. "Come on, the lot of you! We've got to get out of here!"

Midnight and Adon followed Varden and Gratus down two flights of warped wooden stairs into the basement of the building. The old man took the map from Midnight once they reached the musty basement and looked at it again. "The entrance to the tunnels should be right here," Gratus said, pointing to a large, empty bookcase.

The heroes pushed the oaken bookcase a few feet to the side and found a thin sheet of wood covering a small, dark doorway.

For several moments, Varden had been mulling over the comment Gratus had made before they left the room upstairs. "I didn't know what?" the thief finally asked as the heroes peered into the darkened tunnel.

Gratus frowned, but he didn't turn to look at the thief. "Normally the Zhents chop the heads off their victims just to be sure no one's faking," the old man explained. "When you fell, I had to assume you were dead . . . or soon would be."

Varden turned white, and Midnight couldn't suppress a shudder. The realities of war, she reminded herself. She turned away from the tunnel as there was a loud crash upstairs, and Adon heard Durrock barking orders to his men.

"I may be wrong, you understand," Gratus noted calmly as he reached for a torch that hung inside the door. He quickly pulled out his flint and steel and lit the old wooden torch. "But if I'm right, I think we can make the Sembian garrison by nightfall."

Varden took the torch from Gratus and stepped into the tunnel. Midnight and Adon glanced at each other for a moment, then followed the Sembians into the darkness.

* * * * *

Shaking his head to toss his thick, matted hair from his eyes, Kelemvor surveyed his cell. It was a barren little room, really little more than an eight-foot cube, with a wall at his back, bars at his front, and bars to either side of him. Beyond the bars in front of the fighter, there was a poorly lit hallway where two guards were stationed before the cell. Chains bound the fighter's hands and feet, allowing him less than two feet of unimpeded movement from the back wall of the cell.

Heavy footsteps sounded from down the hallway, as if a procession had entered the lower level of the Zhentilar headquarters and was now approaching through the narrow stone walkway. Kelemvor watched as a red-haired man wearing ebon armor entered the corridor and stopped before his cell. The fighter recognized the ornate armor as identical to that worn by the God of Strife in the dungeons of Castle Kilgrave. A beautiful blond woman, wearing an elegant black robe with a brilliant red sash, stood beside the red-haired man, a wicked smile playing across her features.

"Kelemvor Lyonsbane," Lord Bane murmured. "I trust you remember me." The god drew an finely crafted sword from a scabbard at his waist.

"Your dogs address you as 'Lord Bane,' but if that's true, you've changed," the fighter said calmly. "You're not quite as ugly as you were when Mystra defeated you in Cormyr."

The sword shook in the Black Lord's hand. "Do not try to goad me into granting you a quick death!" Bane roared.

Kelemvor winced. Even if this wasn't Bane, Kelemvor realized, his impersonator had control of the situation. Perhaps it wasn't best to provoke him. "What do you want with me?" the fighter asked softly.

"I have come to make you an offer. Choose wisely, for your life may depend on your response," Bane purred, clanging his sword across the bars of the fighter's cell.

"I would expect that kind of offer from someone who threatened a chained, unarmed man with a sword," Kelemvor said, smiling. The fighter looked at Bane and saw shards of crimson dancing in his eyes.

The red-haired man narrowed his eyes. "Do not try to endear yourself to me, either. I know everything about you, Lyonsbane. Perhaps you forget that I was inside your mind when you and your pitiful friends entered Castle Kilgrave."

Kelemvor flinched. This really was the God of Strife who stood before him. No one else could know that Bane had entered his mind and drawn forth illusions based on his fondest desires to prevent him from rescuing Lady Mystra.

"Ah, you remember," Bane noted. "And do you remember the offer your dead uncle made to you in the dream I gave to you?" The fighter looked up sharply. "You can be free of the curse of the Lyonsbanes, Kelemvor—free to be a hero if you wish, without fearing the curse."

Lowering his head, the green-eyed fighter looked away from the Black Lord. "What do you want with me," Kelemvor repeated.

Bane sighed. "Right to business, then. As you might have guessed, my true interest is not in you. You can swing from a meat hook, for all I care." The blond woman at Bane's side giggled.

Kelemvor thought of the body he had found in the Twisted Tower, courtesy of Cyric's handiwork. Those two would be well matched, the fighter thought.

"Open the cell," Bane ordered, sheathing his sword. In seconds, the door was opened and Bane stood within a few feet of the fighter. The blond sorceress followed the fallen god into the cell.

Bane smiled a perversely charismatic grin and put his hand on the fighter's arm. "It's the mage I want . . . Midnight. You know her better than anyone else in the Realms," the God of Strife purred. "And I know you. I know everything about you. Your entire life passed before my gaze in Castle Kilgrave."

Kelemvor looked into the avatar's eyes and nodded slowly. "I want information from you, mercenary," Bane stated, all emotion absent from his voice. "I want an accounting of every time Midnight used the power Lady Mystra granted to her."

"The pendant, you mean?" Kelemvor asked. "The blue star pendant that Mystra gave to Midnight?" The fighter paused and breathed a sigh of relief. "It's gone. It was destroyed in the Battle of Shadowdale. Midnight has no other gift from Mystra, so you can stop worrying about her."

Bane thought of his final moments in the Temple of Lathander. Even though he had taken the pendant from the raven-haired mage, she was still able to cast a spell of far greater power than should have been possible. Perhaps Mystra, who was by then only a magic elemental of sorts, granted Midnight the power directly. Or perhaps Midnight had more power than any of her friends suspected.

"I want you to tell me in detail about every time she used magic since the time of Arrival," Bane said, anger tingeing his words. "And I want to know what her destination is."

Then she escaped! Kelemvor suddenly realized. The assassins didn't recapture her. "I don't know her plans," the fighter said sharply and turned away from the God of Strife. "Besides, why should I help you?"

The Black Lord's hand struck out with blinding speed, and Kelemvor's head snapped to the side with the force of the blow. "If you lie to me, the consequences will be painful." Bane stepped back from the fighter and grinned again. "Besides, you will eventually tell me the truth . . . given the right prompting. So let's not waste my time, and yours, by forcing me to slowly flay you alive."

The blond sorceress moved past Bane and reached up to touch the side of Kelemvor's face, where he had been struck.

"If you refuse me," the God of Strife noted, "I'll let Tarana take your body, then your mind, then your life." Bane covered his mouth his hands, stifling a yawn. "She is a mage. She can enter your mind, just as I have in the past."

The fighter jerked his head away from Tarana's caresses. "Magic's unstable," Kelemvor snapped, fear spreading through him. "A spell like that could kill us both."

"That's true," Tarana cooed and giggled again. "Quite a romantic picture, don't you think?"

Kelemvor looked into the deep blue eyes of the sorceress and felt as if he was gazing into an endless pit of madness. She would gladly kill us both, the fighter realized. He shuddered and turned back to Bane. "What reward do you offer me for my assistance? You know that my curse will not allow me to help you without payment."

The God of Strife smiled. "Before we set a price, my friend, you should know that I want more than information from you." Bane ran a hand through his flaming red hair and paused.

"I assume that Midnight plans to venture to Tantras, with hopes of finding one of the Tablets of Fate that Lord Myrkul and I stole from the heavens." The God of Strife turned away from Kelemvor. "Not that she would ever find it, of course. Its hiding place is a masterpiece of deception. It is nowhere that you would ever expect it to be."

"Stop playing games, Bane. If you're going to kill me once I give you the information, you might as well tell me where you've hidden the tablet," Kelemvor growled.

"Kill you?" Bane asked, a chuckle in his voice. He turned back to the fighter.

Kelemvor frowned deeply. "Isn't that my reward? A quick death?"

All emotion drained from the Black Lord's face again. "I don't want to kill you, Lyonsbane. I want to *hire* you to draw Midnight from her hiding place, then retrieve the Tablet of Fate from Tantras."

Kelemvor was shocked, and it clearly registered on his face. "But why me? You must have an army of loyal followers who would gladly perform such tasks for you." The fighter paused and stared at Bane. "In fact, why don't you find Midnight and retrieve the tablet yourself?"

"She has taken refuge with the Sembian garrison and hides with them. I would have to wage a major assault against the Sembian resistance to recover her. Many lives would be lost, and in the confusion, she could easily escape." The God of Strife frowned. "On the other hand, you would be able to ferret her out of hiding and lead her into a trap with little effort. In short, you would be a perfect spy."

Kelemvor took his eyes away from the god, but Tarana grabbed his jaw and forced his gaze back. Her hands were as cold as the grave.

The God of Strife stared at the fighter for a moment. "Midnight's life is mine, no matter how you decide," Bane noted flatly. "No matter what you do, I will have her. I am a god, after all." The red-haired man took a step toward Kelemvor. "Never forget that."

"Aye," Kelemvor said flatly. The chains were digging into the fighter's flesh, and the pain reminded him of the gravity of his situation. Bane would certainly kill him if he didn't cooperate, and that would put an end to his dream of somehow living a normal life, even for a few years.

And Kelemvor knew that the God of Strife could capture—no, *would* capture—Midnight, whether he helped the fallen god or not. But the fighter loved the magic-user. At least he thought he did. And there was very little he would trade that for.

"I still haven't told you what I offer," the Black Lord said, as if he were reading Kelemvor's mind. "You must know what I am willing to do for you before you can make a decision."

The fighter stared into the blood-red eyes of the god-made-flesh. Bane moved a step closer, and Kelemvor saw his own reflection in the god's eyes.

"I offer an end to your suffering," Bane whispered. "Do as I ask, and I will remove the curse of the Lyonsbanes from you!"

Bane's words hit Kelemvor like a lightly padded mace. For a moment, the fighter's senses reeled as he turned the possibility of release from the curse over in his mind. After a moment, Kelemvor once again focused his attention on the Black Lord.

"My family has sought an end to the curse of our bloodline for generations. How do I know you can deliver what you promise?" the fighter asked, his voice low and taut with emotion. "A bag of gold I can see and feel. Its weight comforts the curse. A promise such as you have made appeals to my dreams, but will likely do little else. After I do your dirty work, then you will renege on your promise."

Smiling, Bane ran his hand over his face. "You forget you are speaking to a god," Bane said, the false grin dropping from his lips. "I do not offer what I cannot produce." The fallen god turned away from the fighter for a moment and struggled to control his anger. When he turned, his smile had returned.

"You know how bargains work, Lyonsbane. You've had to live all your life wondering if a man would keep his word." The God of Strife paused and put his hand around Kelemvor's throat. "That's why I know I can depend on you to keep your part of our bargain *after* I've removed the curse."

Kelemvor's heart began to race. "After?"

"Of course," Bane said flatly. "I cannot expect you to serve me if I haven't made it clear that your curse has ended."

"B—But how can you remove the curse when so many others have failed?" Kelemvor asked breathlessly.

"You keep forgetting . . . I am a god," Bane growled, tightening his grip on Kelemvor's throat ever so slightly. "There is nothing I cannot accomplish."

A heavy breath escaped from Kelemvor's lips.

"You doubt the word of the God of Strife?" Tarana gasped. She backed away from the fighter and drew a small knife from the folds of her robe. Bane shook his head, and Tarana put her dagger away.

"My family has petitioned gods in the past," Kelemvor stated, swallowing hard.

"But not a single cursed member of the Lyonsbanes has ever *believed* in a god before," Bane stated and removed his hand from the fighter's throat. The God of Strife stroked the fighter's face gently.

"That's the key," Bane purred. "A god will grant no mercy and no favors to one who does not believe completely. You may not be a follower of mine—not yet, anyway—but you know what I am. You believe that I am the Black Lord, the God of Strife. You have faith that I am all that I say I am."

Kelemvor nodded slowly.

"That is enough. That faith is all I need," Bane said softly. "And your answer." The fallen god paused and turned away from the fighter again. "What shall it be, Kelemvor Lyonsbane? One final mission, and in return, the fulfillment of all your dreams. Or would you languish here until you die? You must decide."

The blond sorceress had returned to the Black Lord's side, and together, they waited patiently for Kelemvor to give his answer.

❧ 8 ❧

Fatal Decisions

For what seemed like hours, Midnight and Adon followed Varden and Gratus through the secret tunnels that wound beneath the streets of Scardale. Finally they reached a dead end. Panic set in for the mage when she saw the blocked tunnel. She knew that it was only a matter of time before Durrock discovered their escape and followed them. After all, there had been no way to seal the entrance to the tunnels behind them. And the last thing Midnight wanted was to be trapped in the labyrinth beneath the town with the assassins.

"Not to worry," Gratus said as the mage stared at the blockage in front of them. "Look up."

The first rung of a ladder lay a few feet over the old merchant's head. Varden brushed Gratus aside and leaped to grab the lowest rung. After hauling himself up and climbing for a moment, the thief let out a moan when he bumped his head at the top of the passage. Varden strained against the barrier over his head and was relieved to find that the trap door slid aside.

A shaft of amber light, filtered through the dirty carpet that lay over the hole, pierced the tunnel. Cautiously Varden drew his dagger and cut through the rug. The light intensified as the carpet fell away into the tunnel. When the gap in the material was large enough, the thief poked his head through and looked into the room they had found. Varden was surprised to find that he was in some kind of abandoned inn.

A few tables were scattered around the room, which was filled with light from several windows, plus a number of holes in the walls and ceiling. Dust and debris covered everything in the taproom, including the thin amber carpet that surrounded Varden.

"It seems to be clear," the thief whispered as he turned back to the tunnel. "Hurry, though. I'm not exactly sure where we are."

Gratus swore softly and started to climb the ladder, after a helpful boost from Adon. Then Midnight and Adon exited the tunnel. When they looked around the taproom, the heroes saw that Varden was crouched next to one of the few intact windows in the building, surveying the streets beyond.

"I think we're close to what used to be the Cormyrian garrison." The thief paused and turned back toward Midnight. "We're not far from the place where the remaining soldiers from the various garrisons opposing the Zhents have hidden. The Zhentilar call them the 'Sembian Resistance.'"

"I think the Sembians made that up," Gratus chuckled as he led the heroes to the back of the inn. They quietly crept out into an alley, then started off toward the Sembians' hiding place.

On the street, at the front of the inn, there was little activity. Varden took the lead, while Gratus used his knowledge of the layout of Scardale to guide the party to the secret outpost. Resistance fighters from the various garrisons were encountered from time to time, but they recognized Varden and Gratus and presented no problem. There was a close brush with a band of Zhentilar only blocks away from the hiding place, but the heroes managed to evade the soldiers.

Finally Varden and Gratus stopped behind the skeleton of a burned-out butcher shop. The blackened beams stood like dead trees, and a jumble of rubble cluttered the area that the shop had once occupied. Gratus carefully crept to the center of the heap of charred wood, where a slightly singed door lay on the pile, and rapped quietly five times.

After a moment, Midnight heard a voice softly ask for a password. Gratus bent over, and when his face was almost low enough to touch the door, he whispered, "Friends of Sembia."

The door creaked open slightly, and a guard peered out at

the heroes. "Well, well," he whispered, "if it isn't Gratus! And, Varden, you're alive!" The door flew open now. "Come in quickly!"

The heroes rushed through the open door and found a set of blackened, burned stairs leading to a musty cellar. Once the heroes were down the stairs, the guard reset several traps on the door and rejoined them. Then he moved toward a small crawlspace in one of the walls. "Don't worry," he said, turning to Midnight and Adon. "This leads to our hiding place."

After crawling down a short passage, Midnight and Adon found themselves in a stone tunnel, much like the one they had used to escape from Durrock and the Zhentilar earlier. Torches lined the walls, lighting the gray-bricked passage, and Midnight saw a handful of soldiers dressed in the uniforms of various nations. Some rested against the walls, others sat on crates of food, sharpening weapons or rolling dice.

"Wait here," Varden told Midnight and Adon. "I'll go talk to Barth, the leader of our little troop." The thief smiled warmly and walked toward a large curtain that was hung in the tunnel a few yards away.

It was over two hours before Midnight and Adon were given an audience with Barth. Since none of the soldiers made any attempt to talk to the mage or the cleric, they spent the time exploring possibilities for Kelemvor's rescue and discussing all that had happened to them since they'd met in Cormyr.

At one point, the conversation lagged, and Adon spent a few moments looking around the tunnel at the tired, dirty soldiers. For the first time, he noticed that they were huddled in groups—the Cormyrians with other Cormyrians, the men from Hillsfar only with their own, and so on.

The Zhentish invasion changes Scardale little, the cleric thought with a sigh. This was once a thriving, happy place . . . before Lashan's reign, anyway.

In fact, it hadn't been so long ago that Scardale was on the verge of forging its own empire. Under the leadership of Lashan Aumersair, an aggressive young lord, Scardale had had gathered an army and even managed to conquer a few

of its neighbors. But the invasion of Harrowdale, Featherdale, and Battledale drew the attention of the rest of Scardale's rivals for power in the area—Hillsfar, the Dales,
Sembia, even Cormyr and Zhentil Keep.

Lashan was eventually turned back from Mistledale and
Deepingdale by the combined forces of Scardale's powerful
neighbors, and the young nobleman's empire collapsed as
quickly as it had risen. The troops from the conquering
armies soon occupied the town of Scardale itself, though
Lashan escaped and was presumably still in hiding somewhere. Then each of the major powers placed a small garrison in the town, to prevent any one power from rising
unchecked in the dale.

The various garrisons had fought among themselves for
years over petty insults, making the town little more than
an open invitation to lawlessness. Now that the balance had
been tipped in Zhentil Keep's favor, Adon thought bitterly,
the soldiers were treating it like another taproom brawl, another momentary inconvenience. They weren't banding together as allies to save their city; instead, they were huddled
together like groups of thieves in a darkened alley. At any
moment, they might suddenly turn on one another. To
Adon, it was all very sad.

When the heroes finally got to meet Barth, Adon's musings about the soldiers' pettiness were proven correct.

"You expect us to *what?*" Barth exclaimed, his normally
well-tanned face turning bright red. The soldier was
strongly built, with curly black hair and a thick mustache.

"I don't *expect* you to do anything," Midnight growled,
balling her hands into fists. "I'm offering you a chance to
strike back at Bane's forces. You might be safe while you're
inside these tunnels, but the Zhentilar have made you prisoners here just as surely as if they had thrown you in their
dungeons!"

Barth leaned back in his chair, the only one Midnight had
seen in the tunnels, and looked at the mage and her friends.
Contempt showed in the soldier's eyes as he mulled over
Midnight's plan to rescue Kelemvor.

Gratus smiled fatuously and addressed the leader of the
resistance. "The mage has a point." Raising his hand, the old

merchant placed his index finger and thumb together, then allowed a small space to open between them. "Why, we can't even go outside the tunnels this far, even to look for food, without worrying about a Zhentish patrol picking us up. I can't even—"

"Stop thinking of only yourself, you old con man," Varden snapped. "There's a very real chance that Midnight's companion may be enduring torture even as we speak. He might even be dead, for all we know. Bane is going to crush Scardale beneath his black boots. The least we can do is try to strike a blow against the tyrant."

"Enough!" Barth barked, waving Varden away with a meaty, unwashed hand. "Your passion and your beliefs are not the issues. We've already sent messengers to alert Sembia of the takeover. If we wait it out, reinforcements will arrive. *Then* we'll attack the Zhentilar. Not before." The Sembian paused for a moment and picked a bit of his lunch from his teeth with a dagger. "Right now, any attack would be a waste of effort and men."

"There's another reason you need us," Midnight said. She hated to lie, but she was beginning to realize that Barth was going to give her no other choice. "Bane is in possession of a mystical object that we were carrying to Tantras for Elminster the Sage." The Sembian looked up quickly, nearly poking himself in the cheek with his dagger. Midnight smiled and continued. "The object is an amber sphere of great power. If Bane learns what it is and how to control it, he will have the power in his hands to find you whenever he wants to."

Panic flared in the eyes of the Sembian leader. "Perhaps I could spare a few men," Barth said slowly, his mind racing. "Tell me, with this sphere, would you be able to destroy the Zhentil Keep garrison?"

He won't help me for altruistic reasons, Midnight thought to herself, but fear certainly convinced him to assist me soon enough. "No," Midnight said with mock sadness. "Only a god, or a being with a god's power, could accomplish such a task with this object."

Barth paled slightly. "If it's a danger to my, uh, soldiers, I'll assign two men to your party. They'll assist you in your efforts to retrieve this magical sphere . . . and your friend." The Sembian cleared his throat and wiped a thin film of sweat from his brow.

"You have our thanks," Midnight said.

Barth made a futile attempt at a smile. "Yes, well, perhaps you should get going right away. We wouldn't want . . . your friend to suffer any undue danger, would we?" Midnight nodded and silently cursed the Sembian, then led her friends out through the curtain and into the section of the tunnel where the soldiers were gathered.

Almost an hour passed before the soldiers who had been assigned to assist Midnight arrived. The heroes had pulled together a few crates to serve as a table, and the section of the tunnel they occupied had started to look like a military planning room. Maps of Scardale and the outlying areas lay all over the floor. Trade routes and various notations concerning the business districts of the town marked the surfaces of the maps, which had come from a local merchant's looted store, making it impossible to make out some of the map's details.

As Midnight, Adon, Varden, and Gratus huddled over a map of the harbor, two young men wearing grubby, nondescript clothing approached the heroes. The first soldier, a tall, dark-haired man with a pale complexion, stepped forward. He was a tired-looking youth, with deep circles under his eyes. "I'm Wulstan. This is Tymon. We're both from Hillsfar."

The second man was also dark-haired, but his craggy nose appeared to have been broken several times. However, in general, he seemed in much better health than his friend. He nodded to the heroes.

Midnight stood up. "Well met," she said, and proceeded to introduce herself and her companions. "Thank you both for volunteering to help us."

The soldiers glanced oddly at one another, then back at Midnight. "Volunteer?" Wulstan asked incredulously. "Are you serious?"

Varden surged forward, a dark scowl on his face. "You mean the two of you had to be *ordered* to help us attack your enemies?" Wulstan looked away awkwardly.

The thief looked down the tunnel at the other soldiers gathered there. "Is there no one here who has the heart to fight the Zhentilar to regain Scardale?" Varden cried loudly enough for the others to hear.

"Not really," Tymon said matter-of-factly as he walked past Varden and sat down. "But orders are orders, and you will find that neither Wulstan nor I will shrink from our responsibilities."

Varden bowed his head and returned to the maps. "I suppose that your best effort is all we can ask for," Adon sighed and put his hand on Tymon's shoulder. "At least under these circumstances."

Wulstan snorted and rolled his eyes. "Spare us the sermon, cleric." The worn fighter walked to Midnight's side. "Just tell us what we're supposed to do."

Adon narrowed his eyes and started to speak, but Gratus stood up quickly and cleared his throat. "Well, we have a number of obstacles to overcome," the old merchant noted. "We can expect that the Zhentish garrison will be filled to overflowing with Bane's soldiers. To relieve the overcrowding, the fallen garrisons of the Zhent's enemies will be occupied if possible."

Wulstan muttered to himself, then growled, "Once we leave this hiding place, there'll be no other safe place for shelter. Isn't that what you're trying to say, old man?"

Gratus ignored the sullen soldier and continued. "However, we might be able to get lodging in a private house." The old merchant ran his hand over his face and tapped his chin. "The people of Scardale have declared themselves neutral. They won't be interested in harboring fugitives. But I have friends that might be willing to help."

"The Zhentilar will be prowling the streets," Midnight added, "and I wouldn't be surprised if at least one of Bane's assassins is airborne, combing the streets for Adon and me." The mage grew silent.

"So our first problem is getting to the Zhentish garrison in one piece," Varden said flatly. "Then what?"

"The obvious," Gratus answered, rubbing his hand over his bald spot. "Getting inside, retrieving Midnight's belongings, and rescuing her friend. Then the small matter of getting out again."

"At least they're simple problems," Wulstan muttered moodily.

"The Zhentish may be expecting us to make such an attempt," Adon added. "It's possible the Zhentilar may have set up a trap. They might let us get into the garrison with only token resistance, then capture us with ease."

Gratus frowned and sat down. "So what do you suggest?" the old man asked. "If it's such an impossible task, why are we undertaking it?"

Midnight's eyes flashed. "We're doing this because we must!" the mage snapped. "And we have one thing you haven't mentioned that may tip the scales in our favor. The one thing the Zhentish won't expect."

Adon looked up. "Magic!" he breathed softly. "But Bane has your spellbook."

"There's one spell left in my memory," Midnight said, smiling at the scarred cleric. "One I was studying before we were captured."

Varden shook his head and started to object. The two young soldiers eyed the exit from the tunnel. Gratus nervously rubbed behind his ears. "If you mean to teleport us halfway across the city," the old man snapped, "you can count me out right now."

"No," Midnight answered. "That would be madness. We could end up inside solid rock or buried beneath the Ashaba." The two soldiers from Hillsfar glanced nervously at each other and frowned.

"Any spell is dangerous," Varden said. "There are no guarantees—"

"Life itself has no guarantees," Adon interjected, running his hand across his scarred cheek. "Let her finish."

Tymon nodded. "Though I'm afraid to find out what the mage has in mind, I think we should at least hear what she has to say."

Varden frowned. "All right. Go ahead," the thief said, defeated.

"It's a spell of invisibility," Midnight stated, a smile creeping back onto her lips. It casts a cloak of invisibility for ten feet in all directions. If it works, we should stay invisible unless we attack somebody. And since we would plan on avoiding any attack, we should remain invisible for the entire time we make our way through the town."

"I still feel—," Varden began.

"Enough!" Wulstan snapped, standing up and moving to Midnight's side. "The matter is no longer up for debate. I'm no more anxious than any of you to die, but if we can possibly be safe and still follow our orders, then I say we should give the mage her chance."

Midnight's smile grew broader, and Tymon, Gratus, and Adon nodded in agreement with Wulstan. Only Varden looked away from the mage, deep concern lining his face. "Fine. We should leave by the butcher shop entrance immediately," the raven-haired mage said. "And we probably should inform Barth of our plan." The heroes crossed the tunnel to the Sembian's quarters.

The Sembian leader looked shocked when Midnight explained their plan. "At least give me a few minutes to clear the guards from the basement entrance before you begin your sorceries," the burly fighter mumbled. "A good thing we have another exit."

After Barth recalled the guard from the small basement of the butcher shop, the heroes crawled through the tunnel and prepared to leave the Sembians' haven. At the bottom of the stairs, Midnight gathered the components for her spell. From her pocket, she removed a small piece of gum arabic, which she carried especially for this spell. Then she collected a single eyelash from each of the heroes. Finally the mage encased the eyelashes in the gum and began her chant.

Gratus and Varden exchanged nervous glances. The soldiers from Hillsfar trained their attention at the wall beyond the mage and forced themselves to think about anything but what might happen. Adon, however, stood before his friend, smiling serenely. From the cleric's expression, it seemed he would welcome even death itself if the spell went awry and killed them all.

Steadying her nerves, Midnight finished the incantation. Unable to think of a single spell that had worked properly for her since the escape from Shadowdale, the mage prayed that this one would work—for Kelemvor's sake. Soon a blue-white glow began to surround Midnight. The heroes gasped and shielded their eyes as the light intensified, filled the room, then faded.

Gratus looked around the basement at his companions. "Nothing happened!" the old man said, much relieved. "And we're still alive!"

At the same moment, Midnight saw Barth poke his head out of the crawlspace between the basement and the tunnels. A look of amazement filled his face. The burly man's lips moved silently, and the mage laughed.

"What's wrong with you?" Wulstan said as he approached Midnight. "I can still see you. Your spell didn't work. Why should you be laughing?"

Adon pointed toward Barth, and the heroes turned to see the Sembian staring into the room. "I—I can hear you," he whispered, "so the spell must have worked. But I still can't see you. You are there, aren't you?"

"We're just testing the effectiveness of the spell," Midnight said, and the burly fighter started slightly, bumping his head on the top of the crawlspace. "Let's go, then," the mage said, and the heroes left the hiding place.

As Midnight and her allies journeyed across the city, Gratus stopped from time to time to point out various safe houses whose residents were likely to admit them should the need arise. "Lashan had friends in the city," Gratus noted softly as the heroes passed one such house. "And many of them do not approve of Scardale's declared neutrality."

"I've been curious about something, Gratus," Midnight said softly. "Exactly what is it you do in Scardale? You aren't a mage, a fighter, or a thief. How do you make ends meet?"

Varden laughed. "I'm not so sure he isn't a thief."

Gratus leaned close to Midnight. "I was Lashan's Minister of Propaganda," he whispered. "The city pensioned me off, but they refused to turn me over to the likes of these two boobs from Hillsfar on the condition that I keep my mouth shut about Lashan's possible return. Now I sell boots."

Wulstan overheard parts of what the old merchant said and quickly moved to Gratus's side. "You'd better watch what you're saying, old man, if you know what's good for you," the fighter growled.

Gratus replied mockingly, "So the rumor is true . . . people from Hillsfar have no sense of humor whatsoever."

Wulstan reached for his sword, but his partner quickly raised his hand. "Stay your arm!" Tymon warned. "We can't afford to have our invisible shield fade. The moment we attack something . . . anything . . . we will become visible."

Adon stepped between Gratus and Wulstan and looked at the mage. "If only one of us attacks something, will the spell be canceled for us all?" the cleric asked quietly.

Varden took Gratus by the arm and pushed him in front of Midnight. "The way magic works nowadays, I wouldn't be surprised if we are never visible again," the thief said with a grin.

Midnight's flesh paled. She had not even considered the possibility that the spell might work *too* well.

"Imagine the fortune that could be amassed in this town by a thief gifted with invisibility," the thief went on, apparently happy for the first time in hours.

The Hall of Records, where Midnight and Adon had met Gratus earlier in the day, came up on the left. The building looked the same as it had earlier in the day, although a lone Zhentilar stood guard at the doors.

"I was worried they'd burn the place down," Gratus whispered as they passed the guard. "There are some very interesting papers I'd like to retrieve from there."

They continued on to the end of the block, then took a sharp right. Immediately the heroes spotted the warehouse where the assassins had landed and the Zhentish garrison beyond that. As expected, the sounds of revelry floated through the streets from the garrison. A token number of guards were posted outside the fort, and the entire building that served as the Zhentish headquarters was brightly lit.

"Bane must be allowing his soldiers to celebrate with a victory party," Midnight said softly as she led the heroes into an alley next to the warehouse.

"How very different from the way he drove his troops in the Battle of Shadowdale," Adon observed. "I wonder if the Black Lord's defeat has humbled him in some way. . . ."

"I doubt it," Midnight replied. "Perhaps he's simply

learned to recognize the value of his troops. In any case, we might just be able to turn his lenience against him."

"You mean you've solved the problem of how we get in?" Varden asked, running his hand through his blond hair.

"We need to check out the warehouse before we worry about the garrison itself," Midnight said as she turned to Varden. "We should circle around the building and see if there are any other doors."

The heroes slowly moved around the outside of the warehouse, staying as close to the side of the building as possible. Twice groups of Zhentish soldiers passed them, singing bawdy songs and telling off-color jokes, but they never even suspected that six intruders were only a few yards away.

At the rear of the warehouse, Varden discovered another door, though this one was locked. The thief quickly took out his lockpicks, and in a moment the door was open. He opened it slowly and peered inside.

"We couldn't have come at a better time," Varden whispered as he turned to Midnight. "The warehouse looks empty. We should be able to move around freely." The heroes silently filed into the building, with Midnight in the middle so that no one would stray outside the invisibility spell's area of effect.

"Close the door," Midnight hissed when they were all inside.

Wulstan started to follow Midnight's order, then paused and looked at the door's lock. "It looks like it locks both ways," the fighter said, motioning for Midnight to examine the door.

Midnight nodded and removed a piece of the gum that she had left over from her incantation and handed it to the soldier. "Put this in the lock first. The door will shut, but it won't lock. Then we won't be trapped if we need to make a quick exit."

Wulstan and Varden both looked at the mage with surprised expressions.

"An old friend taught me that trick," the raven-haired magic-user said, her thoughts suddenly turning to Cyric. But then Midnight felt a dark, somber mood settle over her, and for an instant, she was almost overwhelmed by her sorrow. The mage closed her eyes, steeled her will, and dismissed the emotion. Cyric's dead, and there's nothing I can do about it, the mage decided calmly. Kelemvor's alive and in need of my help. I can grieve later.

Midnight's thoughts were interrupted when Gratus moved to her side. "Could that be something you're looking for?" the old man asked as he pointed toward the shadows twenty feet to the left of the door.

Midnight squinted. Something sparkled in the moonlight. It looked like tiny shards of amber light.

"It couldn't be!" she breathed, then advanced toward the light. Adon rushed ahead of her and bent down over a partially open canvas sack.

"Midnight, they're here!" the cleric cried, a broad smile lighting up his face. "The sphere of detection and your spellbook are right here!"

"The assassins must have forgotten about them in the confusion caused by our escape!" Midnight said, picking up the sack.

"I didn't forget about it at all," a voice boomed from a darkened corner across the warehouse. "And I was counting on your not forgetting it either." Durrock stepped out of the shadows and into the pale moonlight filtering in through the windows. He wasn't wearing his armor, and his disfigured face was uncovered as he walked toward the heroes.

Midnight nearly gasped as she saw the assassin's face, and a brief flicker of sympathy flared inside her. Then she felt the canvas bag slip in her grasp, and she tightened her grip on it. Quickly the mage realized that, since she didn't have the canvas sack with her when she first cast the invisibility spell, it was still visible!

"Thanks for showing me exactly where you are," Durrock growled as he drew his night-black sword. The assassin was striding straight toward Midnight. "I've been waiting here for you for some time now."

The heroes spread out as far as they dared, and as Durrock came close to the mage, several of them circled behind him. Midnight tossed the sack to the ground and tried to dodge the assassin's attack, but the scarred killer made a feint forward, then reached out and grabbed the mage's hair. Midnight screamed.

Suddenly a large wooden plank crashed over the assassin's head, staggering him and forcing him to release his grasp on the mage. As Midnight scrambled away from Durrock, a blue-white aura enshrouded each of the heroes as the spell of invisibility faded.

Gratus stood behind the assassin, the shattered plank of wood still in his hands. Durrock gripped his night-black sword more tightly and screamed with rage and pain. The assassin's sword flashed out just as Varden grabbed the old man's shoulders and yanked him backward. The sword bit into Gratus's chest and blood spurted from the wound.

Midnight backed away from Durrock in shock. The assassin turned and took a step toward the raven-haired mage, but Adon appeared beside her and took hold of her arm. "Run!" the cleric hissed as he pulled the magic-user toward the door.

Durrock started to follow her, but the two soldiers from Hillsfar stepped into his path, drawing their swords. "Come on, you Zhentish pig. Let us see how you fare against someone closer to your own age!" Tymon taunted as he stood before the scarred man.

Wulstan glanced over his shoulder at Midnight. "Take your treasure and run!" the fighter screamed. Midnight hesitated for an instant in the doorway, then picked up the canvas sack and backed out of the warehouse. Varden was already pulling the wounded merchant to the door, but Adon took hold of Gratus, too, and the heroes disappeared into the night. They slipped into the shadows and were far from the Zhentish garrison before the drunken soldiers even knew what had happened.

*   *   *   *   *

"Wake up!" the guard yelled and clanged his sword back and forth over the steel bars of Kelemvor's cell.

The green-eyed fighter was jolted from his sleep, but he pretending to wake gradually, making a show of shaking the sleep from himself, rubbing at his eyes, and yawning broadly. Two guards stood outside Kelemvor's cell, but the fighter didn't want the men to have the satisfaction of knowing that they had indeed startled him awake, that their little cruelty had affected him.

The fighter knew why the guards had awakened him, too. The Black Lord had expected an immediate answer to his proposition, but Kelemvor had argued that he needed time and solitude to consider the bargain. The fact that Bane agreed to his request had come as a complete surprise to Kelemvor. But now the time to consider the offer was past.

The fighter heard footsteps approaching from down the hall, and from the way the guards snapped to attention, Kelemvor knew who his next visitor would be. It was no surprise.

"You said I had until morning," Kelemvor noted calmly as Bane stepped between the guards.

"Circumstances have changed. The time for you to act is now. Have you considered my offer?" Bane asked sharply. The edge in the fallen god's voice told Kelemvor that something had obviously angered him.

"I've been unable to think of anything else," Kelemvor answered as he rose to his feet and stared into the blood-red flickers of light that danced in the Black Lord's eyes.

It was true. Even the fighter's dreams had been consumed by thoughts of freedom from the curse. Kelemvor had often wished that he was a hero, someone who could do noble deeds for the sole reward of helping others. But the curse had always stood in the way. The fighter believed, without a shadow of a doubt, that Bane could deliver on his promise. The God of Strife could make his dreams a reality.

Which only left the problem of Midnight to consider. If Kelemvor accepted Bane's terms, he would obviously have to betray the trust the mage had placed in him . . . and his feelings for her. But Midnight has betrayed me many times, Kelemvor thought bitterly.

Then the fighter reviewed the insults and petty hurts the mage had heaped upon him, trying to rationalize a decision he had really already made. The mage had left Shadowdale without him. Certainly her words upon Blackfeather Bridge were of love and commitment. Still, the simple truth was that Kelemvor had known Midnight for but a few weeks.

Suddenly Kelemvor wondered just how well he really

knew the raven-haired mage. The fighter no longer worried about whether Midnight had committed the crimes the dalesmen had accused her of. There was no question that she had not. But Kelemvor wondered now if Midnight really loved him.

"You had visitors during the night," Bane said casually, snapping Kelemvor away from his thoughts.

"Who?" Kelemvor asked. The fighter took a step toward the bars of his cell.

Bane narrowed his eyes and sneered. "Who do you think, fool. Midnight and her accomplices. She was here to retrieve her spellbook and whatever other personal items she might have had with her when Durrock and his assassins captured her." The God of Strife paused for a moment, then smiled. "However, she did not try to rescue you."

The fighter breathed a silent sigh of relief. "Obviously the mage escaped again, or you wouldn't be here," Kelemvor said.

Anger burned in the Black Lord's eyes. "She could not escape before one of her party was wounded and two were killed. Do not overestimate your importance in my plans, Kelemvor. Midnight will die. Your participation is merely a matter of convenience. By allowing you to go to her and draw her out, I can minimize the casualties in my own ranks."

Bane's playing this badly, the fighter thought. He's acting like a petty warlord, not a god. Still, the information Bane had just given the fighter about Midnight's visit to the Zhentish garrison answered some of the questions that had been tugging at the corners of his mind.

"Very well," Kelemvor said softly but firmly. "I will accept your terms."

The Black Lord smiled. "Then you have finally come to your senses. There is nothing more precious than life on your own terms," Bane hissed. "It's about time you realized that."

The fighter nodded. "I will find Midnight and win her trust. I'll convince her that I escaped on my own, and I'll pretend to lead her to freedom. Then . . . I'll subdue her at the first opportunity." Kelemvor paused and ran a hand through his hair. "Later, I will travel to Tantras to retrieve the Tablet of Fate that you have hidden in the city. In return for all of this, you will remove the curse of the Lyonsbanes."

"That is correct," Bane said, motioning for the guards to open the cell.

Kelemvor stepped back from the door. "Now that our agreement is settled, where exactly is this Tablet of Fate?" the green-eyed fighter asked.

"You must show a little faith," Bane answered with a sly edge in his voice. "The information will be yours after you deliver Midnight to me. Right now there is another small matter that we must deal with."

Kelemvor's heart was beating wildly. He couldn't control his anticipation as the cell door was opened and the God of Strife moved to his side.

"Guard, give me your sword," Bane ordered sharply. The fires in the Black Lord's eyes suddenly seemed bright enough to light the corridor without the benefit of torches. The guard complied without a word. The fallen god raised the sword high over his head.

The fires in Bane's eyes spread over the dark god's body, and soon his entire form was covered by a blood-red aura. The Black Lord began to recite a complex incantation. Suddenly the sword burst into flames. The voice of the god rose in intensity as he waved the sword wildly. His form began to undulate like the body of a snake.

The sword flashed through the air, and Kelemvor screamed as the weapon pierced his chest, cutting a jagged line from his breastbone to his abdomen. The fighter looked down at the torn cloth and flesh and felt weakness wrap itself around him. Still, the fighter struggled to stay on his feet. Even if he were dying, he would not kneel before the Black Lord.

The flaps of the parted skin on the fighter's chest seemed to bubble and quake, and Kelemvor nearly shouted in terror as he saw the panther's ebon head push its way out of his gaping wound. The fighter suffered agony unlike any he had ever known as the claws of the beast raked at the inside of his body, savaging him in an attempt to break free.

This is impossible! was the only thought in Kelemvor's

mind. Then the fighter's entire world became a white-hot explosion of searing anguish that blurred his perceptions of everything but the pain itself. The beast was tearing its way free, but it was killing Kelemvor from within at the same time.

There was a loud animal roar, and Kelemvor felt an incredible weight burst free from him. Instantly the pain lessened considerably, and Kelemvor saw that Bane had gripped both sides of the beast's head. With a sharp, inhumanly swift motion, the god snapped the creature's neck.

The fighter looked down and stared at his chest. He watched in awe as his torn flesh began to close and mend together. The wounds were healing at an impossible rate.

"It is done," Bane said nonchalantly and dropped the body of the panther at Kelemvor's feet. The god turned and strolled from the cell. "Tell him where to find the mage, clean him up, and send him on his way."

"No!" Kelemvor rasped, his voice little more than a whisper.

Bane looked back to the cell, suspicion crossing his features.

"I should look as if I had to fight my way out," the fighter said and collapsed onto the ground, inches from the panther's still-warm corpse.

The Black Lord smiled. "Very well," he hissed. "But know this, Kelemvor. If you even think of reneging on our agreement, I will know. My agents will hunt you down and kill you, no matter where you hide." The God of Strife paused, and another evil grin flitted across his lips. "Or better still," he added, "I'll put that creature, or one even more horrible, back inside you." The smile widened slightly. "One that would be far more painful to remove than the panther was. Remember that."

The fighter nodded. "It is no less than I would expect," Kelemvor said. "And no less than I would do in your position. Set your mind at ease. I will follow the terms of our pact to the letter."

"This could be the beginning of a long and profitable association," Bane called over his shoulder as he continued down the corridor. "Bring her to me alive, Kelemvor. If that's at all possible."

Kelemvor shuddered and stood up slowly. He didn't look at the guards as he staggered out of the cell. "I shall," the fighter whispered as he followed the same path from the dungeon that the Black Lord had taken.

❧ 9 ❧

A New Leader

Travel through the eastern dales was long and hard for the Company of the Scorpions, but the Zhentilar were well supplied and used to the difficulties of such a journey. Cyric quickly learned from Tyzack that the Scorpions had been on an expedition to Haptooth Hill, searching for an artifact of great power that wanderers passing through Zhentil Keep had made some offhand comments about.

The Company of the Scorpions had received its orders before the Battle of Shadowdale, when Lord Bane had been obsessed with finding any artifacts that might be repositories of magical power. In all the confusion surrounding the battle and its aftermath, the Scorpions, and their mission, had been forgotten by Zhentil Keep—until the time came to amass every available unit of Zhentilar in Scardale. A mystical communication from Bane's new sorceress, Tarana Lyr, had come one night, and the Scorpions had actually been relieved to receive the new orders. Their efforts at Haptooth Hill had been fruitless and extremely tedious.

Two days after Cyric joined them, the Scorpions ran into a small Sembian patrol and were forced into combat, an opportunity for the thief to measure his new acquaintances' skills, and for them to measure his. The battle was swift and furious, but not without cost to the Scorpions. Croxton was killed, though whether by a Sembian hand or a Zhentish, Cyric wasn't sure. Much to Cyric's surprise, Tyzack promoted the thief to second-in-command for his efforts in the battle, with Slater openly supporting the decision and the others saying nothing, though some—like Eccles—were obviously unhappy with Tyzack's choice.

One day after the clash with the Sembians, the Scorpions encountered the first of many Zhentish patrols heading toward Scardale. Tyzack automatically assumed command of the ragtag groups of fighters and thieves that the company met. No one opposed him.

Now, as Cyric rode behind Slater, his mind wandered over a myriad of subjects. But mostly he watched the bright afternoon sunlight pulse through the prism earring the female warrior had taken from Mikkel's corpse and attached to her right ear. The sparks of brilliant, multicolored light shot out from the bauble as Cyric stared dreamily at it, washing away all the thief's concerns and fears.

The line of the horizon was choppy, marred with sharp ridges, and the earth was a strange mixture of grayish green stone, with veins of raw, auburn clay. Small, barren hills and rises surrounded the riders. An immense growth of earth, with a crevice along its spine and serrated, evenly spaced depressions leading off in crooked gaps, lay ahead and continued for miles. Cyric felt that he was looking at all the skeletal remains of an incredible giant, which might have lived eons before the gods ruled Faerun.

It should be the form of a god, towering over the Realms, he thought as he looked at the ridge. Tall enough to reach into the sky and pull down the very heavens, not trapped inside a frail body of flesh, like a mortal.

Shards of light from the stolen earring drew the thief's attention once more, and as the Zhentilar rode—now more than three hundred strong—Cyric realized that he had become just as fascinated with the prism as Slater was.

The hawk-nosed thief watched the slivers of light as they glittered in a beautiful array of colors, and studied each shard. The lights came into existence and passed on in the blink of an eye. Much like a human life, he thought. Gone and quickly forgotten. Cyric wanted more from his life. He thought of the gods and the gift of immortality that they had endangered with their foolish, petty squabbling. The thief felt contempt for the deities like Bane and Mystra, who had allowed their vast powers to be stripped away.

Cyric tried to calm himself. The dry afternoon heat was sweltering, and even the slight breeze he felt did little to assuage the bands of broiling, intense heat that assaulted the company as they trekked along the Ashaba. The heat pressed against Cyric's flesh like scorching, oppressive hands, causing rivulets of sweat to pour into his eyes, obscuring his view of the prism momentarily.

Looking around at dozens of faces that he did not recognize, Cyric considered the fact that each of the Zhentilar rode to Scardale for the sole purpose of answering Lord Bane's call. Nearly all of them would lay down their lives without a moment's hesitation if the Black Lord called for them to do so. Incredibly, it was the Company of the Scorpions that these men had turned to for temporary leadership. The political maneuvering that Cyric had observed Tyzack perform to ensure his own supremacy surprised the thief. Cyric thought the leader of the Scorpions incapable of even conceiving of such well-thought-out plans, let alone implementing them.

The thief cleared his eyes and returned his gaze to the prism. The shards of light released from the earring seemed endless, and as each new shard died away, another took its place. Cyric thought of Tyzack. The man had to have a weak spot, a vulnerability that Cyric could exploit. What was it? the thief wondered. Ahead, Slater reached for the prism earring, caressing it gently. The thief smiled. Perhaps there was a simple way of finding out.

An hour later, Tyzack was off chatting with the commander of a fifty-man contingent from Tasseldale that was located somewhere near the rear of the sizable Zhentish advance. Ren had gone with Tyzack. Cyric moved up through the line and motioned for Slater to join him a few lengths ahead of the Zhentilar. Willingale, one of the Zhentish operatives from Harrowdale, had taken point a few hundred yards ahead of the troops, and Cyric told the others that he and Slater were going to replace him for a while.

"Why are we replacing Willingale on point?" Slater asked as she rode next to the thief. Cyric hesitated, and the flesh of the woman's eyebrowless forehead wrinkled as she flashed her eyes wide open in a gesture that was meant to emphasize her confusion. "What is it you really want with me?"

"Am I that obvious?" Cyric asked as he looked away from

the Zhentish soldier.

Slater grinned. "Don't ask if you don't want an answer," she said.

Cyric chuckled softly as he wiped the sweat from his forehead. "By the gods, it's hot!"

Slater frowned and tapped her fingers on the stock of her crossbow. "If this of your idea of small talk, I think I'll take my leave," she grumbled.

"I was merely making an observation," Cyric snapped, turning to the fighter. "And I was wondering how observant you have been."

The woman's eyes narrowed, and she looked at Cyric with mistrust. "In what regard?" Slater asked.

"I wish to know more about the Scorpions," Cyric stated flatly, looking straight at the woman.

"I can guess why," replied Slater, running her hand across her horse's mane. "It's Tyzack you really want to know about, right?"

This one's brighter than I suspected, the thief thought. "Aye," Cyric admitted, trying to look as innocent as possible. "His actions confuse me. So do yours, for that matter."

Cyric saw that Slater was intrigued. "Explain yourself," she said abruptly.

"You recommended me for second-in-command, when you certainly could have had it yourself. Why would you do such a thing?" Cyric asked, wiping more sweat from his brow.

Slater grinned maliciously. "Survival. People in that position do not seem to last terribly long in the Scorpions."

Though Cyric tried to appear shocked, he was actually quite pleased. It seemed that Slater needed very little prompting to tell the truth. That could be a very useful little quirk. "Yes . . . ," the thief said at last. "I thought that something was odd about Croxton's death. Was there someone before him?"

"Yes," Slater said casually, swatting at a fly that was buzzing around her. "His name was Erskine."

"What happened to him?"

"Dead," Slater stated flatly. "What else?"

"Tyzack killed him?" Cyric gasped, perhaps a bit too melodramatically. "Why?"

The warrior shook her head and shrugged. "Who's to say? We were on our way back from Haptooth Hill. Tyzack, Erskine, Ren, and Croxton had gone off to forage for dinner. Everyone except Erskine returned. We were told that it was an accident. They had separated to cover more ground, and Ren placed a shaft in Erskine . . . by mistake. They buried him in a shallow grave, and we moved on."

This time, they left Croxton for the crows with the dead Sembians, Cyric thought. He didn't even merit a shallow grave. "Maybe they were telling the truth," the lean thief suggested.

Slater bit her lip, then let out a deep breath. "Erskine was a troublemaker. He had known Tyzack for many years, even before the formation of our company. The man was loud and stupid, and he took liberties no one in the company would ever dream of risking. Erskine courted death until, one day, it came to collect him. We were all glad to be rid of him."

"Why are you willing to tell me all this?" Cyric asked after a moment. The thief felt he knew the answer, but he wanted Slater to say the words aloud and commit herself to the course of action they would imply.

The woman looked at the thief for a moment, then glanced back at the Zhentish following them. "Because Tyzack is weak," Slater stated without emotion. "He's not a warrior. His dreams consist of a comfortable place somewhere in the bureaucracy of the Black Network. His reticence to engage in battle has cost us days of travel. By the time we reach Scardale, the war may be over. If not, our task will be to protect Tyzack's life at all cost.

"The other Zhentilar, the ones who follow brave leaders, will be awarded the glory and honor of conquering our enemies for Lord Bane. If I can help it, I will not be denied that opportunity," Slater growled and put her hand back on her crossbow's stock.

"What do you mean to do?" Cyric said, again trying to look innocent.

"Don't be coy!" Slater hissed. "Your talents do not lie in the art of deception, no matter how much you believe they do."

Cyric looked ahead. They would soon catch up to Willingale, the point man.

"I know you, Cyric. You're a thief. You're a murderer. And you're ambitious," Slater growled. "Lie to the others, if you want. Not to me. I can help you . . . and help myself by doing so."

The warrior gripped the mane of her horse as she said, "The time to act may not come until we are in the thick of battle in Scardale. All we may have to do is allow ourselves to be distracted long enough for an enemy sword to take Tyzack's head off."

"Good," Cyric said, dropping his facade of innocence. "And if the opportunity comes sooner?"

The woman narrowed her eyes again and looked at the thief as if she was seeing him for the very first time. "Then we will take it," Slater said. "Afterward, you will give me my own command. Thirty good soldiers would do. That way, if your blood turns out to be as thin as Tyzack's, we will not find each other in opposition. I will take my soldiers to battle. You will do whatever you wish. Agreed?" The Zhentish soldier looked directly at Cyric's eyes now, waiting for his reply.

"Agreed!" Cyric said after a moment, returning Slater's stare.

Willingale was almost within hearing range, so Cyric let the conversation die. And as the Scorpions approached, the heavyset Zhentish soldier turned and signaled them to hurry to his side. "Glad you came out here, sir," Willingale said to Cyric. "You've saved me the trouble of coming back to report." He pointed. "There's something on the horizon."

The thief followed Willingale's finger and saw a bright, steady light in the distance. The pitted, mountainous rise to the right flank of the Zhentish forces provided no cover for the troops from whatever was creating the light. In fact, there was absolutely no sign of natural protection within three hundred yards in either direction.

"It could be a trap," Willingale said, scratching his chin. "Our enemy could be waiting in the ribs off the spine of that rise. The rifts could hold a hundred men or more."

"Perhaps," Cyric answered. "But why alert us to the danger? Why not just lie in wait, then take us by surprise? There must be some other explanation."

"It could be just some natural reflection of the sunlight . . . or even some manifestation of the chaos in nature," Slater noted, reigning in her horse. "The light never seems to change."

"We'll ride back and inform Tyzack," Cyric said to the point man. "Keep watching, and let us know if you see anything else, but don't go any farther. When the company catches up to you, you'll get new orders."

Willingale nodded as Cyric and Slater turned and rode back to the main body of the Zhentish army. The female soldier remained silent for a moment, then noted, "An ambush would give us just the opportunity we're after, Cyric."

"At the expense of how many of our fellow Zhentilar, or even our own lives?" the thief asked gruffly. "There will be better opportunities than this. Besides, we have another problem—Ren. He blends into the background so well that I hardly notice he's around. Yet he seems to be Tyzack's true second-in-command, no matter who holds the actual title. Any plans we make will have to take his interference into account."

The thief and the warrior arrived at the front line of the Zhentish advance. Tyzack and Ren were waiting for them. The leader of the Scorpions trembled with barely controlled rage.

"Would the two of you like to explain yourselves?" Tyzack screamed. The dark-haired man waved his fist in the air as if he were shaking dice.

Cyric looked to Slater, then back to Tyzack. "I don't understand. What did we do that requires explanation?"

"Spare me," Tyzack growled. "Word came to me that the two of you left the ranks, and so I was forced to come to the front and investigate. The penalty for desertion is—"

The thief's features turned as hard as stone. "Am I your second-in-command?"

Tyzack flinched. "What has that to do with anything? You will be treated exactly the same as any other Zhentilar."

"You're wrong," Cyric snapped. "As second-in-command, it's my duty to see that your policies are followed to the letter when you are not present to enforce them."

The dark eyes of the Zhentish leader narrowed.

"Willingale was staying far too close to the main body," Cyric continued, pointing toward the soldier as he spoke. "He is not a Scorpion and does not know your views about serving as point man for the Zhentilar." The thief paused and smiled. "Of course, *we* both know that if Willingale was close enough for our men to see him too clearly—which he was—then he was far too close to be an effective scout. Slater and I informed him of his error." Again the thief paused. This time, however, he turned to look at the Zhentish woman. "That's when he pointed out the strange light on the horizon—right, Slater?"

Ren leaned close to the company's leader and whispered something in his ear. "What strange light?" Tyzack asked as soon as Ren had finished speaking to him. "What's causing it?"

Cyric forced a look of bewilderment onto his face. "We don't know," the thief said. He related what he and Slater had seen—and their personal views of the situation—to Tyzack. "I instructed Willingale to hold his position until you caught up with him."

The black-haired Zhentish leader ran a hand through his tangled hair and grinned a wolfish smile. "All right," he muttered, motioning to Ren. "Let's bring the company to a halt. It may be nothing, but someone is going to have to investigate before we can ride any farther."

The Zhentish leader then turned to the hawk-nosed thief. "Cyric, since you seem to have unlimited amounts of initiative today, the task of discovering the nature of the strange light goes to you . . . and Ren. Slater will remain with me. Your climbing skills may come in handy. Scale that southern rise and follow its path until you can tell what's producing the light."

Cyric's heart skipped a beat as he stared into Ren's narrow face. The man's eyes were cold, emotionless. Ren stared back at Cyric as if the thief were a corpse that didn't have the sense to lie down and allow itself to be buried. In short, Tyzack's orders were a death sentence, and both Cyric and Ren knew it.

"Be careful up there. With all the gaps and rifts, it would be a shame if either of you had an accident," Tyzack said, still grinning evilly. Ren nodded and gestured for Cyric to lead the way.

"Of course," Cyric said cheerfully, pretending that the Zhentish leader's orders had no particular significance. Yet, as the thief kicked the sides of his mount and prodded the beast forward, he growled, "Good-bye, Tyzack . . . Slater."

Ren followed close behind the thief, and the two men were no more than a hundred feet away from the Zhentish column when Tyzack and Slater both screamed. Cyric turned, confused . . . until he saw the shining, diamond-shaped sliver of steel approaching from the east, tumbling end-over-end as it pierced the air, heading directly toward the main body of Zhentilar—toward Slater and Tyzack.

The hawk-nosed thief drew his dagger and tossed the weapon in one fluid motion. Cyric's knife sailed through the air and passed the deadly shard, which was only slightly larger than the dagger itself, an instant too soon. The flechette continued on. Suddenly the sound of metal striking metal echoed through the air. Although it was a small sound, very high-pitched, Cyric started as he heard it.

Ren had tossed one of his own daggers and deflected the steel shard from its path. Slater and Tyzack were safe.

The thief forced his body to relax as he focused his attention on Ren. The Zhentilar was, quite possibly, Cyric's equal with a blade, and that knowledge made the thief thankful that they had been temporarily recalled from their "mission." Cyric knew that it was up to him to make the reprieve permanent.

His original plan had been to kill Ren on the skeletal ridge, then escape over the southern side of the rise and head for the Ashaba. But without a horse or supplies, his chances for survival were slim. Should Tyzack turn vengeful and order just a few Zhentish soldiers to track him down, his chances were downright dismal. And returning to the advance with Ren dead would have been out of the question, too. Tyzack would have executed Cyric on the spot. So, since the mission to the ridge was a no-win situation, the thief knew that he had to find a way to turn the current situation in his favor.

Slater stared at the ground six feet before her, where the two-foot-long sliver of steel had fallen. She looked at Cyric and saw the frustration in his face, then turned to Ren and said, "My thanks."

"I am here to serve," the blond Zhentilar replied, his voice low and scratchy.

Tyzack was staring off at the horizon. "What *was* that?" he asked, visibly shaken.

Ren leaped from his mount and reached down to grab both his dagger and the diamond-shaped metal shard. The blond man picked up his knife, but there was a hissing sound the moment Ren's hand touched the steel sliver. The Zhentilar drew back, holding his right hand in his left.

"Damn!" he growled. "The sliver burns!"

"There must be a sorcerer involved," Tyzack hissed as he tried to regain his composure. "I see no one near, and nothing could have thrown that shard all the way from the rise. It's simply too far away."

The thief instinctively thought of Midnight, then chided himself for the foolish thought. The mage would never be stupid enough to confront a three-hundred-man regiment of Zhentilar. Then a thought occurred to the thief. "If it was a mage, it might explain the light in the distance," Cyric noted aloud.

Suddenly a shadow passed over the Zhentish forces, and an audible gasp erupted from the troops. As Cyric looked up, his hand moving onto the hilt of his dagger, the thief saw a swirling mass of glittering light hovering above them. Squinting, Cyric realized that, although he was looking full into the sun, a curtain of steel fragments hung in the sky, blocking his view. Sparks of light refracted from the myriad surfaces of a storm cloud formed from metal shards.

"What is *that?*" Tyzack cried, his voice cracking. The Zhentish leader reached over and clawed at Slater's shoulder, trying to get her attention. The warrior shrunk away from Tyzack's touch as she controlled an urge to grasp the man's hand, yank him from his mount, and cut his throat as he fell.

Instead, Slater yelled, "Don't touch me!" and shoved Tyzack's hand away.

"Tyzack!" Ren murmured, disquiet showing in his ragged voice. "What are your orders?"

A single shard fell from the heavens like a drop of water dripping from the tip of an icicle that had begun to melt. Tyzack tore his gaze from the skies and covered the back of his head with his arms, then he thrust his face into the mane of his horse. From a hundred feet behind the black-haired leader, there was a scream.

"It got Sykes in the leg!" someone shouted.

Some of the Zhentish soldiers had begun to break ranks, scattering across the flat, open field. "There's nowhere to hide!" someone screamed, and a ripple of panicked cries arose from the troops.

Cyric watched the leader of the Zhentilar quake and moan in fear. "Ren's right!" the hawk-nosed thief growled as Tyzack slowly raised his head. Contempt for the coward raged within Cyric as he cried, "You must give an order!"

Tyzack was about to speak when another shard fell from the sky, this one sailing toward the front of the advance, where the Scorpions had gathered. Praxis was struck in the shoulder by the sliver of metal, and he howled in agony as the sharp tip exited the back of his arm.

"I'm—I'm burning!" Praxis screamed as a grayish black mist rose from the wound. The soldier tried to pluck out the shard, but the effort only caused him greater pain.

Cyric and Ren turned to face the rest of the Zhentish army. Both men shouted for calm, then looked at Tyzack, waiting for the man to speak. Discord was spreading through the ranks, and individual leaders were trying to take control of the individual factions within the force.

"We're . . . dead!" Tyzack whispered as he stared at the heavens. "There is no place to go!"

Cyric forced his horse over alongside Tyzack's. He grabbed the black-haired man by the collar and shook him hard. "Don't say that!" the thief hissed. "You'll lose control of the men." Cyric was surprised to see that Ren didn't make a move to stop him.

"The blades!" Tyzack cried. "There are so many of them, and they're getting bigger! Look!"

Looking toward the sky, Cyric saw that the mass of shining silver blades was slowly descending.

"Ride!" Tyzack muttered, his voice as soft as a child's.

A half-dozen shards dropped from the sky like ripe apples from a tree. Those Zhentilar that had shields now struggled to free them from their backs or their saddles. Screams went up from the rear and center of the advance.

Cyric looked to Slater. "What did he say?"

Ren glared at the thief. "Tyzack said to ride! We must reach the shelter of the southern rise before the shards drop from the sky!" The blond fighter kicked his horse into motion, and a large group of soldiers followed him.

The rain of metal shards increased, as if the bottom of the huge, invisible box that had been holding them were torn open, allowing the flechettes to plummet to the ground. Screams sounded from throughout the ranks. Handfuls of Zhentilar were struck down, dead or gravely wounded.

"Ride!" Tyzack screamed as if he had suddenly realized the danger. The black-haired man kicked at the sides of his mount, propelling the beast forward.

In seconds, Cyric found himself racing toward the auburn, skeletal ridge. The shadow caused by the cloud of knives was deepening, and it seemed to be following the Zhentish army. The cries of the Zhentilar who were struck down by the shards filled the air, their shrill screeches cutting through the dull roar made by hundreds of galloping horses.

The Zhentilar are at my back, Cyric mused. Then suddenly his amusement turned to fear. He felt exposed and very much alone at the front of the horde of charging soldiers. The thief's shoulders tightened, and he strained to listen for any mount that was closing on him, knowing that at any moment the rain of steel from above could end all of his problems.

The thief focused on the ridge, even though he thought their flight was useless. Then one of the rifts leading off from the skeletal hills beckoned, growing larger, its night-black shadow opening wide in front of the soldiers like the maw of a hungry animal. More and more Zhentish riders were struck by the shards. The lucky ones were killed outright. The unlucky ones fell from their horses and were trampled beneath the hooves of their comrades' mounts.

Slater was still riding near Cyric when they finally reached the mouth of the rift, where Ren and a majority of the Zhentish that had followed him had taken refuge. The soldiers' abandoned horses raced around, frantically trying to avoid the burning pieces of metal. From the number of horses either wounded or riderless at the end of the rift, Cyric judged that a hundred men had already taken refuge inside it.

But inside the ten-foot-wide gap, the Zhentish were faring no better than those still out on the plain. "This is absurd!" Cyric cried. Then a flechette smashed into his horse's neck, and the mount tossed the thief onto the ground. Luckily for the thief, however, he was close enough to the rift that the riders behind him had slowed their pace enough to avoid trampling him. Still, Cyric was momentarily shaken by the fall.

Before the thief could utter a word of protest, Slater grabbed him by the arm, and they were forced into the dark, cool rift by the flood of soldiers desperately crowding into the opening. Once in the rift, Cyric grabbed a rough wooden shield from a trampled body and raised it over his head. Slater, taller than the thief, had to crouch slightly to remain beneath its cover. The warm, smelly crush of bodies surrounded the thief and the warrior, and Cyric cursed loudly whenever he was bumped or pushed.

"They're not using their heads!" the thief yelled to Slater, who cowered next to him, listening to the frantic cries of the Zhentish and the hiss of falling shards. Above the Zhentilar, the rain of shards continued. The walls of the rift helped to slow the metal fragments; many struck the rock first, then tumbled with decreased momentum toward the soldiers, burning them but not killing them. But many knives still fell directly into the ranks, and the screams of the dying filled the rift with horrible echoes.

"Use your shields!" Cyric screamed, then Slater joined him in the cry, trying to make their voices heard above the din. A dozen soldiers immediately surrounded the thief, looking to him for orders, their eyes wide and frightened. But Cyric's words seemed to slice through the chaos as surely as the sharp edge of a blade through unarmored flesh. "Use your shields! If you don't have a shield, crawl under a corpse!"

More soldiers turned to Cyric and obeyed his commands.

"Interlock the shields, then—" Cyric screamed as a burning metal shard pierced his shield, striking his arm. There was a hiss, and the hawk-nosed man felt his flesh burning. He gritted his teeth and turned to Slater. "Anchor the shield. I've been hit."

The Zhentish woman complied with Cyric's commands. As the thief pulled his arm away from the shield—and the shard that still hissed at its center—a group of nearly fifty soldiers with shields closed ranks around the thief, near the center of the rift.

"Give the tallest men the shields!" Cyric yelled, holding his hand over the blackened wound. "Those without shields, stay low, under the protection!"

The shards continued to fall, but now the sound of shields being struck echoed through the cavern, drowning out the moans of the wounded and replacing the screams of the dying. Of course, occasionally the steel slivers found the meaty forearms on the undersides of the shields, but no one complained.

Cyric tore part of his shirt and wrapped a hasty bandage around his arm. "Forget the pain!" he cried. "At least you aren't dead!" Then he moved between the huddled men as best as he could to give orders to another segment of the frightened troops, Slater always at his side. "Those of you on the ground, help the wounded. Forget the dead; they can't be helped! Keep those shields up if you want to stay alive!" Cyric yelled, slapping some men on the back, encouraging others as he moved through the ranks.

Cyric's plan was working. Throughout the rift, more than one hundred Zhentilar with shields huddled under the network of protection.

At one point, as Cyric sat resting while Slater rebandaged his wound, she asked Cyric how he had thought of having the men use their shields as one instead of separately.

The thief smiled, or at least came as close to smiling as he had since the deadly rain had begun. "Storming a castle once . . . long ago. It's called 'forming a tortoise,' " the thief said. "It keeps your troops from getting slaughtered when the enemy decides to drop oil on your head or have their archers fire a rain of arrows at you." He looked up at the men holding the shields over him. "It's really quite simple."

"Cyric!" a low, throaty voice called from the huddled soldiers.

The thief spun and saw Ren crawling toward him, without a shield, his shirt torn and bloody from a number of small wounds.

"Tyzack's dead," the blond soldier rumbled. "He froze when death looked him in the eye, the coward."

Both men stood and stared at each other for a while, waiting for the storm to pass. Eventually the steady thump of shards hitting the shields lessened, then stopped altogether. The hiss of the still-warm fragments singeing the shields remained, as did the murmurs of the men and the cries of the wounded. Many of the men holding shields had begun to lower them. but Cyric shouted for them to hold their shields up until he gave orders to the contrary.

The thief turned back to Ren. "If Tyzack's dead—," Cyric began, his brow furrowed.

"Then you're our leader now," Ren said and bowed his head slightly. "I live to serve."

The thief's head was swimming. Cyric quickly considered turning command over to someone else, but that would almost certainly turn out to be Ren, and that would most likely mean Cyric's death. As usual, the hawk-nosed man was sure that he wasn't being given a choice. "But *who* do you serve, Ren?"

Ren frowned. "As I said, I live to serve. You saved the men. You should lead them." The blond man paused and ran a hand across his dirty, blood-smeared face. "There is no reason to fear me . . . for now, anyway."

The thief ignored the last comment. "Show me Tyzack's body," Cyric said quietly.

The two men maneuvered some distance through the shield bearers. Finally Ren pointed toward a dead man lying ten feet beyond the last Zhentilar with a shield. Although darkness was now descending, Cyric could see that a metal shard had pierced Tyzack's chest, very near his heart. And the thief noticed something else: Tyzack's throat had been cut. The shards would not have been so efficient, Cyric thought as he turned to stare at Ren.

The thief stepped out from beneath the shields and looked up at the empty sky. Metal fragments lay on the ground all around him, some still red hot. Ren followed Cyric out from under the shell of shields and joined the new leader of the two hundred or so Zhentish soldiers that had survived the rain of death.

"Tell me," the thief rumbled as Ren came to his side, "what secret did Tyzack bear that was so horrible he had you kill to protect it?"

The blond man paused for a moment and looked down at Tyzack's body. "Lately he'd become frantic that someone would discover what he'd done a long time ago at a small temple to Bane north of here." The guard looked up at Cyric. "Tyzack was hot-blooded and idealistic in his younger days, and he foolishly decided to revolt against the Black Network because they wouldn't accept him as a cleric. He raided a temple and slaughtered the young Zhentarim who had been sequestered there. If anyone from the Zhentarim ever found out—"

"It would mean his head," the thief concluded. Then Cyric laughed. "Tyzack was a fool! What he did might actually have put him in good stead with some of the powers in Zhentil Keep."

The soldier frowned and lowered his eyes. Cyric smiled and whispered, "I've done far worse than Tyzack ever dreamed of, Ren. But you won't have to protect my secrets. I take care of that myself." The blond man's frown deepened, and the thief turned away from him. "We'll wait another twenty minutes. It should be safe to send out scouts by then."

Cyric paused and looked down at Tyzack's body. "And then you can announce me as your new leader," the hawk-nosed man said proudly and walked back to rejoin the ranks of his men.

❧ 10 ❧

The Escape

"There's someone here to see you," Varden said softly as he walked into the small room where Midnight and her allies were hidden.

Midnight turned from her spellbook, which was braced upon a splintering crate, and looked to the figures standing in the safe house door.

"Kelemvor!" Midnight gasped as she watched the fighter step into the amber light of the single small lantern that lit the room. The mage rose so quickly that she nearly knocked her book to the floor.

"You look like hell," Midnight said, glancing at the leg irons the fighter still wore. Her lips trembled as she tried to smile. "How did you—"

But as the green-eyed fighter moved toward the mage, Varden stepped in front of him. As the fighter watched, three other members of the resistance—the old man and old woman who owned the safe house, and a rough-looking Sembian soldier—moved to block the room's exits.

"I escaped from one set of captors into the arms of another, it seems. May I sit down?" Kelemvor asked, gesturing with his fingers toward a vacant chair beside the raven-haired mage. Midnight nodded and studied the fighter as he walked to the chair in a series of short steps that might have seemed comical were it not for the severity of his condition. By the flickering light from the lantern, Midnight could see the scars, cuts, bruises, and burns that lined Kelemvor's body. His clothing had become rags, and Midnight was reminded of the first time she had admitted her feelings for the fighter, in the corridors of Castle Kilgrave. Kelemvor had not looked much better then.

The fighter's hands trembled as he muttered, "I haven't eaten in days. If I'm going to be tortured, can I at least have something to eat first?"

The old woman moved past Varden and Adon to the door. "I need to check on Gratus anyway," she croaked and left the room.

"How do you think he found us?" the craggy Sembian soldier said to Varden.

Looking up sharply, Kelemvor glared at the gruff soldier. "You can ask me if you want to know something about that," the fighter snarled. "I overheard my guards mention this place as a possible safe house. They didn't think I was going to survive, and they talked in front of me as if I wasn't even there, just as you are doing."

The others in the room, including Adon, silently stared at Kelemvor, wondering just how much of what the fighter said was the truth. Midnight, however, had no such problems with her former lover's story. "Are we going to get these chains off him?" the mage cried as she looked around the room at her other allies.

"We can't do that," the old man mumbled, running a hand over his bald head.

"He's right, Midnight. What proof do we have—," Varden began to add.

Midnight stood up and glowered at Varden. "What proof do you need? Kelemvor is our ally . . . *my* friend." The mage paused for a moment and her voice sank into a growl. "And if you don't release him, I will."

"But he came directly from Bane's garrison," the old man said. "He could have led the Zhentilar right to us!"

The cursed fighter bowed his head and sighed. "I wouldn't have to lead them here. They know where you are," Kelemvor mumbled.

The old man shook his head and looked around the room. "Then why haven't they attacked us?" he asked sarcastically. "We're still here, aren't we?"

"Listen to me," Midnight said coldly before the fighter could speak. "I want the chains removed, and I want food brought here. Immediately. Or I'll cast a spell that will raze this entire building."

There was a moment of silence, then the old man stood and muttered, "You win, mage. We'll do as you ask. But I will not have you threaten me again. I don't take well to threats . . . particularly from those who have sought asylum with me."

Varden took out his lockpicks and unlocked the fighter's leg irons, then moved away quickly.

"Now his hands," Midnight told the young thief.

Adon held up his hand to stop the thief from following Midnight's request. "What if you're wrong?" he asked. "What if he's here to capture you?" The scarred cleric pointed at the fighter and added, "He was our friend . . . once. But it wouldn't be the first time he's led a patrol after us."

The raven-haired mage was silent for a moment, then turned toward the cleric. "You must trust me, Adon. I know that Kelemvor wouldn't harm us." When the cleric bowed his head, the magic-user softly said, "Varden, unlock the other chains."

Varden turned away, a scowl on his face. "All right," the thief muttered and did as she asked.

When the irons clanked to the floor, Midnight sighed with relief. "Now I want all of you to leave us alone for a moment," the mage told her allies.

"Absolutely not," said the old man, shuffling forward a few steps.

"Please," Midnight cried. "Do as I ask, and we won't trouble you anymore. We'll leave. Now that Kelemvor's back, we can leave."

"Very well," the old man grumbled. "If that's the way you want it."

"That's the way it has to be," Midnight answered, turning toward the fighter.

Adon, Varden, the old man, and the Sembian filed from the room. "We'll be just outside this door," Adon said, glowering a bit at Kelemvor. In moments, the room was cleared and the door swung shut.

"Oh, Kel," Midnight cried, her emotions threatening to overwhelm her as she embraced the fighter. "You don't know how good it is to see you." She kissed his cheek, then brushed the hair from his face. "Are you all right?"

"I will be," he replied, sitting up straight again.

Midnight kissed him full on the lips, then drew back as she realized that he had not returned the kiss. Something was wrong.

The mage furrowed her eyebrows and looked into Kelemvor's eyes. "What happened? What did they do to you?" Midnight asked as she backed away from the fighter.

"That should be obvious," Kelemvor growled, glancing at the dried blood on his clothes. The fighter stood and kicked the chains at his feet. "I don't want to talk about it. Not yet."

"We tried to rescue you," Midnight told the fighter. "We couldn't get into the garrison. Durrock found us . . ."

There was a momentary flicker of understanding in Kelemvor's eyes.

"Kel, I was so afraid for you. For both of us," Midnight cried, tears running down her cheeks. "We've got to get out of this city."

"It'll be difficult," Kelemvor noted distantly as he looked around the small room. In fact, he found himself looking at anything but the mage's eyes.

Midnight wondered why Kelemvor was being so cold and distant. Anger could have been the explanation, but it made no sense that his rage would be directed at her. Perhaps it was the strain of his recent incarceration. She stared into his eyes and saw it was neither of these. Varden and Adon might have been right.

"Something's happened to you, Kelemvor. And you should know me well enough to understand that you can trust me with whatever has happened." The mage paused and looked at the door. "You can whisper if you must, if you're afraid of the others overhearing," Midnight told her former lover.

"There is nothing to tell," Kelemvor said, smiling weakly. "I just need a meal. I need to clean my wounds. You're letting your imagination get the better of you."

Midnight gazed into his eyes. The fighter was lying.

"I suppose you're right," the magic-user said coldly as she turned from Kelemvor. "Varden knows a way out of the city, but we will require your assistance. Will you help?"

A look of confusion crossed the fighter's face. "Of course I will."

"Then it's settled," Midnight snapped, reaching for her dagger and drawing the weapon from its sheath. "It's settled that you betrayed us!"

Kelemvor made no move as the point of Midnight's dagger found his throat in a ferocious, quicksilver motion. The mage stopped her hand, and the knife's point touched the fighter's skin but didn't break it.

"You are bound by your curse, Kelemvor," the mage hissed. "You can do nothing without promise of a reward. Yet when I asked you to help us get out of the city, you asked for nothing in return. That means that someone has already paid you . . . to lead us into a trap!"

The fighter closed his eyes and took a sharp breath. "Everything you've said is wrong. Even about the curse."

"What?" Midnight cried, confusion on her face. "The curse is gone? Who removed it?"

The fighter swallowed, then his hand shot out and grabbed Midnight's wrist. He twisted until the dagger fell to the ground. Kelemvor spun Midnight around, knocking her from her feet, and wrapped one of his powerful arms around her neck. With his free arm, Kelemvor steadied the mage before she could fall and pinned her arms to her body. Varden and Adon rushed into the room.

The blond thief drew his dagger and Adon hefted the war hammer that the old man had given him when they first entered the safe house. "Let her go, you Zhentish dog," the thief yelled.

"Not until I've had my say!" the fighter growled. "So just stay back and listen." Adon took a step forward and Kelemvor tightened his grip on the mage. "I'll break her neck if you come any closer," the fighter lied.

When the thief and the cleric stood still, Kelemvor began his story. "Bane did send me here to gain your confidence. I was to lead you all out of the safe house, subdue Midnight, and bring her to the Black Lord."

Adon cursed and spat at Kelemvor's feet. "How much did he pay you, Kel? What did you trade our lives for?"

Midnight tried to struggle, but Kelemvor tightened his

grip again. "Bane removed my curse," he hissed. "But I lied to Bane, the way he lied to me. I never intended to bring you to him. I want to go to Tantras with you, help you finish this damned quest . . . because you're my friends." The fighter paused and loosened his grip on Midnight. "Not for any payment. Just because I care about you."

Kelemvor released Midnight and backed away. The mage fell forward, but kneeled where she fell, her back to the fighter. "I want to believe you, Kel. I don't know how I can trust you after all that's happened . . . but I do."

"You can't be serious!" Varden cried, taking a step toward the fighter. "He was going to kill you."

"Not likely," Adon said softly and put down his war hammer. "He could have killed her long before we rushed into the room, Varden." The cleric looked at Kelemvor, who returned his gaze with tear-filled eyes. "I know about suffering, Kel. Mine is not like yours, but all who suffer know what it is to want their pain to end." Adon walked to Kelemvor's side and put his hand on the fighter's shoulder. "Perhaps I'd even lie to a god to end mine, too."

By now the Sembian soldier and the married couple who ran the safe house had rushed to the room. As they stood in the doorway, Varden muttered a curse and turned to them. "It's nothing," he grumbled. "They seem to have worked it out for themselves."

"Well, the sooner you're gone, the better," the old woman croaked as she brought some food into the room on a tray. Then the old couple, Varden, and the Sembian left the heroes alone.

Midnight, Adon, and Kelemvor talked as the fighter ate. And though Cyric was missing, the little time the three heroes had together in the safe house was the happiest they had shared for a long time.

An hour later, after gathering their few belongings and acquiring mounts, clothing for Kelemvor, and supplies, the heroes left the safe house. Varden rode beside Kelemvor at the front of the small band. The thief knew the best route through the city, but the fighter knew how to avoid the Zhentilar.

The heroes secured their horses three blocks from the

harbor and walked the rest of the way. As they reconnoitered the port, Kelemvor began to relax. Despite the Zhentilar that were stationed there, the vast stretches of the shipping yards made the area impossible to secure with any degree of certainty. Only a single watchman stood between the heroes and the *Queen of the Night*, an ebon slave ship used by the Zhentilar to transport illegal cargo and avoid taxation.

"We'll need a boat with speed and power if we're to escape the blockade," Varden said as they studied the slave galley. "What could be better than one of Bane's best?"

On the bow, a huge, half-naked wildman with bright yellow hair had been chained to a post and was enduring the lashes of the galley master's whip. The slave hurled curses and threats at his tormentor, and the heroes were able to see the slave's face for a moment. One of the wildman's eyes was missing, as if it had been gouged out in a fight.

"Had enough?" the galley master called as he lowered the whip.

"Set me free!" the slave wailed. "I'll rip your arms from their sockets and beat you with them. Then I'll tear your head off and—"

Enraged, the galley master cracked his whip again. The slave's threat was never finished. The black-garbed galley master whipped the slave until the man sank to his knees and his head lolled back, a vacant expression in his eyes. "Bjorn the One-Eyed will have his revenge," the slave muttered and passed out.

"Take him below," the galley master snapped to one of the three Zhentilar who also stood on the bow. "We'll resume our . . . discussion after I return from Scardale. I'm going to find a lass to help me relieve my tensions!"

The guards laughed and nodded as they dragged the slave away.

On the dock, Kelemvor turned to Midnight. "Perhaps you could—"

The mage froze the fighter with her stare. "Even if I pretended to be a trollop, it would do no good. These men have been given my description. They would see through the ruse in an instant."

"There's only one place the galley master can go that's close by, and the proprietor is a friend of mine," Varden said softly. "We can take him when he gets there."

Kelemvor watched as the galley master, a short, strongly built man with a thick, black mustache, left the boat and approached the lone watchman near the heroes.

"We should ambush him in the shadows and save ourselves the bother," Adon said quietly, lifting his war hammer slightly to emphasize his words.

Adon's suggestion surprised Kelemvor. "I'll go along with that," the fighter said and smiled at the cleric. "But only if the opportunity presents itself as we follow him to this establishment run by Varden's friend."

The heroes tried to follow the galley master, but the short man kept to streets that were heavily patrolled. Within a few minutes, they had lost him.

"It doesn't matter," Varden muttered as the heroes hid in a darkened alley. "He went in the direction of the Fatted Calf Tavern, just as I thought he would."

The thief knew a short cut, and the heroes were soon at the rear of the tavern, in a dark, dirty alley. "Wait here," Varden whispered. The thief went around to the front of the tavern and vanished inside.

Five minutes later, the tavern's rear door opened, and Varden stood silhouetted in light, grinning from ear to ear. "Good evening and welcome to the Fatted Calf," the thief announced proudly as he ushered the heroes inside. "May I take your order?"

Kelemvor allowed his allies to go in before him, then he closed the door. The room they entered was very small and decorated with beautiful, multicolored veils that were draped from various points in the wall and ceiling. The light in the room came from lanterns, and shades of soft blue and red played across the heroes' features. A bed, a table, and a few chairs made up the furnishings.

"The galley master's name is Otto," Varden noted. "My fiance will be bringing him in here any moment." He turned to Kelemvor, who had hefted a small chair. "Do be careful not to hit the girl."

Midnight laughed. "*You're* going to be married?"

Varden shrugged. "I had to keep telling this wench something to get her to go along with my wild schemes—like this one." He paused and smiled. "Besides, her father owns the tavern. There's money in this family."

There was a sound at the door, and from his position next to the entrance, Kelemvor motioned for silence. The other heroes crowded on the other side of the door, out of the line of view of anyone entering. The smell of bad liquor wafted into the room before the galley master, and the sound of celebration came from the taproom as the door opened.

Otto the galley master stumbled into the room on the arm of a beautiful woman dressed in bright, golden robes, pulled tightly to display her perfect figure. Her hair was the color of honey and matched her clothing. Bits of jewelry sparkled from her hands, neck, and waist. Her features were stunning, and she had captured the attentions of the galley master completely.

Kelemvor grimaced. The woman was on his side of the door. But as she entered the room, Varden's fiance cried out, tripped, and fell forward. The galley master bent instinctively, and Kelemvor crashed the chair over his head. Varden slammed the door shut and locked it behind them.

"I want a ring, and I want a ceremony," the golden-haired woman told Varden. "None of this sneaking about in the middle of the night and getting married in the Hall of Records. Do you understand me, Varden?"

The thief opened his mouth.

"Further, this thieving business is out of the question. You've never made enough at it to convince me it's a viable means of earning a living. I thought you could apprentice with Daddy, then—"

"Shut up and kiss me," Varden said as he grabbed her waist and pulled the woman to him. Their lips met, and the kiss lasted long enough for Kelemvor to drag Otto to the bed and set him on it.

Varden's fiance sighed. "I thought I was going to have to talk about our old age together before you got motivated to do that."

Varden smirked and turned to the heroes. "This is Liane."

The woman bowed slightly, then looked to Otto. "What

are you going to do with him?' "

"The question is, my dear, 'what are *we* going to do with him.'" Varden said.

Adon watched the lovers in silence. There was a time, not very long ago, when he had played Varden's role: the lover, the fool. Liane caught sight of the cleric and shuddered when she saw the scar that lined his face. Adon had grown used to the reaction, but a slight shiver of pain ran up his spine. He turned away to open the door and check the alley.

Twenty minutes later, Varden and Liane stood on either side of the galley master as they dragged him back to his ship. The lone watchman approached, and the galley master mumbled incoherently. The stink of the cheap wine wafted from the short man.

"Tipped back a few too many," Varden said, just loud enough for the heroes to hear him from their hiding place a few yards away. The watchman laughed, made a few crude jokes, and gestured for the trio to move along.

"Say, you're a cute little thing," the grubby dock guard commented to Liane when he noticed the woman staring at him with a wicked grin. "If you go on that ship, we'll never see you again. All the fine young men on board will never let you go!"

Liane sauntered to the watchman's side, leaving Varden to struggle with Otto. "What are my alternatives?" Liane asked as she circled the guard. The man turned to follow Liane with his eyes, and when his back faced the ship's walkway, Kelemvor and the others broke from the shadows and ran to help Varden with Otto. Liane threw her head back, ran her hands through her hair, and slowly traced a path down the luscious, smooth skin of her neck, allowing her hands to come together and follow a straight line to the sash at her waist.

The watchman sighed.

In moments, Varden and the heroes had Otto on board the *Queen of the Night*. Midnight, Kelemvor, and Adon hid as Varden called out, "Fair lady, he's getting kind of heavy, and you're the prize he came ashore to find, not I, a humble serving boy!"

Kelemvor shook his head at the thief's overwrought

performance.

At the walkway, Liane said farewell to the watchman and promised to look him up when she returned from the ship. The woman tried to appear casual and unhurried as she made her way to the boat, although her hands were shaking the entire time.

The heroes dragged the galley master back through the shadows, then below deck, where the slaves waited. Bjorn the One-Eyed sat at his station, mumbling curses. Suddenly the body of the galley master fell before the slave, and he nearly jumped out of his seat. Kelemvor smiled at the slave and pulled back the flaps of the galley master's coat to reveal a huge set of keys tied to the man's waist.

"That's a sight I'll wager you hadn't expected to see this night," Kelemvor noted softly as he tore the keys from the groaning galley master and handed them to Bjorn.

"He was a cruel taskmaster," one of the slaves said from the shadows of the slave hold. "He'd beat us—whip us—for no reason."

"No one escaped his punishment," another slave cried.

The tide of condemnations grew, but the shouts abruptly ended with the sharp, metallic click of Bjorn opening his chains. The wildman stood up, a bit shaky on his feet at first, but proud and tall. In fact, the slave towered over the heroes.

Bjorn grabbed the galley master's hair and pulled the man up to look at him. "Remember the promise I made earlier this evening about what I'd do with your arms and legs?" the wildman growled. The slave grabbed a metal clamp and locked it in place around Otto's throat. "Keep thinking about it." Then the one-eyed man turned to face the heroes. "You've come to liberate us? What for? What do you want in return?"

The fighter smiled and ran a hand through his hair. "Safe passage to Tantras. Then the ship is yours," Kelemvor said.

Bjorn studied the fighter with his one good eye. A smile broke over his face, and he threw the set of keys to the next slave. "A fair deal," Bjorn decided and looked to the army of slaves. "What about the rest of you?"

There were cheers as the slaves were unchained, one by

one. Cries of allegiance to the new captain of the *Queen of the Night*, Bjorn the One-Eyed, filled the hold.

"How many of you men want to see the stars once again?" Bjorn asked. The slaves roared in approval.

Moments later, the sight of the minor skirmish taking place on the *Queen of the Night* between the freed slaves and the few Zhentish sailors still on the ship did not escape the notice of the grubby watchman. As the Zhentish were pitched overboard, alarms were sounded.

On the ship, Kelemvor watched as Adon clubbed a Zhentilar with his war hammer. The soldier was still alive, and the cleric was about to strike again when Kelemvor raised his hand. "A few should be kept alive as hostages. Perhaps they'll have information we can use!" Kelemvor ordered as he lowered the cleric's hand.

"We'd best secure the prisoners in the hold, then," the cleric noted. Looking at the harbor, Adon grimaced. The alarm had been sounded, and a few soldiers raced in their direction.

"They're more observant than I would have wagered," Kelemvor yelled, then turned to Bjorn. "Do what you have to do. Just get us out of here!"

The battle with the few Zhentilar that boarded the galley was very short. Despite their training and their superior weapons, the Zhentilar could not compensate for the large numbers of slaves that waited for them onboard the ship.

When the fighting was over, Bjorn had ordered as many of the slaves as he could spare to take their stations at the oars. The one-eyed man was now the galley master. The rhythmic sound of drums filled the night, and the *Queen of the Night* soon raised anchor and pulled away from the dock.

Soon after they had left the harbor, Midnight rushed to Kelemvor's side. "Look there," Midnight cried, pointing back toward Scardale.

Two of Bane's ships had left the dock in pursuit of the captured galley.

"Wonderful!" Bjorn cried out as he was informed of the news. "Those dogs have given us no choice. We turn and fight!"

In moments, the ship was alive with activity, and the *Queen of the Night* turned to intercept the closer of the Zhentish ships. The catapults on the deck were filled with everything the men could get their hands on, including the Zhentish corpses that had not yet been cast over the side.

From the cries of panic that sounded from the opposing ship as the *Queen* drew close, Kelemvor realized that the Zhentish were hardly prepared for this type of battle. The majority of their crew was probably on shore leave, celebrating the fall of Scardale with the crew of the *Queen of the Night* and the rest of Bane's forces.

"Ramming speed!" Bjorn cried, a maniacal glint in his one good eye.

The ships collided, and a hole was torn in the side of the pursuing Zhentish ship. The *Queen of the Night* withdrew, and the second Zhentish ship moved in to pick up survivors as the *Queen* sailed out into the Dragon Reach. But before the galley could put a hundred yards between it and the other Zhentish ship, there was a cry from the bridge. Kelemvor looked up and saw a horrible shape floating in the air above the galley.

Kelemvor's mind seemed to freeze as he realized that Bane must have discovered his betrayal. Sejanus had escaped the suits of animated armor and now sat astride his nightmare, ready to attack the galley. The assassin's bolos whirled in the air. The fighter looked to the bow and saw Midnight about to throw a spell.

"Midnight, get out of the way!" Kelemvor cried, but he was too late. The bolos flew through the air. In seconds, the weapon would wrap around Midnight's torso, and they would knock her over the edge of the ship, into the water. Sejanus would have his prisoner at last.

Suddenly Varden appeared beside the mage and shoved her to the side. The bolos wrapped around the blond thief's neck, and Midnight heard a sickening snap as her friend's neck broke. Varden fell over the side of the ship, already dead.

"No!" Midnight wailed in horror. Images of Cyric being swept away in the Ashaba flooded the mage's mind. She raised her hands once more. Her fingers moved like quicksilver, and the incantation flew from her lips so quickly that it sounded like gibberish.

The assassin reigned in the nightmare and hovered in place for an instant, the extent of his error suddenly becoming clear. A spiral of light leaped from Midnight's hands and struck the water below Sejanus. He was startled to find no ill effects from the spell. Whatever incantation the mage had tried had gone awry. Ordering his mount to descend toward their prey, the assassin charged toward the *Queen of the Night.*

But as Sejanus raced down through the air, the nightmare he rode slapping fiery hoofprints into the sky, a group of huge, black tentacles burst from the dark green water next to the galley. Pulling a knife from his boot, the assassin looked down and saw the horrible sight. Dozens of writhing, slimy limbs were rising up toward him, curling around the nightmare's legs.

This is only an illusion, Sejanus thought. These figments cannot harm me.

He was wrong.

The tentacles grabbed the assassin and his mount and carefully, methodically pulled them apart. When the last of the black limbs sank back into the Dragon Reach, Midnight collapsed. The few small pieces of Sejanus's armor that had stayed afloat for a moment after striking the water now sank beneath the bloody waves.

Several hours passed, and Midnight would not speak. Liane had been told of Varden's death, and she too had kept to herself. At highsun the following day, Midnight joined Kelemvor in the private quarters Bjorn had set aside for his guests.

The mage was still badly shaken. "How could I have done that?" she asked as she entered the cabin.

"He deserved death," Kelemvor concluded coldly. "An assassin doesn't feel remorse. He doesn't care about the agony he causes to those left behind. You've done the Realms a favor."

"That's not what I mean," Midnight said. "The spell I used. It should have been a fireball spell. That was all I had time to learn when we reached the Sembian's safe house. But something else happened. Something else completely."

Kelemvor shrugged. "Magic is unstable, remember? We both know that."

Midnight shook her head, trying to scatter the unwanted questions that had grown there since the incident. "Was that all?" the mage asked.

Kelemvor sensed the apprehension in his lover's voice. "Aye," he said, reassuring the raven-haired mage. "What else could it be?"

Midnight shuddered. "No more talk," she said as she drew the fighter close to her. "We've been apart for far too long to talk this day away."

Kelemvor kissed her, then smiled. "I told you there would be time for us," he reminded her softly.

It was the following day when the lovers left the cabin. On deck, they noticed Adon talking with Liane. The scarred cleric placed a comforting hand on the woman's back as he gestured out to sea. Liane sniffed the flower she held tightly in her hands, then leaned over the railing and faced east, toward Scardale and the spot where Varden's body had sunk beneath the sea.

"I forgive you," she said quietly and cast the flower upon the waters of the Dragon Reach.

❧ 11 ❧

Tantras

Bane was furious. News of the seizure of the *Queen of the Night* and Midnight's escape from Scardale had driven the Black Lord into such a state that he had refused to speak to anyone the entire day. Now, sitting alone in his chambers in Scardale, the fallen God of Strife muttered and cursed.

Suddenly the doors to his chamber opened and the sorceress, Tarana Lyr, entered. The blond madwoman was practically drooling with excitement.

"Why do you disturb me when I left strict orders that I wished solitude?" Bane snarled, curling his hands into fists.

The sorceress took a deep breath. "There is a man who wishes to see you, Lord Bane. He waits just outside this chamber."

"A man?" Bane asked irascibly. "Not a god?"

The blond sorceress looked at the Black Lord in confusion. "A god, Lord Bane?"

The God of Strife closed his eyes, trying to control his anger. "The presence of another god would have been sufficient cause for you to interrupt my meditation. Not the supplications of a mortal."

"I think you will see this mortal," Tarana purred, rocking back and forth on her heels.

Gripping the arms of his throne, Bane grimaced as he growled, "I do not trust you, mage, but show him in anyway."

Tarana Lyr sprinted across the length of the chamber and threw the door open wide. "He will see you now," she cooed from the door.

A lean, dark-haired man entered the chamber, and the

sorceress quietly closed the door behind him.

Bane leaped from his throne, suddenly, frighteningly aware that Fzoul had reclaimed his body.

"You!" the priest shouted in anger, and images of Cyric firing an arrow into the red-haired man at the Ashaba Bridge coursed through the mind he shared with the God of Strife. The priest's anger pushed the Black Lord's consciousness down into his mind's dark recesses. Fzoul reached out to the sorceress. "Give me your dagger!"

Cyric stood motionless, a thin film of sweat on his brow. "Lord Bane, you must listen—"

Fzoul grabbed the weapon from Tarana and advanced on the thief. "Not Bane, you imbecile! It is Fzoul Chembryl who will taste your blood this day."

The hawk-nosed thief backed away from the red-haired priest. The last thing Cyric expected was to confront Fzoul. He was certain that Bane would have crushed Fzoul's mind completely when he took the priest as an avatar.

Fzoul lunged with the knife and Cyric sidestepped as best he could. But maneuverability was limited in the chamber, and a single misstep could mean death. Cyric couldn't risk drawing a weapon. If he killed the avatar of Bane, the explosion might level the entire port town of Scardale—or the fallen god might choose his body to inhabit next. Worse still, the giggling blond sorceress was chanting and seemed prepared to release a spell.

The red-haired priest feinted to the left, then drove his body to the right, crashing into Cyric. Both men tumbled to the ground. The thief's head struck the floor with a sharp crack, and Fzoul drove the dagger toward Cyric's right eye, then stopped. The priest's eyes turned crimson, and Bane smiled as he stared into Cyric's wide, panic-filled eyes.

"Fzoul's anger surprises me sometimes," the Black Lord said casually as he climbed off the thief and handed the dagger back to the sorceress. "He has a capacity for hate greater than most gods. Excepting myself, of course."

"No need, Lord Bane," Cyric said as he struggled to his feet.

Bane turned his back on Cyric and climbed to his throne. "I hadn't expected to see you, thief," the God of Strife noted.

"Reports from my assassins told me that you were dead. Of course, my assassins have hardly been reliable these days."

Cyric shook his head, and confusion crossed his face. "Wait a minute. What happened to Fzoul?" the thief asked numbly.

Settling back in his throne, the god laughed and tapped his forehead. "The priest struggles for freedom . . . in here. We have a deal, you see. He does certain things for me. I allow him to rail at his fate and curse the world. Sometimes he gets out of control." The Black Lord paused for a moment, then smiled. "He'll be punished later," he said, seemingly to himself.

Looking off at the wall for a moment, Bane listened to Fzoul's cries for vengeance. The smile dropped from the god's face as he turned back to the thief. "I see you wear my colors, Cyric."

The thief looked down at the Zhentilar garb he had taken from the Company of the Scorpions. "I suppose I do," Cyric answered absently.

"Why have you come here, thief?" Bane asked gravely. "You should have known that a slow, painful death is the most you can hope for at my hands. You are, after all, allied with forces that seek my destruction and the fall of my empire."

"No longer, Lord Bane," Cyric stated flatly. "I entered Scardale with a troop of Zhentilar two hundred men strong, and all loyal to my command."

"Oh, I see," Bane snickered. "You seek to usurp my power. Shall I abdicate now, *Lord* Cyric?"

The hawk-nosed thief remained perfectly still, his arms at his sides, his hands open, palms to the god. The sorceress approached Cyric, squinting as she stared into his face. Next she circled the man, examining him from every vantage.

"I have no intention of challenging you," Cyric said, ignoring the giggling madwoman who still circled around him. "I wish to offer my services to your cause."

A single laugh escaped the lips of the Black Lord. In his mind, Fzoul was screaming.

You cannot trust him, the red-haired priest cried to the Black Lord. *He will betray us. The thief will destroy us both!*

Bane sent a horde of gibbering, imaginary terrors to chase away Fzoul's consciousness. *For your impudence, I may just make him your commander when I'm done, Fzoul,* the fallen god taunted to his avatar's mind as it retreated.

The god looked to the mortal who stood before him. "Tell me why I should believe you," Bane growled, the smile suddenly gone from his face. "Your cursed friend, Kelemvor, played this game with me. He made a pact, then reneged on his agreement at the first opportunity. What guarantee do I have that you would not do the same?"

Cyric started at the mention of the fighter's name. Perhaps his former allies were still alive after all. He quickly pushed all thoughts of Midnight and Kelemvor aside, though, and returned to the Black Lord's question. The answer was rather obvious. "None," the thief said firmly.

Bane raised a single eyebrow. "You're honest, anyway." The God of Strife paused, then stood. "Give me some proof that you favor my causes. Tell me about the mage."

Cyric told the Black Lord more than he ever intended to relate. He informed Bane of almost all that had occurred from the time he first met Midnight in the walled city of Arabel, to the time they were separated on the Ashaba.

"I'm intrigued," Bane said as he paced back and forth in front of his throne. "For some reason, I actually think you're telling me the truth."

"I am," Cyric told the god. "I've kept myself alive through much to offer my services to your cause." The thief smiled and then explained the intricate series of deceptions that had kept him alive from the time Yarbro and Mikkel found him on the Ashaba's banks to the present. Tarana stood by the thief with her arms folded across her breasts. The mad mage hugged herself tightly as the bloodshed and violence was exposed by Cyric's casual narrative.

Bane shook his head as Cyric concluded his gory tale. "In the last few weeks, you've betrayed everything you once held dear. What do I offer that you want so badly?"

"Power," Cyric snapped, a little too emphatically. "The power to shake empires one day."

The Black Lord's lips trembled in amusement. "You sound more like a rival than an ally, thief."

Cyric took a step toward Bane's throne. "The Realms are very large, Black Lord. When you have conquered them all, you will certainly be able to spare a small kingdom for me. After all, a true god cannot bother himself with the petty day-to-day operations of an entire world." The thief paused and took another step toward the God of Strife. "Give me a kingdom to run."

The Black Lord was stunned. "You have a gifted tongue, Cyric. Perhaps I should not waste such skills by slaughtering you where you stand, though that would be amusing." Bane gestured for the sorceress to draw near. She had backed herself into a corner, near the door. "Have Durrock released from his torments and brought before me. We are going to give the thief a chance to hang himself."

Tarana bowed and raced from the chamber.

When she was gone, Bane walked to the thief's side. "Now that my insane assistant has scampered away, is there anything about the mage you have not told me?"

A name flashed into Cyric's mind. Midnight's *true name.* The words were poised on the end of his tongue, but he drew them back. With that information, the Black Lord could lay claim to the soul of the mage in an instant, and Cyric wasn't sure that that would be at all acceptable. Not yet, anyway.

"No," Cyric said firmly, looking up into the god's eyes. "There is nothing else."

The door to the chamber opened, and Durrock was brought before the Black Lord in chains. Cyric flinched as he stared at the assassin's disfigured face. Then he realized that the burn marks were very old. Only a few of the scars that lined his body had been inflicted recently.

"I am in a forgiving mood this day, Durrock. I'm sure it won't last," Bane told the assassin, then he returned to his throne. "I have a task for you, assassin. You will travel to Tantras with this thief and spy on his former allies. You know them quite well, since you escorted them into Scardale."

Durrock stiffened and bowed his head. Before the scarred assassin looked to the ground, Cyric saw an intense hatred flash in Durrock's eyes.

Bane continued. "As I told you before, I do not want the mage killed. The cleric is of no consequence. As for the fighter, Kelemvor Lyonsbane, I want his head adorning a gate on this building as soon as possible. Have I made myself perfectly clear?" Bane asked sharply.

"You have, Lord Bane," Durrock answered, his voice a growl.

"You have a question?" Bane said when Cyric didn't answer quickly.

The thief nodded, glanced at Durrock, then looked back at Bane. "What if they discover the location of the . . . *artifact* we spoke of? What if they try to take it from Tantras?"

Bane frowned and gripped his throne tightly. "Then, Cyric, they will *all* have to die."

* * * * *

It had been two days since the heroes left the Port of Scardale in the stolen galley. At night, a glowing spot on the horizon had marked the location of the city the *Queen of the Night* journeyed toward. The cause of the unearthly light couldn't be explained, but as the travelers drew closer to the city, the illumination grew brighter.

Other than this strange light, the journey across the Dragon Reach was uneventful. The slaves prowled the upper decks in shifts, luxuriating in the feel of the warm sun upon their faces. Adon, as usual, kept to himself. Midnight divided her time between long hours with her spellbook and wonderful, tender moments of love with Kelemvor.

After the escape from Scardale, the fighter had been more relaxed than Midnight had ever seen him, though he did have occasional bouts of worry that the curse had not been lifted for good. Although she was happy, too, the mage found herself wondering if Kelemvor would be happier going back to the adventuring life, perhaps even sailing with Bjorn and his crew. She wondered, too, if the fighter desired to follow that course rather than put himself at risk in Tantras. Soon, the question started to plague Midnight. Similar circumstances had driven a wedge between the lovers before, in Shadowdale, and she did not want history to repeat itself.

Finally she confronted Kelemvor as they stood near the bow, looking out at waves ahead and the dark craggy shoreline that they were fast approaching. It was a few hours after morningfeast.

"I am going with you," Kelemvor told her simply. "I have no destiny to fulfill, other than remaining at your side." After a moment, he looked at the mage, a serious look on his face. "You, on the other hand, seem to have a grand destiny, a path laid out for you by the gods themselves."

"But isn't being dragged along in my wake, following me as I follow my destiny, just another curse, Kel?" Midnight asked somberly. "You'll have less control of your life than you did before."

The fighter took her in his arms and kissed her.

"I love you," Midnight said softly, the words escaping her lips before she even realized what she was about to say.

"And I you," Kelemvor whispered and kissed her again. The lovers stood in each other's arms for a moment. "It won't be long before we land," the green-eyed fighter sighed at last. "We should alert Adon." The lovers walked off, arm-in-arm.

Ten minutes later, Midnight and Kelemvor found Adon on the deck. Bjorn and Liane joined them. Tantras loomed in the distance.

"It's not as big as Scardale, but it's not that much different," Bjorn told the heroes. "Are you sure you wouldn't rather go to the Living City?"

"We have business in Tantras," Adon said, the light in his eyes darkening as he spoke.

An hour later, the *Queen of the Night* entered Tantras harbor. The tip of a huge ridge hooked into the Dragon Reach, forming a natural breakwall, and the ship sailed toward a gap in the southern part of the wall. Massive catapults guarded the harbor from positions along the rocky inner wall. The harbor was filled to overflowing with ships, and watchmen signaled the *Queen of the Night* to fly its colors.

"Full stop," Bjorn ordered, then turned to the heroes. "We don't have any colors to fly, so we can't move any closer. You can use a rowboat to get to shore. They won't bother with us if we drop you, then move off."

"Fair enough," Kelemvor agreed and slapped the captain on the back. Each of the heroes was given well-stocked travel bags, and their purses were filled with gold from the Zhentish ship's stores, compliments of Bjorn and the crew. Then the heroes climbed down the rope ladder into a rowboat. Midnight seemed nervous as she settled onto the small boat, and she stared toward land whenever possible. Kelemvor recalled her many near-fatal accidents on the Ashaba and covered her hand with his own.

"I'll row," Adon said flatly, leaving the lovers to themselves. The cleric released the lines holding the boat in place, then looked up at the *Queen of the Night* to see the captain waving farewell. Adon started to move the small boat toward Tantras.

"If we had stayed with Bjorn, it could have been a fresh beginning for us all," Midnight said as she watched the stolen galley move away.

"I doubt it," Kelemvor replied. "We'd be fighting in a week in the close quarters of a ship, at each other's throats in a month."

"You think so little of our relationship?" Midnight asked, genuinely surprised.

"Not at all," the fighter said as he placed his arm around her waist. "But we both need the hint of danger in the air and open spaces to roam, don't we? Makes life a bit more exciting."

Midnight laughed a small, sharp, bitter laugh. "I've talked to gods and seen them destroyed, been put on trial for the murder of the Dales' most powerful mage, and sentenced to death. I was nearly drowned in the Ashaba, and I've been hunted like a dog by the soldiers of a mad god. Boredom would not be unwelcome at this point, destiny or no."

As the boat came within a hundred yards of the port, watchmen pointed the heroes to a small bay near the north end of the harbor. A small delegation of men, including two soldiers armed with swords and crossbows who wore the symbol of Torm—a metal gauntlet—met the heroes as they climbed from the ship and secured it to its moorings.

"Please state your business," a middle-aged man at the head of the delegation asked them, a bored expression on his face.

Midnight explained all they had been through in Scardale, although she left out their true purpose for journeying to Tantras.

"If you've made an enemy of the Black Lord, then you've made an ally of all of Tantras. My name's Faulkner," the middle-aged man told them happily.

As he stepped onto the dock, Kelemvor turned to Faulkner and asked, "What causes that odd light in the sky at night around here? We could see it from our ship when we were just halfway across the Dragon Reach!"

"Night?" Faulkner asked and snorted. "Night doesn't come to Tantras anymore. Not since the time of Arrival, when Lord Torm, the God of Loyalty, revealed himself to us."

"No night? It must be confusing," Kelemvor muttered.

"Tantras is the city of eternal light," Faulkner added and shrugged. "Our god sets the hours of the day for us; he puts loyalty in our hearts and reason in our heads. There is nothing confusing about it."

Midnight realized that Adon was trembling slightly. Whether it was fear or rage that had been locked within the scarred young man, his emotions had been stirred by Faulkner's words. Then the cleric turned and walked from the delegation in silence.

"You must excuse Adon," Midnight told them desperately, her fear of insulting the soldiers evident in her voice. One of the other members of the delegation stepped forward.

"There's no need to worry," a young soldier named Sian said. He was a younger man, with thin black eyebrows and curly, black hair. "It's rather obvious your friend was a cleric. How long has it been since he lost the way?"

As they slowly followed Adon's path along the dock, Midnight explained how Adon had been scarred at the hands of the Gond worshipers in Tilverton, how he had lost his faith in himself and the Goddess of Beauty, whom he had worshiped most of his young life.

Sian nodded. "Many have lost their faith now that the gods walk in Faerun instead of the Planes. Perhaps your friend will find the peace he so requires in our fair city."

Midnight felt Elminster's sphere of detection resting

against her back, through her backpack. "I'm afraid we won't have much time for rest," the mage said in a low voice as she turned and walked with Kelemvor and the delegation to the main buildings of the Port of Tantras. Adon was waiting with the watchmen when they got there.

In the next few hours, the heroes purchased fresh clothing and were given a brief description of the city's layout. Tantras, like most cities, was protected by a wall. In this case, the wall encompassed the vast port city, stretching in a winding path to the rocky shore. A series of towers lined the northern ridge, where the Citadel of Tantras was located. The Temple of Torm—the focus of the city ever since the god himself arrived there—was located in the northern section of town, and most of the streets that led to it were on a sharp incline. A huge bell tower lay at the southern end of the city, with a military complex close by, making the area off limits to civilians. There were several abandoned temples in the area, and a shrine to Mystra in the far south, near the bell tower.

"Other than these landmarks, Tantras is quite unremarkable," Sian concluded.

"Not completely unremarkable," Adon noted, his voice completely flat. "It looks as if you're preparing for war."

Sian narrowed his eyes and stared at the cleric for a moment. "You've just come from Scardale, haven't you? We've had several reports that confirm your description of the city's condition. If Zhentil Keep and Lord Bane are trying to annex new territories and expand their evil empire, what makes you think they'll settle for controlling only half of the Dragon Reach?"

"It was just an observation," Adon replied coldly. "Besides, I would have expected *Torm* to protect you."

"The city wasn't built with the idea of a resident deity," Sian said. "Torm's arrival is fairly recent. The presence of our god should be a deterrent to any enemy, but the people are prepared to fight for themselves anyway."

"I notice a number of refugee camps in the area," Midnight noted, changing the subject as quickly as she could.

"The chaos in the Realms has driven some of our neighbors to seek the protection of our city," Sian replied. "Others have fled south to Ravens Bluff or north to Calaunt. Hlintar has been practically deserted since an unnatural windstorm tore through the town and unearthed the graves of a few thousand of the town's former residents. The skeletons came to life, and now the dead rule the city."

Ten minutes later, the heroes were alone on an avenue that paralleled the harbor, then stretched off toward the business district to the south. A wandering band of mimes and showmen passed the heroes and performed snippets of a half dozen different stories that ranged from bawdy, ribald comedy, to dark tragedy. The heroes tried to ignore the performers, but they had to part with a few gold pieces before the artists left them alone.

Merchants also lined the street, hawking their wares at the tops of their lungs. From the looks of many of the tradesmen, the chaos in the Realms was affecting business for the worst. Kelemvor simply browsed, though, and Midnight found a new braid for her hair. Adon wandered to an outdoor eatery.

The cleric was sampling an odd-looking combination of bread, filleted meat, and a tangy red sauce topped with ground black peppers. "Delicious," the cleric told the vender, then passed the wooden bowl on to Kelemvor, who also sampled the food.

"There's an inn ten blocks from here that posted a vacancy sign this morning," the vender told the heroes. "You should get there before all the rooms are taken."

The cleric paid for the food and thanked the vender for the information. Then the heroes went in search of the inn. After becoming lost three times in the winding city streets and receiving directions that only led them deeper into the twisted city center, the heroes found the Lazy Moon Inn. As they entered, a young man wearing a red frock with gold trim appeared before the heroes.

"How long will you be staying?" the boy asked, his voice cold and efficient.

"We don't know yet, but this should cover everything," Kelemvor said gruffly and slapped a few coins into the boy's hand. "We'll take two rooms," the fighter added. "At least until the end of the week."

The inn was of a simplistic design, with a large taproom, kitchen, and storeroom on the ground floor, and guest rooms on the upper two floors. A shield bearing the symbol of Torm lay on its side in the corner, next to the boy.

The young man insisted on carrying the heroes' travel bags, although he was clearly struggling to keep his balance as he led Kelemvor, Midnight, and Adon up a wooden, spiral stairway that led to the third floor of the inn. After dismissing the boy and checking over their rooms, the heroes met in the taproom. It was well before eveningfeast, so few other people were present.

"Here we are," Kelemvor said. "Tantras." A deep breath escaped the fighter. "Midnight, how will we recognize this tablet of yours? Better still, what are we going to do with it once we find it?"

"If we find it," Adon said darkly, drumming his fingers nervously on the greasy, unwashed table.

"We *will* find it," Midnight noted firmly, turning to look at the cleric. "The sphere of detection Lhaeo gave us will shatter when it's near an object of great magical power, such as the missing Tablets of Fate." The mage paused and turned to Kelemvor. "As to their appearance, Mystra's final message to me at Castle Kilgrave contained an image of the tablets. They are made of clay and stand less than two feet high. Fiery blue-white runes line their surfaces. They radiate powerful magic."

"But magic is unreliable," Kelemvor grumbled, waving for the barmaid to bring him an ale. "Who's to say this sphere of yours is even going to work? And where will we look? We can't cover every square inch of this city on our own. It's far too large." The green-eyed fighter scowled and looked away from his friends. "Besides, we have to assume that Bane will send agents to find us. His people might even move the tablet before we can find it."

Midnight ran her hands over her face and looked to the open doorway. The perfect sunlight from without had not changed since their arrival. "If we are to believe the men who greeted us at the dock, we'll be able to search in daylight. That, at least, will work against many of Bane's agents."

The barmaid brought the fighter's ale, and the heroes were silent until the pretty girl left them. As soon as she was out of earshot, though, Kelemvor pounded the table with his fist and hissed, "We can't go completely without sleep. Do you want to leave yourself open to attack because you're too tired to properly defend yourself? We need a better plan than just searching the city at random until we find the damned tablet."

"Then what do you suggest?" Midnight snapped, the weariness in her soul bleeding through to darken the tone of her words.

The fighter sighed and closed his eyes. "First, we should split up," Kelemvor said. "We can cover far more ground that way."

The mage shook her head. "We have only one object capable of locating the tablet. If I take the sphere, what can you two possibly hope to accomplish on your own?"

Kelemvor ignored the edge in Midnight's voice and tried to calm himself. "I tried to get Bane to tell me where the Tablet of Fate was hidden. He wouldn't tell me directly, but he did say something about 'having faith.' I didn't make anything of the remark at the time, but it could be an important clue."

A thought shot into Adon's mind, and the cleric smiled. "The temples," he said simply. "Bane could have been playing off the word 'faith.' Not unusual for a god these days." Adon ran his hand over his scar. "And Faulkner said there were a number of deserted temples in the city. The Tablet of Fate could be hidden in one of them."

"Well, that's a start anyway," Midnight told Adon, then turned to the fighter. "As to your other question, Kel, there's only one thing we *can* do with the Tablet of Fate when we find it. Elminster explained that there are Celestial Stairways—paths to the Planes—scattered throughout Faerun. Only gods or mages of Elminster's class can see them and touch them. A mortal can walk through one of the stairways and not even know it's there."

Midnight paused and considered her next statement carefully. "I've seen two Celestial Stairways, and I think we should bring the Tablet of Fate to one of these paths and give it to Helm. But first, one of us must gain an audience with Torm. He'll know where the closest stairway can be found." The mage paused again and put her hand on Adon's shoulder. "This should be your task. As an experienced cleric—"

Adon rose from the table, his chair falling away behind him. "I will not!" he shouted, and the few patrons in the taproom turned to stare at him. "I cannot speak with a god!"

A few murmurs ran through the room, and Midnight hardened her heart to the sight of the frightened, childlike cleric. "You must," the raven-haired mage said at last. "Kelemvor is needed to look for safe passage for us, so we can leave Tantras quickly—once we find the tablet."

The fighter took a swig of ale. "Aye," he grumbled. "We must assume the Celestial Stairway will be somewhere far from this city. If it's not, all well and good. But if it is, we must be prepared."

The cleric's hands were trembling, and his flesh had gone pale. When he saw the inn's patrons staring at him, though, Adon picked up his chair and seated himself at the table once more.

"I intend to return the Tablet of Fate to the Planes," Midnight said with a finality that frightened Kelemvor, though he couldn't tell why. "It's the only chance we have of ending the madness that has infected Faerun. As for our immediate plans, we should start the search immediately, and meet back here in two days."

"There's only one thing you're overlooking," Adon noted softly, his hands covering his face as he spoke in a low, trembling voice.

"What's that?" Midnight asked.

"There are *two* Tablets of Fate," Adon answered bitterly. "What happens when you stand before the God of Guardians with only one of them and he demands to know what you've done with the other one?"

"I'll tell him the truth," Midnight said flatly. "Helm has no reason to harm me."

Adon chuckled a strained, nervous laugh. "Strange," the scarred cleric commented. "I remember Mystra trying to do the same thing you propose . . . before Helm tore her, limb from limb, that is." Adon rose from the table and left his companions to ponder the observation alone in his room.

Eventually, though, Midnight and Kelemvor left the table to return to their rooms. The heroes had just reached the stairs, when a white-bearded minstrel carrying a harp entered the Lazy Moon and approached the bar.

"We do not perform charity work," the innkeeper growled with a voice that reeked of snobbery. "If free lodgings are what you seek, I would advise the local poorhouse."

The heroes turned away and walked up the stairs, and the minstrel watched them until they had moved from sight. Only then did the white-bearded man turn his attentions to the innkeeper.

"I have money, and I have very little patience," the minstrel snapped as he opened his hand and displayed a fistful of gold pieces.

"How long will you be staying?" the innkeeper asked politely, his back straightening, his tone instantly changing.

The minstrel frowned deeply. "I don't need lodgings. I need information. What can you tell me about the couple that just went upstairs?"

The innkeeper looked around to make sure that no one was listening. "That depends on what it's worth to you," he whispered slyly.

"It's worth a great deal," the minstrel said as he shook his fistful of gold pieces and stared at the stairway, just where the heroes had stood. The smile faded from the minstrel's face. "More than you could ever imagine."

Fingers greedily kneading the air, the innkeeper grinned. "I have a great imagination."

"Then tell me everything," the minstrel said quietly as he handed the gold to the innkeeper. "For there is little time, and I have much to learn. . . ."

❦ 12 ❦

Temples and Bells

Outside the Lazy Moon Inn, the heroes said their farewells. Midnight kissed Kelemvor for the fifth and final time, then brushed the hair from his face. His strong, proud features were much more relaxed these days, now that the curse had been removed. Today, however, a shadow of worry and doubt had fallen upon him.

"Perhaps we should stay together after all," Kelemvor told the mage. "I don't like the idea of you risking your life—"

The mage placed her fingers to Kelemvor's lips, then calmly noted, "We're all at risk. The best chance we have is to get what we came for and move on quickly. You know that we can cover more ground and accomplish our task faster this way."

The fighter covered the mage's hand with his own. "Aye," he grumbled, and kissed her fingers. "Be careful."

"You're telling me to take care?" Midnight asked sarcastically and patted the side of the fighter's face as she said good-bye to Adon and left the Lazy Moon Inn. She traveled south for two blocks until she came to a one-story, gray stone building with no visible windows. A sign had been placed above the ragged doorway, and it read, "The House of Meager Living."

The mage pushed at the partially open door, but it wouldn't open. At first she thought the door was simply stuck, then, through the door, she saw a man's arm fall to the floor. There was a soft moan from inside the building and Midnight pushed harder at the door. The sound of a body sliding across the floor accompanied her efforts. Once the door was open far enough, Midnight slipped inside the dark building.

The interior of the House of Meager Living was lit by a handful of small torches set in metal braces attached to the main support beams. A dozen metal beds bereft of any covering were scattered throughout the room, and well over seventy men, women, and children crowded the single room that took up most of the building's few hundred square feet. Volunteers moved among the poor, the homeless, and the sick, bringing food from an open kitchen at the rear.

Midnight looked down and saw the man who had been lying near the door. He was in his late forties, and he wore a tunic that might have once belonged to a guardsman, save that there were now holes where any official markings might have been. Sandals made from worn strips of leather hung on his feet, and his hands were pressed tightly to his chest.

"Can I help you?" Midnight asked softly as she took a step toward the man and bent down. Suddenly the man struck out, his movement surprisingly quick. Midnight fell back, avoiding the blow, and realized that the man held a large, rusted spike in his hand. The mage scrambled backward, moving out of the derelict's range. But he didn't try to strike her again. He merely hugged the spike to his chest and stared at the floor.

Midnight felt hands grip her arms, then she was dragged to her feet. The mage turned to face a middle-aged woman and a boy who might have been her son. Both were dressed in the same clean, white clothes as the other volunteers.

"What's your business here?" the woman asked gruffly, folding her arms across her chest.

"I needed a guide to take me around the city," Midnight explained as she got to her feet. "I thought perhaps—"

"You thought you'd get some cheap labor," the woman snapped. "The government has an office for hirelings on Hillier Way. You'd best go there."

Midnight frowned at the woman. "I thought I could find some resident of the city who knew its lore and its customs better than some bored government worker." She paused and pointed toward the roomful of indigents. "And I was trying to help."

"Do you want to start a riot in here?" the woman hissed softly. "If you offer gold here, they'll kill each other for it. Be off with you."

"Wait! I'll do it," the young man said as Midnight turned to leave. "I work for the city government when I'm not here. They take a lot of what I earn, though. You think we can have an agreement just between the two of us?"

"That would be fine," Midnight answered, looking at the excited boy through narrowed eyes. "Just as long as part of the arrangement is that you don't chew my ear with a lot of questions along the way."

"Well," the boy said in mock outrage, his eyes wide. He'd lived for no more than sixteen winters, but he was tall and strong, with thick, black hair that curled at his shoulders. "Privacy, eh? I have no problem with that, as long as the price is agreeable."

Midnight smiled, and the boy turned to the middle-aged woman at his side. "Can you spare me, mother?" he asked, practically panting with enthusiasm.

"Spare you? Would that I never had you," she snapped. "Begone and good riddance. If any of the city's men come by looking for you, I'll tell them you're busy visiting with your crazed aunt from the family's bad side."

A few minutes later, Midnight and the boy were on the street. "By the way," the boy said brightly, "my name is Quillian. You didn't tell me yours."

"That's true," Midnight answered flatly.

Quillian whistled. "Well, if you're not going to tell me your name, will it be all right if I call you 'milady'?"

Midnight sighed. "Under the circumstances, yes. Just remember our agreement. I'll ask all the questions."

One side of the boy's mouth curled up in a wicked smile. "I bet you're a thief, come to rob our city blind."

Midnight stopped and stared at the black-haired boy. She was obviously angry.

"I'm just joking," Quillian said quickly, holding his hand up to stop the mage from admonishing him. "Still," he added after they had started walking again, "if you *were* a thief, I wouldn't mind helping you. This city's robbed me blind all my life."

Midnight shook her head. "You're a bit young to be that jaded."

"Age has nothing to do with it," Quillian noted bitterly. "You saw the conditions in the poorhouse. If my father hadn't died a war hero and left a decent pension for us, my mother and I would be residents in that nasty hole, not just volunteers."

The mage imagined Quillian dressed in a pauper's rags, the spark in his eyes drowned by hunger and want. The mage frowned and pushed the thoughts from her mind. "I'm not a thief, but I'll pay you well. Just do your job and there'll be no problems between us."

Quillian smiled and brushed a stray piece of hair from his eyes. "Where do you want to start?" he asked.

"How about the city's temples," Midnight answered as nonchalantly as possible. "Any place of worship that you know about."

"That's easy enough," Quillian said. "Let's start with the Temple of Torm. That's just—"

"I believe I can find that one without a guide," the mage told the boy as she gestured toward the beautiful spires to the north.

A look of embarrassment crossed Quillian's face. "Reasonable point," the dark-haired lad said sheepishly. "Let's head toward the market, then. It's nearby and there used to be a small house of worship there."

The two walked in silence for a little while. As Midnight and Quillian got closer to the market, the crowds grew in size. Soon the mage could smell food cooking and hear the droves of people haggling about prices and the merchants yelling to attract customers.

"Up ahead, on the right, there's a butcher shop," Quillian noted as they entered a crowded square. "The building used to be a temple to Waukeen, the Goddess of Trade. Are you familiar with Liberty's Maiden?"

Midnight shrugged. "Vaguely. I remember something about a golden-haired woman with lions at her feet."

"That's how they say she appears when she walks among us. I haven't seen her in town," the boy said sarcastically, "so I couldn't tell you if that's true or not. Tantras was blessed with Lord Torm instead."

The mage found the boy's sarcasm surprising, especially compared to the enthusiasm about Torm's presence she'd heard from the watchmen at the dock. "Aren't you a follower of Torm?" Midnight asked.

"Not usually. But I can be when it's necessary," Quillian said.

I'd best change the subject, Midnight decided, noting the anger in Quillian's voice when he mentioned the God of Duty's name. "What can you tell me about Waukeen's temple?" the mage asked.

"There were statues of Waukeen and her lions in front of the place. The Tormites purchased one of the lions to decorate their new temple. I don't know what happened to the other statues or the rest of the fixtures."

The pair crossed the busy square. Midnight stopped in front of the butcher shop, waiting for the crowd to thin out a bit before she entered the busy establishment. She turned to Quillian and put her hand on his shoulder. "I hope that the money I'm paying you will make you less fickle about your service to me than you are about your devotion to the gods."

Before the boy could answer, a voice called out behind the mage. "Fickle? That's not a word you hear very often in Tantras these days. Not since the God of Duty moved in!"

The mage turned and saw an old man with a shock of white hair and a scraggly white beard. He was carrying a small harp, and he brushed his hand across its strings, bringing a flow of beautiful notes that pierced the sounds of the crowd.

"Fickle," the old man repeated. "The word reminds me of a limerick I picked up in Waterdeep. Would you care to hear it? It's of great significance, I assure you."

Midnight stared at the minstrel, examining his features closely. She was sure that he looked like someone she'd met before.

The minstrel stared back at her for a moment, then asked, "Are you feeling well? Do you need a physician? Or would the young lady prefer an epic ballad or a sweet tale of romance to sooth her frazzled nerves?" The minstrel's voice was lilting and sweet.

The mage shook her head. "My apologies," she said softly as she shook her head. "For a moment you reminded me of someone."

The minstrel ran a hand through his hair, then smiled. "Oh? Fancy that," the old man cackled. He leaned close to Midnight and whispered, "A little secret for you. All old beggars look the same to you younger types."

Suddenly the old man's eyes widened in surprise. "To your left, pretty one!" he cried and pointed to her waist with a bony finger.

Looking away from the minstrel for just an instant, Midnight saw a hand reaching with practiced skill for her money purse. Her left hand reached the purse at the same moment as the hand of the pickpocket, while her right hand balled into a fist. The mage punched the would-be thief in the face.

The yellow-bearded criminal's arms pinwheeled madly as he stumbled into a pair of elderly women and lost his balance. Midnight moved toward the cowering cutpurse, and Quillian leaped on the man.

The minstrel, on the other hand, simply stood by quietly and watched.

"This is not your day, rogue!" Quillian cried as he planted his knee in the thief's back and pushed him onto his stomach. Grabbing both of the pickpocket's hands, the black-haired boy pinned them firmly in place behind the man's back. He moved close to the thief's ear and hissed, "Be still unless you want to end up a cripple!"

The fight went out of the thief as a group of locals gathered around Quillian, the yellow-bearded man, and Midnight. The merchants and peasants hurled insults and a few rotten vegetables at the cutpurse. Then a burly man with a red face and short, gray-shot black hair—the butcher who owned the renovated temple—made his way through the crowd, carrying a blood-drenched axe.

"Well, if it isn't Quillian Dencery," the butcher shouted, genuinely surprised. "What have you brought me today, boy?"

"See for yourself," Quillian said as he fished into the sash at the thief's waist and pulled out three money purses.

The butcher raised his axe in his right hand. "Could this be the thief that has been harassing my customers for the last two weeks?" The butcher grabbed a handful of the man's hair with his left, then pulled sharply. The thief gasped and gritted his teeth as he was forced to look into the butcher's sunburned face. "Do you know how much business you've cost me? My loyal customers are frightened to shop here, and they've been giving their business to that cutthroat, Loyan Trey, in the south end of town."

"Fine!" the thief sputtered. "Let me go and I'll work his shop. Then your customers will return!"

The butcher shook his head. "I don't think so." He looked to Quillian. "Boy, spread his right hand flat so we can chop it off. That'll teach him a lesson."

"Please!" the thief begged. "You mustn't! I'll give the money back. I won't ever come here again!"

"Hah!" the butcher shouted as the thief's hand was forced to the ground, fingers clenched tight. "Your type would say anything to save your own skin. Thieves are all alike." The butcher hefted the axe and the crowd gasped, almost as one. "Now keep still so I can get this over with and get back to business. I promise it'll be quick and clean. I can't promise that you won't feel anything, though."

"Wait!" Midnight cried, lunging toward the butcher.

From the crowd, the minstrel watched with growing interest. The butcher's hand had risen into the air, the bright sunlight glinting off his axe. The blade hung above the thief's wrist, as if it were suspended by a fragile thread.

"You were the one he wanted to steal from," the butcher growled, relaxing slightly. "Don't you want justice?"

The mage stood beside the butcher and whispered, "Look around you. If you're so worried about your business, then stop and think about what you're about to do. Do you really want all these fine gentlemen and ladies to remember your shop as the place they saw you maim a thief?" The mage saw the anger go out of the butcher's face, only to be replaced by concern. "Everytime they think of you, that's what they'll remember. Would they think you a good man, then? An honest man?"

The butcher's shoulders dropped as he surveyed the faces

in the crowd. Some were expectant and excited. Most were horrified. Practically unnoticed by all, the minstrel was grinning a wicked grin as he watched the mage. But the butcher realized that the mage was right: he'd lose everything if he harmed the thief. "But he'll just do it again," the butcher growled as he lowered the axe.

"Of course he will," Midnight told the red-faced man. "That's how he makes his living. But that doesn't mean he'll ever be stupid enough to come near your establishment again. If he has any brains, he'll even put the word out that your shop is strictly off limits to all his brethren." The raven-haired mage turned to the thief. "What do you say to that?"

"I will! I'll do everything the lady said!" the yellow-bearded man sputtered.

"Then be off with you," the butcher growled and signaled Quillian to release the thief. "And tell everyone you know in the Thieves' Guild that Beardmere's is off limits!"

The minstrel appeared before Midnight. "Fine lady, I will write a song in honor of your wisdom and courage." And before Midnight could respond, the minstrel turned and vanished into the crowd.

Business quickly returned to normal in the marketplace, and the butcher walked to Midnight's side. "It seems I owe you for your assistance," he told the mage. "How about a month's supply of Beardmere's finest meats?"

The mage smiled. "Thank you, but I'd accept something far less costly," Midnight replied politely. "I'm a scholar. I wish to know how this former temple to Waukeen became your butcher shop."

"Simple enough," Beardmere said. "The government sold me the building."

Surprise registered on the magic-user's face. That wasn't the answer she'd expected at all. Still, Midnight recovered from her surprise quickly and continued her questioning of the butcher. "Were there any artifacts or books left behind by the worshipers of Liberty's Maiden?"

"Ah," Beardmere said, convinced that he had finally pegged the inquisitive mage. "Are you a collector, as well?"

Midnight smiled when she saw Quillian hovering nearby, obviously listening to the conversation. "I am," the mage said, a little louder than needed. The black-haired boy blushed and turned away.

The butcher nodded and led Midnight and Quillian into the back of the former temple, through a few rooms that had been converted for storage and office space. They reached the top of a stairway, then Beardmere grabbed a torch and ushered the mage and her young guide into the basement.

A musty smell assaulted Midnight's senses as she stepped off the landing and found herself in a small, dirty room filled with abandoned items from the former temple. There were empty shipping crates scattered across the rough dirt floor, and waterlogged ledgers tossed here and there around the damp cellar.

"I sold quite a bit of what was left behind, you understand," Beardmere said, wiping a cobweb from his face. "But many of the items were of no value to anyone in the city. Of course, it would have been sacrilegious to destroy them, so I've kept them stored down here. Someone from the city tried to cart them off, but I wouldn't let him. Just wouldn't seem right, somehow."

Midnight pushed aside a crate and gasped as she found herself staring into the eyes of a beautiful, white-skinned woman. It took her a moment to realize this was the statue of Waukeen, the Goddess of Trade. One of the two golden lions that had once adorned her temple lay at her feet.

Withdrawing the sphere of detection from her travel bag, the mage held the magical item close to the statues. She had no reason to believe that Bane would hide the Tablet of Fate in its original form. In fact, the tablets were probably carefully disguised.

But when the sphere touched the statue, nothing happened. The mage methodically searched the entire basement, her heart thundering in anticipation. Each time she touched an item from the temple, though, the results were the same. The magical sphere of detection remained dark and intact.

Beardmere and Quillian watched Midnight as she moved around the basement. "See anything you like?" the butcher asked at last, his attention riveted on the amber sphere in the mage's hand.

Midnight's disappointment was evident in her voice as she put the sphere away. "I'm sorry, no."

Beardmere nodded. "What exactly are you looking for?"

The mage forced a smile. "I can't really say. But I'll know it when I find it."

Midnight thanked Beardmere for his patience as she left the shop. Then the raven-haired mage and her guide took to the streets once more.

"What was that thing?" Quillian Dencery asked, trying to appear casual. "That yellowish orb you were waving around. Is it magic?"

"No questions," Midnight said firmly. She stopped walking and grabbed the black-haired boy's arm. "How many times do I have to tell you that it's better that you don't know anything? Where's our next stop?"

"It's almost time for eveningfeast. I thought we might stop off at the Dark Harvest Festhall to grab a bite—"

Midnight squeezed the young man's arm a little tighter. "Quillian, for what I'm paying you, I expect to be taken very seriously. I do not intend to wander aimlessly, visiting pubs instead of—"

The young man twisted free of Midnight's grasp. "For a scholar, you don't have much patience, do you?"

Midnight said nothing.

"I happen to know that worshipers of Bhaal, Lord of Murder, meet in the gaming rooms of the Dark Harvest almost nightly," Quillian snapped, rubbing his arm. "If you're looking for something specific—and I think you are—you should go there."

"Perhaps I misjudged you," Midnight noted warily, trying to keep the excitement from her voice. Bhaal was an ally of Myrkul, and Bane had stolen the Tablets with Myrkul's assistance. "The Dark Harvest it is."

The pair traveled south for three blocks, then headed east to the festhall. Midnight looked up toward the blinding face of the sun; its position hadn't changed since she first arrived in Tantras. Daylight had continued, as the watchmen at the harbor had warned her, twenty-four hours a day.

Turning her attentions to the festhall, the mage was not surprised to discover that the squat, one-story building had been painted black with blood-red trim. Agents of the Black Lord and worshipers of Bhaal, the God of Assassins, would find the Dark Harvest a welcome sight in this colorful merchant city.

But as Quillian grabbed the door to the tavern, Midnight realized how foolish she was being by entering a place frequented by the God of Strife's allies. "I've changed my mind," the raven-haired mage told her guide. "We'll find somewhere else to dine. We can always come back here for information later, if we're not successful anywhere else."

The young man shrugged and looked away. "Whatever you say, milady. We could head south and pass through the ruins of the Temple of Sune on our way to another place to eat."

At the mention of the Goddess of Beauty, Midnight thought of Adon. For the first time since she'd left the Lazy Moon, the mage was thankful that she had gone to search the temples without her friends.

Quillian quickly led Midnight through a few alleys. Within ten minutes they were at the ruined temple. "It burned to the ground a few weeks ago," the young man told the mage as they stood near the heaps of scorched timber that were once part of the house of worship. "Rumors say the clerics destroyed the place themselves, just to spite the Tormites. The Sunites left the city right after the 'accident'."

Midnight walked through the wreckage with the sphere of detection and was disappointed once again. After a few minutes of fruitless searching, she turned to Quillian and said, "Why did the Sunites leave?"

"I really don't know," the dark-haired boy said. "But there may be a way to find out. In many circles, the Curran Inn is known as the Wagging Tongue. A few discreet inquiries, and you should be able to learn what you want to know."

Midnight shook her head. "Another inn? I suspect you're just taking me there so I can buy you eveningfeast." When Quillian shrugged, the mage smiled and said, "Very well. Let's go to the Wagging Tongue."

Quillian led the mage west, to a small inn several blocks from the harbor. The taproom of the inn was filled to capacity, and raucous laughter could be heard a full block away from the tavern. To get a position at the bar, Midnight had to push between a pair of off-duty guards who wore the gauntlet of Torm. Quillian stood waiting behind her.

Staring at the wiry, dark-skinned man behind the bar, the mage grinned. It had been a long time since the days when she had traveled on her own and frequented noisy, smelly inns like this one. And though she could remember all the points of "etiquette" that one used to be accepted in the company of crude, ill-mannered louts, Midnight felt strange about using it. She wanted to be able to ask her questions, receive the proper answers, and be on her way. That thought would have shocked her three months ago, when she still considered herself a "wild" adventuress.

As Midnight pondered that thought, the innkeeper placed his elbow on the bar and leaned in close to her. His foul breath and bloodshot eyes shocked her out of her musings. "Would it kill you to actually order something?" the man grumbled.

"That depends on what poisons you're trying to pass off as fine ales," Midnight remarked without flinching.

The man tilted his head slightly. "Afraid I'll get you so drunk that you'll fall prey to my charms?"

Though she quickly found that she hadn't lost any of her wit, Midnight soon tired of the little game. She would have ended it and simply asked for some information, but the mage knew that she wouldn't learn a thing if she didn't play along for a while, at least. "Under those circumstances, I'd have to be dead, not drunk."

"Or dead drunk!" one of the two guards flanking Midnight said with a slurred voice, then broke into a fit of uncontrollable snickering. It took him a moment to realize no one else was laughing.

Midnight let a slight laugh escape her as she said, "Give me a double of whatever he's having. Then maybe you can tell me something."

"I can tell you plenty," the innkeeper grumbled as he took a large red bottle out from behind the bar. Both fighters mumbled in agreement.

"I'm sure you can," Midnight sighed. "But what I'm interested in is that burned-out building a few blocks away. I understand it used to be a temple to Sune. I'm curious as to why clerics of Sune would leave a city as beautiful as Tantras. Beauty *is* what they worship, after all."

The innkeeper laughed as he held the bottle close to his chest. "I remember that lot. They used to come in here with their fancy clothes and their fancy ways, talking like a bunch of damn poets all the time. I only let them stay 'cause they had money."

"It sounds like they had it pretty good," Midnight noted, wiping her hand across the greasy bar. "But I still don't understand why they left the city."

The innkeeper snorted. "I suppose it's hard to compete with a temple that's got its own resident god. Once Torm showed up, their attendance fell off and those worshipers who were still foolish enough to worship—"

Suddenly the pair of guards stood up and kicked their stools to the floor. All sound and activity in the inn stopped as the guards stood, glaring at the innkeeper. The guard to Midnight's right, who was wobbling from too much to drink, placed his hand on the hilt of his sword.

Midnight looked at the innkeeper and saw a cold, almost frightened expression cross his face. He took the bottle of liquor and poured its contents onto the floor. "It seems that bottle's empty," the innkeeper said when he was finished. "Is there anything else that interests you?"

"Only a well-cooked meal for my nephew and me," Midnight told the man.

The black-haired boy took that as a cue. "Quillian Dencery," the young man said winningly as he grabbed one of the guard's hands and shook it vigorously.

"Dencery," the man muttered absently. "I think I met your father once. Good man. Fine soldier. This his sister?"

"My aunt on my mother's side," Quillian said as he tapped his head and raised an eyebrow. "A scholar. You know the type."

The guard looked at Midnight, laughed, and turned away. Activity and sound resumed at the inn, and the mage and her guide were shown to a table. As they ordered their meal, Midnight kept a close watch on the guards, but neither of the men even glanced in her direction.

After they ate, they left the inn and Quillian took Midnight to a small, featureless, and deserted building, not far from the tavern. "The worshipers of Ilmater, God of Endurance, used to meet here," the boy told the mage. "The city levied taxes on the church that the priests couldn't dream of paying. When they defaulted, the city guards put them in the poorhouse. Some even live in the House of Meager Living."

Midnight pictured the derelict who had attacked her with a spike in the poorhouse and shuddered. "What kind of taxes?" the mage asked quietly.

Quillian shrugged. "Once word got out that Torm was in the city, Tormites from all over Faerun flocked here, putting a ton of gold in the coffers of the church. Of course, the government took its share, too. After a while, the city told the worshipers of Ilmater to match the taxes paid by the Tormites or get out. You can guess what happened."

"How very odd," the mage noted as she turned to her guide. "In some places, the churches are exempt from taxation. Here, they're driven away by it." Midnight paused for a moment, then recollected her thoughts. "How far are we from Mystra's shrine?" she asked at last.

"Not far at all," Quillian told her brightly. "It's down in the southern section of the city, near the garrisons."

After a long walk, Quillian led the mage up a low ridge to a small footpath that had nearly been worn away from neglect. The path, in turn, took the travelers right to the Shrine of Mystra.

The shrine was a simple stone arch, surrounded by a rough stone wall a few feet high, with entrances at regular intervals around its circumference. Midnight ordered Quillian to remain behind as she walked around the circle of stones, viewing the shrine from every angle. Then she passed into the circle and stood before the small, white statue of the Lady of Mysteries that rested under the center of the arch. Though she wanted to, Midnight found that she could not bring herself to kneel down and pray before testing the shrine with the sphere of detection. She ran from the circle of stones, then stopped.

"You're not a child anymore," she whispered to herself, then took out the sphere and approached the shrine again.

As she got close, the sphere vibrated very slightly.

A residue of spells that might have been cast years ago, Midnight thought. The raven-haired mage turned away from the shrine. A large bell tower in the distance caught her eye. "What's that?" she said to her guide, pointing to the tower.

"A place where children used to play," the boy told her, stifling a yawn. "Legend has it that the bell was made by the great mage, Aylen Attricus. He was one of the founders of Tantras. They say he was a thousand years old when he passed away, a century ago." The boy picked up a small rock and rolled it down the worn path.

"He forged the bell himself, and built the tower, stone by stone, with his own two hands," Quillian continued. "Then he used his magic to weave a spell preventing any mortal from ringing the bell. He inscribed some type of prophecy on the bell, but even the city's scholars can't decipher the code he used." The black-haired boy shrugged and stifled another yawn. "All I know is that the bell has been there for hundreds of years. They say it rang once and somehow saved the city, but I don't believe it."

"Why not?" Midnight asked.

"Because the only people around who still believe that are wizards, and wizards never tell the truth," the boy laughed.

The mage frowned. "I want to see it," she said grimly.

A slight whistle escaped Quillian's lips as he tried to work out a plan. "It's in the Forbidden Area, where the army garrisons are laid out. The soldiers usually won't let just anyone through." He paused and smiled. "But they know me because of my father. You and I both have dark hair and deep skin. Maybe we can get in by playing aunt and nephew again."

"Then let's go," Midnight said.

"There's a problem," Quillian said flatly, his hand on Midnight's arm. "Morgan Lisemore, the commander who would normally give us access, is away from the city until late tomorrow. If I ask anyone else, there'll be a lot of questions, most of which you won't want to answer." As he finished speaking, the boy tried to stifle a third yawn, but failed.

Throwing her hands into the air, Midnight looked away from the young man. We're obviously not going to solve this now," she sighed. "You'd better get some rest. And try to get us a horse for tomorrow. We'll cover more ground that way."

As Quillian turned and started toward home, Midnight put her hand on his shoulder and said, "Thank you for your help, nephew. Meet me at the Lazy Moon Inn before morningfeast."

"Aye, milady," the dark-haired boy said happily. "By the way, you'll want to buy a sleeping mask before you go to bed. If you're not used to it, the constant daylight here can make it difficult to sleep."

It was more than an hour's walk to the inn. Quillian bade the mage good-bye again, then left her. There were no messages from Adon or Kelemvor in the room she shared with the fighter, so the mage tried to relax and sleep.

After nearly an hour of lying in bed, the sunshine causing her to think in the back of her mind that she should be getting up, Midnight dressed and found the innkeeper. The obsequious, smiling man, Faress by name, located a sleeping mask for the mage and parted with it for the price of a tankard of ale, a rather large sum for a piece of rough cloth with a string attached.

Before she went to sleep, Midnight tried to study her spellbook. When that endeavor failed, she sat down at a small desk in the corner of the room and wrote messages for Kelemvor and Adon. She retired then, and after sleeping fitfully, was startled awake by a pounding on her door.

"It's Quillian Dencery, milady," a voice on the other side of the door cried. "You've overslept."

"I'll be there in a moment," Midnight mumbled and dressed hurriedly. The mage and her guide soon resumed their journey, now on horseback, and spent the day visiting deserted temples and places of clandestine worship. Through it all, the sphere of detection never registered more than a slight tremor. At the end of the day, Midnight accompanied Quillian to the military outpost in the southernmost district of the city. There they found Morgan Lisemore, a tall, sandy-haired man who was easily old enough to be the guide's father.

"If it isn't Quillian Dencery," Morgan said ruefully, then listened to the boy's story. When Midnight's guide had finished his tale of addled aunts and research trips, the soldier sighed. "You know I hate to deny you anything, lad. But there are rules to be followed."

The young man shook his head and pointed to Midnight. "She may be called back home at any moment, Morgan. This could be a once-in-a-lifetime opportunity for her."

Morgan looked up at the sky and sighed again.

"Very well. Go on," Morgan grumbled, then motioned for his guards to let Midnight and her guide pass.

Midnight said nothing as she rode with Quillian to the bell tower nearly a half-mile in the distance. They passed a number of hastily erected barracks and were forced to detour twice to avoid groups of soldiers in the middle of training exercises. Soon, however, the Tower of Aylen Attricus stood before them.

The tower was a gray stone obelisk. Within the monument lay a winding stairway that led to a bright, silver bell. The bell itself stood exposed to the cool afternoon air through large windows on each side. Midnight felt an odd tingling sensation in her back as she gazed at the tower and prepared to dismount. The tingling felt like a thousand fingers capped with razor-sharp nails lightly tapping the mage's back. Midnight realized what was happening just as she got off the horse and her feet touched the ground.

"Look out!" Midnight yelled and threw the travel bag from her shoulder. Quillian leaped to the ground. The bag was glowing with a bright amber light as it landed twenty feet from the entrance to the tower. For an instant the bag seemed to be on fire, and then the sphere of detection exploded soundlessly. The tough canvas sack was shredded, and the stone doorway to the tower was seared black from the noiseless explosion.

Midnight walked over to Quillian. The boy was sitting up, but he scampered away from the raven-haired mage as she extended her hand.

"You didn't tell me you were one of them!" he cried and backed a little farther from Midnight.

"One of *who*?" Midnight asked irritably.

"You're a mage! Your stinking art could have gotten us both killed!" Quillian yelled and rose to his feet. "I knew I shouldn't have trusted you!"

The mage turned away from the dark-haired boy and looked at the tower. I can afford to lose a guide, she thought. But not the Tablet of Fate . . . and from the reaction of the sphere, it just might be nearby!

But the sphere was meant to explode when it came within range of *any* object of sufficient magical power, the mage recalled bitterly. It might have exploded because of the damned bell. She moved toward the doorway and Quillian cried out, "We have to leave! Someone might think you're trying to blow up the bell!"

"You leave," Midnight hissed without turning around. "I have to see what's inside the tower."

Entering the tower, Midnight was greeted by absolute silence. The sounds of the garrisons and the training exercises going on nearby, even the noise of the wind from the Dragon Reach, suddenly vanished. The mage looked through the door and could see Quillian moving his lips, shouting a warning, but she couldn't hear his voice. Turning from the boy, Midnight examined the interior of the tower and found it completely bare except for the winding stairway that led to the bell. She climbed to the top of the tower.

At the head of the perfectly carved, spotless stone steps, the mage gazed at the inscription on the bell. Sunlar, Midnight's teacher in Deepingdale, had insisted that Midnight make a study of ancient languages. The message was a confusing jumble of many tongues, but it reminded the magic-user of puzzles Sunlar had created for her years ago. And then, as she stared at the strange letters and words, a blue-white glow erupted from the inscription, and Midnight found she could decipher it quite easily. It read:

This bell was created to throw a shield of impenetrable mystical force over the city I helped to found. To protect my fairest creation from great harm.

Once, my beloved ally, the sorceress Cytheria, rang the bell and saved the city from the dire magics of a wizard I battled nearby. It took great courage to stay and protect our home, though she would have preferred to fight by my side.

Now, only by the hand of a woman with power and heart such as my wife had, and only in the greatest time of need, will this bell ever sound again.

The mage pondered the message as she climbed down the steps and walked out of the tower. The sounds of the day rushed to her ears the moment she walked through the doorway. Quillian was upon his horse, and he had led Midnight's mount to the tower.

"I put in a long day today and I expect to get paid," the dark-haired boy growled. "Now let's get out of here before we're caught."

"Lead on," Midnight said flatly as she mounted.

The mage and her guide rode back to the checkpoint where Morgan was waiting. He waved them through without a word, and the pair rode for over an hour before either spoke.

"Don't worry about me keeping quiet," Quillian grumbled without looking at Midnight. "I don't want to be associated with mages if I can avoid it." After a moment, he added, "I sense there are some hard times in your future, milady. Try not to drag any innocent bystanders down with you."

"I'll keep it in mind," Midnight told him, angry to be on the receiving end of a lecture from the boy. Although there was less than a decade between Quillian and the mage, she felt as if she had aged a hundred years since she called out to Mystra on Calantar's Way two months before. She had seen far too much in the last few weeks to be scolded by a child who had probably never been more than a hundred miles from Tantras in his entire life.

The riders came to the Lazy Moon Inn, and Midnight paid the amount that Quillian was due, along with a bonus for the hazards she had not warned him about in advance. The dark-haired boy rode away in silence, and Midnight entered the inn.

Once inside the room that she and Kelemvor shared, Midnight looked for messages from either of her allies. The cleric had not picked up her letter, but there was a message signed by a priest of Torm next to the door. It was a short note, meant simply to assure Midnight and Kelemvor that all was well with their friend.

The fighter, on the other hand, had been in the room, recently from the looks of things, and had taken the letter Midnight had left for him. In return, he left a scrap of paper with only three words hastily scrawled upon it.

Cyric is alive.

The parchment fell from Midnight's trembling hands and sailed to the floor, where it lay as the mage ran from the inn, her heart thundering with fear.

❧ 13 ❧

Dark Harvest

Outside the Lazy Moon Inn, Kelemvor stood face to face with Midnight as the heroes said their farewells. The mage kissed the green-eyed fighter for the fifth and final time, then brushed the hair from his face. Kelemvor stared into her dark and beautiful eyes, and felt a chill.

I couldn't stand to lose her again, the fighter thought, then said, "Perhaps we should stay together after all. I don't like the idea of you risking your life—"

The mage placed her fingers to Kelemvor's lips, then smiled gently. "We're all at risk. The best chance we have is to get what we came for and move on quickly," she told her lover. "You know that we can cover more ground and accomplish our task faster this way."

Kelemvor reached up and covered Midnight's hand with his own. "Aye," he grumbled as he kissed her fingers. "Be careful."

Midnight made a sarcastic comment and patted the fighter's face. Kelemvor watched as the mage broke from him, said good-bye to the cleric, and walked away.

Kelemvor turned to Adon. "Until we meet again," he said to the scarred cleric, though he was still watching Midnight as she walked down the street. "Adon?"

No response. Kelemvor turned and saw the cleric across the street, already losing himself in the crowd. The fighter shrugged and headed toward the docks. Kelemvor simply studied the area of the waterfront for the first few hours after he left the Lazy Moon Inn and became familiar with a few of the larger merchant ships that were currently docked in Tantras.

If all else fails, we can always join up as crew on a merchant vessel, Kelemvor thought, though the idea repulsed him.

At length, Kelemvor investigated the warehouses, too, but after an hour of doors slamming in his face, the fighter gave up that line of inquiry. Instead, he walked south along the docks, gazing out at the waters of the Dragon Reach. On the horizon, a long patch of purple and blue rose toward the sky and gave way to a field of perfect blue. In all the other cities nearby, the sun was already fading.

"An odd sight, isn't it?" a voice asked from behind the fighter. Kelemvor turned and faced a hazel-eyed man in a brightly colored uniform. The man was a few years younger than Kelemvor, and he sported a brownish blond beard that was immaculately trimmed. His eyebrow was a single, continuous line that stretched across his face, and he had an odd, crooked smile.

"Odd? Not compared with others that I have seen recently," Kelemvor told the hazel-eyed man. "It's actually quite attractive, in a way."

"Men have been driven mad by the eternal light," the man sighed. "To many, it's worse than the blackest, vilest darkness that night ever visited upon Faerun."

The fighter smiled and thought of the horrors he had faced in the Shadow Gap, on the road to Shadowdale. "When the hills of this city rise up to crush the residents between them, then you have cause to worry."

The man laughed. "You speak with the conviction of a man who's seen such terrible things."

"That and much more," Kelemvor said, a tinge of sadness in his deep voice.

"How incredible." The hazel-eyed man held out his hand to the fighter. "My name is Linal Alprin, harbormaster of Port Tantras."

"Kelemvor Lyonsbane," the fighter answered, and grasped the outstretched hand that had been offered to him.

The harbormaster shook his head and sighed. "I've been stuck in Tantras ever since the gods came to Faerun, but I've seen things in the last few weeks that I wouldn't have believed possible a year ago."

Alprin and Kelemvor stood on the dock for a while, trading stories about the magical chaos and instability in nature each man had witnessed since Arrival. After about an hour, the harbormaster turned to the fighter and asked if he had any plans for eveningfeast.

"Well," Kelemvor told the hazel-eyed man, "I was planning to go back to the inn."

"I'll not hear of it," Alprin snapped brightly. "You're coming home to meet my wife and share a few stories over our meager table." The harbormaster paused and smiled. "That is, if you don't mind, of course."

"That would be nice," Kelemvor said. "I'm grateful."

Alprin looked around at the now-crowded docks. Two guards and a handful of sailors were staring at him. "There are venders along the avenue," he said hurriedly, pointing to the south. "Follow that road until you find a stand that sells fancy hats. Wait for me there. I need to pick up a present for my wife on the way home."

Then Alprin left the fighter and disappeared into the crowd. Kelemvor milled about the docks for ten minutes, then headed down the shop-lined avenue.

The only stand that sold fine hats bore a sign that read "Messina's Elegant Boutique." The fighter felt somewhat strange standing outside the rows of beautiful women's clothing, and the occasional stare he received from the women who met in clusters near the shop to gossip made him even more uneasy.

Eventually, Kelemvor noticed a white-haired minstrel who busied himself at a nearby stand and occasionally glanced in the fighter's direction. Just as the fighter was about to walk to the man and question him, a beautiful, silver-haired woman stumbled into him. She seemed frightened, and a huge red welt covered the right side of her pretty face. Clinging to the fighter, she pleaded, "Help me. He's gone crazy!"

Before Kelemvor could say a word, a young man approached the woman, his hands balled into fists.

"That's my property," the man growled at Kelemvor. "Take your hands off her."

The fighter felt his lips curl back in disgust as he looked

carefully at the man. Dressed in a simple brown felt outfit that bore several large stains, the man was small and mean. From his stench and his swagger, Kelemvor knew that he was also very drunk.

"Stand away," Kelemvor said, although in his head a voice screamed, *The curse! What if it's not really gone?* He grimaced and drove the thoughts out of his mind. Now's as good a time as any to find out, the green-eyed fighter decided.

The grubby little man stood still for a moment, shocked at the fighter's words. "You stand away," the man said. "That's my woman."

"She seems to have other ideas," Kelemvor snarled. He put his arm around the woman's waist and gently maneuvered her to his side. Then he drew his sword. The brightly polished steel blade glinted in the sunlight. "But I'll tell you what. I'll fight you for her."

The man's gaze took in the full measure of Kelemvor's blade, rose to the fighter's cold eyes, then moved to the frightened face of the silver-haired woman. The drunken man lowered his head, turned his back, and walked away. Once the little man was out of view, Kelemvor returned his sword to its sheath and faced the woman.

"I know his type," the fighter muttered. "He's frightened now, but he'll return for you." The fighter pulled out his bag of gold. Taking the woman's soft hand, he spilled a fistful of gold into her palm, then gently closed her fingers. "Book passage on the next boat heading for Ravens Bluff. You can send for your things."

A tear fell from the silver-haired woman's eye. She nodded, kissed the fighter, then hurried north, vanishing into the crowd. Kelemvor felt a satisfaction that he had not known since he was a young boy, since before the Lyonsbane's curse first took hold of his life. If I am still cursed, the fighter thought, it's dormant . . . for now, at least.

Suddenly the minstrel was beside Kelemvor, leaning in close. "Young love can be daunting," the minstrel sighed. "Still, that was a good thing you did. Not many would take an interest in the trials of a stranger."

"Good deeds can be their own reward," Kelemvor said quietly and turned to gaze at the minstrel. The old man's face was rimmed by a long, white beard and his eyes were surrounded by a patchwork of endless wrinkles.

"In Waterdeep, they tell a grand tragedy of young love and dark desire," the old man said, looking into Kelemvor's eyes. "Some call the tale's ending terribly sad. Others see the finale as gloriously happy. I could sing it to you, if you like."

The minstrel strummed his harp and opened his mouth to begin his tale. However, before he uttered a single word or played a single note, the old man stopped suddenly and held out his empty hand.

The fighter smiled and put a gold piece into the open hand. "Sing away, minstrel."

"Kelemvor!" a voice sounded, and the fighter looked to his left to see Alprin emerge from the crowd. When Kelemvor turned back to the minstrel, he saw that the old man had vanished.

"You seem troubled," Alprin noted sagely as he walked to Kelemvor's side.

The fighter frowned as he looked for the wandering minstrel in the crowd. "Not troubled, my friend. Just annoyed. I wanted to hear the tale that the old man promised me. Now I never will."

After purchasing a hat for Alprin's wife, Kelemvor and the harbormaster headed east, into the heart of the city, then took a winding road to the north, where the incline of the streets became quite sharp. A moderate one-story house was soon before the riders. Alprin placed the hat, a rose-colored bonnet with pink silk styling, behind his back, then entered the dwelling.

"And how is my poor, neglected wife today?" Alprin called out from the front door.

"She'd be a damn shade better if her husband spent some time with her," a voice cried in response. Moments later, the owner of the voice, a plain woman with straight black hair and a dark complexion, came into view. She uttered a little scream of delight when Alprin showed her the hat.

"For you, my love," the harbormaster laughed as he rested the hat on his wife's head, then kissed her.

"Who's this?" the woman said suspiciously, pointing to Kelemvor.

Alprin cleared his throat nervously. "A dinner guest, dear," the harbormaster said innocently.

"I might have known," she huffed. Then a smile crossed her face and she reached out to take Kelemvor's hand. "I'm Moira. You're welcome if you're a friend of my husband."

An hour later, over the finest meal the fighter had tasted since he left Arabel, Kelemvor spoke of the many strange sights he had seen in his recent travels, although he was careful to leave out many of the reasons for his journeys through Faerun.

"Such madness you've witnessed," Alprin gasped delightedly and turned to his wife. "To think, Moira, you and I could be free to travel, to see such amazing sights."

"Why don't you just leave the city when you want?" the fighter asked with his mouth half-full of bread.

Moira immediately stood and started to clear the table. Alprin's expression grew serious. "Kelemvor," he said somberly, "if I can secure safe passage for you and your companions, will you leave Tantras as quickly as you can?"

"That's my intention . . . eventually," the fighter told his friend. "But why are you so anxious to see me go?"

"People have been vanishing," Alprin whispered flatly. "Good people."

Moira dropped a metal goblet, and it clattered noisily to the floor. Alprin bent to help his wife clean up the spilled water and she whispered, "He might be one of them! Watch what you say!"

"What sort of people have been vanishing?" Kelemvor asked, not letting on that he had overheard Moira's hushed comments. "Strangers, like myself?"

Alprin shook his head as he deposited a damp cloth on a plate. Moira fixed him with an angry glare, then took the plate and went into the kitchen. "I wouldn't blame you if you thought I were mad once you've heard my story," the harbormaster murmured.

"I don't think that at all," Kelemvor said, surprise evident in his voice.

"A friend of mine, Manacom, disappeared," Alprin began. "One day he was here, the next day he was gone. No one in the guards or the city government would talk about him. All of his records disappeared from the city's books.

"I tried to find out what happened to him. Within a few hours, I was caught by a band of robbers and beaten within an inch of my life. I tried to fight back, but there were too many of them." Alprin paused and looked into the kitchen, where his wife was cleaning plates. "Moira had some healing potions that someone had given to us as a wedding present. I might have died if not for them."

"Couldn't the clerics of Torm heal you? If their god is nearby, they should have the power to heal," Kelemvor said.

"The power, but not the desire," Moira grumbled as she entered the room once more, wiping her hands on her apron.

"Who do you think took your friend?" Kelemvor asked quietly.

Alprin shook his head. "I don't know. But I have my suspicions. It's best that I don't involve you."

Kelemvor laughed. "You've already involved me just by telling me anything about this. You might as well finish what you started. At least you can tell me what you think is going on, even if you won't tell me who's doing it."

Alprin sighed and nodded. "I think that someone has been quietly pushing all those who believe in gods other than Torm out of the city. I've heard rumors that a few clerics, like Manacom, refused to leave, and so they were killed," the harbormaster guessed. "And whoever took Manacom must believe that I know too much, that I'll snoop around until I uncover their plot."

The fighter shook his head. "Then why not just kidnap you now?"

"Because that would arouse too much suspicion," Moira whispered. "Alprin's well known around here. His disappearance would cause quite a stir. And that's the last thing they want right now."

Alprin shook his head. "But if you and your friends go nosing around after religious artifacts, as you've said you were going to, you're sure to draw their attention." The harbormaster paused and wiped the sweat from his forehead. "I couldn't save my friend. Maybe I can save you, Kelemvor."

Kelemvor started to get up from the table, but Moira put

her hand on his arm. "Stay," Moira told the fighter firmly. "We may have put you in danger just by talking to you. The least we can do is put you up for the night."

Alprin smiled. "Anyway, I can't tell you how long it's been since Moira and I have been able to tell stories with guests until late into the night. And if you do stay, I can give you the names of some men who will likely take the lot of you away from Tantras. I know personally most of the captains who stop in this port."

"And perhaps you can talk my husband into booking passage for the two of us as well," Moira whispered as she leaned close to the fighter.

Kelemvor sighed and sat back in his chair. "Very well. I'll stay."

Kelemvor slept in a room that had been meant as a nursery, until Moira learned that she was unable to bear children. He had a fitful sleep, and a few hours later, the fighter woke to find that Alprin had already left for the harbor. Moira fixed a late morningfeast for the fighter, and the two talked for a little while. Soon, though, Kelemvor returned to the Lazy Moon Inn. There he found a letter from Midnight. His lover related her limited successes of the previous day. She also told Kelemvor of the strange goings–on at the temples throughout the city.

Kelemvor read the letter through to the end, then left the inn without writing a reply. Midnight's comments on the temples in Tantras seemed to concur with the harbormaster's fears of conspiracy. The fighter wanted to investigate a little before he alarmed Midnight needlessly, though, so he went in search of information, the final words of Midnight's letter echoing in his mind.

"The Dark Harvest is dangerous. Avoid it at all costs. Will explain later . . ."

At the harbor, Kelemvor found Alprin and learned that tentative arrangements had been made for him and his companions to leave Tantras on a small galley from Calaunt. The captain was a superstitious fellow, but trustworthy, and the ship would be in port for at least a few more days. Alprin made sure, for security's sake, that no member of the ship's crew would be apprised of the additional passengers until just before they left the port.

Satisfied with the arrangements, Kelemvor asked Alprin about the criminal underground of Tantras and the Dark Harvest.

"Those two things are one and the same," Alprin spat, looking around the docks nervously. "The city leaves that particular festhall alone because some of their spies get their information there. It's the slimiest hole in the city, a stinking pool of depravity and foul worship."

It was suddenly obvious to the fighter that Midnight's fear of the Dark Harvest was understandable. Still, Kelemvor thought of himself as an experienced professional, a sea-soned adventurer. He knew that the best way to uncover in-formation on dark dealings was to dig through the filth with the criminals, even if it meant getting dirty along the way.

"And who would be the best person to contact there for information?" Kelemvor whispered, "Someone who has knowledge of the entire underworld of this city?"

Alprin scanned the faces of the dozen or so people that were within a hundred-foot radius. No one appeared to be watching. "Why do you ask?" Alprin said suspiciously, run-ning a hand across his weatherbeaten face.

"My friends and I came here for a purpose that I can't dis-cuss," Kelemvor told the harbormaster. "I've got to ask you to trust me on this." The fighter picked at a wooden railing for a moment, then leaned on it.

Alprin sighed and shook his head. "Now you do sound like Manacom." He turned away from the fighter. "Look, I thought we had this discussion last night. Besides, we shouldn't be speaking of such things in the open. The dan-ger is too great. Wait until tonight."

"I can't wait until tonight," Kelemvor snapped, his anger rising, the volume of his voice attracting unwanted stares. His hands had balled into fists, but the fighter forced his body to relax. "My apologies," he whispered. "But tonight could be too late for what I need to do."

The harbormaster turned back to the fighter, then leaned on the railing next to him. "I don't like it," Alprin grumbled sourly. "But if you're determined to go to the Dark Harvest, the one you want to ask for is Sabinus. He's a smuggler with ties to the city government and the Tormites, too. Now go. I've told you too much already. If anyone suspects I've told you—"

"They'll never know." Kelemvor smiled as he patted the harbormaster on the back. "You've been a true friend, and you have my gratitude. I owe you for this."

"Then repay your debt by getting out of this city in one piece," Alprin grumbled and walked away, scanning the crowd as he went.

Kelemvor nodded, and walked from the harbor. The fighter moved along the streets quickly, and stopped only long enough to receive directions to the Dark Harvest Festhall when he got lost.

An hour later, the fighter stood before the one-story, ebon and scarlet building, shaking his head. He could understand why the sight filled Midnight with trepidation. The festhall even *looked* corrupt. Kelemvor suppressed a shudder and walked inside.

"Are you expected?" an ugly, obese man asked sharply as the fighter entered the Dark Harvest.

"Good news is never expected," Kelemvor growled. "Just tell Sabinus that the owner of the Ring of Winter is here, anxious to relieve himself of some excess baggage."

The fat man snorted. "You don't have a name?"

"Sabinus doesn't need my name. He only needs to know what I possess," Kelemvor snarled.

"Wait here," the guard said as he eyed the fighter suspiciously. Then the fat man passed through a set of double doors. The sounds of gaming and laughter flooded into the lobby the instant the doors were open, then disappeared as they shut again.

A few minutes later, the guard returned and motioned for Kelemvor to follow. They entered the festhall, and the sights and sounds of unbridled decadence rushed at the fighter. There were five bars with men and women two-deep. Dancers from far-off lands gyrated on the bars, and some leaped from table to table, taunting the men and taking their money.

Gamblers wagered with stakes that were sometimes their own lives, but more often the lives of others. A beautiful woman lay on a table between two old men who rolled a set of dice to see who would possess her for the evening. At another table, the scene was reversed: a handsome, muscle-bound man with golden hair lay smiling between two women gamblers.

The whole room smelled of spilled liquor and decaying rubbish. Strange beasts ran along the crowded floor. Fur brushed Kelemvor's leg, and he saw a lump of matted hair and fangs speed away, swallowing anything that happened to be loose on the floor. He had no idea what the strange creature was.

Soon, though, the fighter was led to Sabinus's table, and he was surprised to see how young the notorious man really was. The smuggler could not have been more than seventeen winters old. His red hair was cropped short, and his complexion was almost as red as his hair. And though he looked young, there was a feeling of dark wisdom about Sabinus—the same air that surrounded old, musty secrets and ancient, decaying cursed artifacts. The smuggler motioned for Kelemvor to sit. The fighter did so and rested his hands above the table, empty palms facing up, in a standard gesture of trust.

"You have aroused my interest," Sabinus hissed. "But do not think to waste my time. The Dragon Reach is filled with louts like you whose reach exceeds their grasp."

"I would never consider wasting your valuable time," Kelemvor lied. "I bring something of great value."

The smuggler squirmed in his seat slightly. "So I'm told. The Ring of Winter is not an item to be taken lightly. I thought it was lost for all time."

"That which has been lost can always be found. Now let's stop fencing and get to business," Kelemvor told the boy flatly, moving his hands beneath the table.

A dark, toothy grin passed over Sabinus's face. "Good. To the point. I like that." The red-haired smuggler rocked in his chair, almost giddy with anticipation. "If you have the ring, produce it."

"You think I would have it with me? What kind of fool do you take me for?" Kelemvor asked bitterly.

"That depends on what kind of fool you are," the boy

snapped. "Are you the kind of fool that would dare lie to me about such an important matter? The Ring of Winter is power. With it, a new ice age could be brought down upon the Realms. Only the strongest, or those prepared for the disaster, could hope to survive." Sabinus ran his hands through his hair.

Kelemvor narrowed his eyes and leaned toward the smuggler. Two guards nearby stiffened and reached for daggers, but Sabinus waved them away. "I can give you the precise location of where the ring is hidden. I can tell you the dangers involved in retrieving it *and* how to get around them," Kelemvor told the boy.

"What do you want in return?" Sabinus asked warily.

I want you to tell me where the Tablet of Fate is, the fighter thought sarcastically, but I'll settle for some clues as to its whereabouts. What he said was, "Information. I need to know why the followers of Sune, Ilmater, and any god other than Torm have been driven out of the city . . . and by whose order."

"Perhaps I could tell you that," Sabinus murmured. "Tell me more about the Ring of Winter. Your words may loosen my tongue and jog my memory." The boy leaned forward.

Kelemvor frowned. He thought of the ice creature that guarded the ring when last he saw the artifact and of all the people the creature had slaughtered. Then the green-eyed fighter told Sabinus all that he knew.

Across the festhall, in a shadowy corner of the window-less building, two men sat and watched Sabinus and Kelemvor. One of the men wore a black visor with slits for eyes. The other man was lean and dark, and felt very odd as he watched the fighter fall neatly into his trap.

"Sabinus plays his part well," Cyric said casually as he leaned back into the shadows.

"I don't like this," Durrock growled. "No more than I liked being shipped across the Dragon Reach in a crate that was more like a coffin."

"You didn't even have to get into the crate until we were in sight of land," Cyric snapped. "Are you that superstitious? Do you really believe that lying in a coffin one day means you'll draw your final breath the next? If that's true, Durrock, perhaps we should go before you've had your contest."

"No," the scarred assassin grumbled and slid his hand toward his knife. "I've failed my god. I must make amends. But I don't want to see that crate again." And I'd like to see you dead, thief, he added silently.

Cyric shook his head and laughed. "How many times must I explain this? With your face, we never would have gotten into the city. You have a reputation, Durrock. You are famous, as assassins go. The crate and Sabinus's connections at the docks were the only way to get you into Tantras without sounding alarms."

Durrock looked away. Even with the interference of the visor, Cyric could tell the man was brooding.

"Look there. Sabinus is leading him away," Cyric noted as he picked up his flagon and took a drink of dark, bitter ale. "They're heading downstairs, to the arena. You'd best hurry. The instant Kelemvor thinks he's been betrayed, he'll try to escape." The thief put down his ale and smiled. "And Bane would be very unhappy with you if that happened again, wouldn't he?"

"With both of us," Durrock reminded the hawk-nosed thief and stood up.

"May fortune shine upon you," Cyric told the assassin as he watched him follow Kelemvor and Sabinus to the south end of the festhall. There, the fighter and the smuggler passed through a private doorway and walked down a winding set of stairs. The stairs, in turn, led into a darkened room, a lightless hole that seemed to hungrily absorb the flickers of light from Sabinus's lantern. They reached the landing, then moved into the darkness.

The fighter was tense, his senses alert. "You have records stored down here?" Kelemvor growled impatiently as he tried to focus on any distinct object in the dark room.

"Where else could I keep them?" the smuggler laughed. "In fact, I have one document nearby that contains a seal and a signature you might find interesting. It is a warrant of execution."

The edge of a large, white platform loomed out of the darkness before Kelemvor and the smuggler, and suddenly a dozen torches were lit, revealing the trap Kelemvor had foolishly stumbled into. At that moment, the fighter realized that the festhall's basement was some type of arena, with a platform in its center and balconies where spectators could view the proceedings from above. The fighter could see that almost a hundred people had gathered there already.

"The warrant is for your execution, of course!" Sabinus cried as he dashed toward a doorway near a row of seats on the ground level. Before Kelemvor could move after him, a bright flash of light caught his eye. He looked up and saw a huge man wearing a black visor standing upon the staircase. Torchlight reflected off the surface of the visor.

"Durrock," Kelemvor hissed. But the fighter quickly put aside his surprise and got into a defensive stance, drawing his sword with a liquid grace. The scarred assassin silently descended the staircase, his night-black sword, marked with crimson runes, gripped in his hand.

The assassin was dressed in dark leather, with metal bands at his ankles, thighs, waist, and biceps. As Durrock reached the arena's floor, he raised his hands and crossed his arms. When his wrists touched, there was a sharp sound, and the metal bands flipped up and became razor-sharp ridges. Durrock then ripped the visor from his face and threw it to the ground.

Kelemvor backed away, shocked at the deformities of the assassin's face. The crowd, silent until now, erupted into chaos, and cries and jeers rained down on the two men in the arena. The fighter leaped onto the white square, thirty feet at each side, and stared at Durrock's face as the assassin jumped onto the platform, too. There were few hints of humanity left on the killer's twisted visage.

Suddenly Durrock raced forward, his black sword spiraling through the air. The assassin moved like lightning, dancing around Kelemvor and slashing at the fighter. Then the scarred man backed away before Kelemvor had a chance to return the attack.

By all the gods! the fighter thought. Where was Durrock trained? Kelemvor's own talent labeled him as more than a fair swordsman, but the assassin was a master.

The assassin backed up a step, then spun and kicked Kelemvor in the stomach with his full weight. The fighter recoiled from the blow, his hair flying forward, over his face. Durrock spun once more, this time slicing down with his blade, too.

A handful of black hair lined with grayish streaks sailed forward. Durrock snatched it from the air with quicksilver reflexes.

"This could have been your neck, scum," the assassin said to Kelemvor as he held out the tuft of hair. "You might as well surrender now!"

The crowd roared. "Twenty gold pieces on the misshapen freak!" one of the spectators cried.

"Fifty gold pieces on the ugly brute with a scar for a face!" a woman screamed, and laughter erupted in the shadowy balconies.

Angered by the taunts, Durrock shouted and brought his sword down upon the fighter with a crude, overhand swing. Kelemvor blocked the blow with his own blade, and a rain of sparks pierced the shadows surrounding the arena. Still, the attack drove Kelemvor to his knees.

"Draw some blood, you freak!" a spectator shrieked. "Draw some blood or we'll chain you to the festhall's front door to frighten the little children away!"

"I'll kill you, then I'll find your little mage," Durrock hissed as he turned and drove the hilt of his sword into Kelemvor's forehead. The fighter fell back, and the assassin delivered a kick that tore open a bloody wound on Kelemvor's chest.

Kelemvor thought of running, but he knew that the only way he would ever leave the Dark Harvest alive would be to kill Durrock first. The green-eyed fighter ignored the burning pain in his chest and threw his sword high into the air, then scrambled toward the assassin. Durrock's gaze followed the sword for just an instant, but that was long enough for Kelemvor to kick him in the side, then grab his sword as it fell to the ground.

There was a sickening sound as the fighter's sword bit through the assassin's knee and leg. The tip of the blade had only passed through an inch of Durrock's knee, but it was more than enough to cripple him. Durrock shifted his weight to his uninjured leg, sprang away from the fighter, and fell to the floor.

The crowd watched with breathless excitement as Kelemvor leaped over the downed assassin. The fighter's blade swept through the air, and Durrock rolled and struck with his black sword. As the fighter leaned into his attack, a splatter of blood flew from his shoulder. Fearful that Durrock's well-aimed slash had severed an artery, the fighter ducked into a crouch, one hand instinctively clamping over the cut.

Losing the use of one leg had barely slowed Durrock. The assassin drove his blade into the floor, pushed off with his good leg, and vaulted toward Kelemvor, twisting in midair to position his strong leg outward. In the split second before the assassin met his enemy, Kelemvor rolled away from the razor at Durrock's ankle, which was aimed to rip open the fighter's throat.

Kelemvor raised his sword as Durrock landed over him. The flat of the assassin's blade struck the fighter full in the face, but the green-eyed man focused all his strength on a single forward sweep of his sword. Then Kelemvor felt his weapon pierce flesh and crack bones as it struck the assassin's chest. The fighter collapsed onto the white canvas as Durrock fell upon him.

The razor on the assassin's left arm grazed Kelemvor's forehead as he tried to move. The fighter's sword was trapped beneath Durrock's weight, stuck in the scarred man's body. Panic raced through Kelemvor as he tried to free his arms and saw the razor beside his face move a few inches. He looked up and saw Durrock's twisted, scarred face only a few inches from his own. Blood was leaking from the assassin's mouth as he tried, but failed, to speak. Durrock's face fell forward, and Kelemvor knew that the assassin was dead.

There was commotion in the balcony, and the fighter heard the sounds of men racing onto the surface of the arena. The corpse was dragged from Kelemvor, and the fighter threw his head back in exhaustion. When he opened his eyes, Kelemvor focused on the balcony in front of him. He simply wasn't prepared for the sight that greeted him.

Cyric stood just beneath a flickering torch, staring down at the bloodied fighter in shock. The two men locked eyes for a moment, and a wicked grin crossed the face of the hawk-nosed man. Someone passed in front of Kelemvor at that moment, blocking his view. When the fighter looked into the balcony again, the thief was gone.

A short, almost completely bald dwarf helped the fighter to his feet. Rising unsteadily, Kelemvor knew that he would have to try to catch Cyric. But the fighter also knew that the thief, and Sabinus, too, would be long gone.

"A true champion!" the bald dwarf called out, then turned to face Kelemvor. "What would you like? Gold, women, power, secrets? Tell me, and it is yours. We haven't had such an upset in this arena for years."

"Secrets," Kelemvor hissed wearily.

"Come with me, then," the dwarf bellowed. "We will bind your wounds and tell you all you wish to know."

Twenty minutes later, Kelemvor had discovered that Durrock's blade had not hurt him badly, and he was already recovering from the loss of blood when he left the festhall. He stopped at a nearby stable and bought a horse, for he was far too weak to walk to the harbor and then to the inn.

As the fighter rode to the docks, he tried not to let his anger get in the way of the task he had to perform. In the Dark Harvest, Kelemvor had learned that a city official by the name of Dunn Tenwealth had been linked with the disappearances Alprin had mentioned. Tenwealth had also been placed in charge of the salvage of all religious artifacts that had been not been taken away or placed in storage by the various abandoned temples in the city. Many of these items had been locked in a vault that was located "beneath the hand of Torm."

If the Tablet of Fate had been hidden in one of the temples in Tantras, it was possible that Tenwealth had unwittingly acquired the item, then locked it away, ignorant of its power. The man would have to be questioned and his vault would have to be searched. But there was something else Kelemvor wanted to deal with first: Cyric.

The thief must have aligned himself with the Black Lord, the fighter concluded. But Kelemvor wasn't going to let the thief escape to his master. Cyric would now be returning in a hurry to whatever ship he had come to Tantras in. Yes, the fighter decided bitterly, I'm going to find that vessel, catch up to Cyric, and beat the Black Lord's plans out of him before hacking off his head.

At the harbor, Kelemvor tried to find Alprin to help him search for the Zhentish spy ship, but the harbormaster was nowhere in sight. The fighter made a few inquiries, and learned that Alprin had received a message that so filled him with fear that he ran from his station as if a fire giant were running at his heels.

The fighter walked away in silence, wondering what could have gone wrong to panic the harbormaster so. "Alprin," he said aloud as he realized what must have happened. "Not his wife!"

Kelemvor ran from the harbor, collected his mount, and raced to Alprin's home. The building was in flames when Kelemvor arrived, but he could still get close enough to peer through an open window. Alprin lay on the floor, a bloody smear behind his head. Moira lay beside him. The dead man's hand had been placed around his wife's body in a mockery of the tenderness they had shared in life. A message had been written on the wall behind his body.

I was unfaithful. This is my penance.

A frightened crowd was gathering in the street, calling for the bucket brigade to put the fire out before it spread to their houses and shops. Kelemvor clamped his hands over his mouth and stumbled away from the burning building. All thoughts of finding Cyric were lost in the fighter's grief for the moment.

Horribly shaken, the teary-eyed fighter returned to the Lazy Moon Inn, and scribbled a three-word note to Midnight. By now, the fighter realized that he had little hope of finding the Zhentish spy ship. Cyric had escaped. For now. So the fighter turned his thoughts to the name he'd been given in the Dark Harvest, and set out to find Dunn Tenwealth, a lust to revenge the harbormaster's death burning in his mind.

For many hours, Kelemvor reconnoitered the Citadel of Tantras and the adjacent buildings. The trail had led first to the citadel, the center of Tantras's government. Then it took Kelemvor to the Temple of Torm. There the trail ended, and Kelemvor knew that he did not dare try to barge into the well-guarded place of worship, searching for a murderer.

When Kelemvor finally returned to the Lazy Moon Inn, he found Midnight waiting in their room. The mage was frantic with worry.

"I spent half the night on the docks trying to find you," Midnight cried as she embraced the fighter and they kissed.

"What did you mean by that note?" Midnight whispered as she pulled away from the fighter and wiped the tears from her eyes.

"Exactly what it said. Cyric is alive, and he tried to kill me. I've seen him, and I have no doubt he will make other attempts on my life . . . or your life," Kelemvor growled and stomped across the room. "Is Adon in his room? We should leave the inn and hide for a while. There's a slum near the docks where we can maintain a much lower profile."

"Adon hasn't returned yet," Midnight said.

Kelemvor's face turned white. "He's still at the temple?"

"Yes. Why?" the raven-haired mage asked in a low tone.

Reaching for the door, Kelemvor gestured for Midnight to follow. "We'll have to find him. Adon's in terrible danger from the Tormites. I'll explain on the way!"

Midnight nodded and followed the fighter out of the room, stopping only long enough to grab the canvas sack containing her spellbook.

❧ 14 ❧

TORM

Outside the Lazy Moon Inn, Adon watched as Kelemvor and Midnight said their farewells. The concern the lovers showed for one another was touching, if a little maudlin. Still, the cleric knew that searching the city alone was dangerous and they might never see one another again. But it was better that way. Midnight and Kelemvor could search for the tablet wherever they pleased, and Adon wouldn't slow them down.

"Adon," Midnight said, and the cleric snapped to attention. The mage smiled at him warmly. "Try not to worry. We're going to be fine."

"So you say," the cleric mumbled.

Midnight gripped the young man's arm tightly. "And stop feeling sorry for yourself," she whispered, then turned and walked away. Kelemvor stared at the mage as she headed down the street, while Adon made his way across the lane, then merged with the crowd.

The cleric expected his mission to the Temple of Torm to be a simple matter. Having visited the clergy of many different gods in his travels, Adon was familiar with the protocol for calling upon priests of rival denominations. Holding both hands side by side, palms facing up, thumbs stretched as far apart as possible, was almost universally accepted as a sign of peaceful intentions. By showing this sign and saying, "There is room for all," a cleric could expect to gain admittance to most temples quite easily.

But as the cleric of Sune passed through the Citadel of Tantras, he felt that gaining entrance to Torm's temple might not be so easy. People stared at him as he passed, then looked away and pretended that they hadn't noticed the young man. Others pointed at Adon and whispered amongst themselves. The number of guards Adon encountered increased as he moved farther toward the temple, too. He had the feeling that he was heading toward an armed camp, not a house of worship.

The spires of the citadel were impressive, but Adon expected their allure to pale beside the rebuilt Temple of Torm, a living god. He was stunned by the sight of the plain three-story building that had been surrounded by protective walls and a series of interlocking gates. Pairs of simple one-story towers, with covered walkways leading from one to another, served as gatehouses.

Warriors wearing the symbol of Torm waited outside each gatehouse. Adon approached the first pair of well-armed guards, performed the ritualistic greeting, and announced himself as a worshiper of Sune. Though it pained the young cleric to claim he still worshiped the Goddess of Beauty, he knew that he would be allowed into the temple more quickly if he appeared to be a visiting priest.

The warriors failed to answer the greeting in the customary manner. Instead, one guard ran off to alert his superiors. Then two more armed guards appeared, and Adon was taken into one of the gatehouses, where he was subjected to a series of interviews. Various clerics and members of the town government asked the scarred young man a wide variety of questions about everything from his hobbies as a boy to his opinions about various philosophical matters. Adon was as helpful as possible, but when he expressed his confusion at the odd treatment he was receiving, he received no explanation. Strangely, what Adon thought would be the most important question—his reason for visiting the temple—was never brought up.

"Why is this questioning necessary?" Adon demanded of the fifth interviewer, a bored civil servant who looked out at the cleric through dark, hooded eyes. It was now several hours after eveningfeast, and the cleric had begun to wish that he had forced himself to eat something before he left the Lazy Moon.

"Why do you worship Sune?" the bored man asked Adon

for the fifth time, then looked down at a sheet of parchment that rested on the table before him.

"I'll answer no more questions until I receive some information in return," Adon said flatly, crossing his arms over his chest. The civil servant sighed, folded up his parchment, and shuffled out of the sparse, stone room. The scarred cleric heard a bolt slide into place on the other side of the door. With the door now locked and the small window in the cell filled with strong, iron bars, Adon knew that it would be futile to search for an escape route. So he waited.

It was almost six hours later that a cleric wearing the robes of Torm entered the chamber where Adon had been left to wait. Introducing himself, the scarred cleric performed the ritual of greeting and waited for a response.

"We have no temple to Sune in Tantras," the bald Tormite told the prisoner, ignoring Adon's downturned eyes and opened hands. "Lord Torm walks among us. He is all. Our god sets the hours of the day, the loyalty—"

"The loyalty in your heart, the reason in your head. I've heard it all before," Adon snapped, his calm facade splintering. He stood up and took a step toward the bald man. "I want to know why I have been subjected to this insulting test of endurance."

The Tormite narrowed his eyes, and his features turned cold and lifeless. "You have no business being in a temple dedicated to Torm, Adon of Sune. You will be shown out immediately."

As the bald man turned, Adon subdued his anger. "Wait!" the young cleric called. "I meant no insult."

The bald man turned back to face Adon, a sneer on his face. "You are not a practicing cleric. I've already been told that," the man growled. "You have no real business in *any* house of worship."

Adon felt his heart race with anger and confusion. He had mentioned nothing to the interviewers of his recent loss of faith.

The bald man must have read the confusion in Adon's eyes, for he growled, "The nature of the questions we have asked you allows us to make inferences with a very high degree of accuracy. You are as easy to read as any book in our library."

"What else do you know about me?" Adon asked, worry beginning to well up inside of him. If the Tormites had discovered anything about the Tablets of Fate from his answers, Midnight and Kelemvor might now be in danger, too.

The cleric of Torm walked to Adon and stood directly in front of him. "You are disillusioned. That scar on your face is recent. And you *want* something from us."

"I seek an audience with Lord Torm," Adon told the bald man, meeting the Tormite's look of disgust with one of quiet anger.

The bald cleric tried to hide his surprise at Adon's audacity, but he failed miserably. "That is hardly a request to be made lightly. Besides, why should the God of Loyalty see a faithless wretch such as you?"

"Why shouldn't he?" Adon asked, shrugging. "I have been witness to sights that only a god or goddess could interpret or appreciate."

The bald man raised one eyebrow. "Such as?"

Adon looked away. The cleric knew that he would have to choose his words carefully. "Tell the God of Duty that I have seen Lord Helm stand at the head of a Celestial Stairway. I have heard the guardian's warning to the fallen gods."

The bald man's lips curled back in a snarl, and he raised his hand as if to strike Adon, then stopped. The Tormite paused for a moment, then forced himself to smile weakly. "Since you have come to Torm with this knowledge, my superiors may wish to speak with you further." The bald man gently grabbed Adon's arm and led him from the room. "Come. We will find a place for you to sleep in the barracks outside the temple. It may be some time before my masters can find a moment to speak with you."

Adon rested that night on a warm cot inside the building outside the gate to the temple. The cots were usually reserved for guards who were stationed on call, but, on this night at least, there were more cots than guards. For a short time, Adon actually managed to sleep. The rest of the time he spent mulling over his relationship to the gods and forcing images of Elminster's final moments in the Temple of Lathander out of his mind.

During his periods of wakefulness, Adon strained to listen to the guards' conversations on the walkway outside the gate. If he concentrated, the young cleric could hear fragments of various discussions that went on outside his window. Most of the talk concerned women or drink, but a few statements caught Adon's attention.

"To have seen Lord Torm's face is enough. I understand there are those who have even touched his robes . . . ," one voice said in a reverent tone.

Adon felt a sickness in his heart. The voice had been so pitiful, so awestruck. Would he sound that way if Sune had appeared before him? At one time, perhaps, but certainly not now.

A few minutes later, two more figures paused beside the barracks. "Dangerous talk!" a woman said, her voice full of fear. "Don't let anyone hear you say that. Do you want to vanish like the others?"

Later still, another man said, "I've heard talk of a fringe group that worships Oghma, the God of Knowledge. I have their names and addresses. With Lord Torm's grace, by the end of the week—"

"Lord Torm does not need to be troubled with such matters, my friend!" another voice snapped. "Just give the information to me. I'll see that the situation is handled properly. . . ."

Finally, just before the hour of dawn was announced, a man stopped directly outside Adon's window. "He must never find out," the gravel-voiced man grumbled. "It was all for him, all in his name." He paused. "But Lord Torm might not understand, since he has been removed from the world for so long. He must never know all that has occurred." Then the men were gone.

As dawn was announced, Adon suddenly realized that a priest had silently entered the barracks and stood no more than ten feet to the side of the cleric's cot. Rising from the cot, Adon gave the ritual greeting and felt relief flow through him when the priest returned the gesture. This Tormite was very tall, and his platinum hair was combed straight down, nearly touching his silver eyebrows. The priest's eyes were sky blue, and his smile was so warm that it instantly set Adon at ease.

Suddenly realizing that his hair was unbrushed, rather dirty, and probably sticking up in places, Adon tried to brush his locks into place with one hand. The priest looked on with amusement. Adon laughed and gave up.

"My clothes have been slept in, my hair is a mess, and I haven't eaten since yesterday," Adon said with a sigh. "I suppose I'm hardly what you expected as a cleric of Sune."

The priest put his hand on Adon's shoulder and guided the young cleric out of the small building, past the gatehouse, and onto the walkway leading to Torm's temple.

"Do not concern yourself, Adon of Sune," the priest murmured reassuringly. "We will not judge you by your appearance. As for morningfeast, I have arranged for a private meal to be delivered to my chambers. We will share this, and I will tell you everything that you need to know."

Adon and the platinum-haired priest entered the temple through a gate. A thousand stone gauntlets lined the doorway, and Adon felt uneasy as he brushed past one of them. It seemed to the faithless cleric that the stone hand might reach out and grab him, might prevent someone who didn't have faith in the God of Duty from entering his home. Of course, nothing happened.

The two men passed down a long corridor lined with oaken doors. Each door was adorned with a painted gauntlet, and sounds of chanting and worship drifted through each of the chamber doors.

Soon the corridor forked into two diagonal pathways that stretched for twenty feet in either direction. These smaller hallways ended in doorways. The priest turned to the left, followed the hallway to its end, then opened the polished oaken door. It creaked open, revealing a simple chamber. A straw mattress dominated the cell's floor, and devotional paintings of the God of Duty covered the walls.

The meal that the platinum-haired priest had promised was there, and Adon quickly sat on the floor. A plate of warm bread, along with cheese and fresh fruit, lay on a platter. As the Tormite stood silently over him, the scarred cleric started to eat hungrily. Noticing that the priest was staring, Adon put down his food and waited as the man uttered a prayer over the meal.

Adon started to eat again, and the priest sat down across from him. The platinum-haired man's first words caused the cleric to choke.

"Will you do penance for not blessing your meal?" the Tormite asked softly.

Adon's face turned white, and he got a small piece of bread caught in his throat. He coughed several times, then shook his head vigorously.

The priest leaned forward. "So it's true, then, Adon, that you are no longer a cleric."

Adon began to feel ill as he realized that this was just another interrogation session. He put the chunk of bread he was eating back on his plate.

The platinum-haired man frowned. "A cleric is nothing without belief, and yours is very weak." He paused and studied Adon's eyes. "Have you come here seeking guidance? Is that why you made up that wild story about delivering a message to Lord Torm?" the priest asked sadly.

"Perhaps," Adon whispered. He tried to force a look of shame onto his face to hide his growing fear.

The priest, a broad smile covering his face, clutched Adon's shoulders. "You have just taken the first step toward accepting Lord Torm, the God of Duty. Today you will be allowed to wander the temple freely. You may enter any door marked with the symbol of Torm. All others are off limits to you . . . for now." The Tormite paused, and the smile left his face. "There are serious penalties if you ignore these warnings. I'm sure you understand."

The priest allowed his perfect smile to return, but now Adon saw that expression as threatening somehow.

The scarred cleric cleared his throat and tried to return the platinum-haired man's smile but failed. "You haven't told me your name," Adon said.

"Tenwealth," the Tormite told Adon happily. "Dunn Tenwealth, high priest of Torm. Now, put on a cheerful face, friend Adon. There is reason enough to feel fear and depression outside these walls." The priest stood up and threw his arms open wide. "While you are here, you are safe within the gauntleted hand of Lord Torm."

Tenwealth helped Adon to his feet, then patted him on the shoulder. "I must leave you now," the platinum-haired man said. "I have other duties to attend to."

Adon stayed in the chamber for a little while after Tenwealth left, then spent the morning and half the afternoon observing services and rituals that were so commonplace the scarred cleric soon grew bored. Adon had been a traveler in his youth. He had once seen a pagan ritual performed on the lip of a violently churning volcano that was at once beautiful and terrifying. Although the cleric could appreciate the well-ordered, perfectly respectable rites the followers of Torm performed to honor their god, he was not impressed.

In the middle of the afternoon, Adon sent a messenger to deliver a note to Midnight at the Lazy Moon. Adon then found himself alone in a lush garden that lay at the rear of the temple. A beautiful statue of a golden lion stood in the center of the garden, seeming to stare lazily at Adon as he sat on a stone bench.

Allowing his facade of contentment to drop, the cleric mulled over all that he had seen and heard since he entered the gatehouse almost a day ago. Obviously something sinister was going on in the temple, and it seemed likely that Lord Torm knew nothing about it. Like all the fallen gods, the God of Duty was forced to rely on a human avatar. But Torm was also locked away in a palace, where only smiles of adoration could penetrate the carefully guarded walls. Adon shivered and closed his eyes.

"The gods are as vulnerable as we are," Adon murmured sadly after a few moments.

"I've long suspected it," a voice said nonchalantly. The cleric opened his eyes, turned, and saw a man who was as ruggedly handsome as anyone Adon had ever seen. The man's hair was red, with touches of amber. A neatly trimmed beard and mustache accentuated his strong, proud jaw. The eyes that gazed into Adon's were a rich blue, with flecks of purple and black. Staring at the man's face was not unlike watching a setting sun.

The man smiled warmly, genuinely. "I am Torm. My faithful call me 'the Living God,' but as I gather you already know, I am just one of many gods in Faerun these days." The man held a gauntleted hand out to the cleric.

Adon's shoulders sagged. This was no god. It was merely another cleric sent to test him again.

"Don't torment me!" Adon snapped. "If this is another test of my worth—"

Torm frowned only slightly, then gestured toward the statue of the lion. Suddenly a roar filled the garden, and the golden lion padded toward the red-haired man. Torm caressed the creature's head, and the beast lay obediently at the fallen god's feet. Torm turned to Adon and asked, "Is that proof enough for you?"

The scarred cleric shook his head. "There are many mages who could do that trick," he said flatly.

Torm frowned deeply now.

"And even though your god resides here," Adon added, "you are a madman or a fool for attempting that illusion. Magic is a dangerous force to wield, and I have no desire to endanger myself by remaining in your company." The cleric stood and started to walk away.

"By all the Planes!" the God of Duty cried, then stretched. "You don't know how long it's been since someone has dared to stand up to me! I am, above all, a warrior, and I respect that kind of spirit."

Adon snorted. "Please stop the jests, mage. I don't wish to be taunted any longer."

The god's eyes grew dark, and the golden lion stretched and moved to Torm's side. "Though I may value spirit, Adon of Sune, I will not tolerate insubordination."

Something told Adon he had made a mistake in angering the red-haired man. He looked at Torm and saw the purple and black fragments swirling around angrily in his eyes. The cleric saw power in those eyes, too—power and knowledge far beyond that possessed by any mortal being. At that moment, Adon knew that he was looking into the eyes of a god.

The cleric bowed his head. "I am sorry, Lord Torm. I expected you to travel with an entourage. I never thought to meet you wandering in the gardens alone, unguarded."

The living god stroked his beard. "Ah. You now have faith in my words, I see."

Adon shuddered. *Faith?* he thought bitterly. I've seen gods destroyed as casually as pigs on a market day. I've seen the beings most of Faerun's humans worship act like petty tyrants. No, the cleric realized. I don't have anything close to faith . . . but I do recognize power when I see it. And I know when to bow to save my own life.

The God of Duty smiled. "I left an image sitting upon my throne. It rests there, brooding, and I left orders that I was in an inhospitable mood and would severely punish any who dared to disturb me," Torm said.

"But how did you get here without being seen?" Adon asked, raising his head to look at the god once more.

"The diamond corridors," Torm told the cleric. "They begin in the center of the temple and connect to every chamber. They are designed as a maze, so that few can travel them without becoming lost." The fallen god paused and stroked the lion's mane. "I've heard you have a message for me . . . that you have seen Lord Helm." The god sat down again, and the lion slowly lowered itself to the ground at Torm's feet.

The cleric told as much of the story as he could, leaving out mention of the murders that Cyric committed and Elminster's claim that one of the Tablets of Fate was hidden in Tantras.

"Bane and Myrkul!" Torm growled as Adon finished his tale. "I should have known those treacherous curs were behind the theft of the tablets. And Mystra dead, her power scattered throughout the weave of magic surrounding Faerun! Dark and shocking news." The God of Duty closed his eyes and sighed. Adon could almost feel the fallen god's sorrow.

A man wandered into the garden and froze when he saw Adon and Torm, then ran back inside the temple. The God of Duty seemed to have missed the man's entrance and hasty exit, but Adon did not. He knew that the garden would be filled with Tormites very soon.

The god opened his eyes. "I regret that I cannot help you with your quest to save the Realms," Torm told the cleric. "I am needed here. I have a duty to my faithful." The God of Duty put his hand on Adon's scarred cheek and said, "There is something I *can* help you with, though. You must look inside your heart if you are to banish these dark, guilty thoughts that consume you and make you so bitter. What were you before you joined your order?"

The cleric pulled away from the god's touch as if it were fire. "I was . . . nothing," he whispered. "I was a burden upon my parents. I had no true friends."

"But now friends and lovers grace your life," Torm noted, smiling once more. "From what you have told me, the mage and the fighter seem loyal to you. That, above all, is important. You should honor them, in return, with faithful service to them and their causes. You cannot do that if you are consumed by your own sorrows."

Torm balled his gauntleted hand into a fist. "Don't waste your life in self-pity, Adon of Sune, for you cannot serve your friends . . . or your god, if your heart is weighed down with grief," the fallen god said.

Adon heard voices from inside the temple. People were coming. The scarred cleric leaned close to the God of Duty.

"Thank you for sharing your wisdom, Lord Torm," Adon whispered. "Now let me fulfill my duty to help you. All is not as it seems in your temple or in Tantras. There are forces around you that could tear the city apart. You must look to your clerics and find out what they are doing to serve you. Not all dutiful service is done with justice in mind."

The voices grew louder, then a dozen high priests entered the garden and fell to their knees before Torm. The lion roared in annoyance as the men babbled an almost endless torrent of problems that required their god's immediate attention. Torm rose, smiled at Adon, and turned to the temple's nearest entrance. The golden lion and the crowd of priests followed the god as he left the garden.

Several minutes later, Adon was taken from the garden and locked away in a dark chamber that was devoid of any furnishings. The room reminded the cleric of the cell he had shared with Midnight in the Twisted Tower, but he tried to push those thoughts aside as he waited. It was several hours before a tray of food was brought to him by a silent, surly guard.

"I'm not hungry," Adon mumbled, his grumbling stomach betraying his lie. "Take the food away and tell me why I'm here."

The guard left the food, then departed. An hour later, Adon had finished the meal, which consisted of slightly stale bread and cheese. Soon afterward, a familiar, platinum-haired man entered the chamber, a large smile hanging artfully upon his lips.

"Tenwealth!" Adon gasped and stood up.

"It seems you had quite an adventure today," the priest said. The tone he used would have been suitable for a child. Adon felt insulted. "Would you care to talk about it?"

"What is there to say?" Adon grumbled, a frown pulling at the scar on his cheek, darkening the wound. "I had my audience with Torm. Now I'm ready to leave. Why are your guards unwilling to release me?"

"My guards?" Tenwealth said through the false smile. "Why, they are Torm's guards. They serve the God of Duty and are only doing his will."

"And have I been kept here under his orders?" Adon asked, taking a step toward the priest.

"Not exactly," Tenwealth admitted, running a hand across his chin. "You're not being 'kept' here at all. There's no lock on your door, no guard outside." The priest paused and opened the door. "Of course, there is the danger that you could become lost in Torm's maze before you reach the exit. That would be most unfortunate. Some who have been lost in the diamond corridors have never been heard from again."

Adon looked down at the floor. "I understand," he said dejectedly, then slumped to a sitting position against the wall.

"I thought you might," Tenwealth noted confidently, his perfect smile gleaming in the darkened chamber. "Have a good rest. In a few hours, I'll return for you. You have an audience scheduled with the High Council of Torm. That should set your mind at ease."

The priest left the chamber, and Adon considered the hopelessness of the situation for a little while, then fell into a deep, dreamless sleep. Several hours later, Tenwealth returned with two guards. Adon was fast asleep, and the priest had to shake him roughly to awaken him.

As Adon followed Tenwealth out into the corridor, a plan began to form in his mind. The cleric decided that he would grab a weapon from one of the guards as soon as they were clear of the corridors and fight his way out of the temple. He knew that it was probably suicide, but it was a far better way to die than to be executed in secret. So Adon kept careful watch on the proximity of the guards and played the fool as they marched along. Though Tenwealth became annoyed at Adon's idiotic patter, Adon noted that the two guards relaxed considerably.

Adon was about to make his move against the nearer of the guards when, at the end of the corridor, he saw a white-bearded old man carrying a harp. Suddenly the cleric grabbed a torch from the wall, broke away from Tenwealth and the guards, and ran toward the old man. The platinum-haired priest cried out an order, and the guards raced after the scarred cleric.

"Elminster!" Adon cried as he raced down the hall. "You're alive!"

The old man looked up in alarm. He had been arguing with another priest of Torm, and a momentary flicker of surprise passed across his face when he saw Adon racing toward him. Then he frowned and stood perfectly still.

The young cleric stopped directly before the old man. The blazing torch bathed the minstrel's face in warmth and light, and the heat from the flames made the white-bearded man draw back. And though Adon was certain that he had recognized the man from farther down the hall, closer examination revealed the old man to be someone other than Elminster. The scarred young man was about to turn away from the minstrel when he saw the tip of the old man's nose begin to melt.

"Elminster!" Adon said, his voice cracking, just as Tenwealth's guards reached out for him.

The minstrel looked around, gauged the confusion of the Tormites, and cast a spell before anyone was aware of his true intention. The air crackled, and a shimmering mist of blue-white energies filled the corridor.

"All of ye will accompany Adon and me out of the temple and beyond the citadel. Then ye will return and act as if nothing has happened," Elminster ordered. Tenwealth, the two guards, and the priest nodded stiffly.

The sage smiled. The mass suggestion spell had actually worked! It was the first incantation that had gone right in some time, too. The old mage decided that it must be the close proximity of Torm's avatar that was stabilizing magic a bit, then thanked the Goddess of Luck for good measure and gestured for the Tormites to lead the way out of the corridor.

Adon stood frozen, staring in a mixture of shock and relief at the sage. "Elminster, what are you doing here?"

"My intention was not to save thy worthless hide, I assure ye," the mage growled, wiping a bit of wax from his nose. "Unfortunately, ye left me no choice." Elminster started after the Tormites. When Adon didn't move, he turned back and said, "Ye were hit with that spell, too. If ye dally long enough to make me suggest a course for ye to follow, ye'll not like where it takes ye."

Adon gladly followed the sage. Memories and thoughts whirled in the cleric's mind. Adon knew only that he was relieved to see Elminster alive. Tears of joy streamed down his face.

"Wipe that silly grin from your face and those tears from your eyes," Elminster grumbled as they left the corridors and entered the temple's courtyard. "We don't want to arouse any suspicion."

"But I have so many questions—," Adon began breathlessly.

"They can wait," Elminster snapped.

Adon followed the sage's commands, and within a short time they were several blocks away from the Temple of Torm. They tried to lose themselves in the crowd as soon as Tenwealth and his men headed back to their home.

After a few minutes of pushing their way through milling crowds, Adon turned to Elminster and asked, "Now can you give me some answers?"

"Not until we're safe," Elminster grumbled.

Adon's relief was quickly giving way to anger. Grabbing the sage's arm, the cleric forced the old man to stop. They were on a crowded main street that led to the highest of the citadel's towers, and that building's golden spires were in full view from where they stood. Shops lined the avenue around them.

"Listen to me, old man," the scarred cleric growled. "We'll never be safe as long as we remain in Tantras. The Council of Torm will send its agents after us no matter where we hide. Where we stand at this instant is as good a place as any for you to explain yourself. Now tell me what I want to know."

"Unhand me," Elminster said calmly, his eyes as narrow as a cat's before it springs. "Then I'll tell ye what ye wish to know."

Adon let go of the sage's arm. "Tell me what happened to you in Shadowdale at the Temple of Lathander. I thought you'd died . . . and that it was my fault," Adon said. He felt anger bubble over inside of him and he added, "You can't imagine the hell I've been through because of you!"

"I can readily imagine," Elminster sighed and turned away from the cleric. "Considering where that rift took me."

A voice rang out. "Adon!"

The cleric recognized the voice as Midnight's, and he turned around to look for the mage. A horrible realization dawned upon the cleric then, and he immediately whirled around and grabbed the old sage's arm. Adon looked at Elminster. The mage was ready to walk into the crowd that surrounded them.

"You're not leaving my sight," Adon said. Elminster simply scowled and crossed his arms.

Midnight arrived, with Kelemvor directly behind her. When she saw Elminster, she wrapped her arms around the sage, nearly crushing him in her embrace. The old mage grumbled in protest and pushed her away.

"I'd never have believed it!" Midnight cried as she stepped back from the sage. "I thought I saw you once, yesterday, but I convinced myself that I was only hoping too hard that you'd survived." Tears were streaming down the raven-haired mage's face.

"Never do that again!" Elminster shouted, gesturing with the harp he'd forgotten that he held.

Kelemvor had been surprised to see Elminster, too, but he was now feeling angry, not overjoyed, that the old sage was alive. "Quite a singing voice you have there," the fighter commented sarcastically. "It's too bad you use it to cause so much trouble."

Adon stood a few feet away, staring at the old sage, a barely subdued fury roiling across his features. "You weren't even going to tell us that you were alive. You cruel old buzzard. We're here, risking our lives on your damn quest—"

"Lady Mystra set ye on thy quest," Elminster reminded the cleric. "I simply helped ye along the way."

"We're wanted criminals," Midnight told the mage softly. "Adon and I were nearly executed in Shadowdale for your death."

"That charge has been dropped," Elminster mumbled as he rubbed his neck and motioned for the heroes to follow him. Passersby were beginning to stare, and the heroes agreed that it was probably best to move along.

"I've been to Shadowdale," the sage added. "Ye are no longer suspects in my killing. But there is still the matter of six guards that were murdered during your escape. That ye will still have to answer for."

"You were spying on us," Kelemvor noted flatly. "That's what you were doing here. Checking up on us."

"What else could I do?" Elminster grumbled. "If the charges against ye are true, then ye're hardly fit to serve as champions of Mystra and all of Faerun."

Kelemvor explained that it had been Cyric who'd committed the murders, without Midnight or Adon's knowledge or assistance. The fighter noted, too, that Cyric was now in the employ of the Black Lord.

"You don't know that for sure!" Midnight snapped, shooting the fighter an angry glance. "When you arrived at the safe house in Scardale, you were pretending to work for Bane just to get free of him. Cyric might have been forced into a similar position." The mage turned to Elminster. "I never saw him commit any of the murders of which he's been accused, and Shadowdale has a history of convicting innocent people, as far as I'm concerned."

Adon folded his arms over his chest, and his eyes grew wide with surprise, but the surprise was tinged with fear. "Cyric's alive! He'll come after us next, Midnight."

The raven-haired mage shook her head. "Adon, we have no proof—"

The cleric stopped in the middle of the street. "Cyric is dangerous, Midnight. And not just to us. After the trip down the Ashaba, you should understand that!"

"Let's keep moving," Elminster whispered, scanning the crowd for guards or priests of Torm. "I have a sanctuary nearby where the two of ye can continue thy discussion."

Adon walked to Kelemvor's side, but Midnight put her hand on Elminster's arm. "We'll go, but first, tell us what happened in the Temple of Lathander," the mage ordered. "Adon and I were convinced you'd died. How did you survive the rift?"

Elminster glared at the heroes. "Must we do this now?"

"Aye," Adon said. "*Right* now."

The sage rolled his eyes and motioned for the heroes to follow him into a nearby alley. "My attempt to raise the Eye of Eternity went afoul because of the instability in the magic weave that surrounds and envelops all things. When I examined the rift, I saw that the spell had opened a gate to Gehenna, a terrible place filled with awful, nightmarish creatures."

The sage paused and glanced up and down the alley. "I knew that the only way to seal the rift was to do it from the other side, where the effects of the magical chaos were very slight and my spells were almost certain to succeed. I let the rift pull me into Gehenna, and once I was through, I cast the spells that sealed the gateway. There was only one point of difficulty."

"You were trapped outside of the Realms?" Midnight gasped, her eyes wide with wonder.

"Escape from the Plane of Gehenna, where Loviatar, Mistress of Pain, made her home before the gods were cast down, was not a simple matter. I was forced to fight my way through imps, mephits, and every form of unholy creature imaginable." Elminster shuddered and rubbed his hands up and down his arms. "Eventually I found an area even the monsters feared to tread. Mystra had blessed a patch of ground on that terrible plane centuries ago during a dispute with Loviatar."

A cleric of Torm appeared in the crowd at the end of the alley, and Elminster started to make his way farther up the passage. "When I returned to Shadowdale," he said over his shoulder, "there was little to do but pick up the pieces. And now I am here, wasting time jabbering with ye three even as the damned palace guard makes preparations to hunt us down."

As the heroes walked through the alleys to Elminster's lair, they discussed what they'd discovered. Kelemvor couldn't believe that Adon and the sage had Tenwealth in their grasps and let him walk away. But when the cleric explained Tenwealth's status in Torm's temple, Kelemvor put the final pieces of the puzzle together.

"Torm's high priests are running all those who are faithful to other gods out of the city," the fighter whispered. "Then they take the abandoned temples and add the property to their own."

"That must be why the Sunites burned their temple to the ground, along with everything they couldn't carry away," Midnight added. "They didn't want the Tormites to get it!"

Adon frowned and ran a hand through his dirty, tangled hair. "So most of the sacred artifacts that have been confiscated from the city must be hidden in the Temple of Torm."

"Right!" Kelemvor snapped. "And if Bane disguised the tablet, as we suspect, and hid it in a temple, the Tormites probably don't even know what they've got! Tenwealth probably believed it to be just another trinket when he saw it."

"This is just as I suspected," Elminster noted as he narrowed his eyes and looked at the heroes closely. "And it's the reason why I was at the temple this morning, too."

"Then you agree?" Midnight whispered in surprise.

"Yes, Midnight. I believe ye're right," the white-haired mage said. "The Tablet of Fate is hidden in the Temple of Torm. . . ."

* * * * *

The port of Scardale had seen more activity during the past five days than it had in the previous five months. The theft of the *Queen of the Night* had brought about serious ramifications for the city. Bane's headquarters had been moved from the Zhentish garrison to the port itself, and every ship in the harbor had been placed under the direct control of the Black Lord's troops.

A chamber inside the largest building in the port had been converted into a war room. The room was filled with maps and charts, all of which were lined with marks indicating past and future troop movements. Now, Bane sat at the head of a large, polished table covered with such maps. And as the God of Strife listened to his generals' schemes and complaints, the sorceress, Tarana Lyr, stood behind him.

The soldier closest to the fallen god, a man named Hepton, rubbed at his temples, then folded his hands and dropped them to the table. "Lord Bane, you must address the rumors that have been circulating throughout the ranks concerning Tantras. Do you intend to mobilize our forces again so soon after taking Scardale?"

"To do so would be a grave error," Windling, a general from the Citadel of the Raven, interjected. There were murmurs of agreement from the other Zhentish leaders.

"Enough!" Bane shouted, slamming his fist on top of the thick wooden table. The sound of the table splintering silenced the men. Tarana's quiet giggling was the only sound in the room for a minute or more.

"The Battle of Shadowdale was a disaster," Bane noted casually, his eyes narrowed in anger. "The loss was, of course, unexpected, and the casualties much higher than anyone could have anticipated." The god paused and looked at the silent generals. "And while we managed an almost bloodless coup in the taking of Scardale, it is only a matter of time before the armies of Sembia and the Dales attempt to retake the city."

The generals nodded their agreement. Bane uncurled his fist and stood up. "If we use our forces to attack Tantras, then our victory here will have amounted to nothing. It is clear to me that a majority of the occupation force must remain in Scardale." The God of Strife smiled and ran a hand through his red hair. "But I am a god. And gods have options not open to mortals."

The doors to the chamber flew open, and Cyric rushed in. Bane looked up and scowled slightly. Inside the Black Lord's mind, Fzoul screeched in anger at the sight of the hawk-nosed thief.

Cyric looked around the room and realized the mistake he'd made in interrupting the session. The thief quickly lowered his head and backed away. "Lord Bane, I didn't mean to disturb—"

"Nonsense!" the God of Strife snapped. "You aren't interrupting anything important." The generals looked at each other, then slowly began to stand. "I didn't say our meeting was over," Bane growled, and the Zhentish leaders quickly sat down again.

"Lord Bane, I can come back later," Cyric said quickly, noting the anger in the generals' eyes. These were certainly men he didn't want to anger.

"Give me your report," Bane cried, his voice impatient. "Prove to my generals that the Tantras situation is well under control."

Cyric cleared his throat. "I can't do that."

Bane leaned forward, putting his fists on the table. The cracked wood creaked under the god's weight. "What happened?"

"Durrock is dead. Kelemvor killed him," Cyric told the Black Lord, his head still bowed. "The assassin put up a spectacular fight, but the fighter tricked him."

"Why didn't *you* kill Kelemvor?" Bane asked.

"After Durrock failed, my duty was clear. I had to return to you and inform you that Kelemvor, Midnight, and Adon are in Tantras." The thief swallowed once and hoped that the other information he had for the God of Strife would appease him—for the moment, at least. "And you should know, Lord Bane, that Tantras appears to be preparing for war."

A wave of surprised whispers rolled through the room. Bane looked at the worried faces of his generals. "Prepare the ships and man them with as few of our Zhentilar as possible!"

"No!" Hepton cried. "This is a grave mistake!"

"Silence!" Bane shouted. "News of our victory in Scardale has obviously spread to Tantras. The city is preparing its defenses, and it is certain to call upon its neighbors for help if we give them time to do so." The Black Lord leaned toward Hepton and snarled, "I want my banner to fly over Tantras within the week. *I* want it. Do you understand?"

Hepton nodded weakly, and the generals rose from the table and began to file out of the room. Cyric breathed a sigh of relief and turned to leave, too.

"Not you, Cyric!" Bane snapped. The Black Lord gestured for Cyric to come closer. Tarana gripped the back of the Black Lord's chair.

"Shall I kill him for you, Lord Bane?" Tarana asked, her eyes taking on a dreamy glaze.

"No," Bane said casually, then waited until the last of the generals had left before he spoke again. As the door closed, Bane whispered, "The Company of the Scorpions is still under your command—is that correct, Cyric?"

The hawk-nosed thief nodded and smiled slightly. It was clear that the news of Tantras's preparation for war had turned the fallen god's thoughts away from murder.

"I wish you and your troops to become my new personal guard. But know this," Bane snarled and placed his hand on Cyric's shoulder. "If any harm comes to Fzoul's body, it will be *your* flesh I will inhabit next. And I will not be as generous as I was with Fzoul. Your mind will be utterly destroyed. Is that understood?" The God of Strife squeezed the thief's shoulder until the bones felt as if they were about to break.

Wincing in pain, Cyric nodded, then hurried from the war room.

The Black Lord turned to his sorceress and pointed toward the door. "Make sure the door is locked, then summon Lord Myrkul for me," Bane commanded and sat down.

The sorceress checked the door, then cast an incantation. There was a brief shimmering of the air, and the amber skull of the God of the Dead floated in the air before the Black Lord.

"Congratulations on your victory in Scardale," Myrkul told Bane, and the disembodied head bowed slightly.

"That is unimportant," Bane grumbled. "I need to take care of a problem in Tantras. I'll be taking some of my fleet and—"

The God of the Dead smiled a rictus grin, showing a row

of rotting teeth. "And I am to have a part to play in the battle," he noted flatly.

"I need the power you gave me in Shadowdale, the soul energies of the dead," Bane said, drumming his fingers on the table. "Can you do it?"

"I need a large number of people to die at once in order to empower that spell," Myrkul said suspiciously, rubbing his chin. "You sacrificed your troops in Shadowdale. Who will pay this time for the increased power I can give you?"

The God of Strife sat still for a moment, silently turning the problem over and over in his mind. He certainly couldn't use his soldiers and priests for Myrkul's spell again, yet the souls would have to be aligned to his cause or it might prove difficult to control them. Then the Black Lord realized whom he would make the victims of Myrkul's spell.

"The assassins," Bane whispered through an evil smile. "The assassins have failed me time and again since the night of Arrival. They failed me in Spiderhaunt Woods, in Scardale, and now in Tantras. For this, all the assassins in the Realms must die to give me the power I need!"

The God of the Dead laughed. "You've become as mad as your assistant. The assassins are valuable to me."

"Are they?" Bane asked, arching one eyebrow. "Why?"

The God of the Dead frowned, and as he did, his cheekbones protruded through his decaying skin. "They provide my kingdom with souls. There is a pressing need—"

"Ah, yes . . . the Realm of the Dead," Bane said dryly. "Have you been there lately?" Tarana giggled.

Myrkul was silent for a moment. When he spoke, there was no trace of amusement in his rasping, hollow voice. "I have not come here to listen to you state the obvious. We are, of course, both barred from our kingdoms."

"Then any measure that could help us to regain our rightful homes in the Planes cannot be deemed extreme or worthless, can it?" Bane noted as he stood.

"Only if the effort is wasted," Myrkul grumbled as the Black Lord walked toward the hovering image of the God of the Dead.

"I seek to reclaim the Tablet of Fate that I hid in Tantras, Myrkul!" Bane screamed. The Black Lord wished that his fellow god was in the room with him so he could strike him for his insolence. "Powerful forces may move against me—against us—if they discover that tablet. In Shadowdale, I was overconfident, and I paid the bitter price of defeat. I would rather die than face that again!"

Myrkul took a moment to consider the Black Lord's words. His expressionless, skeletal visage seemed to shimmer and fade for an instant, causing the God of Strife to reel with barely controlled panic. Finally the image resumed its full strength, and Bane relaxed. The Black Lord knew from Myrkul's eyes that the God of the Dead had decided to aid him even before he spoke.

"If you feel so strongly about this matter, then I will help you to recover the tablet," Myrkul said, nodding slowly.

Bane tried to act confident. With a shrug, he noted, "I had no doubt that you would aid me."

"You had every doubt," Myrkul rasped harshly. "That is the only reason I chose to help you. I am pleased to note that you are no longer blindly stumbling into situations that you know nothing about." The God of the Dead paused and fixed Bane with an icy stare. "But there is one thing you must consider: You may not have my assistance the next time you need it, Lord Bane."

The God of Strife nodded, dismissing Myrkul's threat as so much pointless rhetoric. Then the Black Lord mocked a look of concern and noted, "Bhaal will not be pleased if you kill all his worshipers."

"I will deal with the Lord of Murder," Myrkul said, rubbing his hand across his decaying chin once more. "I will contact you when all is in readiness." The Lord of Bones paused for a moment, then added, "Have you given thought to what form you will use to hold the soul energy my spell will channel to you?"

Bane said nothing.

Rage danced in Myrkul's eyes. "Your human avatar couldn't handle the strain in Shadowdale, and the rite you wish me to perform will likely yield you far more power than the one I used then!" The God of the Dead shook his head and sighed. "Do you still have the small obsidian statue I used to contain your essence in the Border Ethereal?"

"I do," Bane said, a look of confusion on his face.

"This is what you must do," Myrkul told Bane. The Lord of Bones quickly listed a complex series of instructions and forced the God of Strife and his mad sorceress to repeat them several times. Then, as soon as he was satisfied that Tarana and Bane knew how to prepare for the rite, the God of the Dead's image disappeared in a flash of gray light and a puff of stinking, yellow-and-black smoke.

🌸 15 🌸

The Tablet of Fate

In a darkened chamber, surrounded by a dozen of his most faithful worshipers and high priests, Lord Myrkul stared at the five-tiered stage that had been set for his performance. Emerald and black marble slabs floating in midair formed a stairway, one step for each of the five ceremonies the Lord of Bones had to perform to kill all the assassins in Faerun and grant Bane the power of their stolen souls.

From somewhere nearby, the God of the Dead heard the tortured screams of souls crying for release. Myrkul shuddered as he listened to the cries and thought of his lost home, his Castle of Bones in Hades. And even though the sounds Myrkul now heard were made by unfaithful worshipers who were receiving punishment and were nowhere near as horrifying as the screeches of those confined to his realm, the Lord of Bones enjoyed them nonetheless.

"Priests, attend me," Myrkul said as he pushed the memories of his home out of his mind, raised his bony arms, and walked to the first platform. Robed men bearing sharpended scepters made of bones approached and placed their offerings in the fallen god's hands. The robed men then knelt before Myrkul, raising their chins and baring their necks.

The fallen god started to chant in a hollow, rasping voice. In moments he was joined by the robed men at his feet. As their deep voices reached a crescendo, Myrkul used the scepters to tear open the men's throats one by one. The corpses fell backward onto the floor, their mouths hanging open in wordless protest at the unexpected agony of their final moments.

Far from Myrkul's hidden chambers, Lord Bane waited in a large abandoned warehouse in the port of Scardale. Tarana Lyr stood behind the God of Strife, and Cyric stood nearby, with five members of the Scorpions, Bane's new personal guard. Slater stood at the hawk-nosed thief's side, and Eccles remained close, staring wild-eyed at the fallen god. All of the Scorpions were heavily armed.

At the center of the warehouse, the faceless obsidian statue stood, for all the world like a child's toy. A complex series of runes covered the floor around the figurine. The strange, mystical markings wound outward from the statue to fill the entire warehouse.

"Come, Myrkul, I don't have all the time in the world," Bane muttered, and a shadow passed across an open window. The Black Lord looked at the statue in anticipation just as a column of swirling green and amber light burst through the ceiling and engulfed the obsidian representation.

"Finally!" Bane cried, raising his fists into the air. "Now I will have true power. . . ."

At that moment, far from Scardale, at the base of the mountains to the west of Suzail, a council of twelve men sat at a long rectangular table that had once been the dining table of the former lord of Castle Dembling. Now, Lord Dembling and his family were dead, murdered by the Fire Knives, a clandestine group of assassins who had sworn to kill King Azoun IV of Cormyr and had seized the small castle near his kingdom as their new base of operations.

The leader of the meeting, a dark-eyed, pug-nosed man named Roderick Tem, was tired of the small-minded bickering that had disrupted all of his attempts to organize his band of assassins into a productive company.

"Fellow assassins, this argument is getting us nowhere," Tem proclaimed, slamming the handle of his knife on the table to get his comrades' attention.

Before he could say anything else, Tem's eyes widened and his body stiffened. A green and amber light exploded from the pug-nosed man's chest and snaked around the room like a burst of lightning. In just a few seconds, the mystical fire from Tem's chest had pierced the hearts of each his friends. All the assassins fell over, dead.

Stalking the back alleys of Urmlaspyr, a city in Sembia, Samirson Yarth caught sight of his prey and drew his dagger. Yarth was a hired killer with an impressive record. Not one of his intended victims had ever escaped his blade. Yarth had even taken enough lives to personally warrant the attention of his deity, Lord Bhaal, on more than one occasion.

On this particular day the assassin was enjoying the hunt. His prey was a circus performer suspected of seducing the wife of a high-ranking city official. The purchaser of Yarth's talents, a seemingly mild little man named Smeds, had offered twice the assassin's normal fee if he could bring the performer's heart to him while it was still warm.

As Yarth watched, his victim leaped through the open window of a countinghouse. The assassin followed the young man into the semidarkness. There, he found his victim and saw the fear in his prey's eyes as the performer realized that he'd been cornered. Yarth raised his weapon.

Suddenly a blinding, green and amber light tore through the assassin's chest, and the killer's blade struck the ground a few feet from his intended victim. Samirson Yarth had failed to complete his first contract.

Far across the Realms, in the city of Waterdeep, Bhaal, the inhuman Lord of Murder, was visited by a sensation unlike any he had ever known. An incredible feeling of loss settled upon the God of Assassins, and for a brief instant he actually knew fear. Running from his chambers, the fallen god found Dileen Shurlef, an assassin who served as his faithful servant. Just as Bhaal opened his twisted, bestial mouth to speak, a green and amber flash filled the hallway. Shurlef gasped and cried out as if his soul was being torn from him. With a mind-numbing certainty, Bhaal realized that was exactly what was happening.

At the warehouse in Scardale, the obsidian avatar had grown to a height of over fifty feet, and the expansion of the magical statue showed no signs of slowing down. A large, steady stream of green and amber light poured into the warehouse and filled the black figurine.

Bane stared at the form of what would soon be his new avatar as if he were in a trance. "Myrkul is preparing to step upon the final tier," the Black Lord whispered to Tarana. The sorceress backed away and gestured for the Scorpions to do the same.

Beside Cyric, Slater cursed her hands for shaking. "Lord Bane is in communion with Myrkul," Cyric whispered. "This is exactly what he said would happen."

Before the Scorpions, the God of Strife opened his arms, and a tongue of green and amber fire swirled around him. "After I depart this avatar, its flesh will be weak, its mind disoriented. Tarana, you will stay behind to safeguard Fzoul and protect my interests in Scardale."

"I would give my life—," Tarana started to cry.

"I know," Bane murmured, holding up his hand to stop the madwoman's oaths of loyalty. "And one day you shall. Take comfort in that, for now I leave you."

A reddish black cloud burst from Fzoul's mouth and shot toward the obsidian avatar, trailing a line of green and amber flame. The red-haired priest moaned softly and fell backward into Tarana's arms. The essense of the God of Strife entered the huge statue and an incredible scream burst forth. The cry echoed across all of Scardale and nearly deafened those who stood in the warehouse.

The statue's arms slowly raised, and Bane's new avatar clutched the sides of its head and continued to wail, though it still had no mouth. Sharp spikes, similar to those on Durrock's armor, burst from the arms, chest, legs, and head of the obsidian avatar. Finally the swirling mists stopped flowing into the room, and the roiling colors inside the statue changed from amber and green to reddish black.

An evil, leering mouth and a pair of glowing red eyes appeared on the statue's face. Bane stopped screaming and looked down at his hands.

"Hollow," he said in a voice that was unmistakably that of a god. "My world is hollow. My body. . . ."

On the ground, Cyric stared up at the God of Strife in disbelief, his heart threatening to burst from his chest. To have such power! the hawk-nosed thief thought. No matter the price, one day I will strive with beings like Bane.

Suddenly the Black Lord began to laugh. A frightening, cavernous roar filled the warehouse. "I am a god. At last, I am once again a god!"

The huge, obsidian avatar of the God of Strife rushed forward, bursting through the front wall of the warehouse as if it were tearing at frail paper. The Scorpions, save for Cyric, helped Tarana carry Fzoul away from the warehouse before the roof collapsed.

The Zhentilar made it to the street just in time to see Bane reach the edge of the port. A vague greenish amber aura enshrouded the God of Strife as he stood on the shore of the Dragon Reach and looked out toward Tantras. The fallen god was sure that nothing could stop him from regaining the Tablet of Fate.

* * * * *

The sudden death or disappearance of all the worshipers of Bhaal who frequented the Dark Harvest—in fact, all the assassins who lived in Tantras—troubled Tenwealth and the other members of the Council of Torm greatly. The assassins had proven themselves to be a considerable asset, despite their blasphemous alignment, and the council members, usually united, were now finding it difficult to locate men willing to rid the city of heretics for a flat fee.

The council had other troubles, too. There had been occasions recently when members had argued that Torm should be made aware of their efforts to unify the city. But as Tenwealth frequently told the council, the God of Duty had only recently taken the body of a mortal; he might not understand the unfortunate measures they had to take to convert most of the population or rid the city of unbelievers. Actually, the council members had stood united in their cause until Tenwealth had recommended that they hire assassins to deal with citizens too unreasonable to convert or leave.

Then, those council members who had failed to see the true value of Tenwealth's plans were killed, too. The high priest had ordered those murders with the same zeal he'd felt when he'd plotted the harbormaster's death, as well the demise of several dozen other intractables. And Tenwealth truly believed he was serving Lord Torm throughout all the bloodshed.

In fact, Tenwealth had just received word that some of his men had taken care of the small sect of Oghma worshipers in town when the order to appear before Lord Torm arrived. Leaving his room, the high priest walked to the audience hall with a light step and the knowledge that all he had accomplished over the years had been for the sake of his god. He knew, too, that Torm would eventually thank him for it. After all, the Tablet of Fate was safely hidden in the temple's vault, and when the city was united behind the God of Duty, the high priest planned to give the tablet to Torm. His god could then triumphantly return to the Planes, an entire city of devoted worshipers behind him.

Tenwealth smiled at that thought. But the smile left the platinum-haired man's face as he entered the private chambers of Torm and found a large group of people gathered there. When he recognized all twelve members of the council, along with many of their subordinates, Tenwealth's heart skipped a beat. The doors slammed shut behind the high priest just as he noticed a group of five old men standing in the corner, their eyes burning with anger.

The worshipers of Oghma, Tenwealth thought frantically. The followers of the God of Knowledge are alive! I've been deceived!

The rest of the room was filled with heavily armed guards. Lord Torm himself sat upon his throne, a gray stone gauntlet with its palm resting parallel to the floor. The golden lion to which the God of Duty had given life the day he spoke to Adon in the garden prowled back and forth at his feet. Tenwealth had placed the statue there himself after taking it from the abandoned Temple of Waukeen.

The lion roared, and Torm leaned forward to address his followers. "I hardly know where to begin," the God of Duty growled, his voice low and burdened with emotion. "My disappointment and my outrage cannot be measured by human standards. If I had learned of the horrors this council has committed in my name while I was still in the Planes, I would have used my power to burn this temple to its very foundations."

Tenwealth's entire body began to quake as he wondered how much Torm really knew. He felt an impulse to run, but the high priest knew that there was nowhere to go, nowhere to hide.

"For the past three days, the mortal who has served as my avatar has assisted me in a charade," Torm told the assembly of traitors and pounded the arm of his throne with his gauntleted fist. "While he has sat upon my throne, I have journeyed into the city, possessing the bodies of a few of my true worshipers and learning first-hand the state of affairs in Tantras." Torm paused and gritted his teeth. "What I discovered has sickened me to the core. There is no punishment great enough for what this council has done, but know this: you *will* be punished."

Tenwealth's legs gave out beneath him and he fell to his knees. The members of the council quickly mimicked his actions. The Tablet of Fate, Tenwealth thought desperately. He might not know about the tablet yet! There is still a chance to save our holy cause!

"All that we have done has been in your name," the platinum-haired high priest cried. "For your honor, Lord Torm. For your glory!"

The golden lion roared as Torm leaped from the throne. The god crossed the room in a few running steps, then grabbed Tenwealth by the throat and yanked him into the air.

"How dare you say that!" the God of Duty screamed. Holding Tenwealth with his left hand, Lord Torm raised his fist to strike the priest.

A wave of total fear washed over Tenwealth and he blurted out, "We have the Tablet of Fate, Lord Torm!"

Torm stared at the mortal for a moment, then dropped him to the floor. "How could *you* have the tablet?"

"It was hidden in the vault beneath the temple. On the night of Arrival, when the fireballs split the sky and the one that bore your holy essence crashed through the temple, I found it. I had no way of knowing what the object was at the time, but—"

"Then I told you the true reason the gods suddenly appeared in Faerun, and you understood the greatness and the power of the object you held," Torm said, closing his eyes. "What were your plans for the Tablet of Fate, Tenwealth? Were you going to sell it to the highest bidder? Bane and Myrkul, perhaps?"

"No! Have mercy," Tenwealth begged. "Let us prove our loyalty to you, Lord Torm. All that has happened was done in your name!"

The god shuddered and looked down at Tenwealth. The high priest lay quivering at the God of Duty's feet. "Stop saying that," Torm whispered. "You know nothing about my wishes."

The fallen god clenched his gauntleted hand into a fist, turned his back on the council, and strode to his throne. He sat down and tried to force his anger away, but couldn't stop quivering with rage. Torm had suddenly recognized the extent of the damage wrought by Tenwealth and his perverted plan. All this time, when the Realms were torn by chaos and good people suffered, the God of Duty had possessed the means to make things right, to fulfill his *duty* to Lord Ao. And his priests had hidden it from him, supposedly for his own good.

Torm looked out at the frightened priests and awestruck guards, and for the first time, he saw himself through their eyes. I'm just another petty tyrant to them, the God of Duty realized. I'm nothing but a very powerful despot whom they will do anything to please.

"We were going to give you the tablet when the time was right. We—," Tenwealth wailed.

"Silence!" Torm shouted. "Where is the Tablet of Fate now?"

"In the vault," Tenwealth said softly. "I had an illusion cast over the tablet to disguise it, and mystical wards keep it safe."

The God of Duty stood up again and pointed at Tenwealth. "You and your council will be held until I decide what to do with you," Torm growled. "Guards, take—"

A wild-eyed messenger burst into the room. "Lord Torm! There are Zhentish ships on the horizon! They're heading this way!"

The priests all gasped and got off their knees. The messenger stopped moving toward the God of Duty when he saw the golden lion at his feet. "Go on," Torm said. "What else do you have to report."

The messenger swallowed hard and spoke again, never taking his eyes off the lion. "There is something else crossing the Dragon Reach, too. A night-black giant, over fifty feet tall. The goliath wears spiked armor, like one of the Black Lord's assassins!"

"Bane!" Torm yelled. The lion roared and leaped to its feet. "He's come for the Tablet of Fate!"

The fallen god was then silent for a moment, and he considered the city's dilemma. After a moment, he said, "Issue a summons to all of my faithful. I wish them to meet in the outdoor cathedral in one hour."

"We are your faithful!" Tenwealth cried and took a step toward the God of Duty.

Torm looked at his former high priest. "In one hour, each of you will have a chance to prove that." Gesturing to his guards, the god added, "Take them to the cathedral. Watch them. Then tell the soldiers to prepare to defend the harbor from the Zhentish ships. The Black Lord will be my responsibility."

The hour passed quickly for the god as he formulated his plan and waited for his faithful to gather in the temple. Soon, he was standing on a platform, looking out over a throng of priests and fighters. The Council of Torm stood near the stage, chains around their wrists and ankles.

"There is little time to waste this day," the God of Duty cried. "By now, all of you know that our city will soon face an attack by Zhentish forces. Lord Bane, God of Strife and Tyranny, conqueror of Scardale, approaches the harbor of our city in the form of a giant warrior." The fallen god paused and listened to the frightened, excited murmuring of the crowd. After a moment, he added, "I can stop Bane. But to do so, I need the power that only your belief . . . and your sacrifice can give to me."

The noise from the crowd grew louder, and Torm raised his gauntleted hand to silence them. "My avatar has volunteered to be the first to offer me his essence." A deep sadness filled the God of Duty's eyes. "You must follow his example, do your duty as followers of my word, if Tantras is to be saved from destruction."

With those words, Torm plunged his hands into his avatar's chest and pulled out his heart. A torrent of sky-blue energy swirled around the staggering body of Torm's avatar, then engulfed not only the frail, human form, but also the golden lion that raced to protect its master. When the swirling lights faded, a golden man more than nine feet tall stood before the worshipers of Torm. His head was that of the mighty lion, and his body crackled with energy.

"Your duty calls you," Torm roared from snarling lips of his new avatar. "There will be no pain. I would not bring suffering to my faithful. You need only accept your destiny, and you will pass quietly."

In unison, a dozen worshipers cried, "Take us, Lord Torm!"

With expressions of complete bliss, the worshipers fell to the ground. From their gently parted lips, sky-blue mists flowed and rushed toward the God of Duty. Torm opened his arms and embraced the souls, which lost their individual shapes and became a large pulsating mass of light. The lion-headed avatar absorbed the energy and started to grow.

Soon the cathedral was filled with corpses, and the fallen god towered over the proceedings, the golden avatar now nearly fifty feet tall. Soul energy flowed toward the avatar from all across the city as word of the god's need spread. In the temple, Tenwealth and his fellow members of the council were among those who had not yet surrendered their lives.

"So beautiful," one of the priests wept as he looked up at the golden avatar. "Yet no matter how strongly I wish to join Lord Torm, he will not accept my life!"

"We were such fools!" Tenwealth cried. "Forgive us, Lord Torm! Accept our sacrifice! Let us prove our loyalty!"

The lion-headed avatar stared down at the council members. He could feel their desire to join him and almost taste the anguish in their hearts now that they recognized the price of their failure.

Torm closed his eyes and opened his arms. Tenwealth and the rest of the Council of Torm died, and their soul energies rushed to the avatar's embrace. The God of Duty absorbed the energy, let out a deep, loud roar, and pushed through the back wall of the temple. Then the lion-headed avatar went off in search of the God of Strife.

* * * * *

At the bow of the *Argent*, a Zhentish trireme, Cyric stared at a city on the horizon. The thief had not expected to return to Tantras so quickly, but Bane's orders had been explicit. Slater and a few of the other Zhentilar whom Cyric commanded were given orders to stay behind in Scardale, but the majority of the thief's men were assigned to the *Argent* and ordered to follow Bane. Dalzhel, the leader of one of the contingents of Zhentilar who joined the Scorpions before Tyzack's death, had been made Cyric's lieutenant. Dressed in an ebon cloak that was pressed against his sleek body by the heavy winds, Dalzhel ran his hand over his bushy, black beard.

"You're worried when you shouldn't be," Dalzhel noted. "There should be no doubt as to our victory. Lord Bane himself leads us to Tantras."

"Of course," Cyric replied, his voice distant. Realizing that Dalzhel was staring at him, the thief assumed the posture of a confident warrior. "We will bathe in the blood of our enemies."

Dalzhel was still staring. Cyric thought for a moment, then realized his mistake. "If we are forced to engage them, we will slaughter the Tantrasans. Lord Bane's orders are not to be taken lightly, no matter how badly some of us may wish to engage these dogs and drive them under our heels."

The lieutenant looked away. "Were you privy to the ceremony where Bane took his new avatar?"

"I was," Cyric replied and felt a warmth spread through his body. "It was a spectacular event to witness. It was almost inspirational."

Dalzhel nodded. "I understand that three beholders were summoned from Zhentil Keep and Lord Myrkul himself was in attendance."

"That is something of an exaggeration," Cyric noted and proceeded to tell Dalzhel all that he had witnessed.

After reaching the harbor, the obsidian juggernaut that Bane had inhabited was forced to enter the Dragon Reach from the east side of Scardale, while most of the Zhentilar fleet, four sailing ships, three galleys equipped with rams, and the *Argent*, left from the Ashaba port to the south. Triremes were noted for their speed and superior handling, so it wasn't surprising that the *Argent* quickly pulled ahead of the fleet and passed the southeast tip of Scardale in time to see Bane's mammoth avatar enter the water.

The sun had been directly above the avatar as it waded into the Dragon Reach. Brilliant white light enshrouded the unnatural creation with an aura of blinding luminescence. Despite the glare, though, Cyric could see reddish black mists swirling inside the smoky body. The obsidian giant now hummed with a throbbing tone that rose and fell in time with the movements of the crimson light within its massive chest.

During the journey, only the head, shoulders, and parts of the God of Strife's arms were visible as he waded and swam through the Dragon Reach. The waves Bane caused made it impossible for the fleet to follow closely, and so the god was always far ahead of the ships.

Now, as Cyric told Dalzhel about the birth of the obsidian avatar, the Zhentish fleet's two–day trek was almost at an end. Bane had broken away from the main body of the fleet, taking two ships with him as he prepared to enter Tantras from the north, where the temple of Torm resided. The Black Lord justified the move by claiming he was going to destroy Torm, and thereby plunge Tantras into chaos.

Cyric knew better. The Tablet of Fate was all that concerned Bane, and the thief now knew that the tablet was somewhere near the Temple of Torm.

The *Argent* had been ordered to take up a position at the northernmost end of Tantras's harbor, closer to the scene of Bane's imminent raid upon the Temple of Torm than any of the other ships sent to blockade the western borders of the city. The *Argent*'s orders had been to stand ready, but take no action unless it was necessary.

Cyric, however, had plans of his own.

* * * * *

Elminster's lair was a filthy hovel in the low–rent district of Tantras. The heroes had spent the better part of three days hiding there from the priests of Torm. They passed the time by arguing about a plan for the retrieval of the first Tablet of Fate.

"I think we should just charge in and grab it," Kelemvor grumbled sarcastically as he stared at the sharp edge of his blade. The fighter looked up suddenly as he remembered something Adon had mentioned about the Temple of Torm. "What about the main worship room in the center of the building? The vault might be there."

Elminster stared at the ceiling, his fingers absently playing with his beard. "Ye sound much like the lummox I always took ye for, Kelemvor," the sage sighed. "The tablet must be in the *diamond corridors* that Torm warned Adon about and Tenwealth threatened him with."

The fighter mumbled something rude about the old mage, but Midnight spoke before Elminster had a chance to reply. "So how do we get to the tablet, then?" the raven-haired mage asked. "If we teleported or even opened a gate—"

The sage threw his hands into the air. "Far too dangerous," he snapped. "With the instability in the weave, ye might find thyself a mile beneath the earth or somewhere beyond the reach of the sky. Ye might even find thyself halfway across the Realms, in a place like Waterdeep . . . but then, ye'll be going there soon enough anyway."

"That's the second time you've mentioned Waterdeep in the last few days," Adon said angrily. "Why do you think we'll go there soon?"

Midnight's eyes narrowed. "Yes. You mentioned Waterdeep when we were in the market, too. Why?"

Elminster thought it over, then looked at the mage. "Ye can get to the second tablet through the City of the Dead, next to Waterdeep," the old sage sighed. "I learned this from . . . reliable sources during my time in the Planes. But whether or not ye are worthy of the task of retrieving both tablets—"

Kelemvor punched the rickety wall that stood a few feet away from him. "No!" he cried, then looked to Midnight. "We're not going to go chasing after the other tablet, too. We're getting nothing in return for this. Let the old wizard get the artifact himself."

"Still the mercenary, aren't ye, Kelemvor," Elminster snapped. "If it's a reward ye seek—"

"Don't talk to me of reward," Kelemvor shouted. "Now that my curse is gone, I can take other things into consideration—like Midnight's welfare and our future together. Besides, even if I was interested in making a pact, you'd be the last being in Faerun I'd deal with. You reneged on our last agreement."

"I was indisposed," Elminster grumbled. "If ye could have waited for me to return instead of striking a bargain with the Black Lord, perhaps I would be more impressed with thy words."

"We'll search for the other Tablet of Fate, too," Midnight said softly, then put her hand on Kelemvor's arm. "But only because it's our duty and our choice. I refuse to be a pawn any longer."

Torm's words about duty and friendship echoed in Adon's mind as he moved forward and said, "We should wait a few days before we try to retrieve the tablet. Let them think we've left the city. Then we can get the artifact in the temple and head toward Waterdeep."

"But that still doesn't settle *how* we're going to get the Tablet of Fate from the temple's vault . . . if that's where it's being kept," Kelemvor said, and the heroes started their argument all over again.

They were still debating about how to retrieve the tablet when the shouting began outside. The heroes stepped out of the small, ramshackle building and saw that the entire city had suddenly been engulfed in chaos. Worshipers of Torm, wearing pendants or patches with the god's symbol, flooded from their homes as news of the deity's summons spread.

Adon grabbed a messenger and asked what was going on. The scarred man's face was pale when he returned to the heroes to report. "It's Torm," the cleric told them, his voice quavering. "He's asking his faithful to come to the temple. He needs their help to fight Lord Bane, who's coming from Scardale even as we speak."

The heroes quickly set off toward the Temple of Torm. As they traveled through the city, they found the streets littered with bodies, though none of the corpses carried wounds of any sort. Supernatural winds ripped through the city, dragging strange, sky-blue vapors in the direction of the temple. Man-sized wraiths walked or flew toward the golden spires in the distance.

"Look there!" Kelemvor said, and pointed to a young man at the other end of the street who fell to his knees. The man was dressed in the robes of a Tormish priest, and he shouted, "For Torm's eternal glory!" before he dropped to the ground. A burst of sky-blue flame rose from his body, then took to the unnatural winds.

"We'd best gather a few mounts and hurry to the temple," Elminster suggested and pointed toward a stable. The stableboy and the owner lay in the street, dead. The heroes took four horses and set off down the twisting streets as quickly as they dared.

As they looked toward the spires of the citadel and the temple that stood beyond it, Midnight and her allies glimpsed an impossible sight. A golden-skinned giant with the head of a lion towered over the temple. The strange winds flowed toward the monster, and the sky-blue lights that had once been the soul energies of Torm's worshipers were absorbed into his body. The lion-headed giant turned from the temple and looked toward Tantras's north shore, beyond the ridge of hills and the wall that protected the city.

"It's Torm!" Elminster cried, reigning in his mount. "He's created a new avatar to use in his fight with Bane."

"We'd best get to the temple before the battle starts," Midnight told the old sage. "If Torm loses, Bane will certainly recover the tablet." The mage kicked her horse into motion again and clattered off down the street.

In minutes, Midnight, Kelemvor, Adon, and Elminster passed the citadel and dismounted before the main gates of Torm's temple. All three sets of gates lay wide open. The guards had vanished from their posts. The gatehouses were ominously empty. The silence inside the temple was frightening, too, and a dire contrast to the constant sounds of chanting and worship that Adon and Elminster had both described. And as the heroes expected, corpses lined the halls.

"They've given their lives for Torm," Adon said softly. "Just like the others we saw in the streets." The cleric shook his head and ushered the party toward Tenwealth's chamber.

"If there's a vault in the temple," the cleric noted as they walked, "there will probably be a door to it in the high priest's quarters."

But as Adon reached the door to Tenwealth's room, a guard called out from behind the heroes. "You there! Where do you think you're going?"

"Go ahead," Elminster hissed. "I'll take care of this dolt. Ye just look for the vault."

Midnight stopped to protest, but Kelemvor grabbed her and pulled her into Tenwealth's room. Adon slammed the door closed behind the fighter. "Quickly," the scarred man said. "Look for a secret door."

Midnight and her allies could hear Elminster's laughter, along with the guard's, as they searched. Then there was silence in the hallway. Midnight went to open the door, but Kelemvor pulled her back. "Just find the door," he grumbled. "Then you can worry about the old man."

"But there's no doorway here," Adon cried at last, exasperated.

"None that we can see, anyway," Kelemvor noted sourly as he sat down in front of the door to the hallway.

Midnight put down the bag containing her spellbook and looked around the sparse cell. "You're right. Why should we think Tenwealth put the door in plain sight? It's probably hidden by magic!"

The fighter stood up quickly, and the heroes circled the room, rapping on the walls. Finally, Kelemvor found a hollow section in the center of one of the walls. "I'd say there's a doorway right here."

Midnight and Adon examined the wall. The cleric frowned and shook his head, but the mage wasn't discouraged so easily. "I think a sequester spell has been used to hide the doorway," she said. "But how are we going to know for certain?"

Midnight knew that the only answer was another spell, but the thought of using magic, even a simple incantation, frightened her terribly. Ever since the Temple of Lathander, Midnight had been terrified that the next spell she cast would injure someone . . . or even kill one of her friends. As she turned the problem over in her mind, though, the mage remembered Mystra's final words to her at the Battle of Shadowdale.

Use the power I gave you.

Midnight sighed and hung her head. "Get as close to the door as you can. Both of you." She walked to the section of the wall Kelemvor had pointed to.

"Don't do this," the fighter pleaded. "You don't know what could happen."

"I'll never know unless I try," Midnight replied. "Besides, we didn't come all this way to give up now."

The mage recited the spell to detect magic. A blue-white pattern of energy shot from Midnight's hands and struck the wall. For a moment, nothing happened, then the wall began to shudder. Shards of mystical energy exploded from the hidden doorway, cutting harmlessly through the heroes' bodies, and pure white daggers of light flashed into Midnight's right eye. As suddenly as it had started, the shower of light ended.

Midnight stood in front of the door, trembling. "I think I can see it," she gasped, wavering on her feet. "I see the door to the vault."

But the image the mage saw was strange, as if two different pictures had been placed, one over the other. If she kept both eyes open, Midnight saw this confusing blur. However, the mage's vision cleared when she closed her right eye. Then she saw things normally. She looked at the wall and saw only stone and paint.

When Midnight closed her left eye and looked only through the orb that had been struck by the daggers of light, she could see the secret door clearly. In fact, through this eye, physical objects like the floor or the wall or even her friends appeared as ghostly gray shadows. Only the magic of the sequester spell seemed distinct or tangible.

Kelemvor took a step toward his lover. "Wait for Elminster to come back!"

"No, Kel," Adon said softly as he grabbed the fighter. "It's up to Midnight now. There's nothing we can do."

"It *is* a sequester spell that prevents us from seeing the door," Midnight noted, holding a hand over her left eye. Her voice was low and distant, as if she had just awoken from a dream. The mage shivered. "I think I can open it now."

The mage reached for the wall. Kelemvor and Adon saw a doorway suddenly appear in the wall, then open. Pale light flooded from the large room the heroes saw through the secret entrance.

"I see a lot of magical traps in there," Midnight noted dreamily. "Tenwealth has been very busy." The mage stepped into the vault's antechamber.

Before anyone could react, the door slammed closed behind her.

The antechamber was a small room, no more than ten feet wide and ten feet long, lit by four bright globes that hung in the corners. Midnight covered her right eye for a moment and looked around. There wasn't much for the mage to see, at least not with her left eye. The room was completely barren, save for a huge mosaic of Torm's gauntlet embedded in the north wall and a large diamond-shaped trap door in the center of the floor.

When Midnight looked out into the room with her right eye, though, she saw a vast web of spells hanging over the trap door and snaking around the room. The spells hung like strands of silk from the ceiling and walls, intertwined and pulsing. The mage followed the weave and pattern of a few of the simpler spells, for the wards all seemed to have slightly varying colors, and she easily identified a few of them.

Tenwealth had ordered a number of spells to be placed on the door to protect whatever was hidden there from thieves. One ward raised an alarm if the door was opened. Another caused a cloud of fog to appear, which would blanket the room and obscure vision. A third spell was meant to keep the trap door magically locked. But when Midnight looked at the wizard lock spell through her right eye, she smiled. Written in the weave of the magic was Tenwealth's password.

She followed the pattern of the wizard lock spell for a moment, just to make sure that it wasn't backed up by another spell. The mage then discovered that a few of the other wards, including the alarm and cloud of fog spells, had actually been linked with the wizard lock. Midnight realized that the password might disable the handful of spells that were connected to the lock—or set them all off.

And not all the wards Tenwealth had placed on the trap door were as harmless as an alarm spell. Midnight recognized the pattern of a spell meant to deafen the person who tripped it. Another set off a fire trap, causing a burst of flame to shoot from the door. Worst of all, there was a feeblemind spell attached to the lock. If this was set off, it could wipe a spellcaster's mind clear, lowering his or her intelligence to that of a moronic child until another powerful spell was cast to heal the wizard's mind.

The secret door from Tenwealth's chamber opened again, and Elminster poked his white-bearded head into the antechamber. "What do ye think ye're doing? I said ye should find the door, not open it!"

As the old sage started to step into the room, Midnight saw the weave of a few of the spells tighten. "No," the raven-haired mage cried. "Elminster, don't come in here. You'll set off Tenwealth's traps!"

Elminster froze and looked around the room. "What traps? I don't see any traps!" he sputtered.

"They're magical wards. I can see them hanging over the trap door," Midnight said without taking her eyes off the web of spells. "Somehow, I can see the spells themselves."

Elminster arched a bushy eyebrow and ran a hand slowly through his long, white beard. "Ye can *see* the spells, ye say? Can ye dispel them?"

Midnight swallowed hard. "I don't know," she said softly. "But I'm going to try." The mage paused for a moment, then added, "And I think you should wait in Tenwealth's chamber, with the door closed. If something happens and a spell . . . misfires, Kelemvor and Adon will need your help to get the tablets."

"Can't we do something?" Kelemvor cried from the priest's room.

Midnight heard Elminster sigh. "She's right," the old sage said solemnly. "There's nothing for us to do but wait."

Kelemvor was cursing, and Midnight could picture him stomping around Tenwealth's room. Adon, on the other hand, stood quietly by the door. "Good luck," the scarred cleric said softly. Then Elminster backed away from the secret door and Midnight heard it close.

My luck's been pretty good with magic so far, the mage sighed to herself. None of the spells I've cast since magic became unstable have backfired too badly. I haven't accidentally tossed a lightning bolt at a friend or lost an arm because of a spell misfiring. Not yet, anyway.

The raven-haired mage took a deep breath and spoke the words that Tenwealth had set to disarm the wizard lock. "Duty above all."

The web of spells tightened and quivered. The golden weave of the wizard lock spell glowed brightly for an instant, then the spell was gone. Most of the other wards disappeared, too. After the strands had stopped flaring and vanishing, two spells still hung over the entrance to the vault.

The remaining spells were incomplete, filled with gaps where other wards had been linked to them. Though the mage couldn't identify one of the patterns, she did recognize the tendonous black strands that wove around the room. They were parts of the feeblemind spell she had seen earlier.

After closing both her eyes and concentrating for a moment, Midnight called the incantation to dispel magic into her mind. The mage knew that Tenwealth had probably paid a powerful wizard to cast the wards on the vault, so she should have little hope of dispelling the magic. Still, she said a silent prayer to Lady Mystra—though she knew the Goddess of Magic couldn't hear the plea—and cast her spell.

The green web that comprised the spell Midnight couldn't identify vanished instantly. However, the black coils of the feeblemind spell quickly curled around the mage. "No!" she screamed, and in desperation repeated the incantation again. A flash of blue-white light filled the room. The feeblemind spell was gone.

Midnight opened the diamond-shaped trap door. A set of iron handholds led down into a small chamber lit by two more magical globes. The mage entered the vault and found herself surrounded by much of the wealth of Tantras's temples. Gold and platinum plates, silver candlesticks, and finely wrought icons were piled in crates. A priceless tapestry depicting the Goddess of Trade was stuffed against a wall. And somewhere in the cramped little room lay the Tablet of Fate Bane had hidden in the days before the gods were cast from the Planes.

Midnight knew that the tablet could be disguised as anything, but the illusion cast over the artifact would be visible to her enhanced vision. The mage quickly held a hand over her left eye and scanned the room. A bright red light leaked from a small box in the corner, and Midnight rushed to open it. She quickly pulled the cover from the long steel case. For an instant, Midnight saw the illusion Tenwealth had chosen for the tablet—that of a large, mailed fist—then the intensity of the light that burst from the box blinded her. She stumbled backward a few steps.

In a moment, the raven-haired mage's vision cleared. Her right eye had returned to normal, and she could no longer see the glow of magic. The world appeared as it always had. The mage looked in the box, and the Tablet of Fate lay before her.

She picked up the artifact and saw that it matched the vision Mystra had given her before the goddess's death. The stone tablet was less than two feet long, with sparkling runes carved into its surface. Holding the artifact with one hand, Midnight turned and carefully climbed the iron handholds into the antechamber.

Kelemvor looked up the instant Midnight passed through the secret door. The fighter raced to her side, and Midnight held the artifact out to him. "That's not a tablet," the fighter cried. "You've got the wrong thing!"

Midnight sat down on the rough mattress in Tenwealth's chamber. The absurdity of the fighter's remarks finally struck the mage and she started to laugh. "It's an illusion," she coughed between bursts of laughter. "Just disbelieve the illusion and you'll see the tablet as it really is."

Adon and Elminster had moved to Midnight's side, too, and the heroes stood for a moment, staring at the Tablet of Fate. Midnight stopped chuckling, and Kelemvor and Adon helped her to her feet. She slid the tablet into the canvas sack that held her spellbook.

Kelemvor hugged the mage, a wide grin upon his face. "Now we can leave this place before anything else happens!"

Elminster frowned and shook his head. "Ye still have things to do here before ye can be off to Waterdeep. Do ye happen to recall what happened when Helm and Mystra battled on the Celestial Stairway outside Castle Kilgrave?"

"None of us could ever forget," Midnight answered, slinging the sack containing her spellbook and the Tablet of Fate over her shoulder. "The devastation went on for miles in every direction."

Adon nodded slowly. "And if one of the gods manages to slay the other . . ."

"Tantras will be destroyed," Kelemvor concluded.

Midnight turned to the sage. "There might be a way to save the city even if Torm and Bane destroy each other. The Bell of Aylen Attricus. They say the bell was only rung once—"

"I know," Elminster snapped, a sly grin crossing his lips. "Legend has it that the bell has the power to throw a shield over the city, protecting it from harm." He turned and raced from the room. "We must go there at once!"

The heroes raced after Elminster and they only caught him when he had stopped outside the temple. "But the bell is at the top of the southern hill of Tantras," Midnight panted. "That's an hour's ride from here, provided we push our mounts to the point of exhaustion. The avatars will be at each other's throats long before we get there."

Elminster stood away from the heroes and began to gesture. "*If* we ride."

The sage cast his spell so quickly that the heroes didn't have time to object. An intricate blue-white shield of light formed in the air and engulfed all four of them. Kelemvor was seized by a fierce panic when he saw the mage cast a spell, and a fear that Elminster might try to teleport them to the bell tower grabbed Adon. But the old sage finished his incantation, and the heroes found that they still stood in front of the Temple of Torm.

"Are ye ready?" the sage asked. The heroes looked at one another in confusion. The sage frowned. "Take their hands, Midnight."

The raven-haired mage did as Elminster asked. Kelemvor started to protest, but he swallowed his words as the white-haired sage grabbed Midnight's hand and the heroes all rose from the ground. In a few seconds, they were high above the city.

"I just hope this spell doesn't fail halfway to the tower!" Adon cried.

Elminster pointed to the west. The golden, lion-headed avatar of Torm stood ominously still, towering over the city wall, waiting for the black-armored avatar of the God of Strife to leave the Dragon Reach. "It's worth the risk," the old sage said grimly. "The gods'll not wait for us to trek to the tower on foot."

❧ 16 ❧

As Gods Battle

As Elminster and the heroes flew over Tantras, they looked down at the chaos that gripped the city. People rushed through the streets. Worshipers of Torm were still dying everywhere. As they surrendered their lives to the God of Duty, the faithful sent their souls—sky-blue streaks of light—through the avenues, forming beautiful patterns. Then the souls mingled and flowed toward Torm's lion-headed avatar.

The Tantrasan military was out in full force, too. The soldiers attempted to direct the people rushing away from the avatars toward the garrison in the south. Most of Tantras's citizens simply ran blindly in that direction anyway. In the harbor, ships were being prepared for battle, and the catapults on the breakwater were being loaded. The small Zhentish fleet remained just out of reach of the weaponry and made no move to advance into the harbor.

Kelemvor had never flown before, and the high, thin air that rushed at his face made him light-headed and giddy. As the green-eyed fighter looked at the sky, he marveled at how close he was to the clouds and how far he'd have to fall before hitting the ground if Elminster's spell failed.

Flight was new to Adon, too, but the scarred cleric stared at the city, not the sky. A strange sense of wonder passed through him. Is this how a god sees Faerun from the heavens? he thought. A world filled with thousands of tiny beings frantically scurrying about? The cleric shuddered and closed his eyes.

Midnight looked back toward the temple and could see Torm standing near the shore of the Dragon Reach, on the edge of a high cliff. A huge, dark shape covered with spikes was climbing out of the water. The mage thought back to Mystra's battle with Helm outside Castle Kilgrave, and a sickness filled her soul. Midnight knew in that instant that Mystra was not the last god she would see die before the Tablets of Fate were returned to Lord Ao.

Elminster, on the other hand, fixed his gaze dead ahead and thought only of maintaining the flight spell.

In the near distance lay the clearing that held Mystra's shrine. Soon the heroes could clearly see the tower that housed the Bell of Aylen Attricus. Within minutes, Midnight and her allies found themselves at the foot of the large stone obelisk.

Midnight turned to the north. Torm still stood perfectly still, watching Bane, who now stood on the shore. "The battle has not yet begun," the raven-haired mage cried. "There's still time!"

The white-haired old sage rushed to the entrance to the tower, gesturing for Midnight to follow him. The instant he entered the tower, though, all sound stopped. Midnight joined him. Elminster looked around, puzzled.

Without trying to explain the magical silence, Midnight looked up and saw the rope coiled beside the bell, almost a hundred feet above them. She cursed silently and ran to the narrow, twisting stairway that led to the bell. Reaching the top, the raven-haired mage looked out the window and saw the Black Lord moving toward the lion-headed avatar. She uncoiled the rope and allowed the knotted end to fall to the sage.

Ring the bell! Midnight screamed in her mind and gestured frantically for Elminster to pull the rope. From the window, she could see that the obsidian giant had moved closer to Torm. Kelemvor and Adon appeared at the door. Both looked confused by the unnatural silence.

Elminster gestured for Midnight to come back down the stairs. The old mage had no idea how the bell would work, and he certainly didn't want Midnight to be needlessly hurt when he used it.

Midnight was about twenty feet from the bottom of the long, winding stairs when the sage wrapped the rope around his hands and tugged with all his strength.

Nothing happened.

Elminster tried again, but the bell made no sound. It didn't even move. Adon and Kelemvor grabbed the rope and all three tried to ring it. Still nothing happened.

Red-faced and sweating, Elminster gritted his teeth and pointed at Midnight, who had just left the stairs. The old sage pushed Adon and Kelemvor back and held the rope out to the mage.

The raven-haired woman nodded and took the rope. It felt very cold, and her sweaty palms seemed to burn as she passed her hands over the line, attempting to get a secure grip. She thought of the thousands of people in the city who would die because of Torm and Bane, and all those who had already laid down their lives. In her trembling hands was the power to save the city. Midnight held her breath and pulled on the rope as hard she could.

The sound that echoed through the bell tower was so slight that Midnight feared for a moment that she'd only imagined it. Then the mage felt a rush of cool air descend from above. She looked up and saw that the bell was now surrounded by a soft amber haze. Streaks of black lightning played over the surface of the bell, then shot out through the tower's windows.

"Ye usually can't trust 'em, but this time the prophecy was right!" Elminster croaked, clapping his hands together. "It took a woman of power to save the city."

Kelemvor and Adon rushed to the doorway and watched as the black lightning reached out for two hundred feet in every direction. The bolts then stopped as if they had reached a barrier. Next, the lightning formed an intricate network of arches that curved down into the earth from the tower, forming the skeletal frame of a dome. The amber haze vanished from the bell, then filled in the gaps between the arches of lightning until the area around the bell tower was encased in an arcane shield.

The green-eyed fighter ran to the edge of the dome, found a stone, and threw it at the barrier. The rock bounced off the amber curtain as if it had struck a solid wall. The city was still visible beyond the dome, and Adon could see that the avatars still stood to the north, beyond Tantras's protective wall.

Elminster, too, was staring out at the barrier, but from inside the tower. He turned to Midnight, who stood with her eyes closed, the bell's rope still in her hands. She felt as if every bit of strength had been drained from her body.

"Are we safe?" she asked softly.

"We are, but the city isn't!" Elminster cried. "Ye must try again! The bell must be rung fully. Its sound must carry throughout Tantras."

Sweat on her brow, Midnight looked up at the bell and dropped the rope. The cord dangled limply before her. Failure will put the blood of all of Tantras on my hands, she thought. But I gave everything I had last time, and the bell barely sounded.

Midnight sighed. Duty above all, she reminded herself sourly, looking down at the bag containing the Tablet of Fate. Then the mage forced away that thought and reached for the rope.

Elminster turned from the raven-haired woman and looked out the doorway, to the other side of Tantras.

Across the city, Torm and Bane stood face-to-face on the edge of a cliff overlooking the Dragon Reach. Both avatars were now well over one hundred feet tall. As each god stood, silently studying his opponent's avatar, a cold smile formed on the Black Lord's face.

"Lord Torm," Bane murmured sweetly. "My spies told me that you were in Tantras, but I never expected such a showy reception."

"Is it true?" the God of Duty growled, the bestial features of his lion-headed avatar curling as he spoke.

"You'll have to be more specific," Bane sighed.

"Did you steal the Tablets of Fate?" Torm screamed. The god's voice echoed over the city. "Are you the one responsible for the chaos in the world?"

"I cannot take all the credit," Bane noted calmly. "I had a fair amount of assistance. I'm sure you know by now that the Lord of Bones aided me in the theft itself. And, of course, Ao's vast overreaction to that theft has played no small part in forging the unsettled state of the world."

The God of Duty curled his huge hands into fists and took a step toward Bane. "You're insane," he growled. "Don't you realize what you've done?"

Torm raised his right fist high over his head. There was a burst of light, and a metal gauntlet covered the hand. Next, the lion-headed giant waved his gauntleted fist and a huge, flaming sword flashed into existence, seemingly from the air itself. Finally, the God of Duty bent his left arm slightly, and a shield bearing his symbol appeared. Torm took another step forward and raised his sword to strike.

The God of Strife stood his ground and sighed. "You have no idea what you're doing, Torm. If you destroy me, your pitiful little encampment will be wiped from the face of Faerun."

Torm stopped for an instant, then took another step forward. "You're lying."

Bane laughed, and the deep, bellowing noise shook the roofs on the houses near the city wall. "I saw Mystra destroyed in Cormyr, you fool. She tried to return to the Planes, and Helm simply murdered her." The obsidian avatar paused and smiled. "And when she died, bolts of energy swept the land and destroyed everything for miles around. It was actually rather pleasant."

Torm stood in shocked silence, so Bane continued. "I am here to retrieve something of mine that I left in Tantras a short time ago. Allow my soldiers to take my property to one of my ships, and I will leave," the Black Lord lied. "There need not be any violence between us."

"Something of yours?" Torm asked, shocked out of his silence. "You mean the Tablet of Fate that found its way to my temple."

Bane was genuinely surprised. If Torm had the tablet, why hadn't he simply returned it to Helm? the dark god wondered. Actually, it didn't matter, as long as the tablet was still in Faerun and not in Ao's hands. "I placed the Tablet of Fate in your temple myself, only a few hours before Ao cast us out of our homes," Bane said, trying to seem at ease. "I thought it was a rather amusing little joke, hiding something stolen by an unfaithful servant in a temple to the God of Duty."

Torm gripped his sword tightly. "Turn back, Bane. I will not let you take the tablet. It belongs to Ao and it's my sworn duty—"

Bane snorted. "Please spare me the lecture on duty, Torm. You should know me well enough by now to realize that an appeal to honor is the last thing that would impress me."

"Then we have nothing else to say, Lord Bane," Torm spat. "If you will not leave, prepare to defend yourself."

Bane took a step back as Torm's sword sliced the air in front of him. Bane willed a night-black shield to materialize on his arm, and he raised it just in time to block Torm's next blow. There was an explosion as the mystical sword and shield met. Both items shattered into fragments of energy and dissipated.

Bane surged forward and rammed into Torm. The God of Duty had raised his shield in time to protect himself from the deadly spikes jutting from the obsidian avatar, but the shield itself shattered from the blow. The God of Duty and the God of Strife stumbled together, back through the twenty-five-foot wall that surrounded Tantras. The giants crashed into Torm's temple, and part of the building collapsed.

Bane pushed Torm against the remains of the temple, and huge chunks of stone toppled to the ground. From somewhere close by, the God of Duty heard tiny screams. Panic seized Torm as he realized that the cries were coming from the few people left in his house of worship.

The God of Duty struck Bane in the throat. When the God of Strife fell back from the force of the blow, Torm struck him again and again in the same spot. The God of Strife felt a slight crack open in his neck, and he reached out in desperation to grab Torm's mailed fist.

At the same time, the God of Duty opened the massive jaws of his lion head and leaned toward the Black Lord's face. The God of Strife fell backward to avoid the rows of jagged, golden teeth, and Torm's mouth snapped shut in the air near Bane's neck. Seeing that the Black Lord was off balance, Torm drove his foot into the obsidian giant's chest and pushed him back outside the crumbled city wall. The God of Strife crashed to the ground, sending tremors throughout Tantras.

Torm stood over Bane and raised his mailed fist. The Black Lord struggled to rise, but the huge spikes in his armor had been pushed deep into the hard earth by his fall. Torm's fist crashed into Bane's throat again, and the tiny, almost imperceptible fissure there opened wider. A tiny flow of reddish amber light seeped into the air.

But Torm did not escape this attack unharmed either. As Bane thrashed about, trying to defend himself against the God of Duty, one of the spikes on the Black Lord's armor punctured Torm's lower arm. The lion-headed avatar wailed in pain, and he fell back, clutching his ragged wound.

As the God of Duty stumbled away from the Black Lord, toward the edge of the cliff, he felt a horrible weakness. Looking down to the wound Bane had inflicted, the god saw a steady flow of sky-blue light pouring into the air. He felt a morbid fascination as he watched the soul energies of his worshipers pass from the ragged hole. Torm looked away from the wound just in time to see the Black Lord's fist crash into his face.

Stunned by the ferocity of the attack, Torm was unprepared as the God of Strife struck him again. After the second blow, the God of Duty swung wildly at the Black Lord and hit him in the face with the back of his hand. Bane's head snapped back and a small chip flew from his face. The God of Strife instinctively raised his hand to the wound. In the shiny black of the avatar's hand, the fallen god glimpsed a reflection of the tiny jet of the greenish amber flame that escaped from the hole. With a scream, Bane leaped forward and tackled Torm.

Both avatars tumbled over the edge of the cliff. As the giants fell, they separated. Bane struck the mountainside twice before he landed on the rocky shore. Torm, another hole in his shoulder from the spikes on Bane's body, reached out and tore a tree from its roots in an effort to slow his descent. The effort was futile, of course, and he crashed to the beach several hundred yards from the Black Lord. For the avatars, though, this was a distance that could be crossed in seconds.

Torm rose first. As he stood up, he saw two ships that

bore the Zhentish flag wallowing in the Dragon Reach, far from shore. A few small boats were rushing to shore, up the coast a little ways off. The God of Duty swore a silent oath that he would kill every Zhentish invader he could catch . . . as soon as he had slain their master.

The Black Lord was only now beginning to rise. As he lifted his head from the sand, Bane looked down and saw another crack in his chest. More reddish black vapors streamed from the opening. "You fool," the God of Strife hissed. He looked up and saw Torm standing over him.

The God of Duty held a boulder over his head. The chunk of stone was so large that the giant, lion-headed avatar was using both hands to hold it up. "You must pay for your sins," Torm said flatly, then smashed the boulder over Bane's head. The rock burst into pieces and more of the obsidian avatar's face cracked. In return, Bane impaled the God of Duty's leg with one of the spikes on his arm. Torm stumbled back, a geyser of soul energy rising from his wounds.

"I'm dying!" Bane cried as he staggered to his feet. He looked at his wounds, saw his energy draining away. The Black Lord's eyes blazed with crimson light as he lowered himself into a crouch. "Come, Torm. We will visit Myrkul's kingdom together."

Before the God of Duty could get away, the Black Lord charged to his side, grabbed his shoulders, and drew Torm into a deadly embrace. A dozen spikes pierced the lion-headed avatar, and Torm roared in pain.

The juggernauts teetered back and forth for a moment, standing only because they were supporting one another. Bane laughed, low and hollow, and the sound drifted out over the Dragon Reach. Torm looked into the Black Lord's eyes, then opened his sharp-toothed maw and slowly brought the rows of teeth down upon Bane's throat.

The God of Strife's laughter abruptly ceased.

On the southern hill of Tantras, Midnight released her hold on the bell's rope. It was no use. She had tried time and again to force the Bell of Aylen Attricus to sound once more, but she had failed.

"Try again!" Elminster snapped, then turned to look out at the sky over Tantras.

"Elminster, I can't," Midnight cried, her shoulders sagging with exhaustion.

The old sage did not take his gaze from the strange lights above the city. The frail bonds of reality seemed to be coming undone and lines of force were snaking out across the sky. The center of this web of energy rested just above the avatar's battleground and took the form of a swirling vortex that rose toward the clouds. Sky-blue streaks of power intertwined with amber, green, and reddish black strands. The souls of the followers of the Black Lord and the God of Duty battled for control of Tantras, even beyond death.

Huge, glowing meteors had begun to rain down upon the city, too. The fiery balls struck the earth in every direction. Some demolished buildings, others devastated ships in the harbor. As Adon watched, one fireball tore a hole in the side of a Zhentish craft and the galley foundered, then sank in the Dragon Reach.

Still another meteor struck the amber dome that protected the bell tower. Though it couldn't reach the heroes, the glowing chunk of rock bounced off the magical wall and fell into the hundreds of panicked Tantrasans who had seen the shield from the distance and had flocked around it. Kelemvor had to watch in helpless anger as the meteor killed two dozen people and injured a score more.

Inside the tower, Elminster felt his aged heart racing. "Ye must try again," the sage said slowly, turning back to the raven-haired mage.

Midnight fell to her knees, the rope in her hands. "Can't you teleport some of the refugees inside the shield?"

"Magic won't penetrate this barrier," Elminster grumbled. "Ye should know that."

The old sage paused and walked to Midnight's side. He helped her to her feet and rested his hand on her shoulder. "Midnight," Elminster said in a comforting tone the mage would never have associated with the cranky old sage, "ye alone have the power to complete this task. Mystra believed in ye. It's about time ye did the same and justified her trust. Now, force away thy fears and concentrate on saving this city."

With those words, the old sage turned and left the tower. Midnight stared up at the bell and imagined it ringing. For a moment she could almost see the bell swinging back and forth in the tower, its rich tones filling her ears. She closed her eyes and the image remained. In that instant, Midnight finally understood the reason for the magical silence that gripped the tower before the bell was rung. Only by blocking out all distraction, by concentrating fully on the task of ringing the bell, could a mage hope to make it sound.

For a moment, Midnight did not think. She did not feel. For an instant, she didn't even breathe.

Then, the raven-haired mage pulled the rope, and the Bell of Aylen Attricus sang out again, its song of power so loud that it nearly deafened her. The bell tower glowed with a bright amber light, and a terrifying chill flowed down and engulfed Midnight. Amber waves of energy and black lightning flashed in the tower, then leaped from the high windows to the dome that protected the heroes. The walls of the shield quickly spread outward, and the huddled Tantrasans suddenly found themselves safe within its confines.

Midnight ran to the tower's door and watched as the dome continued to expand. She gasped, though, as she saw that the shield was slowing as it moved across the southern hill. She raced back inside and grabbed the rope once more. The mage pulled with all her strength, ignoring the blasts of cold and the maddening sound of the bell tolling. She pulled on the rope again and again, with no regard for herself. All that mattered was the city.

Still, Midnight was only human, and after a time that seemed like an eternity to her, the mage felt her arms grow limp, her hands slide from the rope, and her legs buckle beneath her. She collapsed to the floor, gasping for breath. When Midnight opened her eyes again, only a moment had passed, but Elminster, Kelemvor, and Adon were now inside the tower with her.

The green-eyed fighter fell to his knees and threw his arms around Midnight. "The shield is over the city," Kelemvor said. "It's over."

"I don't think so," Adon whispered as he turned back to the door.

The cleric saw that the shield was still expanding, although it had not yet reached the citadel and the Temple of Torm. Suddenly there was an explosion that made the sound of the bell tolling seem like a small child clapping his hands. A massive, night-black form rose over the north hill of the city. The shape was amorphous, and a blood-red spiral of energy curled within its center. A second shape rose behind the ebon blob, but it was sky blue with an amber core that looked not unlike a shining sun.

The unprotected part of the city, which contained both the Temple of Torm and the citadel, was covered by a wave of searing flame. The land turned black, and the waters of the Dragon Reach bubbled and changed to vapor under the intense heat. The Zhentish ships exploded as the waves of flame struck them. Bane's troops died instantly.

On the shore to the north of the city, the discarded bodies of the avatars lay upon the rocks, charred and brittle. Bane's obsidian giant was shattered in a dozen places, and its head lay yards from its body. The golden-skinned avatar of the God of Duty had been ripped to shreds, and its proud lion's head lay twisted, its soulless eyes staring up toward the essences of the rival gods that hung over the coast.

In the sky, the pulsating essences of Bane and Torm were dragged upward, caught in the pull of the vortex created by the freed souls of their followers. The vortex swallowed the shimmering, swirling masses that had once been gods, and a blinding white flash filled the air. The crimson spiral, the heart of what had once been Lord Bane, the God of Strife and Tyranny, and the amber soul of Lord Torm, the God of Duty and Loyalty, met in the whirlwind. A high-pitched shriek, the final cries of both gods, filled the air. The vortex swallowed the deities and the screams stopped. Both gods were dead.

At the Tower of Aylen Attricus, Kelemvor and Adon helped Midnight to her feet. Together, they walked from the stone obelisk, Elminster trailing behind them. A group of Tantrasans had gathered around the tower, and the crowd was suddenly silent as the heroes stepped outside.

Midnight smiled when she saw the people gathered around, safe from the destruction that had savaged the northern shoreline, but when she looked closer and saw the awe in their faces, she shuddered. Their expressions were composed of the same look of fear mixed with adoration that the mage had seen on the faces of those who'd given their lives for Torm.

Softly, she asked Adon and Kelemvor to give her a moment alone with the old sage. As soon as her friends had walked away, Midnight turned to Elminster and asked, "What do you know about my powers?"

"I have *suspected* many things since the first day ye arrived at my doorstep in Shadowdale. As for the true nature of your talents or what grand schemes ye may use them to pursue, I cannot help ye." Elminster paused and smiled. "Mystra has blessed ye, I think. Perhaps the Council of Wizards in Waterdeep may be willing to hear your tale and offer some guidance. I could put in a word for ye, if ye like . . ."

Midnight sighed and shook her head. "Why do you feel it necessary to taunt and tantalize and drive us to fits of near-insanity just to get us to follow your suggestions, Elminster?" the raven-haired mage asked. "If the second Tablet of Fate is in Waterdeep, then we'll go to Waterdeep. Just tell me the truth: Do you know where in Waterdeep the tablet has been hidden?"

The sage shook his head. "Sadly, I do not."

"That will make the task difficult," Midnight noted sadly. "But probably no more so than finding the first of the pair." The mage hefted the bag containing the tablet and slung it over her shoulder.

"Aye," Elminster laughed. "Difficult, but not impossible." He turned away from the mage and looked out over the city. "But we can discuss this later. There are more pressing matters that call for our attention at the moment."

Elminster pointed to the refugees that had been wounded by the meteor earlier. Kelemvor and Adon were already moving through the ranks of the injured, trying to give whatever aid they could. Midnight smiled as she watched her lover and the scarred cleric.

After a moment, the raven-haired mage looked up at the sky. The vortex was gone, and sunlight streamed through the amber shield that still hung over the city. Midnight gasped slightly when she noticed that the position of the sun was changing. The sky was actually getting dark. By eveningfeast, the eternal light that had graced Tantras since the time of Arrival would only be a memory. They'll be better off without it, Midnight decided and walked with Elminster toward the refugees.

Epilogue

The death of Torm and Bane had forged a crater at the northern end of Tantras, where the citadel and the Temple of Torm once stood. The rocky shore of the Dragon Reach north of the city was now as slick as glass, and a large section of the cliff leading down to the shore had been vaporized in the blast. Strands of amber, red, black, blue, and silver were woven in beautiful designs in the rocks of the glassy shore and blasted cliffs. Fragments of the shattered avatars lay in the surf at the edge of the glass beach.

In the hours after the shield had finally faded and disappeared, Midnight and Elminster journeyed to the ruins caused by the gods' battle. But as they approached the crater, a sudden fatigue overwhelmed the raven-haired mage and she fell to her knees. "Elminster," she cried. The world seemed to spin for an instant, then Midnight dropped to the ground, unconscious. The white-haired sage was feeling a strange weakness, too. He called out to a young man with short-cropped red hair who was prowling through the wreckage of Torm's temple.

"Ye there!" The sage cried and gestured for the man to come closer. "Help me carry the woman."

The young man seemed ill-at-ease, but he did as the sage requested. Elminster and the red-haired man carried Midnight back to the edge of the ruins. They gently put her down upon a patch of bare ground. The young man stood staring at the raven-haired woman. "Off with ye now!" Elminster snapped. "Thank ye for thy help, but I'll take care of her from here."

"What?" the young man asked. "You're not going to pay me for my help?"

The sage grumbled, flipped a gold piece at the red-haired man, then turned back to Midnight. When the young man had moved on, Elminster stroked his beard for a moment and considered the situation. "Something is amiss here," he muttered and took out his pipe.

In a few minutes, Midnight awoke to the smell of the old sage's pipeweed. She coughed twice, then sputtered, "What happened?"

"I believe the area is magic dead," Elminster pronounced. "Nothing magical, not even wizards, can enter it."

"But how is that possible?" Midnight asked as she sat up. "I thought the weave touched every part of the Realms."

Elminster sighed and put out his pipe. "Once, perhaps," he said, then helped Midnight to her feet. "Not since Arrival, though. The death of the gods here may have torn a hole in the weave. Perhaps the magical chaos is unraveling the weave itself."

"Are there more of these magic dead areas in the Realms?" Midnight asked as they walked back to their horses.

"Aye," the old sage said. "In places, they're much larger than this."

Before she mounted her horse, Midnight looked back to the ruins, a look of fear in her eyes. "Can the weave be repaired?" she whispered.

Elminster looked away and didn't answer her.

Twenty minutes later, Midnight and the white-bearded sage reached the harbor. Kelemvor and Adon were waiting on the pier where the fighter had first met Alprin, as they had planned earlier in the day. The cleric and the fighter had spent the last few days helping the Tantrasan military to restore order in the city. They served on patrols to stop looting. They helped to move the wounded to the makeshift hospitals set up around the city. They even worked at rebuilding a few important shops so commerce could pick up again.

Now, when the fighter saw his lover, he took her in his arms. They held the embrace until Elminster cleared his throat noisily.

The old sage turned to Midnight, a wicked gleam in his eye. "As much as I enjoy our little chats, I'm afraid I must depart. Urgent matters require my attention elsewhere. I will see ye all again soon, in Waterdeep."

"Wait!" Midnight cried as the old sage turned away. "You can't just go!"

"Oh?" Elminster asked, not stopping to face the heroes. "Why not?"

"Because you're sending us into danger. You should be there to help!" Kelemvor yelled. Elminster stopped and turned around.

"Ye should understand that the mission ye are going on is vital for the survival of Faerun, but it isn't the only important thing that needs doing!" Elminster snapped. "I'm needed elsewhere now, but ye'll see me again in Waterdeep."

Without another word, Elminster walked back toward the city. No one tried to stop him.

Midnight, Kelemvor, and Adon stood silently looking at the ship on which they were to leave Tantras. After a moment, Midnight smiled and said, "We've done pretty well so far, considering what we're up against. I'm almost looking forward to going to Waterdeep."

Adon, his clothes cleaner than they had been in a long time, turned to face the Dragon Reach and frowned. "I wonder if Cyric was on one of those Zhentish ships that got destroyed."

Midnight shook her head. "He's still alive. I just know he is."

"He won't be for long, though," Kelemvor growled. "Not when I get my hands on him." The fighter put his hand on the hilt of his sword.

A cloud of anger crossed Midnight's face. "You should give him a chance to explain—"

"No!" Kelemvor snapped, turning his back on the raven-haired woman. "You can't make me believe that Cyric was acting against his will at the Dark Harvest. You didn't see the look of surprise on his face when he saw that I'd survived his trap. You didn't see the *smile* on his lips when he saw my wounds."

"You're mistaken," Midnight said coldly. "You don't know Cyric."

"I know that animal better than you do," Kelemvor growled. He turned around, his green eyes flaring with rage. "You may have been taken in by Cyric's lies, but I learned long ago never to believe him. The next time we meet, one of us won't walk away."

Adon nodded. "Kel's right, Midnight. Cyric is a threat to all of us, to all of Faerun. Do you remember how he acted on the Ashaba? Can you imagine what would happen if he got his hands on the Tablets of Fate?"

Midnight turned away from Kelemvor and Adon and walked toward the ship they had booked passage on. She clutched the pack containing her spellbook and the Tablet of Fate tightly as she climbed aboard.

Kelemvor cursed loudly and stormed to the ship behind the mage. "Hurry up, Adon," he grumbled. "Our mage has decided it's time to go."

Adon took one last look back at Tantras and thought of Torm's words to him in the temple's garden. The scarred cleric smiled. Yes, he thought, my duty is clear. My friends need me. Adon paused for a moment and straightened his hair, then joined Midnight and Kelemvor aboard the ship.

In the shadows of a warehouse near the pier, the young red-haired man who had helped Elminster earlier watched as the heroes departed. As soon as Adon had climbed aboard the ship, he ran for a small boat that bore a sign declaring it off duty. The red-haired man tore the sign from the boat, threw it into the water, and kicked the brawny man who lay asleep in the bow.

"I was beginning to think you would never show," the boatman rumbled, rubbing the wart on his bulbous nose.

"You're not being paid to think. Just get this heap of rotting wood moving," the young man spat. "You know where to go." He climbed into the boat, and the brawny man pulled out a set of oars and started to row.

The small boat soon left the harbor and made its way along the shore south of Tantras. A night-black trireme stood in a small cove a few miles away. The red-haired man signaled the ship as he got close, then climbed aboard.

The captain of the *Argent* was waiting to greet him.

"Sabinus," Cyric said happily as he helped the red-haired man climb aboard. "What have you to report?"

The smuggler told all that he had heard and described the ship in which the heroes were leaving Tantras. The young man laughed as he showed Cyric the gold coin Elminster had given him.

Cyric smiled. "You've done well. You'll most certainly be rewarded."

"Tantras is no longer safe for me," the red-haired man told the thief. "You promised me passage to a place far from here."

"And I will deliver on my promise," Cyric said casually, putting his arm around the smuggler's shoulder. "I always do."

Sabinus never heard Cyric's dagger leave its sheath, but the smuggler felt the biting pain as the blade bit into his neck. He stumbled. The thief stabbed Sabinus again and pushed him over the railing. The red-haired man was dead before he hit the water.

Cyric looked down at the body. "Nothing personal," he muttered. "But I have no further need of your services."

Turning from the railing, the hawk-nosed man called for his lieutenant and told him that they were going to follow the ship that carried the heroes. In return, Dalzhel saluted his captain, then barked a string of orders to the sole survivors of the Zhentish fleet from Scardale.

Earlier that day, when Cyric saw the strange vortex form above the city, he had ordered the crew to take the *Argent* out into the Dragon Reach, away from the battling avatars. The ship and its crew survived thanks to that command. Cyric knew that his men's gratitude would serve him well in the days to come.

The thief stared out at the blood-red sun setting over Faerun. He thought of his former allies and all that Sabinus had told him about Kelemvor's threats and Adon's comments. For once, the hawk-nosed man thought sourly, the fighter and the cleric were right.

Cyric had decided days ago that when next he met Midnight and her allies, he would offer them no mercy if they dared to stand in his way.

Calling all fantasy fans –

FOR THE BEST IN PAPERBACKS, LOOK FOR THE 🐧

In every corner of the world, on every subject under the sun, Penguin represents quality and variety – the very best in publishing today.

For complete information about books available from Penguin – including Pelicans, Puffins, Peregrines and Penguin Classics – and how to order them, write to us at the appropriate address below. Please note that for copyright reasons the selection of books varies from country to country.

In the United Kingdom: Please write to *Dept E.P., Penguin Books Ltd, Harmondsworth, Middlesex, UB7 0DA*

If you have any difficulty in obtaining a title, please send your order with the correct money, plus ten per cent for postage and packaging, to *PO Box No 11, West Drayton, Middlesex*

In the United States: Please write to *Dept BA, Penguin, 299 Murray Hill Parkway, East Rutherford, New Jersey 07073*

In Canada: Please write to *Penguin Books Canada Ltd, 2801 John Street, Markham, Ontario L3R 1B4*

In Australia: Please write to the *Marketing Department, Penguin Books Australia Ltd, P.O. Box 257, Ringwood, Victoria 3134*

In New Zealand: Please write to the *Marketing Department, Penguin Books (NZ) Ltd, Private Bag, Takapuna, Auckland 9*

In India: Please write to *Penguin Overseas Ltd, 706 Eros Apartments, 56 Nehru Place, New Delhi, 110019*

In Holland: Please write to *Penguin Books Nederland B.V., Postbus 195, NL–1380AD Weesp, Netherlands*

In Germany: Please write to *Penguin Books Ltd, Friedrichstrasse 10–12, D–6000 Frankfurt Main 1, Federal Republic of Germany*

In Spain: Please write to *Longman Penguin España, Calle San Nicolas 15, E–28013 Madrid, Spain*

In France: Please write to *Penguin Books Ltd, 39 Rue de Montmorency, F-75003, Paris, France*

In Japan: Please write to *Longman Penguin Japan Co Ltd, Yamaguchi Building, 2–12–9 Kanda Jimbocho, Chiyoda-Ku, Tokyo 101, Japan*

Another stunning fantasy adventure series from the
publishers of the DRAGONLANCE® Saga

FORGOTTEN REALMS®

Travel to a land beyond time ... and join princes and heroes
in the fight against evil forces.

already published or in preparation:

The Icewind Dales Trilogy

R. A. Salvatore

Book 1: The Crystal Shard

Book 2: Streams of Silver

and **Book 3: Halfling's Gem**

Imagine the coldest, most hostile, most desolate place men dare
to live. Imagine battling fantastic creatures and deadly enemies
as the frigid wind bites your flesh, even through the heaviest of
furs and leather. Such is Icewind Dale – the subarctic tundra
wilderness of the Forgotten Realms. Here an unlikely quartet of
heroes must combat assassins, wizards, golems and more in the
struggle to preserve their homes and heritage.

Another stunning fantasy adventure series from the publishers
of the DRAGONLANCE® Saga

FORGOTTEN REALMS®

Travel to a land beyond time ... and join princes and heroes in
the fight against evil forces.

The Moonshae Trilogy

Douglas Niles

Book 1: Darkwalker on Moonshae

Book 2: Black Wizards

Book 3: Darkwell

Enter the Moonshae Isles – a world filled with bizarre creatures,
dire occurrences, wondrous events and bitter struggle – in this
bestselling trilogy.

A deep, dark hole is eating away at the spring sunlight, sapping
its strength. The portents are not good. The evil beast is growing
stronger by the day, and its followers, the Firbolg, are craving
the sight of blood. To halt the spread of darkness, Prince Tristan
Kendrick must rally the Citizens of Moonshae...